IN PLACE
OF DEATH

During his twenty-year career in Glasgow with a Scottish Sunday newspaper, Craig Robertson interviewed three Prime Ministers and attended major stories including 9/11, Dunblane, the Omagh bombing and the disappearance of Madeleine McCann. He was pilloried on breakfast television, beat Oprah Winfrey to a major scoop, spent time on Death Row in the USA and dispensed polio drops in the backstreets of India. His debut novel, *Random*, was shortlisted for the CWA New Blood Dagger and was a *Sunday Times* bestseller.

Also by Craig Robertson

The Last Refuge
Witness the Dead
Cold Grave
Snapshot
Random

CRAIG ROBERTSON

IN PLACE OF DEATH

**SIMON &
SCHUSTER**

London · New York · Sydney · Toronto · New Delhi

A CBS COMPANY

First published in Great Britain by Simon & Schuster UK Ltd, 2015
A CBS company

1 3 5 7 9 10 8 6 4 2

Simon & Schuster UK Ltd
1st Floor
Gray's Inn Road
London WC1X 8HB

www.simonandschuster.co.uk

Simon & Schuster Australia, Sydney
Simon & Schuster India, New Delhi

A CIP catalogue record for this book is available from the British Library

Trade Paperback ISBN: 978-1-47112-778-6
eBook ISBN: 978-1-47112-780-9

Typeset in the UK by Hewer Text UK Ltd, Edinburgh
Printed and bound in Great Britain by
CPI Group (UK) Ltd, Croydon, CR0 4YY

MIX
Paper from
responsible sources
FSC

Simon & Schu... ...committed to sourcing paper that ...s made from
wood grown in ... ...d supports the Forest Stew...dship Council,
the leading inte...national forest certification organisation. Our books displaying
the FSC logo are printed on FSC-certified paper.

To my much-loved grandmother,
Mary Robertson 1915–2015

This city is what it is because our citizens are what they are.

Plato

Chapter 1

Remy Feeks always felt his heart beat a wee bit faster when he took that first step. It didn't matter whether it was up a ladder, through a fence or into a tunnel like now. The first step was the no-going-back step. It was the one that meant it had begun.

It didn't mean he was scared. He *was* but it wasn't that. Not just that. A little bit of fear was natural anyway. Sensible, too. Going into the unknown was supposed to be frightening. And thrilling. Exhilarating. Liberating. All those things and more. It was why he did what he did.

He shuffled down the bank until he stood in the water, feeling the pinch of cold even through the toes of his waders. Standing still for a few moments, he enjoyed the anticipation and tried to get his head round it. He was going to walk back in time, nearly

1

one hundred and fifty years, deep into the heart of old Glasgow. It was a walk that only maybe a handful of people had ever done. And the good bit, the great bit, was that he couldn't be sure where he'd end up. Or even if he'd come out at the other end.

Deep breath. First step. Heart thumping. Go.

He stepped into the tunnel, the Molendinar Burn at his feet and Victorian Glasgow somewhere in front of him. Man, this was going to be awesome.

With just one step, the city was above his head, out of sight and almost out of mind. Or maybe he was out of his. He laughed, knowing full well how crazy some people would think he was. The chances were they were right but being their kind of sane was a hell of a boring life.

Remy worked in a supermarket. A bloody supermarket. Four good Highers had qualified him to round up trolleys that lazy sods couldn't be bothered putting back in the right place. Hefting a couple of dozen of them back to the front of the store a thousand times a day was like putting your soul in a car crusher. He knew all about living life the boring way. No reason for him to spend his free time living it like that too.

The stream turned from neon-dappled brown to murky and dark in an instant. No going back. Just on. To wherever the hell it was.

The beginning of the road to this unknown hell was Duke Street, near to the old Great Eastern Hotel. Or rather, underneath it all. He loved the fact that somewhere above his head people were tumbling in and out of pubs, going into bookies and shops, walking to ordinary places, and they had no idea that he was doing his thing beneath their feet. That was the kick.

His old man had told him all about the Molendinar, how the burn was here before Glasgow was. St Mungo came to the dear green place, a wood beside the burn, and founded the settlement that grew to become the second city of the empire. His dad knew all that stuff. He was a welder but history was his thing. That and his son were about the only thing he loved more than his twenty-pack of Embassy Regal. And it wasn't the history that had nearly killed him.

He'd told Remy how the Molendinar used to mark the eastern boundary of the city and how it provided the water that powered the mills that industrialized the revolution. It split the cathedral from the Necropolis, separating life from death, and had the Bridge of Sighs built above it so that corpses could be carted into the cemetery. Glasgow grew on the back of the burn but it grew so much that it didn't have room for it any more. In the 1870s, they covered it with a culvert and hid the Molendinar from view. Now it still flowed but under Duke Street, along the length of Wishart Street next to the cathedral, under Glasgow.

Hardly anyone knew it was there and fewer still knew that there was a way in. That was what made it fun. And what made it scary.

He was enjoying this. The rush, the edge, the adventure. He'd thought of doing it for ages, after he'd heard about the one guy that was known to have done it

3

before him. Another guy like him. Another guy who did this.

The tunnel took a sharp turn to the right, a fine curve of stone wall facing him as he ducked under the arch. Rectangular slabs of old stone, two feet by one, perfectly laid. His nose was filling up with the smell, stale and musky. It was the pungent, beautiful smell of decay.

You maybe wouldn't think that was something you would like, right? Takes all sorts. It's nothing weird. It just smelled of the history of the city. His city. His old man's city. You could smell every year of it.

The arch of the ceiling was less than a foot above his head but he enjoyed the luxury of that while he could. He knew it would get a lot lower. Maybe so low that he wouldn't be able to get through. Time would tell. The stone slabs gave way to brick showing orange and white and grey in the beam of the torchlight. The burn flowed over his ankles, cold as the grave.

The first time he'd done an explore, he'd climbed high rather than hit a tunnel and it had scared him enough that he'd nearly crapped himself. He'd started off full of courage that was poured from a tap in the Hielan Jessie but that beer buzz evaporated in an instant when he realized just how high the roof of the cathedral was. High enough to die from, that's how high. For five long minutes, he'd clung on to the one spot, petrified. It wasn't until he was back on the ground and in one piece that he breathed and told himself he'd enjoyed it.

4

But all the next day, he was buzzing in a way that no amount of beer had ever done for him. He'd actually done that. And it felt fucking good. From then on he was hooked.

This explore was everything Remy had wanted it to be. The buzz ran through him like he'd known it would. Like a charge. Like drugs. Like something you couldn't resist even if you wanted to.

The brick lining changed to concrete, low stuff that had him bent double and his pulse throbbing. It was a good fear though, he told himself. Sensible. He went on because it was what he did. No going back after that first step.

Jesus Christ. Steel piping. He never expected that. A glistening silver tunnel that spiralled in front of him, the water golden at his feet. It was almost mirrored as the steel walls threw corrugated images from one to the other. Man, this was a mindbender. It was like he was tripping and maybe, in his own way, he was.

He had three rules when he did his stuff. The same three everyone who did this had. Be safe. Don't break in. Take nothing away with you. The least important of those was being safe. That was the one he only paid nodding observance to.

The other two were sacrosanct. Never break in anywhere. For a start, it means criminal damage and that means jail time. And it's cheating. Use your brain instead. Don't take anything because the idea is to uncover, to celebrate these old places as they were. Leave them that way.

The steel piping came to an end like all good things do but it was replaced by a beautiful burrowing tunnel of red brick that let him stand upright again. Maybe the worst of it was over and he'd be able to walk upright the rest of the way. Anyway, he enjoyed it while he could, a long stretch of walkway, a long stretch of the leg and the back.

When it changed, he wasn't sure whether to celebrate or not. He was forced to duck again, not just because of the reduced height but also the stalactites that appeared like daggers from the ceiling. He bent low beneath them, on and on until the forest became a field, so many spears that the brick disappeared and he'd have sworn he was in a cave. He wasn't back a hundred and fifty years; it was more like a thousand, ten thousand.

He was at half-height now and getting lower still. The walls grew around him, thick with solidified deposits that crowded in and suffocated. No going back. It was a stupid rule but it was his.

The ceiling was no more than two feet high now and his back was at breaking point. If he still had an adrenalin rush, he couldn't hear it above his breathing or the pounding in his chest. It was hard work and it might be going nowhere. Nowhere that he could get through.

He was firing his torch straight ahead in the desperate hope of seeing more than the miserable amount of space he was being forced to crawl through. Wait. What was that? Darkness blocking the way forward.

His heart sank at the prospect of it being the end of the journey. Another bit of him was secretly glad. Enough was enough on this jaunt.

He inched closer and saw that it wasn't the tunnel closing up but a shape much the same size as him. Holy shit. His heart nearly stopped. It was someone else. He could make out a backpack, like the one he always took with him. Some other mad bastard was doing the same thing.

'Hey! Are you stuck down there?'

No answer.

'You hear me? Can you not get through? Maybe we'd better both back up.'

He waited for the reply that didn't come. No way the guy couldn't hear him. Shit. He crept closer, the walls tightening around him, barely able to squeeze any further. Maybe the guy *was* stuck.

When he got near enough, he reached out for the man. His arm extending cautiously, despite a voice inside him screaming the truth. In one moment he could see that the man had enough room not to be stuck. He saw this just as the smell hit him and he put his hand on the guy's shoulder and tugged.

When the entire arm came away in his hand, he screamed so loud that it must have been heard all the way to Duke Street and back again.

Chapter 2

The tug on the guy's arm put Remy fully on his knees, the cold water of the burn surging over his lower legs. Worse, much worse, the man's body toppled back onto his. Suddenly he could barely breathe, suffocated by this fucking corpse that was on top of him.

He leaned back but the body simply came with him, the head falling so it was next to his and staring at him through blank eyes. Oh Jesus Christ, the eyes had been eaten away. Remy stretched his head as far from the other as he could, straining his neck muscles to put distance between him and the flaking, decomposing face that leered at him.

He took it all in at once, the full horror of it. The man's throat had been cut. From behind by the look of it. Slit from side to side and his front was washed in blood. The blood was rusty and dry, like spilled gravy, all over the white T-shirt and navy-blue fleece. Man, his face was all purples and reds, like a patchwork quilt. There were chunks out of it too, rats probably and whatever the hell else was down here.

And the smell. It was horrendous, like nothing he'd ever smelled before. He knew what it was though. Death. Decay. It filled his nostrils and made him gag.

He was desperate to get the thing, the man, or what was left of him, off him but there wasn't enough room to extend his arms and push the body away. Instead, he pulled his arms in so that he could push up, not wanting to touch it but having no choice. He shoved at the body and at the same time tried to scrabble out from underneath. The man's back felt thin and wet and he knew that the cloying, sweet stink was now all over his fingers. Gagging again, he levered the body higher, dragging his own knees along the floor of the burn as he slid away.

He kept his hands under the corpse even once he was free of it, lowering it gently onto the ground in front of him. He took his hands away as quickly as he could and thrust them into the water. He scrubbed at them, rubbing them together as he stared at the body.

He brought his hands out, drying them on the front of his jacket, and all the while edging away from the dead man. The murdered man. He backed up as far and as fast as he could, until he could stand up again. Then he ran.

Remy sat in his car, parked just a couple of hundred yards from the opening to the burn, and shivered. He didn't know how much was cold and how much was shock. He just knew he couldn't stop shaking. A puddle of water had formed at his feet and he stared into it, watching the drips land.

Did that really just happen? To him? Remy Feeks, the man nothing ever happened to? He'd never seen a dead body before. Who the hell had? No one he knew. And not just dead, obviously murdered. What the hell was he going to do?

Report it. He had to call it in to the cops. But. He didn't want to be part of this. He wanted to go back to collecting trolleys at Tesco and looking after his dad. He didn't want *this*. He shouldn't have been down there in the first place. He'd been trespassing. He had the guy's DNA all over him. Holy shit. They'd think he did it. That's what they do.

It took him a while to realize that there were tears running down his cheeks and trickling into the puddle at his feet. When it dawned on him, he drew the back of his hand across his eyes then rubbed at his nose. Grow a pair, he told himself. You've no reason to feel sorry for yourself: think of that poor bugger killed in the burn. He did think of him and remembered that his hands had been on the man's rotting corpse and felt sick that they'd just been on his eyes.

He flipped the angle of the rear-view mirror and stared at his reflection. His eyes were red and wide. 'Arsehole!' he shouted at himself, then got scared in case anyone had heard him.

He twisted and reached into the back seat where he

grabbed his trainers. He pulled off the waders and changed into his proper shoes. With one final look at himself in the mirror, he got out of the car before he could change his mind and went looking for the first phone box that worked.

He walked half of Duke Street before finding one and had nearly given up and jumped in to use the one in the Crown Creighton instead. But that would have been just as stupid as using his mobile. He'd found some guts but not enough for that.

'Emergency. What service do you require?'

'Police. And ambulance, I guess.'

'What is your emergency?'

'There's a body. A dead ... I mean ... I just ... found it.'

'What is your name, caller?'

'No ... I ... I don't want to ... Look, someone's been murdered. I need to go. Just let me tell you where.'

'Can you give me your name, please, caller?'

'No. Listen, the body's in the Molendinar Tunnel. Under Wishart Street. Or maybe further, I'm not sure. You get in at the entrance near the Great Eastern. The man's been murdered.'

'Calm down, sir. Are you sure this person is dead?'

'Yes! He's very dead. Been dead for ages. Not years but weeks or months. Look, I need to go.'

'How did you find the body? You were in this tunnel?'

'I was just ... I was just exploring. You need to get him out of there.'

11

'Please, stay on the line—'

He hung up. And ran like a coward.

He actually started the engine to drive home but he didn't move. Driving home was the sensible thing but he didn't do it. He wasn't sure why but it was like when he made that first step into the tunnel or up a ladder or through a fence. No going back. He wanted to see what happened. Had to, really.

For the longest time, he thought they hadn't believed him. They got a lot of hoax calls and this must have sounded like one. A body in the tunnel under Wishart Street. Right, sure thing. And he'd been down there for a walk. Sure. Of course they didn't believe him.

What would he do? Go back down there and drag the body out himself? He didn't have the balls for that. Maybe he could go down and take a photograph of it, send it to the cops and make them believe him. Maybe he'd just wait and see.

It must have been forty minutes before he saw the police car pull up. It was dark now and he saw the car's lights as it turned and parked on the other side of the street near where the Molendinar was exposed. Two cops got out, their yellow hi-vis sparking under the street lights. Neither seemed in a hurry. One of them was pointing and shaking his head. Now they were both shaking their heads, not happy.

They pulled waders out of the boot of their car, heaved them on and made their way very reluctantly to the bank. The two cops, one tall and broad, the

12

other smaller and most probably a woman, although he couldn't be sure from this distance, disappeared from sight.

It was like they'd never been there apart from the sight of the car sitting lonely in the dark. He was tempted to go over, tell them about the tunnel and what they'd find if they went in there. He didn't. He sat and fretted.

Every few minutes he turned the ignition key over once and watched the time flash about on the dashboard display. He was scared of doing it too often because the battery on his old heap wasn't in the best of shape. He didn't want to get stuck there: that would be too tough to explain. The time crawled by and he tried to work out in his head where they might be, how far down the tunnel they'd managed to get. The bigger cop was maybe too big to get all the way to where the body was without getting stuck. The lady cop would need to go on her own. That was a bit unfair.

There they were. Both of them climbing back over the fencing and onto the street again. They were moving a lot quicker than when they'd gone in and one of them was on the radio. They were both still shaking their heads though.

It was just ten more minutes before the road in front of the old Great Eastern was flooded with flashing lights, police cars, an ambulance and some unmarked cars. Two minutes after that, the area was taped off and people had started to gather to gawp. He still just sat there in the dark and shivered some more.

When there were maybe twenty to thirty people on his side of the tape, Remy slid quietly out of the car and joined them. He was just another rubbernecker. Not a witness. Not the person who found the body.

There was a lot of chat behind the tape. *It'll be a junkie. Bound to be, man.* Remy knew it wasn't a junkie. *Some'dy try to drown themselves?* In that wee burn, don't be stupid. *I heard some'dy was shot.* No they weren't. *It'll be gangsters, man.* Yeah, maybe. Maybe.

Chapter 3

There's a phenomenon in astronomy called light echo. When a rapidly brightening object such as a nova is reflected off interstellar dust, the echo is seen shortly after the initial flash. It produces an illusion, of an echo expanding faster than the speed of light.

Tony Winter didn't know all that much about astronomy but after years of photographing dead bodies, he knew all about the differences between light and dark.

The echoes of the flash from his camera bounced from wall to wall in the close confines of the Molendinar Tunnel, reverberating from brick to opposing brick in a heartbeat. Even if he cared, he couldn't tell which flash was a reflection of the other. All he knew was that they were lighting up death and giving its ugliness a sheen of undeserved beauty.

The tunnel was bathed in it, the bricks glowing golden and warm and making the corpse with the wide, empty eyes seem even colder by comparison. Winter was tight against the bricks now, feeling their rough edges against his skin and clothing as he fought to get enough room to capture the body from every angle he could without disturbing it. The head, what was left of it after the tunnel creatures had gnawed and nibbled, filled his viewfinder. Dead for a month or so, he guessed. A patchwork face of pale purples and washed-out reds on a canvas of dirty beige. Most definitely not a pretty sight but an irresistible one.

The gaping, festering wound to the throat had been a clean cut once. A sharp blade had let life rush out, just as surprise had escaped from the mouth and terror from the eyes. Whoever he was, he quite literally hadn't seen this coming. There was something else about him though, something that Winter couldn't quite . . .

'What do you see, Tony?'

The shout from twenty yards or so behind him came from Rachel. Newly promoted Detective Inspector Rachel Narey. His significant other. His girlfriend. His partner. Rachel.

They both had new jobs, on paper at least. She'd become part of the West's Major Investigation Team while his paymasters had been rebranded from the Scottish Police Services Authority to the snappier Forensic Services. The truth was that this brave new world was much the same as the bad old one. She investigated murders, he photographed them.

The difference for Narey was that killer-chasing was now more of a full-time occupation. The MIT was part of Police Scotland's newly formed Serious Crime Division and they'd taken responsibility for all homicide inquiries. There would still be other crimes on the sheet but the murders were theirs.

There was an average of a murder a week in the West of Scotland, more than enough to keep a squad on its toes. If they got backed up then the new regime meant MITs could be brought in from the other two Scottish areas to help out with cases. Inevitably, those being shipped in were about as welcome as a clown at a funeral. This time though, it was as local as it could get. It belonged to Glasgow, dear old Glasgow toon.

Narey and Winter had been meant to be going out for dinner before the call came in. It was to have been a rare and, for him, encouraging venture out together as a couple. She still wanted their relationship to be kept from her colleagues in the force but she was less agitated about that than she had been. He wasn't what you might call an expert on relationships, particularly his own, but he was sure they were in a good place. Well, they were but for the fact they were in a damp tunnel in the dark. No one could say he didn't know how to show a girl a good time.

Her voice came to him again, sharper this time. 'What do you see, Tony?'

'Just what the uniforms said. Dead guy. Throat cut.'

'Hurry up, will you?' The more distant voice was the pathologist, Angie Morton. 'I don't want to be down here any longer than I need to be.'

It had been like the start of a very bad joke. A cop,

a photographer and a pathologist go into a tunnel. The difference was everyone knew the punchline.

Normal procedure hadn't been an option. There was no way a team of forensics could have gone in there and done their stuff. Instead it had been decided to send in a mini task force of talents instead. They were to do what they could and then get the body the hell out of there.

Winter had gone first, as was always the way. At any crime scene, photographs had to get done before anything else. It had to be recorded as was. Not as was after forensics had brushed, scraped, daubed and dusted. The photographer's work was always primary but in Winter's case it was also primal.

'I'll be as long as it takes.'

His voice rolled back down the Molendinar towards where Narey and, a bit further back, Morton were waiting, obviously impatiently, to take their turn. He had to do his job first though and do it thoroughly. It was down to him to record the scene and take it back above ground so that it could be re-created by everyone that needed a bit of it.

'Yes, well, don't enjoy yourself too much. Get your snaps and get back out.'

Enjoy yourself. The jibe hurt more when it came from Rachel.

Winter's liking for his work was well known and not particularly approved of by the cops. He had an enthusiasm for it that they and forensics regarded as unhealthy. Or else they just thought he was weird.

Maybe he was but they didn't get it because they simply didn't understand.

Maybe he didn't either.

He'd been trying to change, trying to be less . . . less like he was. Or at least be less obvious about it, he wasn't sure which. He'd never shake it but he could handle it better.

How could you not find this interesting though? He had been buzzing with anticipation from the moment the tunnel walls had started to shrink in on them. Dead. Down here. Throat cut. It set off old feelings and memories that ran deep.

They'd tried to keep the darkness at bay with jokes as they'd walked, the kind of whistling through the graveyard stuff that was the default for those who had to see and do things that most would run a mile from. Through all the nonsense, Winter's nose had twitched. He doubted the other two were so different though. You couldn't, wouldn't, get into the game if crazy stuff like this didn't get your blood flowing. Winter's arteries had a tsunami pumping through them.

The wide-eyed screamer in front of him was perhaps in his late twenties or early thirties. So difficult to tell beneath the decay. The damp denims that held his legs in place were soaked from the knees down and looked set to disintegrate. He wore a light blue cagoule over a white T-shirt and a navy-blue fleece, decent walking shoes on his feet, and a backpack that threatened to pitch him head first into the burn. His scalp, scarred with tracks and bites, was visible below dirty reddish-blond hair.

19

Winter stared at him, his mind itching with something he couldn't place. Dots were joining somewhere deep inside him and he didn't like it. He swore under his breath, telling himself to get on with it, and edged back to fire off a succession of closing shots. The poor bastard, sitting in his own River Styx waiting for a call that had already come. He doubted that there was a coin to be found in the man's mouth, no payment for the ferryman.

'Okay. I'm finished.' He shuffled backwards down the tunnel, Narey and Morton doing the same until the space was large enough for all three to stand, crouching slightly, under the ceiling. The two women looked at him but he just nodded in return as he spoke behind the protective mask on his face. 'Job done.'

Angie Morton blew out air anxiously. 'How bad is it down there?'

'The space or the body?'

'The space. I'm hardly going to be bothered by the body. That's my job.'

'Pretty tight. I didn't know you were claustrophobic.'

'Neither did I till now. Okay, wish me luck.'

She ducked and crept forward warily, her back receding into the near distance until Winter and Narey were left standing alone. His hoarse whisper was tinged with annoyance.

'Don't enjoy myself too much?'

'Sorry. It just came out. Old habits. You know I didn't mean it, right?'

'Right.'

20

She lifted her face mask from her mouth and did the same with his. Raising her head, she leaned forward to kiss him firmly on the lips. 'Am I forgiven?'

'You are. Are you not taking a chance on being seen or heard? Angie's not far away.'

She shrugged. 'I'll live dangerously. Anyway, maybe it wouldn't be the worst thing in the world. You look hot without a mask.'

'Careful, Rach. You almost sound like someone who could deal with this the way normal people would.'

'Oops, my mask slipped.' She eased the protective cover back down over her mouth. 'You had your chance . . .'

He grinned at her, liking it. Claustrophobic tunnel or not, they were in a good place.

She smiled back with her eyes then snapped into professional mode. 'What did you make of the victim?'

'What's left of him? Looks like he was set for a day on the hills. No sign of his hands having been tied. No obvious injuries at all except the cut throat.'

Narey shook her head slowly. 'I don't suppose there's any chance it could have been suicide?'

He laughed. 'Can't see it. There's no knife lying around for a start. And anyway, why would you? Come down here to kill yourself, I mean.'

Narey looked round. 'Why would you come down here to kill? Or be killed? Or at all? I mean, look at this place.'

'Wherever there's places other people won't go, there will always be people who want to go there.'

She narrowed her eyes. 'Did you get that from an episode of *The Twilight Zone*? Or somewhere even darker? Like inside yourself?'

'One of those. Getting this guy out is going to be a barrel of laughs. He's ready for falling to pieces.'

'So is Angie,' she grinned wickedly behind her mask. 'I'm betting this will be the shortest examination she's ever done. We're going to have to get a team down here and do an inch by inch of the tunnel once we're finished. Ha. Here she comes now.'

Morton was lifting and wriggling her shoulders. 'That freaked me out. It was the thought of getting stuck there even though I knew I wouldn't. It's beyond me why anyone would choose to come down here.'

Narey looked at Winter and raised her eyebrows. 'Ask Tony. He'll get all deep and meaningful about it. Anyway, my turn.'

With that she made her way further down the tunnel, the plastic covers over her shoes singing dolefully as they slipped through the shallow water of the burn.

'Does nothing bother her?' Morton was looking at Narey's retreating figure with what seemed to be a mixture of respect and irritation.

Winter hesitated. Rachel had seemingly given him some hint that maybe their relationship didn't have to be as secret as she'd previously demanded. At least he thought she had. Still, he knew better than to answer anything other than carefully. Not too defensively or protectively.

'Plenty, I'm sure. But not enough to stop her doing her job. I guess she just shuts out what she needs to.'

'Well I get that. You have to when you're dealing with the dead. Unless you're *you* and actively enjoy it.'

Winter groaned loudly. 'Give me peace. Did you go through his clothing?'

Morton shook her head. 'Too risky. I'll do it once I can get him laid out in the morgue. We will be able to move him easily enough. Hopefully it won't be in bits. Will you do it?'

'What? That's not exactly ... You're kidding me, right?'

'There's only room for one person down there and I'd really rather it wasn't me. You've just got to—'

'Yeah I know. We've been through it. You could ask Rachel.'

'I'd rather not. Please.'

Winter breathed out hard. 'Yeah, okay. Just don't make any crack about how it's going to be some kind of fun.'

'I won't. I know it's not.'

Fun was the last thing it was going to be. Rigor had been and gone from the victim's body, leaving it as limp as he was when his lights and his life had been turned off. There was still enough density in the bones to keep him upright but whether that would stand the test of movement they'd only know when they tried. When *he* tried.

The plan was to ease him back onto the light stretcher they'd brought with them, hopefully causing as little

23

damage as possible, then float him back down the burn until the ceiling lifted again. Then they'd carry him the rest of the way. More like Baby Moses on bulrushes than a corpse ferried from the battlefield.

He looked up from his thoughts to see Narey beginning to stand up from the crouch that had carried her back through the lower part of the tunnel.

'Anything?' Angie Morton asked her.

Narey shrugged. 'Whoever he is, he was left here thinking that he'd never be found. No attempt to hide him. No point when the body's already well out of sight. The killer must have thought this guy would be dust by the time anyone found him. If anyone ever did.'

'Maybe *that's* why he was here in the first place,' Winter suggested.

'Maybe,' she agreed. 'But came here or brought here? And why would you come to a place like this with someone who might do that to you?'

'Do you have an answer?'

She shrugged again. 'No but I did find this.'

Narey held up a blue-gloved hand and they strained to see what it was she was holding between finger and thumb. It was wooden and rectangular, the size of a matchbox but thinner with a metal ring on the end.

'What is that, Rachel?'

She held the object slightly higher so they could see. 'A key ring. With . . .' She held it higher. 'The letters *RH* on it.'

Chapter 4

Remy watched four men in white paper suits, the hoods over their heads, pitching a tent near the fence where the body would come back up. How the hell were they going to get it out of there without destroying evidence? Evidence. The word hit him over the head. It wasn't just that the dead guy's DNA was on him. His DNA, his clothing fibres or whatever, were all over the dead guy.

He wanted to step backwards like he did in the tunnel. But he couldn't. There was a whole new lot of people in behind him. He was trapped just like the dead guy. It felt claustrophobic all of a sudden and he wanted to tell them all to get the hell out of his way. They just kept talking, leaning into him to get a better view, crowding him.

He could smell them, their sweat and their curiosity. Blood lust, that's what they had. They wanted to see the body, wouldn't leave till they did. He'd seen it though and could tell them it wasn't nice, not nice at all. *What's going on?* someone near him shouted to the cops. *His some'dy been shot? Huv they?*

The tent that the forensics had put up was near the fence but not right at it. So when the first two heads appeared over the rise, the area lit up by temporary floodlights, the whole crowd saw them at once. Two cops at the head of a stretcher, others coming in to help to make sure it got over the fence safely, another two holding it at the back. The body was on its side; he could see that under the paper blanket that covered it. Probably with his DNA all over it.

There was a surge behind him as the crowd wanted closer and he let them slip past, a flood of the nosy bastards going by until he was at the back. All he could see above their heads was the gloved hands of the cops by the tape, telling them to stay where they were. Even if they hadn't seen enough, he had.

He turned away, collar up, weaving his way through some new arrivals. Back to the car, opening the door and slipping inside. He sat in the dark for another five minutes, wondering how he was going to explain to his old man how he was this late in making his dinner for him.

His dad lived in a faded tenement in Adelaide Street, part of the East End's changing landscape south of Duke Street and north of the Gallowgate. Like in many industrial cities, the East End of Glasgow was where the poor and the huddled masses traditionally lived, yearning to breathe free. Instead, they breathed in the pollution that blew in on the westerly wind from the factories and the yards in the city centre. It was their lot.

A whole slew of Adelaide Street had disappeared over the past few years and there was more still to go, maybe all of it. Its problem, apart from rising damp and a lack of decent heating, was that it was on the battleground where the money men were looking to expand their borders, creeping east when they thought no one was watching.

The East End was to become the new West End. That's what they were trying to tell people. Remy took it to mean it was going to become too expensive to live in.

They hadn't actually come out and said they wanted to demolish the whole area and build new houses that only those with good jobs could afford to buy but nobody doubted that was what they were up to. Remy's dad wasn't for moving though. As far as Archie Feeks was concerned, the only way they'd be getting him out of there was in a box.

There had been another letter from the company that owned the building, turning up the heat a few degrees as they pushed to get him out. Apparently, Mr Archibald Feeks was holding back the redevelopment of the entire East End and preventing his neighbours from enjoying the fruits of regeneration. Yeah, like his dad or his mates had any use for coffee shops or craft breweries or cafés that sold pulled pork served by bearded hipsters. Or rents that they couldn't afford.

27

Not that Remy understood his dad's attachment to the place. For a start, the stairs weren't ideal for someone with a chronic lung disease but then again, neither was breathing. It was just something that had to be done.

He'd stopped at the Merchant Chippie on the High Street and picked up fish suppers for both of them. Cooking wasn't an option now and this was the simplest thing. Anyway, some hot battered fish wrapped round Remy's heart might just slow it down enough for him to talk.

He knocked on the front door then let himself in. He was greeted by the sound of the television coming from the front room and shouted out to his dad, 'It's me. Sorry I'm late.'

'In here.'

His old man was sitting, as ever, in his favourite chair about five feet from the TV. He didn't take his eyes off the screen as Remy came in the room but his nose twitched and his eyes slid over.

'Here I was thinking that you'd fallen and broken your watch again. But you might be forgiven. That's the smell of fish and chips.' He sniffed again. 'Merchant Chippie, I'd say. And . . . wait a minute, there's pickled eggs in there too.'

'Brilliant, Dad. You should go on *Britain's Got Talent*.'

'Son, my lungs are worth tuppence ha'penny but there's nothing wrong with my nose. Or my memory. It's what you usually get. Come on, get them open. I'm so hungry I could eat a scabby-headed wean.'

Remy's dad was a big little man, the kind that Glasgow specialized in. He carried himself like he was six foot two and no one had dared to tell him he was really only five foot five. It was all about the size of the fight in the dog. The toes of the slippers on his feet were pointed as ever at the television, like they were praying to his own Mecca.

Archie Feeks, former foreman and welder, built ships on the Clyde the same as his dad before him, but retired through ill health before he was sixty. The frustration of that was choking him but he wouldn't let himself become a moaner. He knew the fault was his own. No one else had forced that cigarette smoke into his lungs.

Remy grabbed a couple of plates from the kitchen and set the fish suppers on them, handing one to his dad and sitting in a chair with the other. He was hoping the food would occupy his dad's mouth enough that he wouldn't have to answer any questions. He should have known better.

'How come you're so late? You been seeing that wee lassie of yours?'

'She's not my . . . No, I haven't been seeing her. I was just in town with a couple of pals. Lost track of time.'

His dad's head slowly turned, eyes narrowed. He'd always been able to tell when Remy was lying and he'd obviously not lost the knack. It was probably because Remy was so bad at it. He looked at him for a bit then glanced down, seeing that he hadn't eaten any of the fish supper.

29

'Not hungry, son?'

He was. He was starving but he just couldn't touch it. He'd gone into the toilets in the Star & Garter and washed his hands before going for the chips but it still didn't feel right. He wasn't sure it would ever feel right again. He stood up.

'Yes, they're just a bit hot. I'll give them a minute. Forgot to wash my hands.'

His old man looked doubtful. 'Okay . . .'

Remy walked into the kitchen and turned on the hot tap, letting the water nearly scald him. He fired soap onto his hands, washing-up liquid too, and slathered them together. He stood in front of the sink with his eyes closed, screwed tight shut, and wished it all away. He dried his hands on a tea towel and took a fork out of the drawer.

Of course, his dad was all over the fork like an interrogation officer as soon as he saw it.

'A fork. You become posh or something? Hands not good enough for you?'

'I told you, they're too hot.'

'Too hot to touch but not too hot to eat?'

''Sake, Dad. Can I just eat it, please?'

They watched the news, Remy in silence barely noticing it, and his dad providing a running commentary.

'What's the world coming to, son? Killing kids with missiles? They should be ashamed of themselves and so should anyone that's not stopping them. And how can kids still be dying in Africa just because of a drought? We should be sending our money over there, not

30

arming people to bomb weans. Who said they could sell off the NHS? Tell me, who? Flogging it off to their mates so they can have even more money. It's disgusting. Wouldn't have happened if we'd voted Yes.'

He liked hearing his dad rant, showed there was still plenty of fight left in him, but the normality of it freaked him out. It was like nothing else had happened that night. How could the world just turn the same?

There was nothing on the news about Glasgow though, not that he expected there to be. Not quite yet and not on the national programme. Maybe on the regional news.

When it came, it mentioned the closure of a factory that had been making baths for a hundred years, sparking another rant from his dad.

'We used to make things here, son. Ships, trains, carpets, engines. Now we just eat things, use things, buy and sell things and throw them away. Same with people. Use them up and throw them away.'

And finally, news just in. Police say the body of a man has been found in the Molendinar Tunnel which runs underground through the East End of Glasgow. Police are still at the scene and the area has been cordoned off while investigations continue. The man, thought to be in his early thirties, was found earlier this evening. It is not yet known whether his death was suspicious. Now here's Eleanor with the weather . . .

That's it? That's all they've got? Didn't know if his death was suspicious. Yeah, right. They knew. They would know *much* more than they were saying.

Chapter 5

Saturday morning

'So, tell me about this guy, Rachel. Mr RH.'

DCI Derek Addison had his long legs stretched up on his desk, an oversized sandwich in his hands and heading for his mouth. Hearing about a month-old corpse with a slit throat was no barrier to his ever-healthy appetite.

'Well for a start, we don't know that he *is* Mr RH. I'm working on the fact that he might be but the key ring might not have been his. It could have been left there at some other time or it could belong to someone else. It could belong to whoever cut his throat.'

'Now wouldn't that be nice.'

She nodded. 'It would but how often do we get that lucky? Anyway, I can tell you more or less what our man had for his last meal but I'm not sure that vegetables and beef are going to get us that far.'

'It wouldn't get me far,' Addison agreed, his mouth full of pastrami and cheese. 'But maybe it tells us that he last ate in the afternoon. That doesn't sound like a breakfast or an evening meal. What else do we have?'

'Not much at all. He was five foot eleven, reddish-fair-haired, probably weighed a little over twelve stone. No tattoos, no scarring, no sign of any major operation. Tox report came back clean so no alcohol or drugs in his system. Clothes were mainly regular high street, bought in their thousands. No identification in his pockets. Fingerprints were intact but they match nothing on the system.'

Addison sighed. 'You've got some good news that you're saving for me, right?'

'Wish I had. The post mortem drew a blank other than estimating death at five to six weeks ago. The killer was probably right-handed but because of the low ceiling we can't make a guess on his stature. The angle of the cut tells us nothing because everyone would have crouched down to the same height.'

Addison swallowed down another mouthful. 'You're trying to get DNA from the key ring, I take it? Make a match to him?'

'We're trying. Sam Guthrie says she'll have something for me by the end of the day.'

Addison nodded and Narey enjoyed the discomfort that the mention of Guthrie's name caused him. He and the forensic chemist had dated more than a few times but she played the game by rules that he just wasn't used to. She was in charge and Addison couldn't

33

quite handle that and he couldn't quite walk away from it.

'Yeah well, we'll see what she comes up with. Okay, so where are you going to go with this from here?'

It was Narey's turn to sigh. 'I'm going to slog it out. No one has been reported missing in the time frame that would fit the description so he maybe lived alone or is from overseas. Maybe he is someone that goes off the radar for long periods so no one's too concerned. I'm going to run a search for anything remotely similar, if there is such a thing. We've got as big a team on the ground as I could muster and they're doing door-to-door in the area. And I'm also going to keep spinning the plates on all the other cases that I have on the go.'

'I hope that's not you moaning about workload, DI Narey.'

'As if, sir. I'm just grateful that a wee lassie like me even gets to play at cops and robbers in the first place.'

'Quite right and don't forget it. Okay, so here's the obvious question. What the hell was this guy doing getting himself killed in some stupid underground tunnel that no one knew existed? Why was he there?'

Narey exhaled wearily. 'Funnily enough, I did wonder that. The same goes for the guy that phoned in the 999.'

'Assuming he wasn't the killer.'

'Yes, assuming that but it doesn't seem likely. Why phone it in weeks later and leave a recording of your voice when all you had to do was walk away and the body would probably never have been found. Doesn't make sense.'

'No but I'd still to want to interview this nutter, whoever he is.'

'Me too. I'm on it.'

'Okay, keep me up to date and I'll weigh in when I can. What else are you working on that I need to know about?'

She held up a clenched right fist and began releasing fingers one by one as she reeled cases off. 'A serious assault on an asylum seeker in Sighthill. The victim's still in intensive care. A rape and beating in Renfrew Lane. An attempted murder on Garscube Road. A gang fight in—'

'Jesus, Rachel,' he interrupted. 'It's like when someone asks you how you are. They don't really want to know, they're just being polite. I meant what do I *need* to know about.'

She smiled. 'Just so you know I'm not slacking.'

'Ha. Sometimes I wish you'd slack. You make every-body else look bad. Now piss off and let me eat.'

Narey was halfway to the door when Addison spoke again.

'Rachel, I meant to ask. How's your dad doing?'

She turned and he saw the energy seep out of her, her face telling him all he needed to know.

Her father, former Detective Chief Inspector Alan Narey, had Alzheimer's. He'd moved into a care home three years earlier. Her mother had died a few years before that.

'Good days and bad days. Well . . .' She hesitated. 'Bad days and some not so bad. He only recognizes me maybe one visit in four. The worst is watching him disappear, like watching a rowing boat going out to sea and not being able to stop it. You know, some days are actually good and they're something special. I'm going to visit him later.'

'Tell him I was asking . . . Just look after yourself, Rachel. And him.'

'Are you . . . are you being *nice*, sir?'

'I'll deny it if you ever repeat it. Now piss off.'

Winter was waiting impatiently in the office of Campbell 'Two Soups' Baxter, the scenes of crime manager, one of many people who were his boss. Baxter was one of those least happy to be in that position and yet one of the happiest to order Winter around. As far as Two Soups was concerned, Winter was an unnecessary anomaly. Baxter often loudly declared that his photographic skills weren't needed when the scene examiners did the job just as well.

It was true and it wasn't.

Winter was an anomaly all right. In more ways than one if he was being honest. He was a throwback to the days when the job was done properly, when police photographers used film and their brains and had limited chances to get things right. When skill was needed, not just a speedy trigger finger and an HNC. A previous Chief Constable of the old Strathclyde force, Sir Ed Walker, had kept Winter on, much to the irritation

36

of the likes of Baxter. Neither a change of chief nor the unification of the country's eight forces into Police Scotland in 2013 had changed the situation. Not yet, anyway.

But what wasn't true was that the examiners did the job as well as he did. They did it more cheaply and, as far as the bean counters were concerned, more efficiently. They didn't do it as well though. It *was* his job. They were proficient photographers, he was an expert. He was a specialist.

They had to be chemists and biologists, detectives and administrators, more than jacks of all trades. They had to keep up with scientific developments that were changing daily as more and more tools became available to them. Tools that they had to master immediately before those tools were out of date and replaced by something better. They had to do all that while he had the luxury of concentrating on one thing and doing it right.

His self-congratulations were interrupted by the door opening behind him and Baxter storming through it. Two Soups was a man who did not get his name by dining on soup. He weighed in at a very round twenty-stone-plus on a frame that didn't seem engineered for it. He was only five foot seven with incongruously slim legs. Winter always thought of him as a dancing hippo, albeit one with a thick salt-and-pepper beard and a permanently crotchety nature.

Baxter fell heavily into the chair behind his desk, throwing a folder onto the wooden surface as he did so. Winter wasn't overly happy to see that it contained prints from the Molendinar crime scene.

Two Soups sat there and stared at him, clearly enjoying the moment. Men of little joy take what pleasure they can in being a pain in the arse to others. Power is of no use to them if it can't be abused.

'Well?'

'Well what?'

Baxter bristled and reddened, the fury of the righteously indignant rising within him. 'These.' He dismissively waved a hand at the folder. 'What have you got to say about these?'

Taking a breath to stop himself from biting back, Winter reached for the folder, took the prints out and let them fan onto the desk. The half-eaten victim of the burn looked back up at them and the blistered, festering cut to his throat smiled blackly. Winter again got a flash of familiarity.

He counted to ten. Then did so again. 'The photographs. What about them?'

Baxter shook his head slowly, a schoolteacher having to admonish a particularly stupid child. 'These . . . these are the work of a *specialist,* are they?' He spat out the word as if it were poisoning him.

When Winter did nothing except set his face harder, Baxter smirked and carried on. 'They are not exactly good, are they? Badly lit. Poorly structured. Oddly angled. Am I really expected to serve these up to the Procurator Fiscal and have him present them as evidence in court?'

'Badly lit?

'They are dark.'

'It was in a tunnel. Without daylight.'

Two Soups sneered and waved his hand at another print. 'And that. What is that supposed to be?'

It was a head-on shot of the victim, catching the man's full thousand-yard stare into the void. A stare that went all the further for the lack of eyes. The composition was less than square, a slight tilt from left to right as it framed the man's face. Baxter twisted his head as he looked down at it, exaggerating the effect. 'You think that is . . . adequate?'

Winter made a tight smile. He wasn't going to give Two Soups the satisfaction of getting angry. Inside though . . . inside he was ripping Baxter's head off and shoving it up his arse.

'That is not only adequate, it is a minor masterpiece of composition. There was no way to get to the other side of the victim to face him and take a frontal shot. There was no room to do so. If you'd been down there yourself . . .' Winter paused and made a show of looking at Baxter's girth. 'If you *could* have gone down there yourself, you'd have seen that.'

A muscle twitched and tightened on the jowls beneath Baxter's beard. Winter continued.

'I had to reach through and over the dead guy's arms and position my camera in front of him to get a face-on shot in situ. It was like trying to take a selfie on a smartphone.'

'A what?'

'A smartphone. It's like a step up from a digital watch but you can talk to people on it.'

Two Soups looked a heartbeat away from combustion, his face flushing furiously. 'I know what a *smartphone* is. What is a *selfie*? There's no such word. Never mind. It doesn't matter. I'm talking about these poor excuses for photographs. They are not fit for purpose.'

Winter slowly pushed the prints apart with the tips of his fingers, saying nothing but spreading them across the desk so that each was visible.

'Do you see that? That is where the initial incision was made. We can see that not only by the angle of entry but by the clarity of the photograph. By the fact that it is entirely central to the frame. You can blow that up a hundred times and you will still have quality. You will still have *adequacy*. And see here? How these two photographs in conjunction show the precise body position in relation to the tunnel and how *these* use what light there is to show the gap round the body and how *this* clearly shows the decomposition in situ yet avoids the inherent danger of the flash over-illuminating the face? *That* is why I'm employed as a specialist. The scene examiners are very, very good at what they do. But this is what *I* do.'

Baxter squirmed uncomfortably in his seat and his face flushed but none of that translated into any words that might have conceded the merit of what Winter had said. Instead he pulled himself upright and scowled.

'That is indeed the case at *present*, Mr Winter.'

A thin smile danced across Baxter's fat lips. He was not a man who readily displayed any kind of good humour and Winter couldn't fail to notice or be bothered by it.

'At present? What's that supposed to mean?'

Baxter sneered. 'Just what it says. Things change. Even you must be aware that various departments have seen adjustment since the unification to Police Scotland. The review of all services is continuing.'

He let the reply sink in, staring into Winter's eyes with a glee that dared a response. Winter fought the urge to rise to the bait.

'That sounds like a very general remark.'

'Does it? You may take it any way you wish, Mr Winter. Although however you take it will not stop the process. The winds of change will be blowing. I have already heard the rustle in the trees.'

Winter could feel his pulse racing as he tried to take it all in at the same time as he longed to punch Baxter in the face. He needed to know but he wouldn't give the fat bastard the satisfaction of asking him.

'Well whatever, Mr Baxter. You keep blowing Russell in the trees if that's what floats your boat. I've got photographs to take. Excuse me.'

'For now, Winter,' he heard Baxter shout as he pushed through the door to get away. 'You've got photographs to take *for now*!'

Chapter 6

Saturday evening

The outside of Clober Nursing Home was possibly the most depressing sight Narey had ever seen. It wasn't the drab exterior walls, pebble-dashed in rainstorm grey, or the anonymous uniformity of the curtained windows. It wasn't even the miserable little sign that apologetically declared its name to the world. It was the knowledge that her dad was inside.

He had Alzheimer's. The cruellest, meanest little bastard of a disease that she knew. It had robbed her of him, and him of a meaningful, dignified life. It had mercilessly attacked a man who hadn't deserved it, picking away at his being like a raven at a corpse. It had condemned him to this soulless shithole of a care home.

It was the best soulless shithole that she could pay for but the sight of it still filled her with guilt and despair. It wouldn't matter if the staff were actual angels with wings and haloes, serving him nectar, ambrosia and thirty-year-old single malt on a golden tray, she would still hate the place because he was seeing out his life in it. She shook her head slowly, breathed deeply and got out of the car.

She walked through the home on auto-pilot, treading the well-worn path to his room. No matter how often she went, it would never be enough, not in her own head. She would always owe him more than she could give. Did the walls of this place really have to be such a soul-destroying shade of bloody yellow?

Halfway along the last corridor, the narrowness of it squeezing the remaining drops of hope out of her, she had to stop when a young woman emerged from one of the rooms and stepped across her path. She looked up to see Narey and her mouth twisted.

'He's not had a good day.'

Maybe it was meant as an early warning, maybe it was supposed to be sympathetic or helpful. But she heard it as reproachful.

The carer's name was Jess and Narey had never liked her. She was in her late teens or early twenties, small and slim with dark hair pulled back tightly from her face. She would probably have been very good-looking if not for the near-permanent scar of irritation that she wore on her face. It seemed something was always bothering Jess and it was always someone else's fault. Narey frequently wanted to slap her.

43

'He's broken a glass and the lampshade next to his bed. And he's had an *accident*.'

Narey bit her tongue and confined herself to a sharp nod to say that she'd heard. She eased past the girl and opened the door to her dad's room. He was sitting up on the bed, fully dressed and staring sadly towards his lap. He didn't stir when she was fully in the room and she cleared her throat to say she was there.

He looked up as if he'd been caught doing something he shouldn't and for a second she saw him as a ten-year-old, tousled fair hair and boy's blue eyes. That moment passed when his eyes clouded over in doubt, wondering who she was and why she was there. It was like a dagger to her heart every single time.

Three years he'd been in this home now. Three long years for her and well, who knows how long it seemed for him. Time was a slippery fish for her dad, a wriggler that writhed in his hands and turned head over tail in the blink of an eye. Ask him the date he started with the police or the day he got promoted to Detective Chief Inspector and he'd trot the answers out. Ask him the name of the song he'd sung to her mum the day they learned she was pregnant and he'd have no problem. Ask him about the broken glass or, God forbid, the little accident, then chances were he'd have no recollection. Not this day anyway.

'How are you, Dad?'

It was always a tough choice whether to call him Dad when he didn't recognize her. Sometimes it frightened him, confused him further. Sometimes though it ticked a box, joined a set of dots and a smile would spread over his face. Not this time.

'I don't know you. Do I know you?'

'It's Rachel, Dad. Your daughter.'

His face scrunched up in deeper puzzlement. His mouth bobbed open and closed a couple of times but no words came out. After a bit, he let his gaze fall disconsolately to his lap again.

She sat gently on the edge of the bed, wary of going too close too soon. If at all.

'It's cold out there tonight. Freezing wind too. You're in the best place in here.'

He looked up. 'I could go out. If I wanted. But if it's cold I'd need to wear a . . . wear a . . .'

She'd learned not to finish his sentences for him. Better to let him get there himself, however slowly, than to demean him further by filling in the gaps. Better too not to correct him when he got it wrong. Upsetting him would just mean upsetting them both. Lots of tears had proven that little truth.

'A coat. I'd need a coat. A warm coat.'

There you go, Dad. Well done. She scolded herself for patronizing him even if it was just in her own head. Every little triumph, every small bit of joy was to be savoured. He remembered *coat*. That meant a synapsis had correctly conversed with another synapsis. It meant a path he could walk on and she was grateful for every single one of them.

She reached out a hand towards him.

'Yes, you couldn't go out without a coat. Far too cold tonight. Feel my hand.'

He looked first at the hand then at her. Then at the hand again. Slowly, he reached out his own, large and soft where it was once strong, peppered with liver spots and streaked with veins. He placed it over her hand and held it gently.

'Oh yes, you're right. Very cold. You need a coat. And gloves. You need gloves.'

He didn't take his hand away after checking her temperature; instead he left it there for a bit then slid it underneath so his fingers curled into hers. They sat in silence, he looking at the bed and she at him. Occasionally, he squeezed and she knew it was her dad doing that, calling to her from inside.

With one particularly firm squeeze, he looked up sharply and she felt the tug of want inside her, pleading for him to make the connection. The flesh and blood he was holding was his own, surely he felt it, sensed it. His eyes furrowed and she waited, barely daring to breathe. Nothing. Not this time.

She sat for as long as she could. Talking about the weather and her job, sneaking in references to her mum, his wife, to holidays they'd taken when she was a kid. Nothing registered. Not today. Still she talked and he listened. And he held her hand. Winning small battles in a losing war.

After he'd warily let her kiss him on the forehead and she'd closed the door behind her and left, she stood for a moment with her back to it and contemplated bursting into tears. Any prospect of that disappeared when Jess the carer loomed into view from the other end of the corridor.

'I could have told you he wouldn't know you tonight. He's not had a good day.'

Narey was torn between keeping on the right side of this girl who would be left alone with her dad or grabbing her by her hair and smashing her face against the wall. As she moved swiftly towards the girl, she wasn't entirely sure which option she was going to take.

She put the brakes on just in time and stood close enough for the little bitch to feel her breath on her pinched face. She paused just long enough to see a flash of worry across the girl's features.

'I'm just popping in to see Mrs McBriar. I want to pay for the glass and the lampshade. You'll make sure my father is comfortable, won't you?'

Jess nodded as quickly as she could.

'Good.'

Narey looked into her eyes and nodded back. Message understood.

She knocked briskly on the door of the woman who doubled as the home's owner and manager and entered without waiting for a reply. McBriar looked up from behind her desk, clearly surprised.

'Miss Narey. Is something wrong? Can I help you?'

'Yes you can. I'd like to talk to you about Jess.'

Chapter 7

Robert Henaghan. Richard Hendry. Ravindra Hegde. Ryan Hughes. Robert Hillman. Rohak Handoo. Reggie Haynes. The seven adult male missing persons in the UK with the initials RH. Narey already knew the names off by heart and recounted them over and over as she walked round the mortuary at the Southern General. It wasn't the perfect place to be immediately after a visit to the nursing home but it was where she needed to be. She needed to work.

Henaghan. Hendry. Hegde. Hughes. Hillman. Handoo. Haynes. It became a verse in her head with a rhythm all of its own, singing to her as she worked her way through the clothing and meagre belongings of Henaghan, Hendry, Hegde, Hughes, Hillman, Handoo or Haynes.

The first evidence bag contained the navy-blue fleece. Size large. Department store label. Pretty cheap. It was streaked with damp and smelled of death and the tunnel. It was lined and elasticated with a zip all the way to the neck.

She didn't like the new mortuary much. It was brand-spanking-new, state-of-the-art shiny, with every possible facility required to host mortuary and forensic services under one roof. But it lacked soul. Maybe that would come with time but for now it left her as cold as the stainless-steel tables with a bank of cameras pointing at each.

Everyone else had gone home for the night and she was alone with the evidence bags, the clothing and the seven. Henaghan. Hendry. Hegde. Hughes. Hillman. Handoo. Haynes.

Ravindra Hegde didn't seem a likely name for a white man with reddish hair. Neither did Rohak Handoo. She wasn't naïve enough to rule them out on that alone but both were also too short. The rumour was that Hegde had owed money to the wrong people and that he'd never be found. Handoo had had a bust-up with his in-laws but beyond that no one had said anything about where he might have gone.

Henaghan, Hendry, Hughes and Hillman. Henaghan, Hendry, Hughes and Hillman.

The two-tone blue nylon cagoule had survived better than the fleece. It was a good make, expensive. Large. The label at the neck had been snipped off. Odd thing to do with a designer brand. The part of the label that remained had the hint of lettering in black felt pen.

Robert Hillman from the Western Isles would be

forty-nine now. He had learning difficulties and his elderly parents had started a poster campaign that was carried across the country. It was thought that maybe he'd fallen into a river or walked into a peat bog and never got out.

Henaghan, Hendry, Hughes and Haynes.

She missed the low red brick of the old City Mortuary near the High Court on the Saltmarket. Sure it was cramped, cold and outdated but it was the real thing. Bricks and mortar. Rough and ready. Memories and legends. The victims of Bible John and Peter Manuel had been laid out there. It had an atmosphere that you couldn't miss. It had scared her witless the first time she was in there on her own. The new place couldn't scare her if it tried. Its ghosts were all just children.

Reggie Haynes was of Jamaican parentage and his photographs showed he had a distinctive hooked nose. The age and height would have fitted but nothing else seemed to.

Henaghan, Hendry and Hughes. Henaghan, Hendry and Hughes.

She picked up the bag containing the dead man's disintegrating shoes. The fact that they'd survived as well as they had was testament to their good quality. They were lightweight and flexible hiking boots, Gore-Tex lined with a tough rubber sole. Expensive. Size nine.

Robert Henaghan had dark hair and was just five foot seven. He'd said goodbye to his wife at breakfast and left to go to his office but never arrived. There had been debts and doubts but no one ever knew if he'd simply disappeared or if something had happened to him.

The white T-shirt was cheap and mass-produced. Medium. Shop's own label.

She'd gathered her MIT squad together in Pitt Street and tasked them with brainstorming ideas of who the man was and why he'd been killed where he had. The suggestions had come thick and fast, some more helpful than others. Loner. Geologist. Local historian. Dealer looking for somewhere to hide his stash. Hermit. Schizophrenic. Potholer.

Did any of these tags apply to their man? Was Hendry a geologist, was Hughes or Haynes a hermit? Was Henaghan a risk taker? Did Hillman go willingly with his killer and, if so, why?

All the loose thoughts would be examined, every thread pulled until something unravelled. Hopefully. These would be hard yards. Nothing more than a methodical slog.

Ryan Hughes had been missing since he was seven years old in Swansea. God only knew what height he was or where he had been living. No one even knew if he'd reached eight. For a while, the broken faces of his parents had become familiar on television, then they too slowly disappeared from view.

Rico Giannandrea was on her MIT squad. Until a few months earlier, they'd both been DSs at Stewart Street and the situation would have been awkward if it had been anyone else. Not Rico though. If he had to ride shotgun then he'd be the best shotgun in town; there on time, full of bright ideas and positivity. He'd be that way as a DS until he wasn't a DS any more.

It was Rico who had suggested they might be looking at someone reckless. A risk taker. Maybe someone who'd done something equally stupid before. Maybe something a profiler could work with.

Why the hell would anyone need three torches? Three of them tucked away inside the nylon backpack along with spare batteries. Had he intended to live down that tunnel for a month? The Swiss Army knife made sense if he had been hillwalking or camping but why three torches?

The mortuary was silent and cold. Not cold like the old place where it made you shiver on a summer's day. Sterile cold, like the sluiced-down tables and floors you could eat your dinner off. All she could hear was the faint buzz of electricity and the names that danced through her head.

The squad was sure that the location meant that the killer knew Glasgow well. They guessed that maybe five per cent of people even knew the Molendinar Burn existed. Less than half of those would know you could get into it or where. She remembered scribbling on her whiteboard. *Local. Knowledgeable.*

Richard Hendry was already five foot eleven when he'd disappeared aged seventeen. Chances were he'd grown more than enough to be taller than the man in the tunnel. He'd been in his last year at school when he failed to return from a night out with friends. The search for him had gone viral, hitting every teenage Facebook page in the land, but he was never seen again.

Rico had been sure that killer and victim had gone into the tunnel together. The chances of the murderer stumbling across him there were minuscule. Yes, he could have followed him but it seemed much more likely they'd gone down there together. Narey had written on the whiteboard again. *Killer known to victim?*

No one knew how many people went missing in Scotland or the UK every year. The best guess was far too many. Some went missing but were never reported, others were reported out but never back in again. The ones old enough to be thought capable of looking after themselves, they could bugger off and go where they liked. More difficult these days of course when every transaction leaves a digital trail but still quite possible to do.

She had interviewed too many distraught parents whose grown-up baby had done a disappearing act and had to tell far too many of them that there was nothing she could do. Not until the kid was harmed or broke the law. If they ended up living under an underpass or begging for change in London then there was a good chance they'd disappear forever.

Henaghan, Hendry, Hegde, Hughes, Hillman, Handoo and Haynes. She wandered round in the room's harsh white light and hummed the tune to herself as she walked and thought.

She'd already decided that an artist's impression of this guy wasn't going to cut it. They were going to need a facial reconstruction. She'd put in a call to a friend, Professor Kirsten Fairweather at the Centre for Anatomy and Human Identification at Dundee University, to ask if her department would do a 3D reconstruct. Kirsten had been only too happy to help and was making arrangements to get the process started. It would, of course, take time, and until then there was no choice but to continue to do it old-school.

Dental records were en route for all seven RHs on her list but she knew they were unlikely to match. None of the seven seemed a fit to the man in the tunnel but their names still worked for her, giving her a beat to work to, the rhythm of the lost.

She left the room and wandered the corridor for a bit, following her thoughts and staring idly into one of the smaller rooms used to counsel bereaved families. It was a halfway house between the living and the dead, all pastel colours and adjustable lighting. Would there be anyone to come and see the remains of the Molendinar Man? Anyone to say yes, that's my son, my husband?

She turned and retraced her steps, feeling suddenly anxious to be with the evidence bags, to hold the clothes again and see the man that wore them, her thoughts coming together and a puzzle falling into place.

What did the clothing tell her? A mismatch of sizes

and quality. The victim was either a man who just didn't care much about what he wore or didn't have much choice. She knew plenty of men who didn't give much thought to their wardrobe, Tony for one, but they generally at least wore clothes that fitted them.

The cagoule with the cut-off label had to be second-hand. It looked it too. The rest was cheap but functional. All except the shoes. They'd been bought new and the man hadn't skimped on the price.

Clothing worn, definitely seen better days. Maybe worn for longer than the time in the tunnel. A fleece *and* a cagoule? It wasn't that cold yet, not unless you were outside a lot. Good shoes that fitted him but not the pattern.

They'd wondered about him being a farmer, a postman or a road sweeper but there were plenty of reasons other than a job for someone to spend a lot of time outside. Perhaps the lack of a job.

She had an idea but the torches, all three of them, didn't fit in any way that made sense. Still, at least it was a place to start.

With a final crashing note, the song in her head stopped. Goodbye Henaghan, Hendry, Hegde, Hughes, Hillman, Handoo and Haynes. The man in the tunnel wasn't an RH at all.

Second-hand clothes, worn and dirty. Good footwear an essential. No one to know he'd gone missing. No employer or loved one to call the police. No one can miss you if they don't know you're there to begin with.

She picked up the evidence bag with the little wooden key ring in it, staring at the initials and seeing them for what they really were. She signed the bag out and slipped it into her coat pocket, switched off the last of the lights and left the building.

The initials didn't stand for a person's name at all. It was a place. And she was sure she knew where.

When she phoned the operations room the next morning, she couldn't help but sigh inside when it was Fraser Toshney, one of the DCs, who answered. She guessed he'd have to do.

'Fraser, meet me in the car park in about ten minutes. Never mind why. We're going to do some visiting. We're going to start at the Rosewood Hotel.'

'The down-and-outs' place? Really?' He didn't sound best pleased.

'Yes, really. And after that maybe every shop doorway between here and Dumbarton. And, Fraser? Take that moaning look off your face. Don't think I can't see it.'

'Yes, Boss.'

Chapter 8

Sunday morning

Remy was off work. He'd managed less than half a day collecting trolleys at the store before declaring himself sick. And he was, just not in any way he could explain to them.

He'd probably always known that his hobby would get him into trouble one day. Going in places he shouldn't. Climbing up things he shouldn't. That's why the word *shouldn't* had been in there. And that's why he'd always done it.

Now he was paying the price. His old man had always said that nothing was free in this world. There was an old coffee table in his dad's front room that he'd 'got free' by collecting Kensitas Club coupons that came with his cigarettes and then exchanged at the shop in Cambridge Street. Of course, it wasn't free at all and he paid for it by acquiring progressive lung disease. Not much of a deal really.

Remy wasn't exactly what you'd call a rebel. No marching to ban the bomb even though he thought they should, no protest against globalization or Starbucks or Nestlé or Disney. He was more of a quiet rebel, a personal rebel, making his protest against the world by ignoring *No Entry* signs. He didn't need them to tell him what was good for him or bad for him or whether an old building might fall on his head. It was *his* head.

Maybe loving buildings was his problem. Or loving Glasgow. Or being a bit weird. People might have thought he was odd if they knew he explored derelict hospitals, old schools or abandoned factories but what the hell would they think if they knew he had found that fucking body?

He couldn't stop thinking about it. Every time he closed his eyes it was there, its face staring back at his. Those empty eye sockets. The chewed cheeks. That poor bugger killed down there and left to rot. Stuck in that tunnel forever if he hadn't been down there to find him. Now the cops would be examining every bit of him.

Two years on and off, Remy and Gabby had been going exploring together. Two years in which they'd become best friends but not boyfriend and girlfriend. He was a boy, she was a girl. They were friends. That was it.

They'd trawled the muddy old railway tunnels that ran under London Road where they danced on the rusting remains of an ancient car. They managed to get into the former Woolworths building on Argyle Street and wandered through the basement, the boiler room and the upper floors. They'd roamed the disused Gray Dunn biscuit factory in Kinning Park, searching its spooky warren of floors.

They explored the shell of St Columba's Episcopal Church at midnight, having their own mass as a full moon streamed through the remaining stained-glass windows. They got into the former Transport Museum where they walked the cobbled street and sat in the Black Maria and imagined they were chasing themselves. They had an impromptu picnic on the rubble behind the façade of the old Woodilee Hospital at Lenzie.

They'd even climbed onto the roof of Glasgow University, clinging on for dear life and trying not to giggle as they looked down on the inner quadrangle and the chapel. They couldn't believe the little walkways, doors and balconies that were up there. It was a bird's-eye view of Hogwarts.

It hadn't all been urbexing. They'd go out for drinks, as friends did. She'd been round at his dad's flat a couple of times, one Christmas Eve and once for his old man's birthday. He even got an invite to her sister's wedding as her plus-one on the strict understanding that everyone would know that he wasn't *with* her.

So they stuck to old buildings and a platonic

relationship that killed him a little. The year before they'd climbed the Finnieston Crane on his birthday, both with a bottle of beer tucked in their backpacks, and then sat high above the Clyde to toast him being twenty-six. A couple of weeks after that they'd nearly got caught 'swimming' in the empty pool of the old Govanhill public baths.

They did all that and much more and yet he never had got round to asking her if maybe, you know, one day, they might actually go out on what normal people might consider to be a date. In a normal place. He knew why he hadn't asked. In the back of his head he was scared that if he did then she'd say no and it would all be over.

His phone beeped to signal a text. It was her.

Fancy trying to get into the Sentinel Works at Polmadie?

If anyone would know it would be her; she knew him better that anyone else. If he didn't get his shit together then she'd see through him in two seconds flat. She had this knack of interrogating him, staring at him until he couldn't stand it any more and he'd crack every time. He certainly didn't need any of that.

Not feeling well, he texted back.

So he stared down onto London Road watching people walking back and forth as if nothing had ever happened. For all he knew, Tesco's car park was covered in rogue trolleys and there was a long line of lazy shoppers just standing waiting for them to magically appear at the front of the store. He couldn't give a toss.

He wasn't eating either. Just a couple of slices of toast and some cereal. Sometimes he thought it had all been a weird dream and he hadn't even been down the tunnel in the first place. That was tempting to believe but he knew the truth. He could still feel the fabric of the guy's jacket and the sense of the arm crumbling under his touch. He could still smell the body lying on top of him.

He'd washed his hands a hundred times over the past few days. Scrubbed at them, used every soap and shampoo he had. He could still feel it though. Still knew it was there.

Come on loser. U can't be that sick. I hear the Sentinel is well worth a look.

He ignored it.

Okay if not the Sentinel, how about we go to the old biscuit factory? It's ur favourite place.

He ignored that too.

Okay please urself. Going on my own. Ur loss.

Great. Now Gabby was mad at him too. How the hell had it come to this?

61

Chapter 9

Narey and Toshney parked up outside the Rosewood, got out of the car and looked at each other. They'd have been as well painting *POLICE* on the side of her car. And on their foreheads come to that. Neither of them was wearing uniform but there weren't clothes plain enough that they wouldn't stand out a mile here.

It didn't look too terrible from the outside. It had been repainted in the last few years, a whitewash that hadn't yet surrendered to the elements, all the letters in the blue signage were currently in place and it had handsome, if worn, art deco features. One step inside though and you saw it was carrying a title it couldn't justify. This was no hotel.

Instead it held one hundred and seventy guests. Residents might be a better term. Home from home for the homeless. All men. Every one of them a prisoner of drink or drugs or both, signing over their housing benefit to pay for a room in the Rosewood.

The reception area was behind a protective grille, a design feature generally underemployed by the Hilton or the Ritz. The grubby linoleum flooring felt sticky underfoot and there was a sickly smell that seemed to grow with every second. A handful of hard plastic chairs were strewn around reception and looked as welcoming as the man behind the desk.

Shaven-headed with a tattoo running down his neck, the guy was in a blue tracksuit top and grey bottoms. He sported a few days' dark growth on his chin and a small scar on one cheekbone. Glancing up, he saw Narey and Toshney approach and a silent swear word slipped his lips. This seemingly wasn't going to brighten his day any further.

'Help you?' The question was as grudging as he could manage.

'We're looking for Mickey Doig. Is he around?'

The man considered this and seemed to conclude that Mickey was indeed on the premises. He turned and walked a few paces to his left and pushed a door open. As it swung on its hinges, he shouted inside. 'Mickey! Cops are here to speak to you.'

A muffled 'Fucksake' came back in reply. Moments later, an unhappy-looking forty-something appeared, drying his hands on a towel and eyes darting round the room. When they settled on Narey, his face crumpled and another bit of life went out of him with a sigh. He clearly couldn't catch a break.

He was skinny with close-cropped dark hair and silver-rimmed glasses, maybe just five foot eight, and had a nervous look about him. His green sweatshirt hung loose and the sleeves were rolled up to the elbow.

'DS Narey. What do you want?'

'It's DI Narey now and it's nice to see you too, Mickey. We wanted to ask you some questions.'

'Ask *me*?' Doig's tone was defiant. 'Don't see how I can help you. I don't know nothing about nothing. And everything's above board in here. Completely kosher.'

With that, Doig flashed a look at his colleague behind the desk, the man hanging keenly on every word of the scene in front of him. Narey got the impression that Doig was posturing for Tattoo Man's sake. Time to split them up.

'No one's saying everything's not legit in here. But I'd like to have a look around. Make sure for myself. That okay with you?'

'You got a warrant?' It was the guard dog behind the desk. Narey smiled at him.

'No we don't, Mr . . .?'

A sullen pause. 'Thomas Cochrane.'

'We don't have a warrant, Mr Cochrane. Only looking to give the premises a quick once-over. That a problem?'

It seemed that it was. 'I thought you wanted a word with Mickey.'

'We do. A word about the hotel. We can do our talking while we're walking. Okay?'

Cochrane shrugged sourly. 'I'll need to phone the owners. Let them know.'

'Of course, sir. You do that. In the meantime, Mickey can give us the guided tour.'

Narey turned her back on the desk, gesturing for Toshney to follow before Cochrane could argue any further. She then flipped out her thumb and suggested that Doig get moving. Mickey sighed theatrically and looked over at the desk, his hands held out wide. What choice did he have?

Doig led them to the harshly lit smoky stairwell and began to climb, his shoulders suitably slumped. 'Just keep walking, Mickey,' Narey whispered behind him. 'We'll talk further up.' Doig nodded.

Footsteps above their heads signalled someone descending. Narey and Toshney looked up to see the soles of worn trainers coming unsteadily down the stairs. A tall, bulky man followed, shuffling one step to the side for every one forward. He stopped, peering down to study them from behind thick spectacles. He swayed in thought.

'Got any dolly on youse?' he slurred. 'Methadone, any of youse?'

'For fucksake,' Mickey huffed, clearly not impressed by the man's timing. 'Down the stairs, Billy. Away with you.'

The man flattened himself against the wall, hearing the warning in Mickey's voice, and watched him and the cops walk on by. 'Nae problem. Was only askin'. Not a problem.'

Narey waited until they'd climbed a few more steps. 'Everything kosher, that right, Mickey?'

Doig sighed. 'I only work here. I don't make the rules, I don't make this dump the way it is and I don't make these guys the way they are. I just do what I'm told.'

'The get-out clause for arseholes everywhere,' Toshney chimed in.

'Look, what is it you want? DI Narey, I thought you and me were square.'

'Square?' She laughed. 'You know that's not how it works, Mickey. Keep walking. You don't want it to look like you're helping us out. You just want to be sure that you do. We're looking for someone that's maybe been living here.'

Doig raised an eyebrow nervously. 'Living here? Name would be at the desk. Everybody's registered. Have to be to get benefit paid by the council.'

'Yes and the money straight into the owners' pockets. No, we don't know for sure that he'd been living here. You tell us.'

Doig glanced around. 'Tell me.'

'He's in his early thirties. Reddish fair hair. Five foot eleven. Quite fit. Wore a light blue cagoule and a navy-blue fleece. Carried a grey-and-blue Nike backpack.'

The man's eyes stretched in disbelief. 'That's all you got?'

Narey and Toshney looked at each other. 'Pretty much. We don't think he was an alcoholic or an addict.'

'*Was?* This guy dead?'

Narey nodded.

Doig threw up his arms. 'Listen, I don't know this guy. Description means nothing. If he wasn't a boozer and wasn't using then he wasn't staying here. Them's the only kind we got.'

'The description doesn't ring any bells?' Toshney asked him. 'In here or anywhere else? DI Narey, did I imagine this or did you say something to me about still knowing where Mr Doig's lock-up was?'

'Fucksake . . . I'm not always on duty, I don't know everyone we've got. Okay, look, come and I'll get you to talk to Walter if he's here. It's not lunchtime yet, chances are we'll catch him before he's out of things. Walter's old-school. Just the drink for him. He goes outside more than any of them and knows most of the guys in Glasgow. If anyone can help you it's him. I'll introduce you then I'm out of it.'

'Mickey, you'll be out of it when I say you are.'

Doig led them down a dingy corridor, the walls dirty and wallpaper torn. Halfway along, he skirted to one side and avoided a pool of vomit drying on the patterned carpet. 'Not my job,' he muttered before they could ask.

'I suppose he's not your job either?' Narey was pointing to the far end of an adjoining corridor where a man sat slumped unconscious against a fire door. She strode away from them to where the man, hoodie pulled down over his head, was sprawled. With a familiar rage growing inside her, she pulled gently at the man's arm and lifted his head. She walked back, shaking her head animatedly, and got right in Doig's face.

'Alive but sleeping in another world. You going to do something about him?'

Doig's mouth opened to complain but instead he nodded grudgingly. 'Once we're done here.'

'Make sure you do. I mean it, Mickey. I'm holding you responsible for this place whether that's fair or not.'

He nodded again, more resentfully this time, but recognizing the look on her face said nothing. At the end of the corridor, he stopped at a chipped white door and rapped on it with the back of his hand. He knocked again and when there was no answer, he produced a key and opened up.

Over Doig's shoulder, they could see that the room was tiny and bare. A single bed was pushed up against one wall, a single sink against another and the windows were barred. The unmistakable stench of stale urine seeped out. They could see why Walter spent so much time outside.

Her head spun with thoughts of another miserable little room, another life sentence without a judge or jury saying a word. She realized her fists were clenched and had to force herself to release them.

'I've seen prison cells bigger than this. Better equipped too.' Toshney sounded as angry as she was.

Narey didn't, couldn't, take her eyes off the room. 'Difference is that you get to leave prison eventually. Usually, the only way to get out of this place is in a wooden box. That right, Mickey?'

Doig had the good grace to look guilty. 'Aye. Most die or top themselves. Let's try the TV room for Walter.'

Narey turned and moved quickly towards Doig. A startled Toshney managed to move between them in time. Through clenched teeth, Narey nodded at Toshney that she was fine. 'TV room. Let's go.'

They made their way down another flight of stairs along an identical corridor to the one above, picking their way through a small group of men sitting on the floor, sharing cider from a bottle and smoking roll-ups in the gloom. None of them seemed aware of the cops strolling by, or of much at all. The door to a communal toilet and shower area opened as an old man lurched out, pools of what might have been water or urine on the floor behind him, and an almighty stink overrode even the smell of the corridor.

The TV room held maybe a dozen men, most slumped over or holding each other up. All were old before their time and the truly old ones looked ancient, like drunken Methuselahs. A single TV screen on the wall held the attention of a couple of them but most stared into space or argued over cigarettes. Empty bottles of cider, vodka and Buckfast were spilled round the room and others were on their way to joining them.

Doig signalled for Narey and Toshney to stay where they were and went over to a corner where a small, neat man, much more awake than his brethren, sat reading a book. Doig bent down to talk to him and gestured over to where the cops stood.

'And I thought zombies didn't exist,' Toshney muttered as he looked round the room. 'Just made up pish, I thought, but they've been here all the time.'

'Shut up, Toshney. A bit of respect wouldn't kill you. Right, looks like we're in.'

The man in the chair was nodding and Doig thanking him with a pat on his arm before standing up and going back over to the cops.

'That's Walter. He's sober and he'll talk to you. That's all I can do though. You'll find your own way out?'

'Sure.' She was already past Doig and heading for the old man, Toshney following closely behind. He was aware of the looks that Narey was getting from some of the more awake residents and was uneasy about it. Still, he got the feeling the DI was in the mood to defend herself without much problem.

'Walter? I'm Rachel Narey.' She held out a hand and the man shook it. 'Mickey said why I'm here?'

'He did, lass. Not that I couldn't see you were police. What do you want to know? I'm not a grass. Can't be seen to be one either.'

Walter looked to be about seventy, so Narey guessed him to be five, maybe ten years younger than that. His eyes were busy but dulled, giving the impression of a sharp mind that had been blunted by booze. His shirt, the collar showing signs of fraying, was buttoned to the neck and he wore a heavy V-neck sweater over it, the sleeves rolled double at the wrists to make them fit. His shoes were worn but recently polished. Everything was as trim and in place as he could manage.

'We're not asking you to grass on anybody, Walter,' she assured him. 'The man we're looking for is dead.'

Walter's eyes slid over and he shook his head. 'We're

70

all dying. I don't mean people generally. I don't mean Glasgow. I mean *us,* in here. Killing ourselves right enough but no one cares enough to do anything about it. There's a guy in here who . . . you got time to hear this?'

Narey nodded for both of them. She had time to listen.

'A guy in here named wee Sammy McClune. Nicest wee fella you could ever meet. Do anything for anybody. Get your shopping. Go and see your mammy or your daughter and tell them you're doing okay. Slip you a bit of cigarette when you're short. A gentleman. Always time for everybody, you know? And the best mouth-organ player this side of the Rio Grande. Could play a moothie like Stradivarius could play a fiddle. What most folk don't know is that Sammy had a wee boy that died the day he was born. Broke Sammy's heart. Broke his marriage too and sent him into a bottle of vodka. Then another one. Couldn't find his way out. Sammy died two days ago. We're *all* dying in here, Miss Narey. Every one of us.'

Narey didn't have the words. Her heart was breaking but she knew the man didn't want her sympathy and she sure as hell couldn't tell him anything would be all right. Instead, she nodded with all the understanding she had and repeated the description she'd given to Doig.

Walter thought on it, his right hand massaging at his temples. 'Wasn't a drinker or a junkie, you say? Few of those men on the streets and that's for sure. There was a guy a while back though . . . Aye, it could be him, I suppose.'

71

Her pulse quickened as she sensed a light in the dark. 'Who was he, Walter?'

'A young guy. Young to me anyway. Under forty for sure. He just stayed a few nights. Didn't seem the type for this place, you know? He maybe took a wee drink but no like the guys in here. No like me. And he wasn't a junkie. I called him the Saint on account of him being sober. He asked a lot of questions. Wanted to know how the place worked.'

'And you told him?'

'Course I did, lass. Like I said, he didn't seem the type. You need to learn the ropes quick in here or you'll never survive. Guys think you're soft they'll break into your room in the middle of the night and take your smokes or your booze, whatever they can get. I told the Saint to watch himself. You think it's him? Jesus, I hope I'm wrong.'

Walter leaned in closer before Narey could reply and she managed to bite on her impatience and let him speak.

'What happened to him? If it wasn't the sauce or that junk they put into themselves?'

She didn't want to lie to the old man but she couldn't tell him the truth either. Not all of it at least. 'We're not sure yet, Walter. Looks like he was murdered.'

The man closed his eyes again and he pinched at the top of his nose. It was a small age before he spoke. 'No wonder I drink, hen. No wonder we all drink or get stoned or whatever. What's the point in staying sober when that's all the good it does you. He was a decent laddie, that one, compared to some. What's the point in being decent if you get yourself killed? And wee Sammy's McClune's baby. Never done harm to a soul, never had the chance. See some of them in here? Bad bastards, pardon my language. We all die just the same, good and bad. No wonder I take a drink.'

Narey could see the thirst growing in the man as she looked at him. Walter wasn't going to finish this day as sober as he was now.

'What can you tell me about this guy, Walter? When was he last here? Do you know what his name was?'

'Last here?' Walter looked surprised at the question. 'Hen, I'm no very good with dates. Head's too muddled with the drink if I'm honest. I think his name was . . . hell, let me think. Like I said, I called him . . . Wait. Brian. That's it, Brian. That's what he told me anyhow.'

'I don't suppose you know his surname?'

Walter laughed. 'Hen, you've had all the memory I've got left.'

Narey nodded, her hand resting on the old man's arm. 'Thanks, Walter. You've been a big help.'

The man's eyes were moist now. 'See if you can find out what happened to him, Miss Narey? Will you? If they start killing the saints, what chance have us sinners got?'

'I'll do my best, Walter.'

'And, Miss Narey . . . I wouldn't normally ask but . . . all this—'

'Don't worry about it, Walter. I understand.' She

opened the hand that was resting on his arm just long enough for him to see the two twenty-pound notes that were in it. She then pressed them quietly into the man's fist.

He looked up gratefully and managed a weak smile. 'Thanks, lass.'

Narey and Toshney were making their way back down the stairwell, avoiding fresh dumps of vomit, when he spoke.

'Boss, hope you don't mind me asking. But you do know he's just going to spend that money you gave him on getting plastered, right?'

She turned on him and he took half a step back despite himself, shoved there by the anger that was pouring out of her.

'Of *course* I do, Fraser. Like he said, it's no wonder he takes a drink. Living in a place like this, in a world like this. If it was my dad . . . well I'd rather he was sober than drunk but if he was a drunk then I'd rather someone bought him a fucking drink. I just gave Walter another reason to be drunk by telling him about this. Least I can do is pay for it.'

They stopped by the front desk on the way out and Narey wasn't in the mood to go round the houses this time. She told Cochrane that she wanted to look at their register to see if they had anyone signed in by the name of Brian.

'I don't think I can do that.'

She smiled, glad of the challenge. 'Oh I think you

can. Or else you can just give me the excuse to rip your head off and shove it up your arse.'

He stared back at her for a few moments, trying to think of a way to argue. Finally, he gave in. 'You may as well. It's all public record anyway. I don't remember any guy called Brian though.'

'Do you really care what their names are?' Her insinuation was paper-thin. Cochrane just glared back and pushed the open register towards her.

She went back four weeks and saw no one named Brian. Five weeks, the same result. Then there it was, one entry six weeks back, a booking that only lasted for four nights. The name beside it was Brian Christie.

'What about this guy?' She pointed at the name. 'Remember him?'

Cochrane shrugged. 'Maybe.'

'So tell us!'

'If it's the guy I'm thinking of, he told us he'd lost his job and been thrown out by his wife. He said he'd be signed up for housing benefit by the end of the week. It never came through and he didn't stay long.'

'Five eleven with reddish hair?'

'Could be.

'*Is it?*'

'I think so. Aye.'

'Did you check for a previous address? See any ID?'

Cochrane laughed sourly. 'Why would anyone? Who would anyone want to stay in here if they didn't have to?'

Chapter 10

It wasn't unusual for Narey to want to wash off the dirt of a day on the streets but this one demanded it more than most. She stood in the shower for fully fifteen minutes letting it soak her, lathering herself so much that her feet stood in a pool of bubbles. Staring up into the needles of the shower, she took the hit on her face and let the water run down into her open mouth.

She could feel her fists clenching and forced herself to open her hands wide. She placed them palm first against the tiled shower wall. Being angry wasn't helping but she couldn't shake it off. She slapped her hands against the tiles and liked the sound of it, so did it again.

She stood long enough to calm down. The anger was all still there, curled up and smouldering inside her like a sleeping dragon, but she was fairly sure that she was in control of it. For now at least.

Wrapped up in a towelling robe, she marched into

the front room and dropped heavily onto the sofa. Air rushed from her and her eyes closed over. She wanted wine. It wasn't a good idea though, given that her head was as muddled as it already was.

'Glass of wine?' Tony, mind-reader and bad influence, was sitting in the chair opposite.

'Yes. I mean no. No.' She didn't open her eyes. 'And I really mean no. But thanks.'

'You sure?'

'No.'

'Okay. Want to talk about it instead? I'm guessing it was a bad one.'

Her eyes flicked open but her hesitancy was obvious. There was a line. One or other of them had first joked that it was police crime scene tape and it was there to keep him out. The line had been set a long time ago but they both knew it had become blurred since then. The choice of ditching it altogether was hers though.

'Up to you? Tell me as much or as little as you want.'

She sighed heavily and rubbed at her eyes. 'Okay. But only because this is therapy and an alternative to wine.'

'Okay.'

'You know the Rosewood Hotel?'

'The dosshouse? I've never been in it but yes. I know of it.'

'Of course you've never been in it, why would you? And you don't want to, believe me. It's a hellhole. And it's not a dosshouse, it's a bloody waiting room. Just full of people waiting to die.'

He couldn't miss the emotion in her voice. She was in a bad way and he needed to tread carefully, for her sake, not his.

'Can the owners not be done for something if it's as bad as that?'

'Let's hope so. They will be if I can find something to stick on them.'

'Want to tell me why you were there?'

Another big sigh. 'Oh why not? It's the Molendinar case. We think our man had been living in there for a while. Poor bastard is almost better off dead than being in there. Shit, I don't mean that. Long, long day.'

Winter's itch pulsed. The guy in the burn. The guy lying under the streets. The voice that he couldn't quite hear.

'So you think the guy in the tunnel had been homeless?'

'Looks that way. We think he'd only been in there for four nights though. God knows where he'd been staying the rest of the time. But that place . . . Everyone in this city should be ashamed that it's there. We all just shut our eyes and pretend that places like that – people like that – don't exist. Well they do. It made my skin crawl. It made me . . . so fucking angry.'

He wanted to ask a hundred questions. He wanted to know everything but he was also wary of her shutting down, pointing at the police tape and telling him not to cross. The voice in his head had become quieter. He didn't know anyone who was homeless. At least he didn't think he did.

But he heard something else too in what she was saying. Her anger wasn't just at the Rosewood. He knew it was also at places like it, places where people were left to be forgotten, left to die. He crossed to the sofa and sat with his arm round her.

She made a half-hearted effort to push him away but quickly gave in, her head slumping onto his shoulder. 'I'm supposed to be professional,' she protested. 'Supposed to be detached. Can you just imagine all those sods in the station if they knew how this got to me?'

'I'm not sure you *are* supposed to be detached. How can you do your job if you don't care? You're supposed to be human, not a robot. And you're taking on a lot. You can't save the whole world, Rach. You can just do your best for those who matter most and you're doing that.'

She raised her head so she could look at him. 'I've never thought this before but you might actually be smarter than you look.'

'Thanks.'

'Don't mention it.

'So what happens next with the tunnel guy? Have you got a name for him?'

She banged a small fist lightly against his chest. 'You're pushing your luck. Yes, we have a name. He signed himself into the Rosewood as Brian Christie. It doesn't match anyone on Missing Persons but we're looking.'

Suddenly, the voice that Winter couldn't quite hear

faded away. He felt the whisper of it go from the room and out the window into the night sky. He'd never heard of a Brian Christie. It was a relief and at the same time an odd disappointment. That wasn't something he'd even begin to think of trying to explain to Rachel though. She had enough to worry about.

Chapter 11

Monday morning

It took Narey a moment to realize what the sound on the other end of the line was when she answered the phone. The beeps were from another century and she couldn't remember when she'd last heard them. It was someone calling from a phone box. Finally, a coin dropped and the line cleared.

'Hello? Detective Narey? Inspector Narey?'

The man's voice was old and rather weak. She had just about placed it when he confirmed it for her.

'It's Walter McMeekin. From the Rosewood Hotel. You said to call if I remembered anything else. Well I have, sort of. It's no much, mind.'

She reached for a pen and pulled a notepad towards her. 'Hi, Walter. Thanks for calling. Listen, anything at all could help us. What did you remember?'

'Well, like I said, it's no much. But if you're still

81

trying to find out about that laddie Brian then you maybe want to try down at the City Mission. The boy told me he'd been down there. I remember him telling me that. Before he came to the Rosewood, he'd been down at Crimea Street.'

'Walter, that's great. Did he say why he he'd been to the Mission?'

A pause. 'No really. He said he'd been speaking to the boss man over there. I remember because I know him as well. Malcolm Colvin. Malky is what they call him. The project manager. One of the good guys.'

'Okay, Walter. I'll go down there today and check it out. You've been a big help.'

'Och, no. It's nothing. That poor laddie. Best you find out what happened to him.'

'We will. Are you doing okay, Walter?'

He laughed. 'Ah'm doing how ah'm doing, hen. Better than I will be tonight no doubt and better than I will be tomorrow morning. I could say different but I've known maself for too long.'

'Take care of yourself.'

'Too late for that, hen. Too late.'

The City Mission was nearly two hundred years old, the first of its kind in the world. They were a Christian organization, offering practical care like food and a roof over people's heads when they needed it most. The current offices were on Crimea Street, a narrow warren halfway between Argyle Street and the Broomielaw. It was a new build that resembled a New York loft conversion, all brick and floor-to-ceiling windows over five floors. The sign, GLASGOW CITY MISSION, ran from top to bottom, extended beyond the building's side.

Just a few yards away across the road, at the T-junction with Brown Street, an abandoned building sat in stark contrast, its tall arched windows covered in protective grilles, its ornate doorway bricked up. Narey had paused as she got out of the car, fascinated by it being there in splendid isolation. She couldn't help but wonder what it had been, a tobacco baron's warehouse or maybe his offices. A bit grand for one and maybe too plain for the other.

Toshney caught her looking at it. 'Everything okay, Boss?'

'Hmm? Yes. You never wondered what a building like that used to be in a former life?'

The DC looked bemused. 'No.'

She sighed. 'No, I don't suppose you have. Come on. He's waiting for us.'

Inside the front door, a middle-aged woman introduced herself as Maureen and told them she was the project manager's assistant. A quick call ahead had already let them know her boss was in and would hang around until they turned up. Maureen led them up to the first floor where he sat waiting behind a desk.

Malcolm Colvin was only in his early thirties, a tousled mop of hair and stubble making him look more like he'd walked off a beach with a surfboard under his arm than managed a homeless project.

His casual look was topped off with blue jeans and an open-necked white shirt. Narey noted that he was good-looking in that superficial blue-eyed Greek god kind of way that more shallow women might find attractive. He greeted her with a broad smile and she suppressed the temptation to bite him.

'Mr Colvin, thanks for taking the time to see us.'

'Not at all. And it's Malcolm. Glad if I can help in any way. Please, both of you, take a seat. Can I get you a coffee? Tea?'

Narey and Toshney sat but politely refused the offer of a drink. 'How can I help you, Detective Inspector? You said on the phone it concerned someone I might know who had lived in the Rosewood. I hope he's okay whoever it is and not in some kind of trouble.'

'You assume it's a man.'

'Well ... you're right, I'm making an assumption. But it's a fair guess. As far as the homeless are concerned, men make up 93.3 per cent of our service users.' He shrugged. 'We keep records. And we see the proof with our own eyes. They are almost always men.'

'Fair enough. And yes, it is a man. We're hoping you can help us identify him.'

Colvin looked slightly pained, his pin-up features crumpling apologetically. 'I'll do what I can, Inspector Narey, but this job is all about trust. Both ways. I'm not going to be earning the trust of the guys who come here if I turn them in to the police. I guess it depends what he's done.'

'Malcolm, you don't need to worry about losing his

trust. Unfortunately. What's he's done is died. We're trying to identify a murder victim.'

Colvin's mouth fell open for a moment before he steadied himself, dragging a hand through his hair. He breathed out hard. 'Who was it? Sorry, that's what you want me to tell you. Of course. Anything I can do. *Murder?*'

'I'm afraid so, yes. We have a description of the man plus a possible name for him. As I said on the phone, we think he came down here to talk to you. Do you want a moment, Malcolm?'

Colvin's hand was absently covering his mouth. 'No, I . . . please ask me what you need to. Sorry, I shouldn't still be surprised when things happen to the guys out there. One of our regulars hasn't been seen in a couple of months and he'd stayed at the Rosewood. I've been worried about him. What's the name you've been given of the man from the Rosewood?'

'We think he's called Brian Christie.'

'No, that's not my guy and it doesn't ring any bells. I'm sure I don't know that name. What's the man's description?'

Narey told him. Colvin processed it slowly, clearly taking his time. Finally he shrugged. 'Well . . . no. It could be so many of them.'

'Walter also said this man asked a lot of questions.'

Colvin still looked blank but the assistant's voice came from the corner of the room. 'I don't know the name Christie but the description does sound like someone who came in a couple of times asking questions. His name was Euan though. Not Brian.'

Colvin's eyebrows rose as a penny dropped. 'Yes, you're right, Maureen. Euan. Euan . . . Hepburn. It was maybe the name that threw me because I should have remembered him straight away. He was a bit different.'

'In what way?' Narey asked the question but thought she already knew the answer.

'Well . . .' Colvin hesitated. 'Don't quote me on this but he was different from most of the men that might have come from the Rosewood and most of those who use our service. Most of them have suffered through personal problems and circumstances outwith their control. A lot of them are quite vulnerable.'

She didn't have the time to let him feel guilty about making generalizations about the mission's clients. She'd do that for him.

'Malcolm, are you saying that he was sober?'

Colvin looked uncomfortable but nodded. 'Yes. Made him stick out a bit. He wasn't the only one but it's unusual. He wasn't just sober, he'd *been* sober. And I'm sure he didn't use drugs.'

'And he asked questions?'

'He wanted to know about the Rosewood Hotel. If that was somewhere I'd recommend for him to go. I told him I couldn't do that. There are a lot of places in the city better for those in need than that place. In fact, and again don't quote me, I can't think of anywhere worse. The street would be a better option, honestly.'

'What else did he want to know?'

'Well he wanted to know why I thought it was so bad. Wanted to know about other places in the city for the homeless, good and bad. He asked if people ever got out of the Rosewood in one piece. We chatted for quite a while.'

Narey nodded absently, her lips pursed in thought. 'Malcolm, you said you kept records. Would Euan Hepburn feature in them?'

'He should. After we spoke, I passed him on down the line to get him what help we could. Keeping him out of the Rosewood was the one thing I wanted to do. He didn't strike me as lasting long in there. He didn't belong. I'll get what we have on him.'

When Colvin returned five minutes later, he found Narey staring idly out the window at the old building opposite. They were level with the top of the arched windows and she could now see that the upper floors in red brick were newer than the pale stone of the ground level.

'It's a great building, isn't it?' Malcolm Colvin sensed her admiration . 'I could look at it all day. I love old places like that. Can't get enough of them.'

The man's expression changed when he remembered the single piece of paper he'd come back with. His apologetic look didn't fill Narey with much hope.

'Inspector Narey, I'm sorry but we've no record of him. I spoke to the staff but the only one that remembers him thinks that he just left after speaking to me. We'd asked him to wait so we could help him out but it seems he just slipped away. He must have left us and gone to the Rosewood despite what I said.'

'Shit. So what's this?' She nodded at the piece of paper Colvin held.

The man gave a slightly embarrassed smile. 'My mobile number. In case I can help with anything else.'

Narey caught the birth of a smirk on Toshney's face. It died a sudden death as soon as he saw her looking. She thanked Colvin, said she'd be in touch if they needed anything more and began to direct the DC out the door with a glare.

Colvin called after them, 'Inspector Narey. I might be completely wrong here but Euan . . . well like I said, he was different from most men that come here. I'm not even sure he was homeless at all.'

'Nor me, Malcolm. Nor me.'

Chapter 12

Monday afternoon

It sometimes occurred to Winter that his uncle, Danny Neilson, had never changed in all the time he'd known him. Danny had seemed old to him when Winter was a kid. Old but big and strong, patient and wise. None of that had altered. Danny was one of those people who grew into his age. Being in his sixties seemed to suit him. He'd filled out into what he should always have been.

He'd done his thirty years in the police, mainly as a sergeant, and he still worked a beat of sorts. He spent his nights as a taxi-rank superintendent keeping part of Glasgow safe and the other part in order as best he could. The drunk had not yet been stewed that Danny couldn't keep in line.

Danny was Danny. Solid. Always there when he was needed, gruff, tough and rough but capable of being as gentle as a summer breeze. And the smartest man that Winter had ever known.

When Tony had called wanting to speak, Danny had suggested they meet for a lunchtime coffee in Lola & Livvy's under the Hielanman's Umbrella – the glass-walled railway bridge that carried Central Station's platforms across Argyle Street and was historically a meeting place for Highlanders relocated to the big city. The café was fronted in the green and gold of the Umbrella's refurb, and inside it had a Mediterranean vibe with tiled floors, exposed walls, whitewashed wood and red-leather sofas.

'This place is a bit trendy for you, isn't it?'

Danny shrugged and lifted his mug as evidence. 'Great coffee. Great cakes as well. What do I care what the décor's like?'

'Fair enough. Wasn't trying to suggest you weren't a man of refinement.'

'Yes you were. So how have you been, son? Haven't heard from you in a month or two. Everything okay?'

'Sure. Rachel's enjoying her promotion. Working like a slave but loving it. She's picked up a new murder case and that's always guaranteed to make a girl happy.'

'The body pulled out of the Molendinar near the Great Eastern?'

Winter nodded.

'Odd one. Saw it on the news. Did you do the photography?'

'Yeah. The body had been there for at least a month

so it was in a right state. Hell of a place to work in as well.'

'Sounds right up your street. You'll have been in stranger places than that.'

Winter didn't rise to it, seeing the gleam in Danny's eye and hearing the tease.

'Anyway, I asked how you were, not how Rachel was. So what aren't you telling me?'

He sighed. Danny would drag it out of him anyway so he may as well get it over with.

'It might come to nothing but that twat Baxter had me into his office to give me a bollocking and dropped very heavy hints about me losing my job.'

Danny's eyebrows rose but his expression didn't change. 'They're going to fire you?'

'No. Not this time. The suggestion was that I'd be made redundant. "The review of all services is continuing" was how he put it but he couldn't have laid it on thicker if he'd stabbed me with the trowel he was using. And he was enjoying it, obviously.'

'Obviously. Pompous arse. You think he's serious?'

'It's certainly possible. I probably shouldn't have been there for a few years now. The SOCOs can do what I do. Not as well but they do all their forensic shit too so they come in much cheaper. It will make sense to accountants and it's them that are running the show now.'

Danny nodded soberly. 'You've told Rachel this, I take it?'

'Nope.'

'And you think that's a good idea? Because I don't. Something like that doesn't work well as a surprise. Flowers or a weekend away – that's the kind of surprise women like. You need to tell her, son. You'll be hard pushed to marry her if she's killed you.'

Winter hesitated just long enough for Danny to pounce on it. 'Now, I was just joking but I didn't hear a denial or a piss off, which I'd have expected. You thinking of making an honest woman of her? Because you won't do any better, believe me.'

Winter laughed. 'Thanks for the vote of confidence, Dan. But I'm not about to drag her up the aisle, even if she'd let me. But . . .'

'But what?'

'But I'm ready to . . . I want more. I'm fed up of hiding this. I want us to be like normal people. A couple. And you know, I think she is too.'

'You think?'

'Danny, you know what she's like.'

'Pretty great, I'd say.'

'Yes, pretty great. Amazing. Fabulous. But she is also capable of being stubborn, contrary and argumentative. If I suggest it, she's as likely to dump me as say yes. It's trying to find the best time to talk about it. I'm not sure being landed with this kind of murder case is the best time.'

'*This* kind of murder? They're *all* this kind, son. Dead body and dead ends. If you're going to wait till things are nice and quiet, you'll both be on Zimmers. If you want my advice – and I'm guessing that's why you're going to buy me coffee and one of those big pastries – then you need to grow a pair and ask her.'

'Aye, maybe.'

A beep called from inside Danny's jacket pocket. He pulled out his mobile phone and read the text. Whatever it was, it seemed to amuse him.

'Looks like I'm in demand today. We'll need to wrap this up.'

'Hot date?'

'You could say that.' He typed a reply and slipped the phone back into his pocket. He picked up his coffee mug and looked at Winter over the rim.

'Here's what I think. You can listen or not, up to you. Rachel is the best thing that's happened to you and whatever you decide to do, get it right. And not just right for you, for her too because that lassie's got enough on her plate without you making it worse. If you upset her and she decides to kill you then I'll not be helping you. I'll be holding you down so she can do it. Got that?'

'Yes, Uncle Danny. I've got it. Loud and clear.'

'Good.'

Half an hour later, Danny was still sitting in the same chair with a fresh coffee steaming gently in front of him. He'd had no more than two cautious sips at it when he heard the door open and looked up to see Narey walk in, her collar turned up against the wind.

'Rachel.' He got out of his seat and hugged her. 'Good to see you.'

She'd known Danny for almost as long as she'd known his nephew. There was a shared respect and a closeness between them, him being an ex-cop, and his knowledge and experience had been of help to her in the past.

She looked around at the café and nodded approvingly. 'Nice. Didn't think it would be your kind of place though.'

He half laughed, half groaned. 'Too trendy for me, do you think?'

She kissed him on the cheek. 'Not at all. Looks like you started without me. You want a pastry to go with that?'

The waitress had appeared beside them and looked at Danny as if to say did he really want *another* one. Patting his stomach like a man who'd been caught having a midnight feast, Danny politely said no thanks.

'So you said you wanted to pick my brains?

'And to see you,' Narey assured him. 'But yes, I could do with some help. I need answers that I'm not going to get from Google. I've got a case that—'

'The Molendinar?'

'Yes. How did you know?'

'Lucky guess.'

'Yeah, sure. But that's exactly what I mean. I need some answers from the kind of smart-arse that knows everything.'

He grinned. 'Then you've come to the right place. What do you need to know?'

'The Molendinar. Everything you've got.'

He spread his arms wide. 'Sit comfortably, my child, and I shall begin. History lesson first. In the beginning, God created heaven and earth and Glasgow. But before he created Glasgow, he created the Moldendinar Burn. The Clyde was too big and unmanageable and the land around it was too low and marshy so they built along the Molendinar. The city could never have grown without it but in the end, the burn just got in the way and they covered it over and built on top of it. It's the city's own time capsule. Buried and forgotten. Most folk don't even know it's there.'

'And now it's where the bodies are buried. One of them anyway.'

'So what are you thinking?'

She exhaled hard. 'It's the one thing I can't get away from. Why would someone be in the Molendinar? Whether it's to kill or be killed or to play tiddlywinks. Why there? Who would go in there now?'

'People *do* know it's there. Not many but some for sure. Locals will all know it, kids probably played in or around it. Anyone with any knowledge of local history will know all about it. Engineers will be down there, keeping it clear. The council will have responsibility for it, probably have maps of it. Urbexers would probably see it as a challenge. Teenagers might walk it as a dare. I guess it could be used to stash stolen goods or even drugs. And I'd say it would be a good place to hide a body.'

'*Urbexers?*'

'Urban explorers. They like to go places they shouldn't.

Abandoned buildings. Old places. Tall places. They go in, without breaking in, and photograph what's there. Old schools, churches, factories, tunnels. That sort of thing. There's websites if you want to know more.'

'Maybe . . .' She sounded doubtful. 'And how – apart from knowing everything – do you know about urbexers?'

He shrugged casually. 'I know someone who used to do it.'

'Okay. You really think someone would see it as a good place to hide a body?'

'Not now they wouldn't. Now it looks a pretty stupid place to use. But before . . . you'd think it might never be found.'

'So my suspect list is locals, kids, historians, council workers, engineers, urbexers, serial killers and teen-agers. Have I forgotten anyone?'

'That probably covers it. Can't think what else to tell you.'

'It helps, Danny. Thank you.'

'Any time. Come back if there's more I can help with. What about you, kid? How are things with you and my nephew?'

'Good. Very good, actually. He's behaving himself, not bugging me, generally doing what I tell him. The training is paying off at last. I think I might keep him.'

Danny raised his coffee mug. 'I'll drink to that. So where do you think you two will go from here? You just going to keep playing at secret boyfriend and girl-friend for ever?'

She gave him a warning stare for a moment or two but it melted. There probably wasn't *anyone* else she could talk to about this.

'Maybe not. Probably not. It's maybe time to become adults, Dan.' She said it with a smile.

'Adults, eh?' he mocked gently. 'You sure you're ready for this?'

'No,' she laughed. 'But I can feel us changing. For the better. That time we had apart made me think a lot about what I wanted. Now, I'm pretty sure I know. I love him. I still have my dad to think about, of course, but there's probably room in my life for two men.'

'Three surely?'

'Ha. Of course, three. No show without punch, Uncle Dan. I need to sit down and talk to him about where we go from here. It's difficult though, I need to make sure I—'

'Find the right time?'

'Yes. Exactly. This is serious stuff, Dan. This could go either way. It really could.'

Chapter 13

Tuesday afternoon

'Hold your horses. I just want a last look around before we total the place.'

'What for? It's a dump.'

Jackie Doran sighed and not for the first time he wondered about the philistines he had to work with. Okay, so if he'd wanted to have profound conversations about the art deco movement or the meaning of life then he shouldn't have got into the demolition business. It wasn't exactly choking with philosophers. It still got on his tits though that guys like Murray Inglis just didn't see what was around them. All they wanted to do was knock the place down and get to the pub.

Jackie was older. A lot older. Maybe that's why he appreciated it more. When you were sixty-four and seeing the end of your own working life looming up in the rear-view mirror then you had a feeling for buildings like this that were about to be smashed to bits. It was called empathy. Murray Inglis would probably think empathy was a rap star or whatever they were calling them now.

It was more than that though. He used to be a regular at the Odeon long before Inglis was born. His mum and dad, God bless them, used to take him when he was a kid. He remembered seeing his first movie there when he was eight. *The 7th Voyage of Sinbad*. He'd never forget being amazed at the size of the room. Nearly three thousand people in one huge auditorium. Tell that to the kids today and they wouldn't believe it.

He couldn't swear that he was impressed by the art deco then as much as he was by the movie. But he did remember the ceiling looking like it was fashioned in waves as it moved down over the balcony towards the screen. And at the sides of the stage itself were massive gold-coloured designs like the sides of great church organs, all latticed and glitzy. There was a tea room and ritzy foyers and lounges. It was some place, the old Odeon.

Of course he didn't know or care back then that it had been built by Verity & Beverley, the company that built all the big luxurious cinemas in Britain. This was the only one they built in Scotland and it was a beauty.

Standing here now, inside with the doors long shut, he felt like he was part of it. Looking down on Renfield Street, seeing the world going past but being unseen behind the old building's grimy windows, was exciting in a way that young guys like Inglis wouldn't understand. It was like watching an old movie but in reverse. Like looking out from the screen.

The building on the other side of Renfield Street looked fabulous. It was true what they said about most people never looking up. They missed out on so much, especially in a city like Glasgow. The architecture was stunning. The place opposite had incredible stone balconies, statues and carved heads. Intricate scrolls, beautiful pillars, arches and stonework. All above a couple of modest pubs.

The building diagonally opposite was pretty incredible too. How many people walked past it every day and never noticed the terracotta turrets at the top that looked like they'd been pinched from some German castle above the Rhine? Maybe there was a princess locked up in one of them, or a dwarf. Maybe he'd watched too many movies.

'Jackie, are you going to shift? We're on a schedule here and I'm going out the night.'

Murray Inglis was going out every night. He didn't know any other way to live his life. He would come in every morning with a hangover and go away every evening with an itch for another one. Jackie was too old for that nonsense. A few beers on a Friday night was his lot these days.

'Son, I'm having a last look around. Deal with it. This building's been standing here for seventy years. Another twenty minutes isn't going to kill anybody.'

Jackie wasn't Inglis's boss. Not technically. But he'd

been round the block often enough to get away with just about anything he wanted. They couldn't sack him for it and they certainly weren't going to promote him if he was a good boy. There were benefits in being a year from retirement and being a bolshie bastard was one of them.

Inglis disappeared, no doubt to tell the gaffer that the old bugger was being an old bugger again. That suited Jackie just fine. He could have a wander round in peace.

What else did he see here? *Lawrence of Arabia*. Peter O'Toole appearing through the desert on that big screen. *Bonnie and Clyde*. *Dr Zhivago*. Which everyone had raved about but which lasted over three hours and bored him. *The Dirty Dozen*. And dozens more.

It wasn't just the movies either. The Beatles played there. The Rolling Stones too. He couldn't get a ticket for the Stones and hadn't wanted to see the Beatles. His cousin George had seen the Stones though and talked about it for weeks.

The last thing he saw on the big single screen was *On Her Majesty's Secret Service*. The one with the Australian guy as James Bond where his wife gets killed at the end. That was 1969, just before they ruined the place. Every bit of the old interior, all the beautiful art deco stuff, disappeared. They made it into a three-screen complex and covered the front of the building in dull grey corrugated sheeting. Maybe no one knew it then but that was the beginning of the end.

101

They added more and more screens and took away more and more of the magic. He wasn't even sure of the last picture he'd seen there. It might have been *Wall Street* or maybe *Rain Man*, something like that in the late 1980s. Long time ago now. Seemed like another world.

And now he was part of the team that was going to blast the Odeon into smithereens. He didn't exactly feel good about that but he was just the hangman: someone else had been the judge and jury. Just following orders, the oldest excuse in the book.

The front façade would be kept, safe from the other ravages, and would form the centrepiece of a new ten-floor office development. Nobody seemed to give a flying fuck for the rest of it though.

He walked through what was the main foyer, images of usherettes in tartan dresses and male staff in dark suits tumbling through his mind. The stairs rose from here to the old upper foyer where there had once been a bar, a walk he'd made a hundred times but never like this. This time, the likelihood was that no one would ever make it again.

He walked further back into the building, his torchlight leading the way down memory lane. Jackie had been in a few times since it closed in 2006, including before it had been stripped out. Since then it had lain dormant and such a waste, bang in the middle of the city centre and nothing happening to it.

It was so quiet back here. Only the occasional creak of the building and the distant scurry of rodents broke the silence. He liked that though. It gave it an atmosphere it deserved.

The rooms were all bare but he'd been there when the floors were still covered in dark blue carpets, dotted dirty grey where the chairs had been and marked with the sticky stains of old popcorn and spilled juice. The stage was for ghosts now, the old screens long since taken away and sold off.

There were no numbers on the rooms any more but he still knew which was which. The rooms got smaller as the numbers got bigger. Something great had been chopped up into little bits of something ordinary. Cinema 1 had still been a good size but by the time you got down to what had been Cinema 9 then it was pretty claustrophobic and banked steeply from back to front. It was the space that had been 9 that he went into now, breathing in fifty-plus years of his own thoughts.

He stood and listened, closing his eyes and remembering. It was so small and dark that you could almost hear projectors whirring, reels clacking and people shushing each other. You could feel that buzz, the one you got when the whole crowd felt the same thing at the same time. Fear and amusement and sadness and relief. He could imagine dust whirling in the light of the projector and dancing through it were glimpses of car chases and Westerns and custard pies.

He could still smell popcorn and hairspray, hot dogs and sickly orange juice. He could smell sweat and hope and teenage troubles. There was something else though, something newer and yet older. It was the stench of decay. Maybe the smell of the old place finally about to breathe its last.

Jackie wandered down the steep bank to where the screen would have been, seeking one last bit of nostalgia before he left. He'd always wanted to be up there; not that he'd ever dared tell anyone for fear of them laughing at him. He'd imagined himself in a shoot-out with Clint Eastwood or a punch-up with The Duke. Maybe in a love scene with Sophia Loren. Jeez, his pals would have wet themselves if he'd told them that.

He was up there now though. The silver screen. Even if it hadn't been so much silver as dusty grey. The walls to the side a shabby, peeling blue. Jackie gave a little soft-shoe shuffle, like Gene Kelly or Fred Astaire, and put his hands out like it was show business.

He even gave a little bow to the ghosts and turned as if to walk off into the screen. That's when he saw it. That's when he realized that the smell of decay wasn't just from the building.

It was tucked into a little recess to the side of where the screen would have been, partly covered by a sheet of plywood. There was a foot sticking out though. An ashen-white foot that barely seemed real but he knew that it was.

Jackie really didn't want to look any further. He backed away then stopped himself, breathed hard and went forward again. He took hold of the plywood and lifted it, the stench flooding his nose as he did so. All at once he saw the rotten corpse of a woman, naked and eaten, her flesh chewed and decomposed.

This time, he backed away with his mouth open for three steps until he tripped over the lip of the small, raised stage. He was on his knees when he threw up.

Jackie got to his feet, wiping his mouth with the back of his hand, not daring to look at the body again. He hadn't seen anything like that on the big screen, not once. With his back to it, he ran as fast as his over-weight body could take him, up the slope and out of what had been Cinema 9.

Chapter 14

Narey climbed out of her car onto Renfield Street and saw the old cinema looking like she'd never seen it before. Blue flashing lights threw shadows onto the grimy white walls and the tall windows, somehow looking apt on the 1930s design. It was the opening night for a horror movie.

Half the street had been blocked off to accommodate the two squad cars, two unmarked vehicles and the ambulance that would only be needed to take a body away. Uniformed cops stood guard in front of the crime scene tape while others helped direct the traffic chaos that they'd caused. Between them flitted white-suited ghosts who were waiting to carry out forensic duties.

There was some wire fencing round the exterior, more for show than a real attempt to keep anyone out. She noticed the sign on it as she passed. *Development by Saturn Property. Premises Protected by Mullen Security*. Neither protected nor secure, she thought.

She nodded at the cops on the tape and pushed past them with DC Becca Maxwell at her heels, ignoring the shouts from the journalists who wanted answers as to what was going on. Another officer pulled back the recently reopened front door and let them through. When it closed behind them, Narey allowed a solitary shiver to pass through her as she thought how much the old place felt like an indoor cemetery, quiet and cold. It might only have held a single recent corpse but it still held the presence of a thousand more.

A uniformed sergeant, a broad, dark-haired man in his mid-forties, looked up to see her and Maxwell approaching and dismissed one of his constables with a quiet word before stepping forward to meet them. He tipped his head in greeting, his eyes battle-weary. 'DI Narey? I'm Jack McVean. What do you need to know?'

'Well . . . who found the body for starters.'

'Demolition man found it. Name of Jackie Doran. He's over there.'

Narey followed his nod to see a balding man in his sixties sitting on his own and looking dazed. He was cradling a mug of something hot and probably wishing it was something stronger.

'He was back in the building having a last look around before they got ready to bring the place down. Says he used to come here when he was a kid. Didn't we all? I think he nearly crapped himself when he found the woman. He was pretty shook up, still is, but he phoned it in. Constables Dixon and Corry responded and they've interviewed him. The building's been shut since 2006, stripped out years ago and nothing but rats been in since. Mr Doran says it was last checked out a couple of months ago and been locked up in between. They were about ready to push the button and demolish it.'

'Yeah, I saw it on the news. Shame. Okay, let's see the body then and obviously I'll want to talk to Mr Doran and the constables.'

'This way.'

McVean led her and Maxwell back into the building, through narrow corridors and plasterboard walls marked with painted numbers. She'd been here plenty of times but never quite like this. Her mum and dad had brought her at least once a month, packets of Munchies as a treat, the rare school-night visit if she was lucky. Then she'd been with various friends and boyfriends, fending off groping arms when it suited her. It was positively weird being in here now though.

They got deeper into the shell until they came to a single door in the far recess. McVean opened it and stepped back to let them through. The room banked steeply away in front of her to where a small scrum huddled together near the far wall, the whole tableau illuminated by temporary lighting which threw long shadows onto the walls. Campbell Baxter was there and she recognized Paul Burke as being one of the SOCOs under his white suit and mask.

As she got closer, she saw a single foot poking out between the forest of legs, the instep turned onto the dirty floor. The sea parted as Narey neared and she saw the corpse lying there on its back, one leg tucked under the other and the head broken.

It was badly decomposed and had suffered from however long it had been hidden away in the old cinema. The building must have been full of rats and mice and the body wasn't a pretty sight. The woman had been left naked, stripped of dignity and her life as well as her clothes. Left there to end up under rubble when the place was flattened.

Narey stood silently for a moment, contemplating the type of bastard who would do that to another human being.

'Was she killed where she's lying?'

Paul Burke shook his head. 'There's tissue and blood spatter on the corner of the stage over there. Every indication that's where it happened.'

'When did the demolition guy find her?'

'Less than an hour ago,' McVean told her. 'We had a car here within ten minutes.'

'Anyone estimated how long ago she died?'

Baxter made a face. The one he pulled when making out he'd been asked to make a definitive judgement when all she really wanted was some rough idea to work with.

'I'm not in the business of guessing, DI Narey. If you—'

Another voice cut in. 'I'll make a guess. Five to six weeks by the look of it.' It was Winter, walking across the stage towards them with camera in hand and his kit bag over his shoulder.

She glared at him, resenting both his sudden presence and his manner. She'd known, of course, that he'd be on his way but was still irked at him turning up like this, far too familiar in front of the others. There was a line when they were at work, her line, and he knew he was crossing it. Most of all though, she begrudged the fact that she was going to have to step aside and let him get at the body first.

'*Mr* Winter,' she addressed him coolly. 'This is Sergeant McVean. You know everyone else. Do what you have to do and then let us get on with it.'

He walked past her, his eyes fixed on the body and a strange, almost troubled look on his face. She'd seen him photograph victims many times and had been bothered by the enthusiasm, almost zeal, with which he approached his work. This time his lips were pursed tightly and his brows knotted anxiously. Maybe he had finally developed a sense of fitting solemnity but she doubted it.

'What's up?' she whispered as he readied himself over the corpse.

'Just doing my job,' he murmured back. 'I won't be long.'

She stepped away, unsure how to reply and keen to avoid arguing with him in front of the others. Winter dropped his bag a few feet away from the body and raised his camera to his eye.

The truth was he'd been disturbed since the moment he'd got the call. Not the body or the length of time it had lain there: they were just different shades of an old routine. It was all about the location.

He got to work, doing what he had to do, but with a real and unusual sense of unease. The woman filled his lens in an ugly mass of welts and blistered skin, a war of purples, blues and reds. Her hair was the only thing intact: long and dark it curled in waves under her caved skull. He photographed her from every angle, in whole and in part. Open mouth, twisted leg, outstretched arm, desecrated torso.

He got to his knees and squeezed into the recess off stage so that he could photograph what was left of her face in situ. She could have been anything from early thirties to mid-forties, so difficult to tell. One arm was up near her face, unnaturally so and maybe trapped when she was dumped there. Her nails were still a well-manicured red, their shine barely dimmed.

It made him think of what was probably Enrique Metinides' most famous photograph, *The Death of Adela Legarreta Rivas*. Two cars crashed on Avenida Chapultepec in Mexico City and she was run over on her way from the beauty parlour to a book launch. Metinides photographed her, hand outstretched, eyes open, make-up done perfectly, nails immaculate.

It was the thought of the Mexican photographer that made him tilt his camera slightly and catch the circus that was gathered above and beyond this poor woman's head. Forensics and police, Rachel among them, game faces on, itching to get to work. Well fuck them, they could have her.

He got to his feet, stepped back a couple of paces and took one final, all-encompassing shot before tilting his lens to the floor. Job done but far from happy.

She was by his side, speaking quietly. Obviously trying to suss out why he'd been so short with her earlier.

'Two dead bodies in creepy places in such a short time. You must think it's Christmas.'

'Not really. You know I don't believe in God.'

'Tony? What's wrong?'

'A woman's been murdered and left to rot. I just don't think it's funny.'

He knew she didn't quite buy it but she could hardly argue with his reasoning: the truth of that lay in front of them. It wasn't the truth about why he was troubled but he wasn't ready for telling her that, not quite yet.

Chapter 15

Back on Renfield Street, the air was thick with the sound of car horns being thumped by frustrated drivers. The building was on a busy interchange and traffic had ground to a halt thanks to the cop cars and ambulance that were taking up part of the road.

Tough shit, she thought. You'll get to wherever you're going even if you will be late. The woman in there will never get home.

She knew she was tense, more than was normal. Tony had freaked her out a bit with his reaction and she couldn't figure out what was wrong with him. Maybe she didn't have him as well trained as she thought.

It was more than that though and she knew the second reason, while completely selfish, was the one that had her adrenalin in knots. She could feel the clock ticking on this case already, not just in terms of getting a result but also making it hers. She'd been in the right place at the right time to get the call to the Odeon but she knew keeping it wouldn't be as simple as that. MIT was packed with people who'd want their hands on this and would be trying to rip hers from it.

She could hear them now, forming a disorderly queue to moan about her already being on the Molendinar case, about her only being a DI for five minutes, how she only got her promotion because of reorganization to Police Scotland. And of course, they'd play their big card, their sneaky ace. How she only got promoted because she was a woman, how she was meeting some imaginary gender quota, how the bloody glass ceiling had somehow turned upside down.

Of course it was all complete bollocks but if she wanted this, and by Christ she did, she had to make sure she was stuck to it with superglue.

She glanced at her watch and saw there were still forty minutes of office business hours left and she had to make the most of them. Fraser Toshney and Becca Maxwell were on the pavement a few yards away and she scribbled a note on her pad and ripped the sheet from it then called them both over.

'Becca, I want you to stay here, make sure the uniforms keep the public and the press on the right side of that tape and keep me up to date with anything that forensics find. I also want you to look into *this* when you get back to the office.' She handed the DC the note she'd just written.

Maxwell read it, looked quizzical but nodded. 'Yes, ma'am.'

'Fraser, you're coming with me. We're going to pay the site owners a visit and let them know they've got a bit of a problem.'

Now all they had to do was get through this bloody traffic.

Saturn Property had its offices in Skypark, the vast glass monstrosity in Finnieston that they liked to call a business campus. It had been christened as the New Face of Glasgow. Narey wasn't sure there was all that much wrong with the old one.

She looked up at it disapprovingly before they went in. 'Does no one build anything from brick any more, Fraser? It's all glass and steel and aluminium. Remember the third pig? The smart one?'

Toshney looked confused. Narey sighed. 'No matter how hard the big bad wolf huffed and puffed, he couldn't blow down the house made of bricks. Remember that if you ever go into the construction business.'

'I will, Boss.'

Saturn were on the eleventh floor of Skypark 1 with blue-tinged views over the Clyde through floor-to-ceiling windows. Narey looked down to see New Glasgow below her – the Exhibition Centre, the Hydro, the BBC Scotland building, the Science Centre, the Armadillo and the Squinty Bridge. Some things didn't change though – the Finnieston Crane and the river itself defying all attempts at renewal.

Saturn's managing director had an office that might be described as minimalist. Ready for a quick getaway was another description that sprang to mind. A computer and monitor sat on the sole desk, a black-leather chair behind it, a single filing cabinet and a black-leather sofa. Beige walls and a carpet so nondescript that it almost wasn't there. The only thing that even suggested what they did was a series of black-framed artist's impressions of what she presumed were future projects.

In one stood a row of modernist apartments, all glass and wood frontage with awkward angles and showy features. Standing on a field of pastoral green and under a gloriously sunny sky, they were 'full of Eastern promise' according to the accompanying text. They also looked like a big bad wolf could blow them down with one puff.

A door opened behind them and the office's owner hustled in. Mark Singleton was a sunbed thirty-something in a loud suit, all white teeth and fashioned hair. Narey disliked him even before he looked her up and down without bothering to try to hide the fact.

'Detective Inspector . . .'

'Narey. Thank you for seeing us, Mr Singleton. I expect you'll know why we're here.'

The man gestured them towards the sofa but Narey didn't budge. He shrugged and sat behind his desk.

'I got a call from my site foreman telling me about the body found at our Renfield Street site but I don't see how we can help. This hasn't got anything to do with Saturn other than the fact that someone was trespassing there.'

'Well I don't think we'll be charging the woman with trespass, Mr Singleton.'

The man looked annoyed but didn't rise to it. 'What can I help you with, Inspector?'

'Have you any idea why the woman would have been inside the property?'

'None whatsoever. I'm told the body had been there for some time so she didn't work for us. The site had been secured for a considerable period of time. She had no right being in there.'

'Mr Singleton, I am not looking to make a case for negligence. This isn't about holding your company responsible. It's about finding out how and why the victim was in your property. It's about trying to find out who killed her.'

He blanched beneath his fake tan. 'It was murder?'

'It looks that way. Have you spoken to your security people about *how* she could have got in?'

'I haven't had the chance but it wasn't Fort Knox. People can get into most sites if they try hard enough. Frankly, I'm more concerned about any possible delay in demolition. We're on a very tight schedule and time is money. When can we get the site back?'

She was disgusted and barely hid it. 'Not any time soon. It's a crime scene. The demolition will have to be delayed indefinitely.'

Singleton looked furious. 'Our lawyers will have something to say about that, Inspector.'

'They're welcome to try, sir. Now about your security firm. Did they have the premises covered by CCTV? If so, I want to see their tapes.'

He exhaled, clearly irritated. 'I don't know. I don't think so. It was an empty building with nothing inside to steal. There was no need for cameras.'

'It seems there was. Now, your security. It is provided by Mullen Security. Is that right?'

A shrug. 'I'd need to check but that sounds right.'

'It is right. Have you employed this firm for long or on other premises, sir?'

'I'm not sure why any of this is relevant.'

'Maybe it's not, sir. But I'm curious as to how you came to employ Mullen. They have a certain reputation. The people behind it definitely do.'

Paul and Bobby Mullen made their money through drugs, prostitution and people trafficking, then laundered it through the security firm, pubs, tanning salons and saunas, etc. They were serious players in the city.

'What are you insinuating? If you have a problem with Mullen Security, Inspector, then I suggest you take it up with them. I fail to see how they or their reputation have anything to do with what happened in our building. Do you have any further questions?'

'Yes I do.'

She saw the flare of anger in the man's eyes and it made her happy. He sank further back in his seat but said nothing.

'How often were the premises checked and who checked them?'

'I don't know.'

'Can you find out?'

'Yes.'

'Do you have a list of all the people who have worked in the building in the past few months and may I see that, please?'

'They are mostly subcontracted.'

'That's not what I asked you, Mr Singleton. Will you get me a list of the names?'

'*Yes!*'

'Thank you. Can you provide me with your lead contact for Mullen Security?'

'I really don't see why . . .' He made a small exasperated sigh. 'Okay. I'll get my secretary to look them out. She'll get all the information to you.'

'Thank you, sir.'

'I need that project to restart as soon as possible, Inspector. There is a lot depending on it. What can I do to expedite things?'

She narrowed her eyes. 'You can cooperate fully. As soon as I know who was responsible for this woman's death, you can have your building back.'

'What did you make of our Mr Singleton, Fraser?'

'He's a prick, ma'am.'

'Yes he is. And I don't like him one little bit. Let's see what else we can find out about him.' She took her phone out and began scrolling through her contacts.

'You think he's involved?'

'I don't know. Maybe I'd just like him to be. He's in

119

business with the Mullen brothers and a body's been found on premises they were protecting. That sounds like a good starting point to me.'

'It wouldn't be the first time the Mullen boys were responsible for a body or two.'

'Exactly, Fraser. You're catching on.'

They were sitting in the car in the shadow of Skypark and Narey was determined to push things on before they got back to the station. She needed an edge. She needed someone who knew the property game a lot better than she did.

She found the name she was looking for and called. It was answered on the third ring.

'Rachel! How the hell are you? It's been a while.'

Johnny Jackson was an ex-cop, her first sergeant in CID, who now worked as a consultant for IFIG, the Insurance Fraud Investigators Group.

'I'm good, Jacko. You? How's the fraud business?'

'Plenty of it, I'm glad to say. Always someone trying to screw someone else for the sake of a few quid. Keeps me in beer. So is this a business call?'

''Fraid so. I'm hoping to pick your brains.'

'You do know I get paid for that kind of thing these days?'

She laughed, pleased to hear he hadn't changed. 'How about I owe you a lunch? Sarti's maybe?'

'That will do nicely. What do you need to know?'

'I'm looking for information on a company called Saturn Property. Could you let me know what you have on them? And while you're at it, its managing director. A sleazeball by the name of Mark Singleton.'

'Saturn is familiar but I'll need to look up what we have. It will be tomorrow before I get back to you. It will take a bit of time and I work office hours these days. That okay?'

It wasn't ideal but it would have to do.

'And, Jacko, could you check if you have any info on links between Saturn and Mullen Security?'

There was a long pause. 'Bobby Mullen's firm? That explains why Saturn's name is familiar. If I'm right they had one or two fires at their properties and Mullen's name has come up in connection with it. I'll get it for you.'

'Thanks, Jacko. It's appreciated.'

'Whatever this is about, watch yourself, Rachel. Bobby Mullen isn't known for taking prisoners.'

Chapter 16

Winter climbed the stairs to Narey's Highburgh Road flat with a heavy step. He'd spent most of the previous night thinking about what he would say. Or even if he would say anything at all.

He'd almost blurted it out the day before, standing over the body at the Odeon with all that running through his head. A bit of him had known when he was in the Molendinar. Maybe he'd known as soon as he'd heard a body was in there. But when the second victim turned up at the Renfield Street site . . . he'd had no doubt at all.

For a while he conned himself by saying that she wouldn't want to hear it. That he was only there to take photographs and everything else should be left to the police. God knows she'd used that line or a variation of it on him often enough. If he heeded the well-worn advice then he'd just keep his theories to himself.

Except he was sure it was more than a theory. More than a coincidence. And there was more, the voice whispering at him was back. It nagged away at him no matter how much he tried to ignore it.

She met him at the door with a kiss and two glasses of wine. She let her arms slump round his neck for a while, the wine expertly upright, and her head on his shoulder.

'Long day?'

Her voice came back muffled. 'Uh huh.'

'Worse than usual?'

She lifted her head. 'Yep. I was already juggling a fair bit but two murders in a week have put it onto another planet.'

'You think they're connected?' He wasn't sure if he wanted a yes or a no. Maybe she'd get there without whatever help he had to offer.

'What? No, nothing to suggest it. I've got a line I want to follow for the Odeon. It doesn't link to the Molendinar though. I'm ruling nothing in and ruling nothing out.'

'I'm getting the official press line? At least it wasn't No Comment.'

'Oh shut up and come through. I need to sit down, have someone to lie against and share wine with me. What do you say?'

'I can just about manage that.'

Winter sat at one end of the leather sofa in the front room and she lay along its length with her head in his lap, the wine glass on the floor by her side. He let his right hand trail along the length of her body, occasionally resting and squeezing as the moment seemed right.

She made appreciative noises and her body lifted towards him. 'That feels good. I wish I had the energy to do something about it.'

'I could do the work and you could lie there and think of Scotland.'

'The day that's the way it works then we're both in trouble. We'll scratch that itch soon enough, just not tonight.'

'Sounds good to me.' He stroked her hair and sipped slowly at his own Rioja.

'Did you see the DCI tonight?' He could hear the tiredness in her voice. He and Addison were best pals and drinking buddies.

'Hmm? Yes. We had a couple of pints in the Station Bar after work.'

'Thought you might have. So what was he saying about my murder cases? I can't imagine it didn't come up in conversation. Come on, spill.'

'He's going to chat to you about the Odeon tomorrow. Don't quote me but I think he's going to come in on that one. He's worried you're getting overloaded.'

She sat upright, nearly knocking the wine glass over. 'Is he saying I can't cope?'

Winter laughed and gently pushed her back down. 'You know he's not. Anyway, *you* were saying you had so much on your plate.'

'I know, but I get to say it. So that was it? Just that he was going to pitch in?'

'Pretty much. So what's the line you're following for the Odeon body?'

An elbow came back and caught him in the stomach. 'You know the rules.'

'And I know we've broken them often enough.'

'Not this time, lover. Anyway, it's not much more than a hunch at this stage. The owners have a dodgy connection and I want to check it out.'

'Okay.' It wasn't really okay. He wanted to know more but he'd change the subject for now. 'Have you spoken to your dad tonight?'

Her eyes closed over and she blew a thin sigh between her lips. 'I called him. Didn't get a whole lot of sense though and he didn't know who I was. I cut it short because he was getting distressed.'

Winter massaged her shoulders and kissed the top of her head. 'Sorry. I know how hard it is when he doesn't know you.'

'It's harder for him. All of it.'

'I know. But still—'

He was cut off by a text alert on her phone and she manoeuvred a hand beneath her to pluck it from her back pocket. Whatever she saw revitalized her immediately.

'From Kirsten Fairweather. She's emailed me the facial reconstruction of the Molendinar guy.'

With that she levered herself off him and hurried to fetch her laptop. In moments she was back, sitting alongside him this time as the computer booted up.

'So what do you know about this guy? Off the record . . .'

She gave him a weary look before opening up her

125

mail to find that, sure enough, there was an email from Kirsten. She clicked on it and waited for the image to build.

'*Strictly* between us. He seemed to be homeless, living at the Rosewood Hotel. We think his name is Euan Hepburn. But . . .'

Clocks stopped and traffic noise disappeared. Winter's world missed a beat. The reconstruction stared back at him from the screen. Narey's eyes narrowed as she caught the look on his face.

'Do you *know* him?'

His instinct was to lie but the truth was written all over him.

'Yes. Well, I used to. Years ago.'

'And is he Euan Hepburn?

'Yes.'

'Tony, are you okay? Did you know him well?'

This time he managed to lie. 'No. Not really.'

She studied him for a bit, clearly doubting him and seeing how shocked he was. He had to give her something else.

'I haven't seen him in years. He'd moved to England to work, last I heard. I had no idea he was back in Glasgow. But he wasn't homeless, I really doubt that.'

'Then what? He *had* been staying in the Rosewood.'

'Euan was a journalist. Freelance.'

She just nodded. 'I thought he might be. Explains why he'd been asking so many questions.'

'Questions about what? Or who?'

She put the shutters up again. He could see them rising on her face.

'I don't know yet. That's what I need to find out. You didn't recognize him in the Molendinar?'

Part of him had, he remembered that. The quiet voice that he'd been quick to dismiss. Maybe deeper down he'd known but hadn't wanted it to be. Not Euan.

'The body was so far gone. The decomposition . . .'

'But now, does it fit with the guy you knew?'

He nodded. 'Yes, it's definitely him.'

'Did he have family? I need to contact relatives.'

'He had a sister who lived up north somewhere, near Aberdeen. They weren't close. His parents were both dead.'

'Tony, what the hell would he have been doing in that tunnel?'

He was ready for the question and didn't hesitate. 'I've no idea. Sorry.'

Another extended stare before she nodded. 'Are you sure you're okay?'

'I'm fine.'

'Okay then. I'm going to have a shower. Wash some of this day off me. Dinner once I get out?'

'Sounds good.'

They moved together and he hugged her, staring over her shoulder and through the window to the street-lit sky beyond. There was a ghost out there somewhere in the darkness.

Euan Hepburn. Euan fucking Hepburn.

Chapter 17

August 2006

Winter turned a corner and saw the corridor stretch out endlessly before him, the patterned carpet an eyesore, garish pink walls flocked with flaking paint and closed doors off left and right. The place was infested with asbestos and word was it was basically falling to bits. Hard to believe it was once the most prestigious hotel in Glasgow.

The Central Hotel. Frank Sinatra had stayed here when he was in town. Winston Churchill and John F. Kennedy too. It was the place for all the Hollywood stars when they visited. Mae West, Gene Kelly, Judy Garland, Cary Grant, you name it. Roy Rogers even booked a room for his horse, Trigger. It had been on the way down for years though and now it had come to this. A shithole.

Some said it was a shithole with ghosts. The haunted

spirit of a scullery maid who fell to her death down a lift shaft from the seventh floor. Or of the guest who hanged himself in his room. Just bollocks, obviously. Winter didn't have time for that kind of stuff. The place was creepy though, no doubt about that.

It ran the whole length of the railway station along Gordon Street and a fair way down the Hope Street side too. All the rooms were massive, twice maybe three times the size of modern hotel rooms. The word was that a new company was going to take the hotel over and spend a packet on refurbishing it. For him, that meant going in while he could and seeing it for what it was.

It had been easy enough to find his way in through an unboarded, unbarred window. Laurel and Hardy, Bob Hope, Edward G. Robinson and the Queen: they'd all come in past the doorman at the front.

He stopped at one bedroom window, through which faint morning light was streaming, and looked down onto the station below. It spread out like a vast greenhouse under its glass roof, only a few trains rumbling in and out because of the early hour. One hundred and thirty years trains had been coming and going from down there, the hotel just four years younger. Beyond the station, Glasgow yawned into the distance, its rooftops stretching to begin its day. He had to move before the city arrived with the milk.

He pushed open other doors as he paced along the corridor. Some had curtains and tables, some looked as if they were waiting to be made up for the next

129

guest. In the half-light of a Glasgow dawn, they all gave the impression they had someone sleeping or standing in the shadows.

When he finally got to the end of the passageway, Winter turned and climbed an uncarpeted staircase, a beautiful piece of Victorian craftsmanship that creaked and groaned beneath his feet. He paused for a moment to catch the view outside and instead caught his breath as he heard other footsteps on the floor above him. Or were they below? He stopped and they did too. It must have been an echo. Or maybe just the ghost of the suicidal guest, the man who'd topped himself because of the lurid wallpaper.

He climbed three flights and explored each floor, his footsteps resonating on the stairs in search of friends. Enough noise to wake the dead. A couple of hours slid by as he found empty rooms and rooms littered with cabling, packaging boxes and general rubbish. In two rooms, he lifted the corner of a brash patterned carpet and found that it covered a beautiful Italian marble floor.

He knew that the top three floors used to be used for the staff; waiters and chambermaids and the like; plus servants of the rich and famous who stayed there. These floors were noisier, creaking more than the others and with a constant, unsettling hum as gusts of wind blew through from some unseen hole. The top of the building seemed to be alive, noisily breathing in and out. From somewhere close there was a rustle and a scurry as creatures made themselves scarce at his arrival and he thought he heard a sudden beating of wings from around a corner. The startled cooing of a pigeon confirmed it.

One dark brown door, stencilled *Ladies' Toilet & Bathroom*, was pushed back to reveal intricate green-and-white tiles that must have dated back to the 1920s, a broken mosaic floor and large ceramic baths that held a million bacteria. Large washbasins and exposed wiring also conspired to ruin what it had once been.

Something moved behind him. He turned to see two pigeons fly past the open door, heading along the corridor in the direction he'd come from. Winter strode over and popped his head out but they'd already disappeared from sight. All that was left was their shadows.

The distant sound of the birds and their flapping wings began to merge with the groan of the wind and with floorboards that continued to screech long after he'd stepped upon them. The building was talking to him, complaining about its condition like an old man left in a corner to cough and wheeze.

Breathing deeply, Winter opened the next door and then another, seeing just the same faded normality that he'd seen before. The next, a small attic room, was dressed in dust and a dark colour scheme that could have been brown or grey or just old. What caught his eye was a metal door on the far wall. It gleamed darkly and begged him to come closer for a look.

It was only about five foot high and seemed newer than the rest of the room. An addition. Yet it still gave off a vibe of age, a rustiness that was maybe by design. The metal handle, the same dark brown colour as the door, begged him to turn it. Shaking his head in wonder, he grabbed and pulled.

The door came towards him with a grunt, revealing not another room but a closet, painted a creamy white inside. It was a narrow recess into the wall, maybe five foot high, the same as the door and three or four feet deep. Tall enough for a child to stand up in, big enough to hold an adult if they ducked. His eyes widened and his jaw dropped. The three walls of the closet were lined with razor blades.

He stood on the threshold, crouching and dipping his head, seeing that the blades were indeed razor sharp and had been carefully and firmly pushed into the walls. Behind him another floorboard creaked and the wind sang. There must have been . . . he counted . . . Jesus, there were maybe two hundred blades.

The final floorboard creaked just as he felt a shove in the middle of his back and he was propelled forward into the closet. He didn't dare put his hands out to stop himself for fear of the blades and instead had to brake with his feet as best he could. The door closed firmly behind him and the closet was plunged into darkness.

The urge to move was huge but he had to fight it. He was wary of even turning to face the door to try to open it. The blades were maybe just an inch or two from his face, his chest, his wrists. And he couldn't see a thing.

132

The floorboards squealed again from the other side of the door, close enough for him to feel it.

'Open this door. Open this fucking door!'

Nothing. Nothing but more creaking as if the floorboards were slowly bouncing.

'Who's there? Open this fucking door now!'

He began to edge his feet forward to gauge just where he was. His left shoe nudged forward maybe three or four inches when it hit the wall. He backed up, stopping when he realized he wasn't certain whether there were blades in the back of the door behind him. He swung back his right leg and kicked out with his heel, slamming it into the door and wobbling dangerously as a result.

Laughter came from the other side of the door. A dirty laugh that was trying to be stifled but burst out uncontained. There were slaps against the door that made the metal ring and seemed to shrink the room; then, just as suddenly, there was light. He felt the air as the door pulled back behind him.

A voice came out of the laughter. 'Step back. Straight back. Straight as a razor. Man, if I was any sharper I'd cut myself.'

Winter did as he was told. One step, two and he was out, standing up and whirling as soon as he was clear of the closet. In front of him, nearly doubled up in fits of laughter, was a guy about his own age, tears running down his cheeks.

'Sorry, man. Seriously. Sorry. I just couldn't resist.'

Winter swung his right arm, fist clenched, connected

with the man's jaw and put him flat on his back. The guy lay there, hand nursing his chin, and continued to laugh. He was about five foot eleven with short reddish fair hair, athletically built and with a wicked grin plastered over his face.

'Fair enough. I deserved that. Just couldn't help myself.' A finger of his right hand tested his lips and saw it flecked with blood. 'One shot's all you get though. Okay?'

'You could have killed me, you idiot.' Winter softened as his rage slowly dwindled with relief. 'Okay, maybe not killed me but those blades . . .'

The man held both hands up in surrender. 'You're right. It was stupid. Shouldn't have done it.' He got to his feet, slowly stretching out a hand. 'I'm Euan Hepburn. Accept an apology?'

Winter shook his head and let a reluctant smile cross his face. 'Tony Winter. Apology accepted. Just. You make a habit of doing stuff as stupid as that?'

Hepburn shrugged. 'Yeah, pretty much. Some weird shit in this place, huh?'

'You could say that. So it was you I heard moving around earlier?'

'Either me or the ghost of the woman who fell down the lift shaft. You can never be sure somewhere like this. You know what this is?' He nodded at the razor-clad closet.

Winter shook his head.

'It's an art installation. Weird, huh? I'd heard about it. One of the reasons I wanted to explore in here. Look, how about I buy you a pint to make up for it.'

'A *pint*?' Winter looked at his watch. 'It's only seven thirty.'

Hepburn smiled mischievously. 'Another quick scout round here and then a wee stroll to the Saltmarket. The Whistlin Kirk opens at eight. Need to get a breakfast with the beer, right enough. It's the law.'

'What kind of pub opens at eight in the morning?'

'One that works what they call Grandfather Terms. So they can sell to shift workers. And I feel we've put a shift in going round here. What do you say?'

Winter laughed. 'Why not? My mouth's so dry—'

'It thinks your throat's been cut?'

'Exactly.'

The Whistlin Kirk was in Greendyke Street, just a stone's throw from the Clyde and just enough time to take your tie off if you'd walked from the High Court. It was only just gone eight but already there was a small, happy band with pints of lager in front of them on round tables. Plates held sausage, bacon and egg or filled rolls. The crowd was pensioner age, most pitched somewhere between sixty and eighty, and they all looked happy to be out of the house and still alive.

Hepburn led Winter to the bar where they were greeted with a nod by a woman in her thirties with blonde bobbed hair and a red apron over a black top. She sized them up and didn't see any trouble she couldn't handle.

'Help you, boys?'

'Two pints, please. A lager and a Guinness. And a bacon roll.'

'Needs to be a roll each. It's the law.'

They found a couple of seats in the corner, a bit along from a clean-shaven man in a hoodie who sat looking down silently into a pint of lager, a plate of square sausage and beans sitting untouched beside him.

The bar still had the stale whiff of last night's booze but that was slowly disappearing through the open door along with the hangovers. Some customers chatted quietly, some cracked jokes and told each other lies. They all got what they wanted from it.

'Nice place,' Winter said quietly.

'It is actually. Never any bother, keep a good pint, folk are friendly. Not my bit of town but I'd drink in here if I was local. And it's cheap.'

Winter supped on his Guinness, deliberately letting a creamy crescent settle on his lip before licking it off. 'You not got a job to go to today?'

'Nothing till later. I work for myself so can generally choose when I come and go. I'm a freelance journalist.'

'Yeah? What kind of stuff do you report on?'

He grinned. 'Anything that pays. I do some undercover stuff but whatever pays the bills and lets me not work nine to five is fine by me. What about you?'

'Photographer?'

'Really? I know plenty but never seen you. Who do you work for?'

Winter dropped his voice. 'The cops. Not long started.'

Hepburn laughed. 'That explains it then. Obviously most of the guys I know are snappers for the papers.'

'That's not for me. So were you in the Central doing some undercover work?'

'Jeez no. Just exploring. If I started exploring it to get paid, it would take all the fun out of it. I have a couple of cameras and tend to use one for work and one for urbexing.'

'Really? I do the same. One for work and one for me, although I usually take both to a job with me. Just habit, I guess. So where have you explored?'

They took turns to reel off places they'd been. The old Merkland Street station, the public baths, Govan dockyards, Woodilee Hospital out at Lenzie, the Titan at Clydebank, a succession of old schools, factories, churches and disused railway lines. It turned out they'd unknowingly been following in each other's footsteps across the city. They were each other's shadow.

'This makes a change,' Hepburn grinned. 'I never get the chance to talk to other urbexers. Man, I didn't even know I *was* an urbexer till I read about it online. Until then I thought I was the only eejit going into places I shouldn't.'

'I guess there's a few of us. Guy I met reckoned there were maybe about nine or ten in Glasgow doing it. Can't be sure though. We all just do our thing and no one talks about it – we hardly ever meet each other. How did you get into it?'

Hepburn tilted his head in thought. 'My old primary

school was getting knocked down and made into flats. I thought it was a shame and wanted to have a look around before they flattened it. They said I couldn't, chance had gone. So I figured I'd go in anyway. Getting in was a piece of cake. Looked around the classrooms and the gym, went into the head's office seeing I got called there on a regular basis. I even sat at a couple of my old desks. Amazing how the memories came back. Just as well I went in when I did though because the place burned down a week later.'

Winter groaned. 'Let me guess. They found something inside. Asbestos maybe? The developers couldn't get planning permission and then the place mysteriously caught fire.'

'That's exactly it. Amazing how many times that happens in Glasgow.'

'Always just a coincidence though. Feel good when you were back in the school?'

'Felt great. Being in there but also being in there because they'd told me I couldn't. I got a buzz out of that. They're always telling us we can't go places or can't do things. They treat us like kids, man. Beware of this, danger of that, don't even think of going there. Load of crap. If I get hurt then it's my own fault. I'm not going to sue anyone. Tell me I can't and I want it all the more. You know?'

Winter knew all right. Every word that Hepburn spoke felt like it had come from his own mouth. It was oddly reassuring to find someone of the same mindset. Maybe he wasn't as strange as he'd thought.

It seemed Hepburn was thinking the same thing. 'Do you ever want to do some explores but don't because it's a bit dangerous or too bloody stupid to do them on your own?'

He considered the implication of the question. 'Yeah. What are you suggesting?'

A shrug of the shoulders. 'Sometimes it might make sense to keep an eye out for each other. Places where you'd want someone to be there if you got stuck or fell.'

'Don't know. I'm used to doing this on my own.'

'Christ, I'm not suggesting we get married or anything. Just when it suited.'

'Could give it a go, I guess.'

They clinked their pints together and the deal was sealed.

That's how it started. They climbed all the cranes on the Clyde, they explored most of the buildings that tried to keep them out and they photographed wherever they went. Both of them had a feel for historic buildings and made a vow to get into as many as they could of the ones that were marked for demolition. It was their small rebellion against the gentrification that was cleaning up by tearing down. Schools, offices, factories, libraries, banks. Anywhere that couldn't be turned into a pub or converted into overpriced flats ran the risk of being obliterated so that the land could host some throw-me-up new build.

It helped that they both worked weird hours and

they forged a bond by being up and about when most of the city was asleep. If it was three in the morning and you were in the darkness in a former mental asylum then you needed to be able to trust the person you were with.

For three years it was great. Then it stopped. Euan packed up and moved to London.

He and Winter had already stopped urbexing together by then but that was a different story, one that he didn't like to think about.

Chapter 18

Tuesday evening

Remy Feeks could only stare at his laptop screen. The Odeon. A woman's body. The news report hadn't said much more but then it didn't need to. Not for him.

It couldn't have been anything else. Not after the Molendinar. It was just too much of a coincidence. The Odeon meant urbexing. It had to.

He sat for an age, looking at it open-mouthed and with the feeling that something was crawling over his skin. He'd barely left the house, refusing Gabby's pleas and threats to meet up, instead just sitting there obsessively poring over every bit of news he could find online. Then he'd found this. The Odeon.

He'd been scared before but now he was terrified. For him and for Gabby. More for her. He was hiding away at home and she was out there, exploring places like the Sentinel Works without him there to look out

141

for her. It couldn't be safe. He grabbed his phone and texted her, urging her to be careful, asking her not to go out. She got back ten minutes later to say she already had a mother and didn't need another one.

He had to do something and while he didn't know what that was, at least he thought he knew where to look.

OtherWorld was the main UK urbexing forum. He'd used it for about five years, almost as long as he'd known that exploring old places even had a name. People would gather online, post their photographs, chat and get ideas for places to explore or share leads for new locations.

He didn't think anyone would urbex in Glasgow without knowing of OtherWorld. Most probably, although you just couldn't know, every urbexer would use it.

It was a community of sorts. People who largely didn't know each other but knew enough to say hello in the passing online. Not so different from the real world these days. There were those quick to congratu-late someone on a good explore but there were also those quick to criticize and find fault, keyboard war-riors who took what pleasure they could in being a pain in the arse to others.

Most people were cool though. They just loved what they did and wanted to share. Photography was a huge part of it, not just proof that you'd done what you'd said but to let others see what was out there. Often it was a case of capturing it before it disappeared. In a city like Glasgow which was doing pretty well, places tended to be abandoned for less time. They'd either be quickly demolished or tarted up into something else and pressed back into service. Their job, and lots of them saw it that way, was to get photos for posterity while they could.

It was all pretty much anonymous and that was the way it had to be. What they were doing was basically illegal, even if it was just common trespass, and that was the first reason not to put your real name to it. But also, it was just the nature of the beast. You got in, got out, no need to shout about it. They all liked the fact that it was a bit cloak and dagger. They were evening explorers. Night Ninjas.

At least that was the way it had seemed until now.

Secret identities had seemed cool and exciting. Now though it looked like the forum was hiding something. It was hiding everyone and everything and he didn't like it. The forum was full of names that he knew by sight, but he could brush past these people in the street and wouldn't know who they were. But maybe they'd know him.

Tubz. Digger9. BigTomDog. Ultrabex. DrJohn. SkeletonBob. Jonesy78.

All these stupid names. Did they hide witnesses or victims? Did they hide a killer?

His own user name was Magellan93. It had seemed like a good idea at the time but now it just sounded a bit wanky. He wasn't a real explorer. He collected trolleys, he didn't circumnavigate the earth.

143

He had to figure out what he wanted, what he hoped for. Help, reassurance, friends, answers. All of those. Maybe most of all he wanted to be told that everything would be all right. It was something that he'd doubted even before he read about the Odeon. From the moment he did, he knew there was something seriously bad going on.

The forum had a search facility and he put *Glasgow* into the keyword field and combed through the results. He went through every post and jotted down the name of every user who had replied on it in the past few years and their location. It was a long and laborious process, maybe a pointless one, but he had to feel he was doing something.

There was seven years' worth of reports and a long list of people who'd either posted them or commented on them. All those made-up names, all those masks. The only one he knew in real life was Vixxxen, who was Gabby. He divided the others up into three separate lists. Glasgow. Rest of Scotland. Outside Scotland. He counted how often they'd posted and when. After an hour, he was confident he had the names of all the regular Glasgow urbexers. He had his list.

Tunnel Man was probably among them. In fact, Remy was sure he was. The person that killed Tunnel Man? It scared him silly that he – or she – might be in there too.

There were just fifteen names, a manageable number for what he had in mind. He sent all of them the same private message. If he was right, then at least one of

144

them would be unable to reply. And maybe one of them would be unable to resist replying.

Hi guys. How do you fancy getting together for a forum outing? Just the Glasgow crowd. Nothing too difficult, not the Molendinar or anything stellar like that. I was thinking we could walk down the line to the old Botanics station then go for a couple of drinks on Byres Road. If the Botanics is too tame for some of you then you can just go straight to the pub and meet us there. It's short notice but how about Thursday night?

He pushed send and immediately wondered just what the hell he'd done.

Chapter 19

Wednesday morning

'Jacko. What have you got?'

'Quite a bit, Rachel. Let's just say that Saturn are of interest to us. A colleague has them on his list so I didn't know all I might have but I'm up to speed now.'

'I'm all ears.'

'Well the first thing you need to know is that Saturn is not where this starts. There was once a company called Midas Homes and then one named LDM Holdings. Midas went bust with a trail of debts and a short time later LDM started up with the same client list. Nine months after that, LDM hit the wall and were liquidated.'

'Then they became Saturn?'

'Not quite. First there was Valhalla Homes, the phoenix that had risen from the flames when LDM burned.'

'I thought they hit the wall?'

'They hit the wall and burst into flames. It's a regular occurrence with some companies in this business. Valhalla then led to Hastings Developments, hit the wall and then Hastings became Saturn.'

'I'm slightly confused here, Jacko.'

'You're supposed to be. These kind of companies try to muddy the water as much as possible because when it's clear they just look like the crooks they are. All five firms owned, sold, built and demolished properties around Scotland and the north of England. And all five have been dreadfully *unlucky* at various times over the years. That's what brought them to the attention of IFIG.'

'Unlucky how? Fires?'

'Yes. Nine of them that we know of.'

'*Nine?* And yet they've never been done for it? Nine fires in properties that they owned and yet they still operate?'

'Nine times they haven't been caught. In firms that *technically* aren't connected. And the firms don't still operate, only Saturn. Officially, of course, they have done nothing wrong. Officially, they are the unfortunate victims of firebugs and bad luck. Officially, they are merely companies of interest.'

'And unofficially?'

'I wouldn't trust them to build a Lego house without putting a match to it. They're crooks. They shut down, dump their debt and start again. They torch their own properties if they can't get the planning permission

147

they want or if it's just cheaper to rebuild from scratch rather than renovate a listed building the way it should be.'

Narey scribbled notes on the pad in front of her, underlining *crooks* and *nine fires*.

'So, Mark Singleton. Tell me about him.'

'He's just a front man. On the payroll rather than ever owning the business. I made a call and the word is he likes the limelight, the appearance of being in charge. He's a chancer. A bit of a risk taker, likes getting his photo in the paper.'

'A front man? But I checked myself and he's listed as a director.'

Jackson laughed. 'Almost none of the directors are real. The names you are seeing are wives or children of those serving seven-year bans as directors after the previous companies bit the dust, leaving creditors in the lurch. It's all front.'

'So if Singleton's the front, who really owns Saturn? Could it be the Mullens?'

'I guess it could be, sure. Come on, what's this about, Rachel? You're not chasing fires, I know that much.'

'Saturn owned the old Odeon site. And Mullen Security had their name on the fence.'

She could almost hear his brain joining the dots. 'And that's where the woman's body was found. I must be getting slow in my old age, should have made that connection myself. Okay, what do you want me to do?'

'Keep looking, keep asking around.'

'Happy to do it. Saturn are exactly the kind of company we're after. Our clients aren't keen on paying out for fires that these cowboys have started themselves.'

'Jacko, if I want to get at this mob, where do I look?'

'Well, it's not easy, they're sneaky bastards. But my advice, for what it's worth, is that you don't look for what Saturn are doing but what they've not been able to do. That's when these guys get dirty.'

Chapter 20

The call to DCI Addison's office was always a dubious pleasure and Narey feared this one would be no different. She was armed with the feedback from her chat with Johnny Jackson but she still felt a nervousness she wasn't enjoying.

Addison was inevitably on the phone but cut the conversation short as soon as she stuck her head round the door. Alarm bells rang immediately.

'I'll get back to you, Charlie,' he was saying. 'There's someone more important than you I need to talk to. Yeah – and the same to you with knobs on. I'll call you back.' He hung up. 'Hi, Rachel, good to see you. Take a seat.'

The alarm bells were now ringing like a cathedral had been overrun by a troop of chimpanzees and they were swinging on the ropes.

'I'll stand, sir, if it's all the same. What's the bad news?'

He grimaced. 'Look, Rachel, don't start.'

'You're trying to be nice. Of course there's bad news. What is it?'

He spread his arms wide as if ready to make some plea for understanding then gave up. 'Sit down.'

'No. Just tell me.'

'Fucksake. Okay, have it your way. Rachel, you've got enough on your plate with the Molendinar body and everything else you're working on. You don't need another murder case on top of that. I'm giving the Odeon woman to Jeff Storey and Rico.'

It felt as if she'd been slapped.

'What? No way. There's no need for that. I'm all over this. Seriously, I can handle both. And I *want* both.'

'It's not about what you want. I've got people queuing up who want this. It's about clearing both cases up and doing whatever makes that most likely. You running two separate investigations does not qualify as best practice. I'm taking it off you for your own good and the good of the team.'

'My *own good*?'

'I said don't start. You know there's guys out there gunning for you as it is. Some of them resent your promotion and it's not going to help for you to be running two murder cases. They'll be desperate for you to fuck up and I don't want that to happen.'

'I've no intention of fucking up. And I got promoted because I earned it.'

'I *know* that. Christ, it was me that recommended

151

you. But there's knuckle-draggers out there who can't see past your skirt and won't believe you got it on merit. They're the ones who will stir up trouble and I'm not giving them the ammunition. One murder case is plenty.'

'So you are saying I should give in to guys who are still coming to terms with the fact that women have got the vote? That doesn't work for me.'

'No, I'm *not* saying that. You know I'm not. You're a better cop than any of them and that's all the more reason not to give them any room to slag you off. It's not just about them either. I've a duty to manage resources and having half the MIT team sitting scratching their balls while you take on every case in the book isn't the best way to do that.'

'Leaving me in charge of the case *is* the best way to do it. We've got a probable name for the victim and if dental records match then I'm going to inform the husband.'

'No.'

'I've talked to the guy in charge at Saturn and there's no doubt he's dodgy. I've got Johnny Jackson all over the company history and it stinks. Saturn is a phoenix firm with a history of unexplained fires and they're tied at the hip with the Mullens. I'm *on* this.'

'No!' He was shouting now too. 'The Mullens? Are you *trying* to give me reasons to take you off this? If they are involved in any way then we'll need to liaise with Organized Crime. You're not getting all of that. Storey and Rico can pick it all up quickly enough. We need—'

'This is out of order.'

'Don't push it, Rachel. I've made my decision. And unless you can give me a very good reason not to do this—'

She blurted it out before she could think it through. 'I think the cases are linked.'

There was a bemused pause before he laughed in her face. 'What? They're *linked*. And you've just worked this out now?'

'No, it's a connection I've been looking at. I think it's got legs and it makes sense for me to pursue both.'

'This will be good. Go on.'

She breathed deeply, clutched at a straw, said a silent prayer to Danny Neilson and hoped for the best. 'I think both cases are linked to urbexing.'

His face screwed up as if she'd spoken in Swahili. '*Urbexing*? I knew this would be good. What the hell is that?'

'It's a hobby. A pursuit, I guess. Short for urban exploration. People go into abandoned buildings and the like. Places they're not supposed to go. Places like—'

'Like the Molendinar Burn? Really?'

'Yes. And places like the old Odeon. Both are known sites for urbexers. The people who do this kind of thing.'

Addison scratched his head and was clearly regretting the entire conversation. 'People who break into places. They've got a fancy name now, have they? In my day we called them thieves.'

153

'They don't steal things. That's not the point.'

'So what is the point?'

'The *real* point is that I think the cases could be linked. Yes, it might be speculation. Yes, it might come to nothing. But it's worth a look. And for that reason you should keep me on both.'

He stared at her for a while, long enough for her to see the wheels turning in his head. He was almost there but she saw him pull back.

'No. This is nonsense. You can't just pluck this stuff out of thin air.'

'I've already got Becca Maxwell checking it out. It's not like I've just made it up. What do you take me for?'

She hoped he wouldn't answer that. She *had* got Maxwell to check it out after the Odeon find but with no real expectation that there was anything in it. She still didn't believe it but right then it was all she had.

'Rachel, I've made my mind up.'

'Give me a bit more time.'

'No.'

'Give me till the end of the day.'

He groaned. 'You really think there might be something in this?

'Yes.'

'You'll be the fucking death of me. Okay, end of the day and that's it. Understand?'

'Got it.' All she had done was buy herself some time but it was something.

'Okay, now tell me about the case you *will* be

working. Tell me where we are with the Molendinar guy.'

She breathed for what seemed like the first time in five minutes. 'Well it turns out that although he'd been staying at the Rosewood when he was killed, he wasn't homeless.'

'So what the hell was he doing there?'

'I spoke to the boss at the City Mission, made a few phone calls and got a facial reconstruction done. This guy had been asking a lot of questions, both at the Rosewood and the Mission. He was a journalist named Euan Hepburn, working undercover. Tony knew him and confirmed the facial ID.'

'Tony? And when did you two discuss this?'

She ignored the tease in his voice, pretended to herself that he couldn't be insinuating anything. 'He was there when the reconstruction came through from Dundee. Anyway, I made a few calls this morning and none of the Scottish news desks claim to have commissioned him to do it. He was a freelance so he might have been getting the story first, then intending to flog it to the highest bidder. A couple of the papers confirmed they'd taken stories from him before and they had an address for him for payment. A flat in Cordiner Street in Mount Florida.'

'A journalist. Great. Just great. I take it you haven't released his name to the press.'

'No. I was planning to hold on to that for a while longer. For one thing, we need to contact his sister, the next of kin. We'll run a DNA test on her for confirmation. Anyway, it will do us no harm to keep his identity to ourselves for a bit.'

'Agreed. You checked his flat out?'

'Not yet. I've sent Toshney and a couple of uniforms over. We'll see what they come back with. But if he was undercover then it gives us a motive to play with.'

'The owners of the hotel?'

'Yes. If he was digging the dirt on the place, stands to reason that someone wouldn't be too happy about that.'

'Who owns it?'

'Two businessmen. Thomas Kilgannon and Brian Wells. Neither of them has a record. Although they should have just for running that place. It should have been shut down years ago. If they found out Hepburn was undercover and they had something to hide then they'd need to shut him up.'

Addison levelled her with a stare. 'Okay. And how exactly does that fit in with your urbexing theory?'

Good point, sir, she thought.

'I don't know yet,' she said.

Addison shook his head. 'I'm regretting this already. Okay, let's not get carried away with this pair either. Wanting them to be guilty isn't enough to bring a case against them.'

She sighed heavily. 'Look, I'm not wishing them guilty. Okay, maybe I am a bit. Have you been in that place? It *is* criminal the way those people are living. They are being milked of their housing benefit and left to die slowly from drink and drugs. I'm betting the

owners make a small fortune from keeping those poor
bastards in that shithole and people will do whatever
it takes to keep the money rolling in. One thing we can
be sure of, the people who own the Rosewood aren't
big on scruples.'

Addison spread his arms wide in surrender. 'Okay,
okay. Get down from your soapbox and go bring them
in.' He looked at his watch. 'I'm free later this afternoon. Haul them in and I'll sit in with you. Okay?'

She agreed grudgingly. 'Okay. And it's not a
soapbox.'

'High horse?'

'Common decency.' She was laughing. 'You should
try it sometime.'

'That would involve principles, Rachel. I've got no
time for principles. I'm a police officer. And remember,
end of the day is all you've got for this urbexing thing,
then it's gone.'

157

Chapter 21

It took seven hours to get Thomas Kilgannon and Brian Wells into an interview room. Narey's case to drag them into Stewart Street was weak and no one knew that better than their lawyer. Arthur Constance finally relented and said that his clients would agree to visit the officers out of a sense of civic duty and a willingness to help if they could.

Kilgannon and Wells were both tall men, the former broad and bulky and the latter as thin and sturdy as a rake. They were in their late fifties and dressed awkwardly in suits, carrying themselves the way men do when they are used to being in work clothes but pressed into service for a funeral or an appearance in court.

Constance glided quietly into the station in their wake, a small, bird-like man with the bite of a velociraptor. He had been taking chunks out of cops and police lawyers for years and was feared just as much as the powerful men he frequently represented. Connie was a little man who had grown very wealthy on the fat of others' transgressions.

He and his clients sat on one side of the table while Addison and Narey sat on the other. It was an informal interview, nothing under caution or recorded, an act of assistance on the part of Mr Kilgannon and Mr Wells, as Constance informed them. It was clear who would be doing most of the talking.

'My clients are here to assist in any way they can but I have let it be known that they are as mystified as I am as to how you think they might be able to help you. You say that a deceased person once took lodging at a property owned by my clients and, even if that is indeed the case, their connection to your investigation is tenuous at best, I'm sure you'll agree.'

'If that is indeed the case then your clients have nothing to worry about, Mr Constance,' Addison replied. 'However it would be very helpful if they could outline for us the working practices at the Rosewood Hotel, the number of employees positioned there and their identities. I would also like to ask them for a detailed list of people staying there in the past six months.'

Kilgannon and Wells looked back across the table, their expressions unchanged and their mouths firmly shut. There was a coldness about both of them that would have kept fish fingers frozen for a month.

Constance spread his arms wide, his face a picture of innocent confusion. 'Working practices at the hotel?

As at any other hotel, DCI Addison. Guests are registered, accommodation is provided and payment received. What other practices could you possibly mean?'

Addison was about to tell him just what he meant when the lawyer cut him off by opening a folder in front of him and picking up a number of sheets of A4 paper in a clear plastic pocket. He placed them on the desk in front of the two officers.

'Everything you require is in there, Detective Chief Inspector. It lists five employees. Their names, addresses, National Insurance numbers, employment history and contact details are enclosed within. We would insist that you inform us of any plans to interview any of them as I am their legal counsel and would be present at any such meeting.'

'Only five? For a building that size?'

'It is a well-run, well-organized company run by two outstanding businessmen. Five employees are sufficient.'

Narey's temperature rose a couple of degrees. '*Well run*? You are telling us that place is well run?'

Neither Kilgannon nor Wells blinked but Constance looked at her over the top of his small round glasses. 'Yes, Detective Inspector, I believe that is what I just said. Do you have any reason to cast aspersions on the running of my clients' business and do any such aspersions have any basis in the law or any relevance to the case you are pursuing? Indeed do they have any relevance whatsoever to the basis on which Mr Kilgannon and Mr Wells graciously agreed to be here today?'

'Let's move on.' Addison knew he had to be quick before Narey bit back and he just managed it. 'But you should maybe get off your high horse, Mr Constance, and remember you're not playing to a jury. You're clients' business isn't on trial here. Not yet. But we do want to know if they can help us with why Euan Hepburn was staying in the Rosewood Hotel.'

Kilgannon and Wells, sitting like two fish stuck into suits and overcoats, narrowed their eyes slightly at that and there was a hint of a bored glare towards Addison. Still they didn't speak.

'Detective Chief Inspector ...' Constance laboured the title as if he were talking to a child. 'My clients cannot possibly be expected to guess why one person chose to stay in their hotel. Presumably, and this is my supposition rather than theirs, he wished for a roof over his head. My clients provide a place of warmth and safety for individuals who do not have the luxury of booking themselves into the Ritz-Carlton. They provide a service.'

Narey's kettle began to boil over. 'Bollocks.'

'DI Narey ...' Addison and Constance chimed warnings in different tones. She ignored both.

She lost it. 'The Rosewood Hotel is a shithole and we all know it. Your *clients* are raking in money at the expense of the health and mental well-being of people who are out of their faces on drink and drugs. They don't give a monkey's about the people who stay there as long as they continue to screw them and the tax-payer out of housing benefit. Your clients are morally

161

bankrupt and I'm not sure you're much better for representing them.'

Constance seemed to relish the outburst. 'DCI Addison, are you going to allow the newly promoted DI to continue to speak in such intemperate and undoubtedly slanderous terms? I suggest you might do well to protect her from herself by disabusing her of the notion that she can throw about such remarks without consequence.'

Addison barely concealed a smirk. 'I'd say that DI Narey is perfectly capable of looking after herself without any protection from me. And I've not heard her yet say anything that isn't true. If this was a court of law, which it isn't, I think our lawyers would be calling *veritas*.'

Connie smiled sweetly. 'I do love it when a policeman starts quoting law at me. It invariably means they don't know what they are talking about. Now, shall we proceed with some civility or should we call this conversation to a close? Your choice, officers.'

Narey could see the amusement in Addison's eyes as he turned to her. He loved a fight and it was tickling him that he was the one having to rein her in. 'What do you think, DI Narey?'

'I am all in favour of civility. Let's go with that. Euan Hepburn was a freelance journalist. We believe he was in the Rosewood Hotel to expose the practices that take place there and the callous treatment of the poor bastards – my apologies, residents – who have to stay there. Are your clients aware of any particular failings within the Rosewood that Mr Hepburn may have been interested in?'

Kilgannon and Wells bristled and Constance feigned being indignant.

'Yet more intemperate language, DI Narey? At least you had the good grace to apologize for it on this occasion. I do not believe my clients are aware of any such failings. Nor were they previously aware of Mr Hepburn's rather dubious behaviour, if indeed it was as you describe it.'

'Why don't we let them tell us? After all, they must be better placed than you to say what they were and weren't aware of.'

'Well that is a very helpful suggestion, DCI Addison, and I thank you for making it, but I am here to represent my clients. They are both wary of being tricked into saying something they don't mean. No offence whatsoever is intended when I say that they are aware of police officers employing underhand methods to extract unwitting statements and they do not wish to be duped in such a way.'

Addison sighed heavily and shifted slightly to face away from the lawyer. 'Mr Kilgannon, Mr Wells, do you know of anything in your hotel that may have aroused the interest of a journalist?'

Neither man twitched. They stared at Addison as if he were something stuck to their shoe.

'Anything at all, *gentlemen*?' Narey had had enough. 'Drug taking on the premises, perhaps? Hygiene breaches?'

Brian Wells was beginning to look uncomfortable but Kilgannon wasn't fazed in the slightest. Annoyed maybe but not remotely bothered. She charged on.

'Maybe your employees supplying Class A drugs? Disregard for human life? A blatant disregard for any form of human rights? A regime that encourages residents to be doped to the eyeballs to keep them quiet? Residents being physically attacked and threatened?'

'Rachel ...' Addison's tone held a half-hearted warning.

She ignored him. 'I sat and spoke with a nice old man in your *hotel* who told me that people were just in there killing time before they died. They only leave there in a wooden box. You let them have a shitty little existence in place of death and then they get the real thing. That nice old man deserves better than to be in your dump with people dying around him. Would it never occur to you to let them have a bit of fucking dignity before you order the next coffin?'

Nobody spoke or seemingly even breathed for an age until Thomas Kilgannon offered a loud and obviously fake cough. Constance slowly turned to look at his client who merely nodded his head. The lawyer's eyes snapped to Narey. 'My clients are busy men, Detective Inspector, and I feel they have been more than generous with their time. It's time for us to leave.'

The two men rose lazily from their chairs. Kilgannon's mouth twisted into a sneer as he looked at Narey. They held each other's gaze just long enough to make Addison both hopeful and worried that she would smack him. He stepped across their paths and waved an arm towards the door.

'Mr Constance, it was a pleasure and an education as always. Mr Kilgannon and Mr Wells, thank you for dropping by and rest assured we will speak again.'

The door had closed on the interview room for a full half-minute before Addison turned to her to break the silence.

'Rachel, don't bite my head off as well but that was about your dad, right?'

'Right.'

Half an hour later, she was sitting at her own desk when she looked up to see DC Becca Maxwell approaching from the other direction, carrying a sheaf of papers and looking concerned.

'Everything okay, Becca?'

'Ma'am, you asked me to look into suspicious deaths related to urban exploring.'

It had been nothing more than checking all possibilities rather than a real feeling that there was a connection. The Odeon had brought Danny's mention of urbexing to mind and then she'd thrown it at Addison in a desperate attempt to cling on to the case. And now?

'Yes. Have you found something?'

Maxwell hesitated. 'I think I've found another two.'

Chapter 22

Sometimes you have to be careful what you wish for. Narey held her breath as Maxwell read from the sheet in front of her.

'Derek Wharton. Aged thirty-one. He was found by Constables McColm and Elliot on the morning of 10 September 2014 in the remains of St Peter's Seminary at Cardross. It was called in by a Daniel Gallagher who had gone there to photograph the building. Mr Wharton had a broken neck and head injuries. It had been raining heavily and the thinking was that he fell from one of the upper levels onto the bottom floor. He might not have died immediately but there was presumably no one to call for help.'

Maxwell laid four A4-sized photographs out on the table. The first was of the seminary's wide, concrete façade in three tiers, looking like the world's least fancy wedding cake. It was modernist, brutalist and Category A-listed. It wasn't exactly her cup of architectural tea but she knew it was rated as a world-leader when it was built. Surrounded by trees, it had been a priest's training college near the village of Cardross between Dumbarton and Helensburgh, about twenty miles from Glasgow. Now it lay in near ruins, overgrown and covered in graffiti.

The second and third photographs showed internal shots with the body in position on the solid grey floor. Way above, the ceiling rolled in concrete waves like a sea parted only to let in light from the heavens. Her sense of thrill was still there but it was now accompanied by a definite sinking feeling. The final shot was of the young man's head, cruelly and unnaturally twisted at an impossible angle from his body.

'And there were suspicious circumstances?' Narey asked.

'That's where it gets tricky. The FAI ruled it an accident but the file is flagged up because Wharton had gambling debts and there's still a suspicion this might have been payback. I can put in a call to the attending constables and the detective in charge if you want.'

'It's okay, I'll do it. Leave me a note of the names and numbers. What's the second one, Becca?'

Maxwell turned to the next sheet. 'Christopher Hart. Aged twenty-nine. His body was found at the foot of the Finnieston Crane on the night of 7 August 2013. There was a broken bottle of Buckfast nearby and alcohol in his system. However there were also what were thought to have been ligature marks on his wrists, suggesting they might have been tied prior to

167

his death. He suffered multiple injuries, broken arms and legs, fractured spine and severe cranial damage.'

'Yes, I remember that one. The suspicion was that it was organized crime. Some kind of punishment killing.'

'Yes. No one was ever prosecuted for it though. The case is still open. Do you want to see the photographs?'

Narey grimaced. 'Not particularly but let's have them.'

Maxwell placed five photographs down and Narey immediately knew that Winter had taken them. They were stark but scenic, an almost filmic quality to them. The first was a typical scene-setting shot, the giant of the Clyde a silhouette against the dark blue summer sky. A neon rainbow of city lights shone through the lower part of the crane's lattice structure while a blue hue to the right-hand side signalled the attending cop cars.

The body was as much a ruin as the seminary had been. For a moment, she forgot just why she was interested in these deaths and wondered how her partner could do what he did. She saw plenty of bodies in her job but to see *this* every day . . . Shattered bones, shredded skin, a collapsed skull and shapeless face. Few people would have the stomach for it. What did this do to him? Whatever it was, it didn't stop him doing his job well. True to form, Winter hadn't missed the abrasions to the wrists and, from his sharp close-up, they did indeed look like rope marks.

'What's on Hart's record?'

'Theft. Possession with intent. Assault. Handling stolen goods.'

'Career criminal. Do we know who he worked for?'

'Nothing official but there's a note saying he was believed to be in the employ of the Mullen brothers.'

Narey looked up from the photographs, briefly expecting to see that Maxwell was joking with her. 'Mullen?'

'Paul and Bobby.'

'I know who they are.'

'Of course, ma'am. Sorry.'

She remembered Danny Neilson's verdict on why someone might be found in the Molendinar. A good place to hide a body, he'd said. Did the same go for the seminary and the foot of the Finnieston Crane? These two had been easily found but maybe it *was* a good place if you didn't care if the bodies were eventually discovered. Maybe it was enough that they wouldn't be found until whoever had put them there was long gone.

The crane was far more open than the Molendinar, the Odeon or the seminary. Did it fit? She could well imagine the Mullens – or their enemies – hanging someone upside down there to make them talk or just to scare the shit out of them. And then letting go.

'Whose case is it?'

'DI French's.'

'Okay, I'll call him. Thanks.'

Maxwell hesitated and Narey could see how tense she was. 'What is it, Becca?'

'There's more ma'am.'

'Shit.'

'I wouldn't have found this except that I was looking for unusual locations as well as suspicious deaths. And this isn't suspicious but I thought I'd better flag it up.'

Narey's pulse quickened in perfect time with her heart sinking. 'Go on.'

'The body of a homeless man was found in an abandoned building. Two days ago.'

'Two days?'

'Yes, ma'am. David McGlashan. Aged fifty-three. Of no fixed abode. Found in the former William Cook and Son, File and Saw Works building in Houldsworth Street in Anderston. Initial post-mortem results say probable heart attack, but the body had lain there for approximately ten weeks before it was discovered so it was badly decomposed. No signs of other injury or assault.'

Her mind flashed back to Malcolm Colvin's mention of a homeless client who hadn't been seen for two months. Had Colvin named the man? She didn't think so but would have to call him.

'What do we know about this guy?'

'Not much, ma'am. He's thought to have been homeless for as much as fifteen years. His only record is for a drunk and disorderly eight years ago and a disturbance of the peace last year.'

'What do we know about the saw works?'

'It closed in the late nineties, has lain dormant since then. It is a known urbexing site.'

'Definitely?'

'Definitely. So is the seminary and the crane. There's a website.'

Narey sighed heavily. 'Great.'

'Are these cases connected, ma'am?'

'I really don't know, Becca. I wish I did but I don't. But at least it looks like I didn't lie to DCI Addison after all. This urbexing website that you mentioned?'

'Yes, ma'am?'

'Give me a note of the web address. I think I need to go do some surfing of my own.'

Chapter 23

Narey laid the photographs out on Addison's desk and watched with decidedly mixed feelings as the DCI took it all in.

Derek Wharton's broken neck under the great roof of the seminary. Christopher Hart's shattered body at the foot of the crane. Then David McGlashan's decomposed remains on the floorboards of the saw works, light streaming onto it from attic windows. For good measure, she'd added Winter's photographs from the Molendinar and the Odeon.

He studied them unhappily then looked up at her.

'So you're telling me you might have five cases here.'

'No, I'm telling you I might have one case. Five bodies.'

He sighed heavily. 'Rachel, how sure are you of any of this? I don't see a whole lot in the way of firm evidence linking these.'

'I'm not sure. Of course I'm not. But it's enough to think there's something there. Enough to have me work this as if they are or might be connected. You've got to leave me on the Odeon.'

'I don't *have* to do anything,' he snapped. 'Okay, talk me through your thinking. Convince me.'

Convince you or convince myself, she wondered. She was letting him think she was a step further down that line than she actually felt. There *was* something there. She just didn't know how to play it. For now, she was making it up as she went along.

'Okay, for a start these are too much of a coincidence for us to ignore. That wouldn't make any sense. I've done some research and I need to do more. All urbexing sites. Places where people shouldn't be. Unpoliced, out of the way, unguarded. Maybe a good place to leave bodies, which might bring us back to Bobby Mullen. Maybe someone senses that the people who go there are vulnerable. Maybe it's an opportunity. Maybe it's something else altogether but there is a connection. I just need time to find it.'

He looked down and studied the photographs again. The waiting made her want to scream. At last, he looked up at her, shaking his head.

'Okay, here's what's going to happen. I'm taking over both cases. You answer to me. So does Rico. He'll take part of this.'

She said nothing but her face said plenty.

'Rachel, it's the best I can do if you want to run both sides of this. If these are all linked then it's above your pay scale. If they're not then Storey and Rico get the Odeon. You still think they're linked?'

'Yes I do.'

'Okay. Then you have a choice to make. You are *not* taking all this on yourself. It makes no sense and is a bad use of resources. You understand me? You can work this urbexing wild goose chase or you can keep after the owners of the Rosewood or you can take on Saturn. Not all three. You can have the choice because they were yours first.'

'Gee thanks.'

'*Rachel . . .*'

She had to decide and she had to do it quickly. The thought of giving any of it up was tough – once she got her teeth into an investigation she was always loath to let go. Kilgannon and Wells were dirty, she'd no doubt about that. The same for the property company Saturn and Mullen. But going for either of those effectively meant choosing one case over the other. She couldn't, wouldn't do that. Hell, she could think of no other way.

'Okay, let Rico run with Saturn. I'll get Jacko to bring Rico up to speed on what he's said. I'll go with the wild geese. I'll take the urbexing angle.'

'You sure? This is going to ramp up the pressure on you with every doubter out there.'

'I'm sure. But that still leaves me with Bobby Mullen because—'

'Jesus, no! I'll need to talk to Ken Bryson at Organized Crime and run this past him. If we end up stepping on his toes then he'll have my balls for shooting practice. You stay away from Mullen.'

'*Sir . . .*'

'No.'

'Then I'll have the Odeon victim's husband, as that falls within my remit.'

'Within your . . .' He shook his head at her again. 'Fine. Do it. I get the feeling I've just been had but I'm not sure how.'

Chapter 24

It never got any easier to tell someone that a loved one was dead. Not for Narey anyway. She knew cops who gave the impression that they'd become inured to it over time but she wasn't sure she believed them. Nor did she think it was right. Every time you knocked on someone's door to tell them that a loved one had died *should* feel like it did the first time. It would always feel like the first time to the person you were talking to and you should be the same.

Identifying the body had, for once, been as simple as checking recent missing person reports. Jennifer Cairns, a forty-three-year-old interior designer, was last seen on the evening of 10 September. Her description fitted the victim and so did the date. Dental records had already been requested in case the worst had happened. It had. A match had been confirmed that afternoon and now she and Becca Maxwell were about to deliver the news.

This time it wasn't to be a door of anyone's home but rather an office and that made it more awkward. She could perhaps have waited until the close of business hours but this case was cold enough and she wanted to get her teeth into it without delay.

Cairns and McCormack, Architects, had a floor to themselves in an ornate sandstone building in Hope Street, not far from Central Station. It looked faded grandeur from the outside but was very different once they pushed through the double doors to get in. It screamed design and trying too hard. All black and white with expanses of bare wall broken only by a couple of statement pieces that were as obscure as they were surely expensive. This was an office of people who wanted you to know they were worth the money.

There were maybe five people in the office, all dressed in black as if they were already in mourning. A girl of no more than eighteen greeted her by the front door and asked if she could help them.

'I'm hoping to speak to Mr Cairns,' Narey told her.

'Do you have an appointment?'

By way of answer, she held up her warrant card. 'I don't but it's urgent. Is he in?'

The girl paled and lost all composure. 'I'm not . . . I don't think so. He was . . . let me check with Mr McCormack.'

'Okay. We'll come with you.'

'I should . . . well, um, of course.'

She led them towards the back of the room where two inner offices had been created by frosted black walls. She knocked on the door of one of them and a man's voice called for her to enter. The assistant opened the door and Narey followed her inside before she had the chance to close it, Maxwell taking her cue and slipping inside with her. Flustered, the girl tried to explain but Narey cut her off.

'Mr McCormack? I'm DI Narey of Police Scotland, this is DC Maxwell. Could we have a word, please? In private.'

Consternation clouded the man's face and he instinctively got out of his seat. He was in his mid-thirties, six foot tall with fair hair and dressed in a black suit and dark grey shirt and tie.

'What's happened? I mean, yes, of course. Chloe, could you leave us, please? Unless, do either of you want anything? Water? Tea or coffee?'

'No, thank you.'

McCormack nodded and the girl closed the door behind her.

'What is it, DI . . . Sorry, I don't . . .'

'Narey. I was hoping to speak to your partner. Is Mr Cairns in the building?'

'No, he's . . . Is it about Jennifer? It is, isn't it?'

'I'm afraid I'm not at liberty to say, Mr McCormack. I need to—'

'Jesus. Have you found her? He'll be so happy. This has been . . .' He stopped short, reading the sombre look on Narey's face.

'Do you know where Mr Cairns is, sir?'

'Is she dead?'

'Mr McCormack, I'm sorry but I really am not able to tell you anything. Where can I find your partner?'

The man didn't seem to know whether to be angry or sad. 'He's gone to see a client then he's heading straight home. Why can't you just tell me? She and Douglas are my friends as well as him being my partner. Christ, why didn't you call ahead? You missed him by less than an hour. He needs to know now, whatever it is.'

The truth was she'd *wanted* to turn up unannounced. It wasn't that she suspected the husband but she wouldn't rule it out. Always look close to home, Johnny Jackson had taught her. She wanted to see the man's reaction without him being prepared for it. Heartless maybe but policing was a practical business.

'I have his home address and we can go there now. How long is his meeting likely to take?'

McCormack scrambled at his sleeve to look at his watch. 'I'd think he'd be home in about an hour, maybe slightly less. Let me call him and tell him to meet you.'

'No! I must ask you not to do that, sir. I need to speak to Mr Cairns personally and it will be far from helpful if someone talks to him first, particularly without access to the facts.'

The man's eyes challenged her but not for long. He sat back in his black-leather chair and held his head in his hands before looking up again.

'Okay, Detective Inspector, I won't. But please, go easy on him. He's not been himself at all since Jen

179

disappeared and I'm not sure how much more he can take. If he comes across as . . . well, maybe confrontational, then forgive him. He's really not like that.'

'In what way has he not been himself?'

McCormack hesitated, seemingly reluctant to say any more.

'Anything you can tell me will allow us to be better informed when talking to Mr Cairns.'

He gave a heavy sigh. 'He's been drinking. It's understandable given what he's been through but I think he's been hitting it pretty hard. He's normally very easy-going but lately . . . well he's been short-tempered, argumentative. It's really not what he's like.'

'Has he talked much about what he thinks happened to his wife?'

A change came across McCormack's face and he got to his feet. 'I'm sorry but I think I've said enough. You won't tell me what's happened and yet you're trying to pump me for information about my partner. I'm not going to give you that. Not until you've spoken to him and not until I have to.'

Narey nodded. 'Fine. I respect that. Thanks for your time, Mr McCormack. And please, *do not* phone Mr Cairns. I'd have to regard it as obstructing a police officer and that wouldn't be helpful for anyone.'

Narey knocked, Maxwell beside her, and waited for Douglas Cairns to answer. It struck her that perhaps he'd been waiting on that knock for nearly seven weeks.

180

The door pulled back and she saw the man immediately work out what she was and why she was there. He hadn't been tipped off by McCormack though: this was the shock of the expected.

He was in his early fifties, a dark beard turned silver at the chin and more flecks of age through his shoulder-length hair. With bleary, stressed eyes, he looked like he hadn't had a full night's sleep in those seven weeks and she doubted that he'd get one tonight.

'Mr Cairns?'

'You've found her. She's dead, isn't she?'

'May we come inside, sir?'

'Is she dead? Tell me!'

She deliberated and decided the kinder thing was to tell him there and then. 'Yes, sir. She is. I'm sorry. I do think we should go inside.'

The man stared at the ground at his feet, seeing nothing. He slowly lifted his head and nodded without being able to look at them. 'Come in.'

They followed the man into the large apartment on South Frederick Street on the corner of George Square. He led them into an expansive, modernist, open-plan room with three huge arched windows on the far wall. It was very different to the A-listed traditional stone exterior but maybe not that surprising given that Cairns was an architect.

The man slumped into a seat and stared into space some more. Narey and Maxwell took seats opposite him without waiting to be asked and gave him the time he needed. Once or twice his head came up and

181

he looked at them as if ready to ask questions but didn't dare.

'Mr Cairns, I know this is difficult but I need to tell you what happened to your wife. And I will need to ask you some questions. Is that okay?'

He nodded dumbly.

'A woman's body was found yesterday in a city centre building not far from here. We have made dental comparisons against your wife's records and they confirm that it is her. We shall make further tests but we have no doubt that it is your wife.'

'What happened to her? What building? I don't understand.'

'Your wife suffered severe head injuries. As yet, we don't know for sure how they came about. The building was the former Odeon cinema on Renfield Street. A workman found her body. It had evidently been there for some time.'

She watched his reaction, seeing his head swing from side to side and his forehead crease. 'I don't understand what you're saying. The Odeon? But that's been closed for years. What are you talking about?'

'Yes, sir. It was due to be demolished. Do you have any idea at all why your wife would have been there?'

He became angry. 'What? No! None whatsoever. This doesn't make any sense.'

Narey glanced at Maxwell and she took the hint, speaking for the first time since they'd gone inside.

'Mr Cairns, would you mind telling us the circumstances of your wife going missing? We know you've made a report but it would be helpful if you could tell us in your own words what happened.'

'I've told your people all this already! Who *did* this to her?'

'Please, Mr Cairns,' Maxwell persisted. 'It will help us to hear it from you.'

He just looked back at her for a while as if not understanding, pulling at his beard and rubbing fiercely at the silver on his chin. He jumped from his seat and went to an oak sideboard where he poured himself a large whisky from a decanter and took a mouthful. Then, seemingly calmer, he sat down again.

'It was a Wednesday evening and Jennifer, my wife, was going to meet a client in the West End. Kensington Gate. She left around six and she never came back. I'd fallen asleep maybe about eleven and when I woke she still wasn't home. I called her mobile but didn't get an answer. I wasn't pleased. In fact I was annoyed, more annoyed than worried. I went back to sleep and in the morning she still wasn't there. I called her mobile again but got no answer. I had to go to the office and gave it till lunchtime before I called the police. I'd tried to call her another three times and got nothing. Staying out late wasn't unusual but overnight, without at least a text message, she'd never done that.'

'Who was the client she was going to see?'

'I don't know. She'd told me it was Kensington Gate and that it was potentially a big job. If she told me the name I didn't listen or didn't remember. I checked her diary and she didn't have it listed.'

Narey returned to the conversation. 'Did your wife regularly go to meet clients in the evening, Mr Cairns?'

'Yes. It was usually easier. People work during the day so she'd make herself available at a time that suited them. And she would obviously need to see the space that they wanted her to work with.'

'Do you have a list of her clients?'

'Yes, but none of them are in Kensington Gate. I checked and your colleagues checked. The old Odeon? I don't *understand*.'

'Neither do we, Mr Cairns. But we will. How was your wife getting to Kensington Gate? Did she drive or take a taxi?'

'She drove. I've given her car details to the police but it has never turned up. Her phone stopped responding. I tried to track it but the signal was dead or had been switched off. I think your colleagues thought she had just left me but I knew that wasn't true. She didn't take any clothes and her bank card wasn't used.'

'Tell us about your wife if you can, Mr Cairns. Anything at all that will give us a picture of who she was and what might have happened to her. Her job, close friends, hobbies, anything you can think of.'

His eyes flashed angrily at her and Narey knew it was her referring to the man's wife in the past tense that had maddened him. She'd seen it before and silently cursed herself for doing it.

'Jennifer had her own business. Interior designer. Fashioning homes for people who are either too fucking lazy or clueless to do it for themselves. She'd been doing it for five years and did well. She worked hard.'

'And friends?'

'She had quite a few. The police spoke to most of them after I reported her missing. I assume they'll still have the list I gave them.'

'All female friends or male friends too?'

'*What do you mean*? We had many friends who were couples so the answer is both. What are you suggesting?'

'Nothing, Mr Cairns. I'm just trying to get a picture of your wife's social scene, establish anyone she would have interacted with. I'll get a copy of that list from my colleagues. This is a difficult question, I know, particularly in the circumstances, but would you say your wife was happy?'

The man's eyes darkened and he snapped at her. '*Happy*? How can you ask that?' He glared at her then gulped at his whisky before continuing. 'Yes I would say she was happy. We had our ups and downs. Who doesn't? But our marriage was fine.'

'You didn't have any children?'

Another glare. 'Not that it's any of your business but no. We tried but it didn't happen. I was probably keener than she was but . . .' His voice trailed off sadly.

'What other aspects of your wife's life can you tell us about? Groups or organizations she might have been involved with, people she knew. Anything that might help.'

He banged his glass down on the table in front of him and splashes of whisky leaped into the air and onto the wooden surface. 'Christ. I've already ... Okay, okay. She had a wide circle of friends and acquaintances. She was popular, lively, always on the go. She did charity work, she spent time in galleries, socialized with neighbours. We'd eat out quite a lot, either dinners with mutual clients, sometimes her accountant or with my partner David McCormack. It's a long list and I've already given it to the bloody police.'

She could see he was unravelling and just getting angrier. Any current thoughts weren't going to be much help. One last question, a shot in the dark, then she'd let him be for now.

'Mr Cairns, has your company done any work for a Saturn Property? You're in related businesses.'

He paused, obviously wondering what the relevance was. 'I know of them. I think we've met the directors at networking events.'

'Would it be a Mark Singleton that you've met?'

'Maybe. It was at those part-business, part-social type things. I can't remember. Why? Is it important?'

'Probably not. Okay, I think we should leave it there for today. I'm sorry if I've made any of this difficult for you. I can only imagine what you're going through.'

'Can you?'

'We'll arrange for a Family Liaison officer to call and they will make sure you are kept up to date with every aspect of the investigation. And we'll arrange for

you to see your wife and allow you to formally identify her when you are ready.'

'I'm ready now.'

'That's not possible, sir. Not just yet.'

'I'm ready *now*!'

'We'll let you know when that can be done. We're as
keen as you are to—'

'I doubt that. I really do. Let me know as soon as
possible.'

'I will, sir. I promise you.'

'No. I only need you to promise me one thing. Do
you think you can do that?'

She'd never make the promise he wanted. She
couldn't do it because she couldn't be certain it could
be done. She'd do the next best thing.

'Mr Cairns, I promise you we will do everything we
possibly can to make sure that the person who killed
your wife will be caught and punished.'

Chapter 25

It had been a long, long day but it couldn't be over. Not just yet. Much as she would have loved to just fall asleep or, better still, drive over to Tony's for some physical therapy, she still had work to do. She was at home in Highburgh Road and in bed but she was online and on the case.

Whether it was a good idea or not, she'd put all her eggs in the basket marked urbexing. Now she had to find out what she was actually talking about. The little knowledge she had came from the brief mention that Danny had made of it.

They like to go places they shouldn't – that's what he'd said. Then she remembered. He'd also said he knew someone that used to do it.

She had her iPad open at the website address Maxwell had given her but now it struck her that hearing it from someone who actually did the thing would be more helpful.

He answered after half a dozen rings. She knew he'd be working and probably couldn't hear it over the noise of the taxi-rank queue.

'Hey, Rachel. What can I do for you?'

She could hear cars going by and the chatter of a number of voices. Someone not too far away was singing 'Flower Of Scotland'. She'd be lucky to get long with him so she got straight to the point.

'Danny, when we spoke the other day, you said you knew someone who urbexed. Do you think he would talk to me?'

There was a pause at the other end of the line.

'I don't think so, hen. He doesn't do it any more and I think he wants to put it behind him.'

'Could you ask him, Danny? It's important.'

'I'll ask, love. But don't get your hopes up. Is this because of the body in the old Odeon then?'

She laughed. 'Do you actually know everything?'

'Naw, love. Just most things. And I'm good at guessing.'

'That was no guess. You think there's some urbexing connection between the Molendinar and the cinema site?'

'Rachel, I've no real idea. You've got the facts there, you'll know better than me. I've just got suppositions and an old copper's nose.'

'And what's that telling you?'

'Not to trust coincidences. I'd say it's definitely worth looking at. And so do you or you wouldn't have phoned me about it.'

'It occurred to me when I was in the Odeon but it still seemed a stretch. Now I'm more inclined to think it's the key. Thanks, Danny. Ask your pal for me, will you?'

'I'll ask. But don't expect a yes.'

She finished the call and turned back to the laptop. OtherWorld. That's exactly how it was to her but she had to step into it. She had to learn everything she could.

Winter sat and looked at the laptop in front of him, his fingers drumming distractedly on the keyboard. He hesitated, wary of clicking on the search result that had popped up in front of him. As if there would be no going back. As if it would open the door that he'd promised himself to leave closed.

He stared hard at the screen, wishing some other answer to show itself. The option was to close the lid. He knew that was probably the sensible thing to do. The thing that Rachel would want him to do. If she knew. Holy shit, it was just as well that she didn't.

The room was silent and the only noise came from the street outside; cars driving up and down Berkeley Street, and the comings and goings from the Mitchell Library opposite. His right index finger hovered above the enter button. All he had to do was press.

OtherWorld. It didn't seem that scary in itself. Just a word.

Stuff this, he told himself. Do it or don't. His finger was down before he could stop himself and the screen shifted.

190

The layout had changed since the last time he'd visited. Hardly surprising really: most forums got a makeover every now and again and it had been four, no five years since he'd dipped in. There was a lot familiar about it though. Seemed to be the same old subject categories for a start. High places, military sites, hospitals, asylums, cinemas, underground sites, quarries. It was all there, all you had to do was explore it.

He sat and looked at it for a couple of minutes, drinking it in and searching for familiar names among those that had posted. He didn't recognize any but then he'd been gone for a while and most of those he was looking at were from elsewhere in the UK.

Did his login still work? That was the question. Only one way to find out. Login name, Metinides. Password, snapper1. He pressed enter again and he was in. He was still one of the crowd.

From the moment Remy had sent the messages about the walk to the Botanics, he'd been fretting over their return. He'd refreshed his inbox often enough that the F5 key was in danger of being worn out. It didn't bring replies in any quicker but gave him something to do.

He'd ventured out to check on his dad a couple of times, taking him food and company, making both of them feel a little bit better. That apart, he'd stared at the screen, willing it to change. It turned out that his psychic powers were not all that they might be.

There was a lot of waiting. Replies came in slowly

or didn't come in at all. Ironically, the first was from Vixxxen and he had to steel himself before seeing what Gabby had to say about it.

Seriously, what is up with you, man? Okay, I'm glad you've seen the light and want to go out. Really glad. But a walk to the Botanics? What is this, a Sunday school outing? X

The X at the end was a very good sign and managed to put a smile on his face for the first time in five days. She was making fun of him and that was fine. Of course she hadn't actually said whether she'd go but he could tell that she would. Whether he wanted her there he wasn't quite so sure about but he couldn't not ask her.

After that they'd come in in dribs and drabs, each greeted like a message from above.

Astronut said yes and so did NightLight. Hermit said it wasn't his or her thing. LilythePink couldn't make it. PencilPusher, Spook and Gopher said yes. Crow said maybe. CardboardCowboy, JohnDivney, Tubz, Digger9, BigTomDog and Ectoplasm didn't bother to reply.

Of course, it might have been that one of them didn't reply because he was dead.

It was enough, he supposed. A quorum of sorts. He'd done it. He'd actually organized an outing of the Glasgow urbexers. He suddenly wasn't sure just why he'd done it. Or that he really wanted to go.

He thought of Gabby and the poor bugger in the tunnel and momentarily found some courage. He thought of all that he didn't know and couldn't do and lost it again. This wasn't him, this wasn't what he did. He rounded up bloody supermarket trolleys. That's who he was.

The more he thought about it, the less sense it made. But it was done now. He couldn't reach down the line and grab those messages back.

Narey's eyes were tired and her head was beginning to hurt. Sitting in front of the screen wasn't helping and neither was the amount of information she was having to take in. This really was another world. How the hell was all this going on and she knew nothing about it?

While most of Glasgow slept, others were creeping in and out of its history, climbing its past and exploring its near future. There were so many buildings that she knew and had forgotten about. She'd driven past so many of these places time and time again without thinking to step inside. She walked past so many of them without bothering to look up and be reminded that they were there.

Some of the images posted on the site were remarkable. There were photographs of the old ballroom at Gartloch Asylum and she could hardly take her eyes off them. She'd been to the building once before, with her dad when she was maybe seventeen, but they'd done no more than look in a window. It was incredible. The centre part of the tall ceiling was like the upturned hull of a ship in mosaics of cornflower blue and white. The walls were stripped of paint or paper but were still magnificent with pillars and ornate cornicing. The floor was in pieces, all rubble and old spars, but one look was enough to imagine ghosts dancing across it.

She had to stop herself from being engrossed in them. There were stunning shots from cranes, of old schools and churches, railway lines and subway stations, all places that she knew so well, or so she'd thought. This *wasn't* another world. It was right here, right under her nose and everyone else's. All they'd ever had to do was look.

So who were they, these people who'd looked where she and the rest hadn't? It was a world of mystery, all user names and hidden faces. A lot of fun for them she was sure but not a lot of use for her. They got their kicks in the shadows, playing out of sight and undercover. In investigative terms, it was a frigging nightmare.

Maybe she could petition the court, get the website to cough up email addresses behind the user names, force service providers to give up addresses. It was a logistical and legal minefield but it could probably be done. It would take forever though and just what use it would turn out to be she wasn't sure.

Who was Astronut? Who was LilythePink or CardboardCowboy? Who the hell was Digger9 who had climbed the university roof? Or Hermit who had photographed the old Transport Museum. Or . . . she stopped. Who was Metinides?

She shook her head. It had been a long night and

had already turned into day. Her mind was all over the place and she was seeing tricks when they weren't there. The site was obviously used by lots of amateur photographers. It wasn't that surprising. A bit odd but not so surprising.

She checked names against posts, looking in vain for someone who had recently walked the Molendinar or explored the Odeon. No one had done the cinema but there was one report on the burn, all of seven years earlier. That didn't hold out much promise but she'd try to check it out.

What she got from the website, more than anything, was that it all felt right. The kind of person that might walk the Molendinar would have been on OtherWorld. It was their home. And the Odeon too. It just fitted. Where it left her or the investigation, she didn't know but she was on the right page. That much she was sure of.

Winter had sometimes wondered how many people on the site had ever wondered about his user name. Chosen after Enrique Metinides, the great Mexican tabloid photographer. The man who'd chased fires, crashes, shootings and suicides on the streets of Mexico City for over fifty years. The man who inspired Winter to pick up a camera and photograph dead people for a living.

Even if some knew or guessed then they wouldn't think too much of it. Most of the forum users took photographs; it was intrinsic to the whole thing. Sure, some just went where they went and did nothing more than look but most took images away with them. Some for their own records, some to share the spoils with others, some just to show off. It didn't matter, each to their own.

There were two messages lying unread in his inbox. One just an administrative memo about forum changes, the other from a name from the past. PencilPusher. *Haven't seen you online for a while, mate. Hope you're doing okay. Stay safe.* It was dated four years ago.

It wasn't someone he knew, not as such. They'd swapped messages online, talking about places they'd been or would like to go. *Stay safe.* That advice would have been better sent to someone else.

Winter's fingers moved to the search function and he typed in *PencilPusher*. A flurry of results came up, the most recent being just ten days old. Nothing remarkable about the post, just talk of a potential explore. It meant PencilPusher was still on the go though. Someone he could talk to. All he had to do was send him a message.

Damn it. He still wasn't sure this was something he wanted to do and knew it was something he shouldn't. This stuff was supposed to be locked away in a drawer marked *history,* only to be opened in memories and even then only when he was sufficiently drunk to turn maudlin.

You couldn't always pick your moments though and sometimes it came to him when he least expected or wanted it. Like when his mind drifted back to the last time. To the one that made him give it up.

Chapter 26

Six years earlier

He hadn't wanted to make the climb. Not that night anyway. It was too wet and too windy and it was madness to even consider it in conditions like that. Euan was adamant that they should do it though. You didn't chicken out of climbing Everest because there was snow on the mountain, he'd said. If they waited for a dry night in Glasgow, they'd be waiting a long time.

The argument went on for a while. Winter's position had been pretty simple. The Glasgow Tower at the Science Centre was a big beast and needed to be respected. Climbing it in the rain when they didn't have to was plain stupid. Euan said they'd picked a night to do it and should stick to it. He'd already told his girlfriend Lisa that he and Winter were going for a drink that night and he'd be out late. Winter had said that was fine – they should just go for the drinks instead. No, Euan insisted, they'd checked the tower out, knew where and when to climb, it was all in place and they should just do it. Winter had said the risk wasn't worth it. Euan responded by saying the risk was what made it worth it. Then he accused Winter of being scared. It was a simple tactic but always effective. Few men were capable of resisting it even though they knew that was why it had been said.

Winter hadn't been happy, far from it, but he'd finally given in.

As they stood at the foot of the tower looking up into the night sky, they stared into rain swirling in the black and the neon. The tower itself was a ghostly white, rising ominously for as far as they could see.

'You know this is stupid, right?'

'It's going to make us legends, mate. Anyone can do it when it's dry. Come on, let's climb this bad boy. You know you want to.'

Did he want to? He really wasn't sure. Part of him did. The part that got him into this in the first place was desperate to do it, rain or not. On the other hand, he was pretty sure if Euan wasn't standing there goading him on then he'd have turned round and gone home, waiting for another day. But he was, so they climbed.

The tower was one of those typically Scottish things that people could be proud of yet took the piss out of at the same time. It was a hundred and twenty-seven metres high and the tallest tower in Scotland. It was actually the tallest tower in the world capable of turning through three hundred and sixty degrees.

Capable was the key word as it hadn't worked for more than 80 per cent of its life. Instead it just stood there, crying out for a pair of idiots like them to climb it in the rain in the middle of the night.

They had to scale the outside of the tower, within the wide cage of curved white metal beams that was attached to the main structure and rose with it into the night. The loops that he and Hepburn passed through flamed almost orange in the artificial light and they at least gave Winter a grudging sense of security. They weren't climbing the loops though but the frame that fastened them to the tower and provided a ready made ladder all the way to the sky. It was the scenic route.

Euan went first, climbing arm over arm, occasionally glancing down to grin infuriatingly at Winter. See, he was saying, told you we should have done it. You can't tell me it doesn't feel good. And it did.

The handholds were wet but manageable under gloved hands. They called for care and attention to be paid but maybe that was a good thing, concentrating the mind as it did. It was a long way straight back down. Euan, being Euan, said it was fine because if he fell then he'd land on Winter.

He had to admit it felt great. Clambering higher and higher, the city spreading out before them like food on a plate, there to be devoured by his eyes and his camera. The adrenalin rush grew with every rung that he scaled, surging through him, empowering him. Higher and higher, bolder, stronger. The rain continued to fall but Euan was right, it was only rain. The risk was why they went urbexing at all, a huge part of the thrill of it.

They were almost at their target, the maintenance platform just a few metres below the observation deck, so maybe a hundred metres from the ground, and Winter felt like Glasgow was his.

The Squinty Bridge was winking at him, its purple arc reflected in the midnight black of the Clyde. The Science Centre and the BBC headquarters blazed in blue while the Finnieston Crane glowered disapprovingly grey from the opposite bank. Beyond all that, the city celebrated his ascent in a glow of twinkling gold. What a picture.

That's when his foot slipped.

In an instant, the skyline swept past in a blur of neon and a rush of blood, metal handhold after handhold racing past the desperate grab of his hands. His right wrist smashed against a beam, his left knee did the same, his face clattered into something hard and his heart and stomach lodged somewhere tight beneath his throat. He plummeted, hurtling through the metal frame towards the ground, his hands flailing at the crossbars, his camera swinging wildly but strung to his shoulder.

There was no doubt in his mind that he was going to die. He fell. Maybe it was no more than thirty feet but it felt like a hundred and more to come. The world and his life flashing before his eyes. He saw Hepburn staring down, eyes wide and mouth open.

Then he hit another of the loops: hard. He heard and felt a loud crack in his leg, pain exploding through him, and something in his chest or ribs went too. He grasped desperately with his right hand and somehow it stuck. Pain surged through his shoulder and he felt something wrench where it shouldn't as the entire weight of his body was thrown onto a couple of muscles.

Weirdly, it was only then that he was actually frightened, scared that his grip would loosen. The force of the sudden halt caused his body to shudder and swing, nearly wrenching the hand away. He threw up his other arm and held on for his life.

His left leg was broken, he was sure of that. Probably broken ribs too, judging by the fire that was erupting there. He hung on, suspended by a thread of sinew and tissue, and stared wildly at the neon city from the spindly tower that held him up. It was out of focus, just a riot of colours and lights. As he tried to take it all in, he was aware of his breathing – a heavy staccato, coming in reluctant bursts. In his shock and pain all he could do was stare.

From somewhere above him, Euan's voice broke into his consciousness although he had no idea what he was shouting down. All Winter could concentrate on was not letting go. On not dying. Glasgow swayed before him like a Saturday night drunk and he could feel his consciousness slipping like his foot had done.

He wrapped himself round the beam as best he could and shook his head to keep himself awake. He could not, could not, let go in any sense.

After what might have been one minute or thirty, he heard the nearby metallic clatter of Euan's feet on the frame. His words filtered through for the first time. 'Jesus Christ. Hold on, Tony. Are you okay? Fucking hell. Are you okay?'

In seconds, he felt arms on his. They were at once holding him on and pulling him in. Pain surged through his ribs as they were dragged along towards safety. A loud groan burst out of him, the effort of the cry painful in itself. Euan hauled him, reeling him in inch by inch until Winter was able to get one hand then the other onto the makeshift ladder. He clung to it, doing his best to shut out Euan's questions and apologies. He just wanted to get as much breath back as he could then get off that bloody tower.

'Take your time, mate. I'll get you down. Don't worry. I'll get you down. Christ, I'm sorry, Tony.'

'I'll get myself back down. Don't *you* worry. Just stay out my way.'

The climb back down was slow and agonizing. All his weight had to be taken on his arms and one leg, hopping and dropping from one hold to the next, pain ripping through him at every movement. At the foot of the tower he slid onto his haunches, the ground soaking wet beneath him, trying to let his breathing settle and his anger subside. He was soaked in sweat and rain. And he was shaking like a leaf.

Euan stood over him, his face crumpled. 'I thought . . . Jesus, I thought . . . Thank God you're—'

'Euan?'

'Yes?'

'Get me to a hospital then fuck off and leave me alone.'

Chapter 27

The image on Winter's laptop was of the Glasgow Tower. An OtherWorld poster had climbed it a few months earlier and his photographs were there for all to see. It brought everything flooding back. The fall, the pain, the guilt, the blame.

His leg had indeed been broken and so had three ribs. They healed in time but his friendship with Euan Hepburn never did.

Blaming Euan for the fall was easier than taking responsibility for his own recklessness in climbing the tower that night. No one had actually made him do it, that was the truth, but it wasn't the truth as he saw it at the time.

He'd been mad at him. Furious. Winter had been in no doubt that he was going to die and the fall had scared the shit out of him. No way he'd have gone up there but for the goading. No way he'd have climbed in the pouring rain but for Euan. He'd convinced himself it was *all* his fault. Every bit of pain when he eventually tried to walk, every bit of discomfort when he breathed, that was all because of Euan.

What really got him though was the realization of what almost happened. He could live with the broken leg and the ribs, the severe bruising to his wrist and face, the bang to his knee. But when it was quiet and no one was around, the thought of how close he'd been to dying sneaked into his head and scared him again.

Euan had been distraught but that had just made Winter angrier. He shut him out, refusing to see him in hospital, not taking his calls. He sent one text to say that he wouldn't be urbexing again because he, Euan, had killed his interest. Euan had been eaten up with guilt and wanted Winter to take that away from him but he wouldn't let him off lightly. In fact, he didn't let him off at all.

Maybe he would have done eventually and maybe he wouldn't but he never got the chance. Euan moved to London to get away from it all. It just made Winter angrier at him, feeling Euan had taken away his right to forgive him or be mad at him. He made up his mind not to get in touch and the pair never spoke again.

It took him a long time, maybe even years, to realize that he'd been angry at himself rather than Euan. That *he'd* been the one at fault and he should have been strong enough to just say no, not tonight. He was angry at his own fear and his own failings. By the time he recognized that, it was too late.

Sitting now at his laptop, the OtherWorld page open in front of him, he knew that the nasty truth wasn't that he stopped urbexing because he and Euan had fallen out. He fell out with Euan so that he wouldn't have to urbex again. He'd lost his nerve. Certainly for heights but probably also for any of it. He'd been more scared than he could admit. The thought of being up somewhere like the tower again made his stomach turn. That was natural enough but to bin a friendship because of it and let Euan take the hit was something he'd always be ashamed of.

He'd thought that falling out with Euan was the price he'd paid for stopping exploring. It wasn't. The price was his friend's life. If he'd been with him, the chances were that his death in the Molendinar would never have happened.

All these years it had been locked away and now he had no choice but to open it. He owed it to Euan Hepburn.

He closed his eyes for a moment, exhaled hard, looked at the website in front of him and typed.

Hi PencilPusher. It's been a long time. I've been out of the scene but back and raring to go. Where's good these days? My name's Tony, by the way.

Chapter 28

Thursday afternoon

Laidlaw's was a shabby-fronted pub on a battered side street in the Calton in the city's East End. Its lack of a makeover or even a fresh lick of paint in the previous twenty years was by choice rather than shortage of funds. The faded blue décor, the rust and the scruffy sign were designed to be as much deterrent to new customers as they were comfort to the existing ones. It didn't say welcome, it shouted leave us alone.

It worked.

When Narey pushed her way through the front door, heads whirled in the way they can only when the entire clientele smells a stranger. It wasn't just that she was a woman, which would have been different enough, it was that she wasn't one of them. She wasn't there to soak the afternoon away and she wasn't one of Bobby Mullen's people. She might have passed for a lawyer but big Bobby's smart-suited team were known faces in Laidlaw's. No, she was police and everyone knew it with one look. It didn't bother her in the slightest. It was exactly what she expected and wanted.

The bar had a smell all of its own. It was sweat and bleach and the ghosts of a million cigarettes, abandoned hope and beer-stained bravado. The stink was ingrained in the wooden floor and the patched seating. It swam in the air like flies over a corpse.

The faces that turned to her were either gaunt or bloated, patchworks of ash and red, all with eyes narrowed in defiant curiosity. Some looked her up and down, some looked the other way so she couldn't see their faces. She wasn't interested in them though, not today. She drifted past them towards the thickset man who was standing, arms folded, behind the bar.

'Help you?'

The man's question wasn't exactly coated in warmth.

'I'm looking for Bobby Mullen.'

'Why? Is he lost?'

'You tell me. Is he in?'

The man wore a few day's growth on his face and it rose and fell as he shrugged broad shoulders. 'Dunno. Who's asking?'

She sighed heavily as if there really wasn't any need for him to make her take her card out. She went through the motions of pulling it from her pocket and holding it up in front of her. 'Is he in?'

The man stared back at her to make some point to himself or the crowd before shrugging again. 'I can go see. What's it about?'

'Just tell Mr Mullen that I'd like a word with him. Now.'

The barman made a show of standing obstinately, playing to the audience behind her. She let him have his moment, knowing he'd have to go and talk to his boss. In the end he theatrically shook his head and walked out from behind the bar. A few steps took him to a thickly frosted door leading to a wood-panelled snug in the corner of the pub, the way barred by a shaven-headed hulk in a black-leather jacket. The man stepped aside to let the barman pass and the door quickly closed behind him.

Narey was left standing alone at the bar and turned her back on it. The natives were silently working away at their beer and whisky, nothing more than mouthed whispers passing between them. One chair scraped and a skinny guy in his thirties pushed himself to his feet and strode towards her.

He stood within a couple of feet despite having the rest of the bar to choose from, reeking of beer and stupidity. He leered with a lopsided grin and pushed a hand through a mane of slicked-back dark hair as if convinced it made him look good. She wasn't sure this guy was the full shilling but he was trouble.

'Back off,' she told him, quietly enough that only he could hear. The guy grinned wider and didn't budge. If he moved an inch closer, she decided, his arm was going to be twisted behind his back and his face put flat to the top of the bar. How his pals would react would be anyone's guess.

He didn't move closer, not quite. Instead he did a soft-shoe shuffle from foot to foot, his eyes dancing along with his feet. She could almost see the buzz that was going on in his head and knew she'd have to decide whether to fish through his pockets for dope or pills when she had him held down. The whole pub was waiting on her to make a move. It had to be the right one.

The man continued to shift from side to side, then edged forward and back, then forward again. Right, she was going to have him.

From the corner of the bar, she heard a door open and close, then a voice called out.

'Elvis. Sit on your arse!'

The barman was standing outside the snug, his eyes on Narey and the shuffling punter. The man turned his head to see who'd shouted at him and, seeing him, quickly scrambled back towards his seat.

The barman gestured her forward with a wave of his head. Without a look to the gallery, she walked towards the snug. The barman opened the door as she got there, ushered her in without a word then quietly closed it again behind her.

Four men were inside, three of them with their backs to her. Holding court at the end of the narrow little room and watching her approach was Bobby Mullen. Even if she hadn't seen a photograph of him before setting out, she'd have known without any doubt that this was the boss.

He was a big man, broad and heavy, with a plain face and receding red hair and matching beard. He looked like he was born to chop logs or wrestle cattle. His size wouldn't have been enough to run the operation, not without the brain for it and the backing of his old man and his brother, but it didn't hurt either. It gave him presence and brooked no kind of argument.

He was weighing her up now, not in any kind of sexual or predatory sense, but clearly wondering what it took for her to come into his lair like this by herself. She thought she saw either grudging admiration or an assessment of madness in his eyes. At least one of those things was probably justified.

'Give her a seat. In fact, all three of you move.'

The men got out of their chairs without hesitation and moved back towards the far end of the snug where they stood, filling the space in front of the door. They'd given her room to sit and talk with Mullen but they'd also made sure she couldn't leave.

She thought one of the three, a short, slight man with quick brown eyes, was probably his accountant and right-hand man, John Syme. Word was he was the brains behind the brains and brawn. The other two weren't familiar but she doubted they were in the snug to sell Bibles.

'So you're what? A Detective Inspector? Andy wasn't sure he'd read your title right.'

210

'He did. Detective Inspector Rachel Narey. Major Investigation Team.'

'Uh huh. Am I supposed to be impressed by that? Major investigation. Into what? I can't see how it can be anything to do with me.'

'Perhaps it's not, Mr Mullen, but I'd like to talk to you to find that out for myself. I'm here about the murder of a woman whose body was found in the city centre two days ago.'

She saw something shift in his eyes, just a momentary hardening, but it was enough to quicken her pulse. How many people had seen that and then suffered as a result? The look passed though and he lifted his eyes above her head, looking at his men and laughing out loud.

'A murder? Fucksake. Where do they get them these days?' His eyes switched back to her, cold and hard. '*Detective Inspector . . .*' He drawled the words out like she was five. 'Just what the fuck do you think you're doing coming in here? On your own? Doesn't strike me as being that much of a good fucking idea in any sense.'

She had to admit he had a point.

'Mr Mullen, your company provides protection for Saturn Property, is that correct? Specifically, you protect the redevelopment they're doing on the old Odeon site.'

His eyes didn't leave her but he said nothing. The look flitted across his gaze again though, stronger this time. She pushed on.

'You will know that the body of a woman named Jennifer Cairns was found on site. I'm here to ask you some questions about that.'

Still nothing from him except that malevolent stare. Maybe she had to push it further.

'It doesn't look like you protected the premises very well.'

She heard a muttered 'Fucksake' from behind her along with an angry rush of breath. Mullen looked beyond her to the three men and gave a quick shake of his head. Narey felt she'd just been spared from something but didn't feel much in the way of gratitude.

'So tell me, DI Narey, why I shouldn't have a lawyer present and you shouldn't have another copper with you. You can't take witness statements on your own. Why are you here playing Miss Marple all on your lonesome and doing your best to piss me off?'

Before she could answer, she heard the door to the snug open. She turned her head and saw a wiry guy in his twenties sliding in through it, his eyes going straight to Bobby Mullen. He seemed anxious for permission to go further in or just to keep breathing. Mullen beckoned him with a sharp nod of his head and the rabbit strode forward to pass a folded piece of paper to the big man.

There was something lacking in coordination, something not quite natural, about the way the underling handed the note over that made Narey look at his other hand. She saw that the fingers were crooked, hanging open in a misshapen grip.

She'd heard stories about Bobby Mullen's favoured method of showing his displeasure. The people who seriously aggravated him had a habit of disappearing or getting caught in freak fires. But those who showed disrespect or disloyalty, they got a personal lesson. His signature reprimand was to get people to place their fingers into the jamb of the nearest door. They would be given the choice of doing that or having their knees smashed so that they'd never walk again.

Given the choice of that or taking their chances that Bobby might just be testing them or possibly feeling forgiving, most did as they were asked. Bobby rarely felt forgiving. He'd grip the door in his shovel-like hands and force it fully open, trapping and crushing the fingers of whoever had made him unhappy. It was much better than kneecapping them. Instead, they'd quite literally be walking adverts for the dangers of pissing off big Bobby Mullen.

The mobile billboard in front of her stood looking at the nearest wall while Mullen read the note and crumpled it into his hip pocket. He reached out a hand and pulled the guy close enough for him to whisper in his ear. The message, whatever it was, was understood and the hired help nodded furiously. 'Sure, Mr Mullen. No problem.'

The big man turned in time to catch Narey's glance at his minion's ruined hand. Knowing that she'd made the connection, he smirked, satisfied that the advertising had paid off. He kept smiling quietly as the man left the snug.

213

'So, you were about to tell me why you're in my pub, annoying me.'

'What's your relationship with Saturn Property?'

'Business.'

'Legitimate business?'

'Is there any other kind?'

One of the men laughed behind her. She didn't like that at all.

'Well, I've heard there are other kinds. Like protection rackets.'

It was clearly Mullen's turn not to like what he heard. His mouth curled up at the side and his face darkened. 'You're in the wrong place to be throwing around accusations you can't back up. I'd recommend you be careful about what you say.'

'Is that a threat?'

He laughed. 'Take it any way you want, sweetheart.'

'Did you know Jennifer Cairns?'

'No.'

'Ever heard of her?'

'No. You're pushing your luck, missus. Get to the point. I'm a busy man and I'm no exactly famous for my patience.'

'How can a woman be killed in a property you're protecting? How did she get in? How did the person that killed her get in?'

He shrugged like he didn't care. 'My company protects the site. We don't patrol the perimeter like it's a high security prison. If someone's determined to get in somewhere then they will. Somebody got killed. Tough shit. Nothing to do with me.'

'You'd better hope it isn't. Hope that it's nothing to do with you or anyone that works for you. Because if it is then I'll find it.'

'You've got balls, Detective Inspector Narey. I'll give you that. But maybe you should take them back to Stewart Street before you lose them.'

The remark about the station made her hesitate, wondering about the note that was passed to Mullen and which was now crumpled in his pocket. She wouldn't give the bastard the satisfaction of asking but he had got inside her head. What else was written on that note?

'Do you have CCTV covering the site?'

'No. Now get out of my face. I've had enough.'

The more he wanted her to go, the more she wanted to rattle his cage. 'I'd like a list of all your employees who have worked on the Odeon site.'

'Then get a warrant. Or get to fuck.'

'Do you know Mark Singleton at Saturn?'

'Course I do. We do business together.'

'Singleton builds houses. Jennifer Cairns' husband is an architect. Do you know him?'

'The woman's husband?' Mullen seemed to give it some thought. 'I wouldn't think so. We look after the properties. We don't get asked to design them.'

'Wouldn't think so or no?'

'Okay, no.'

'Is Singleton involved in any of your other business ventures?'

215

'I wouldn't think so. Small world though. Who knows?'

You do, Narey thought. You do. But she tried something else, a little gamble. 'Maybe Mr Syme here knows. He's your accountant – he's bound to know something like that.'

She didn't turn her head to look at the man behind her; instead she just stared at Mullen looking for a reaction. She got one. He leaned forward and banged a large fist on the table.

'Hey! You're here to talk to me. Don't go talking to anyone else. You ask *me*. You don't even look at anyone else.'

'So.' She kept her own voice level. 'Is Mark Singleton involved in any of your other business ventures?'

He stood, towering over her, his cheeks flushed. 'Just get the fuck out of here. Walk out now or regret it.'

One last and risky card. 'What happened to Christopher Hart?'

There was a marked silence from the men behind her, as if they'd all held their breath at once. Mullen's face was like a winter storm about to break. After a few moments, it burst, uncontrollably and surprisingly, into a harsh laugh.

'Jesus, I don't believe you. I really don't. You've some front, lady. Crispy? You're seriously asking me about Crispy?'

He stared but she didn't answer. He was making his own mind up.

'Okay, I'll tell you this and then you go. Crispy

wasn't down to me. And I'm actually fucking offended you even asked. The people responsible, let's call them competitors, were dealt with.'

'And who *was* responsible?'

'Out. Now.'

Narey knew it was all she was getting and far more than Mullen had intended to give. For that, she was grateful. She returned his stare for as long as she dared, which really wasn't long at all, then pushed her chair back and stood up. 'Nice chatting to you, Bobby. We'll talk again.'

'Aye? Well bring a warrant next time.'

'Sure. And you bring a lawyer.'

She walked to the door of the snug in silence, the men parting in front of her and Mullen's accountant holding open the door like a perfect gentleman. The silence continued until she had walked through the bar and onto the street. Then, all she could hear was the rush of her own breath.

She walked on auto-pilot, not caring in which direction she moved but in a hurry to get to the first corner so she could turn out of sight of the pub and let her back settle against a wall. Propped up by brick and adrenalin, she suddenly felt the need to talk to Winter, needed the reassurance of hearing his voice.

The phone rang half a dozen times before he answered. She'd been just about to give up when he spoke.

'Hey. How are you?'

'Um, good question. A bit frazzled, I guess. I could do with a hug.'

She knew it wasn't like her and wasn't surprised to hear him go quiet. That kind of thing, rare as it was, usually threw him.

'You okay?' he said at last. 'Is it the case?'

'Yes and yes. I just let something get to me when I shouldn't. I'm fine. Are you busy?'

A pause. 'Yeah, a bit. Got something I have to do. Can I catch you later? I'll be good for that hug but I can't just now. You sure you're okay?'

She heard something beyond the words but couldn't put her finger on what.

'I'm fine. Are you working?'

Another pause. 'It's a case. Nothing exciting.'

'Okay. I look forward to that hug. You coming to mine tonight?'

'Yes, but it will be late. I'm catching up with some pals I haven't seen for a while.'

'Okay, but make sure you catch up with me too. I have needs.'

She ended the call, breathed out hard and began to walk, leaving Laidlaw's and her doubts behind.

Chapter 29

Winter slipped the phone back in his pocket with a heavy conscience and stared up at the tenement flat opposite him. At least he hadn't lied, not quite.

Cordiner Street in Mount Florida was just a corner kick from the national football stadium, Hampden Park. It was a mix of sandstone tenements and neat newer bungalows. Number 13 was a tenement, two doors along from a nail bar.

It had never seemed right to Winter that Euan Hepburn would be homeless yet that was what he'd been presented with. Homeless and living in a hostel with drunks and addicts. Instead he'd been living here on the South Side for at least six months. It had been easy to track an address; no need to have asked Rachel and much less troublesome not to. But it was easy enough for him to have done it while Euan was alive.

There were eight surnames listed on the ground floor of the tenement and Hepburn was on the top floor of four. Winter pressed the intercom against the name just in case the sister had been contacted and had come to sort through his belongings. There was no answer. The name for the flat opposite was Nicol. That would do.

He pressed a couple of the other intercoms and, after a few moments, a man's voice answered from the second floor. 'Hello?'

'I've got a parcel for Nicol. Could you let me in?'

There was a hesitation then a sigh. It wasn't his problem. Why not?

The door buzzed and Winter pushed against it. He climbed the stairs quickly but quietly, turning his face away from 13e and hoping the neighbour wasn't paying him any attention.

If Euan had been found dead in his flat then the place would have been secured by the police and there would have been next to no chance of Winter getting inside the building, never mind the flat. That wasn't the case though and he was betting – hoping – that there had been no reason for them to think that someone would try to break in.

Of course the cops would have been through everything in the hope of finding out who had killed him but Winter had a better idea than they did of what to look for. Even if he didn't have much idea of *where* to look for it.

They would have taken his PC or laptop away and would be going through his hard drive if they hadn't already. He'd no idea what they'd find on there but he was aware that he was hoping it wouldn't be much. For all that he wanted Euan's killer to be caught, *he* wanted to do this.

Once he was on the top landing, he took out both a thin piece of plastic and the knowledge that his Uncle Danny had given him. In less than a minute, he was inside.

He closed the door behind him and stood in the near darkness for fully five minutes, waiting to hear if he'd drawn attention on the way in. Not that he could have done much in terms of getting away if he had. He'd locked himself in and if the cops came then the options were capture or a drop from the fourth-floor window.

Standing there in silence, his eyes adjusting to the dim light, he could feel Euan all around him. Nothing supernatural, not even a presence as such, just him. His things. His life. It felt intrusive because it was. He couldn't help but see his former friend coming through that front door after an explore, making his way along the hallway to the rooms going off it. It made him more than uncomfortable.

Finally, he moved along the hall himself, picking the door at the far end and finding it to be the living room. Euan was everywhere. There was a framed Nirvana poster on one wall. Two shelves full of DVDs that were so him: early Steve Martin movies, *The Shawshank Redemption, The Usual Suspects*, a box set of *The Thick of It* and what looked like the entire collection of *Bilko*. Other than that there was just

221

clutter, mainly clothes strewn about and a large pile of photographic magazines. This was Euan's flat, no doubt about it.

A desk was pushed against one wall with a comfortable chair in front of it. Behind, there was a tangle of leads that made it clear that it was used as a computer desk. The printer was there but the computer, probably a laptop, was missing as expected.

He sat in the chair and reached out over the desk, imagining Euan doing the same. He ghost-typed, trying to get a feel for where Euan would have looked in the room, for where he would have put things. It was a mistake. All it did was let him feel the absence of his ex-friend, hear him talking and laughing. All it did was ramp up the guilt that he was already suffering.

He shook it off, trying to concentrate on what he'd come for. Information in whatever form he could get it but, above all, the one thing he knew would be able to help him. Euan's camera.

There hadn't been one in Euan's backpack in the Molendinar but there was no doubt he'd have taken one with him. No chance he'd have made an explore like that without a lens. It stood to reason that whoever killed him took that camera, probably for his own protection. Maybe in case he showed up on it.

But if Winter knew Euan owned more than one and would have used a different camera depending on the shoot and his mood. So where was it? Had the cops taken it? Cordiner Street was a decent address but Euan was the cautious type, borderline paranoid even. Not with his own safety, far from it, but with his cameras, definitely. He'd have made sure they were secure, just in case. After all, anyone could break in.

There were no drawers in the desk but then that would have been too easy. Look. See what he would have seen. Think like him. Jesus, this was difficult. He could feel Euan all around him and it wasn't helping him think straight.

He went through the cupboard that formed the bottom of an inset near the window with more hope than expectation. As expected, there were no cameras to be seen. He looked behind and below the worn leather sofa and found nothing. He moved the clothes on the floor and the magazines, he went back to the sofa and lifted the cushions, looked behind the curtains. Nothing.

There were no cameras under the only bed in the only bedroom, nor in the wardrobe or chest of drawers, nothing in the bathroom. The walk-in cupboard in the hall held a couple of bags and a suitcase plus more magazines. No cameras. Euan clearly hadn't lived here for long and hadn't had the time to accumulate much in the way of belongings. What there was had been easy to look through.

He went back to the living room, stung by the very definite sense that he'd missed something. He sat at the desk again and looked, channelling his friend as best he could. The magazines, the DVDs, the lack of much actual *stuff*. It was all so him.

223

The desk and the rest of the furniture looked old, maybe second-hand. The wooden mantelpiece over the fire looked original, maybe stripped back and re-varnished by someone who had the sense to see what it was. The fire had Victorian insets and a grate but there was no way it would be working: city by-laws prevented it. It was for show only.

A bell rang somewhere in his past, memories of a conversation in the darkness of a near-ruin on the edge of the Gorbals. He and Euan had crept inside the old Linen Bank building in the wee small hours. It was a dense maze of rubble and dust, cobwebbed spookiness and creaking floorboards. They explored every nook and cranny they could and Winter remembered Hepburn thrusting his hand up each room's chimney. He'd asked what the hell his pal was doing and was told that if *he'd* been working in the building then that's where he'd have hidden cash or bonds or whatever before they finally closed it down. Winter had laughed at him but now he wasn't so sure.

He jumped off his chair and made for the fireplace at the far wall. Crouching in front of it, he placed one hand on the mantle and reached up the chimney with the other. Nothing. He groped right and left and then . . . there. There. His hand brushed against something solid that wasn't brick. He leaned further in so he could twist his arm round, grabbed and pulled it out.

The camera was safe inside a bubble-wrap bag. Typical over-the-top caution from Euan. If only he'd taken half as much care of himself.

It was a Nikon D750 with a 24-120 millimetre tele-photo zoom lens. Nearly two and a half thousand pounds worth of kit stuffed up a chimney. Only Euan.

With adrenalin coursing through him, he took the camera back to the desk, sat down, punched the on button and began flicking through the photographs on the memory card. The most recent was dated 14 September, less than a week before the date Euan was thought to have died.

It was a series of shots from Gartnavel Royal Hospital on Great Western Road, the old asylum that was known as the black building. Winter was sure he would have recognized the place inside anyway but an external shot, an opening scene-setter, gave that game away. Inside there were blistered walls in faded shades of pink and yellow, laden with graffiti. Steel piping lay across the floor, and an old fire hose, uncoiled. In the next, a table and chairs sat isolated in an empty room surrounded only by fallen plaster. In another, an old bath and sink stood lonely in a room that had other-wise been gutted. There was shot after shot of decay and neglect.

In one of them, a pale blue room with wooden-pan-elled walls and a dirty tiled floor, the light from above had reflected the photographer on the glass doors on the far wall. Except he wasn't alone. Another figure stood by his side, a blurred silhouette standing with his or her arms on their hips. The camera flash had obliterated both heads but Winter had no doubt the photographer was Euan. Who the hell was he with?

Winter enlarged the reflected areas of the image as best he could but there was nothing more to be gained. The other person, surely a man from what he could see, wore a dark hooded sweatshirt and jeans but even a guess at build or height was distorted by the glass and the glare.

He scrolled quickly back through the images, over weeks, desperate to see what Euan had been working on and where he had been in the time leading up to his murder. He saw no other shadows, no other strangers. In a few seconds, he was back seven weeks to a series of dark and stark images. The Rosewood Hotel. He'd never doubted Rachel had been right about that but there was all the proof that was needed. Depressing, disturbing proof.

Men barely awake, barely alive, with sunken eyes, sharp cheekbones and discoloured skin. Rooms littered with bottles drained of booze. Close-ups of vomit and discarded needles. Bedsheets stained with God knows what. Men curled sleeping in corridors and on stairs. Men fighting each other. Feral faces that could have come from a Dickens novel or the siege of Paris.

The photographs were irresistible. Like a car crash or a public execution. Ghastly images of a descent into a hellish existence, men beyond care and way beyond caring for themselves. He and Euan had spent count-less hours together in abandoned buildings but these were abandoned people, out of sight and out of mind just like the decaying places they'd taken such an interest in. No one gave a damn.

Except maybe Euan. He'd had put himself on the line to take these.

Winter forced himself to move on, flipping through the camera's images, on past the shame of the Rosewood and back towards Gartnavel and the most recent pictures. There were a couple of external photographs of the City Mission and some pretty uninteresting shots of what looked like the inside of a Victorian primary school ready for demolition. Nothing that grabbed his attention.

Then, with the date showing just a week before the Gartnavel photos, came a series that stopped him like a brick wall. They were internal shots of a building that was all but empty. A series of steeply banked rooms and a warren of corridors. The flash showed walls that were blue and flaking, a sweeping arc of stairs, a labyrinth of little box rooms and the remains of a section of ornate decoration.

It was the Odeon. Winter's heart jumped. It was the fucking Odeon.

'Jesus, Euan. What the hell have you done?'

Chapter 30

A return to the Rosewood wouldn't have been Narey's first choice given the couple of days she'd had but choice wasn't something that was in plentiful supply. Neither Doig nor Cochrane were working the front desk and the tall, skinny guy who was there didn't put up much of a fight when she showed him her warrant card and said she was going upstairs. She was sure that he got on the phone to the owners as soon as her back was turned but she couldn't care less about that.

She made her way up the stairs, dodging drunks and discarded bottles, stepping over vomit and doing her best not to breathe. A couple of residents took an interest but she pushed past them with a stare that made them think twice.

The TV room was in enough darkness for you not to be able to tell if it was noon or Norway but the set was glowing in the corner, showing just the sort of mindless daytime crap that these men didn't need. In its reflection, she saw him sitting in a chair, his head slumped to one side and propped up on one arm.

The man looked a year older than he had the last time she'd seen him. He was emerging from the wrong side of a massive hangover and he wore the pain of it all over his face. His eyes were red and his skin blotchy and puffy. Drink had been taken and plenty of it.

He didn't notice her until she was standing right over him. He raised his head sluggishly and took a moment to remember who she was. When he did, he also remembered his manners and tried to get out of his chair. She gently pressed him back into place with a hand on his shoulder.

'How are you, Walter?'

He managed a feeble smile. 'Not so great, to be honest with you, hen. All my ain fault but I've definitely felt better. My head's in more bits than a Lego set. How's yourself?'

'I'm fine. Do you maybe fancy some fresh air?'

He looked around the room and took her meaning. Some things were better not overheard.

'Fresh air might kill me or cure me but it's a risk I take every day. Help an old man up, will you?'

She got him to his feet and together they shuffled out of the day room and slowly downstairs until they shrugged off the stink of the Rosewood and found themselves in the overcast gloom of a Glasgow afternoon. They walked and talked, his arm in hers, in the mutual pretence of him giving her support. It was the same unspoken deal she had with her dad.

229

'Thanks for phoning me, Walter. It helped a lot.'

'Nae bother, hen. Had he been at the Mission right enough?'

'He had, yes. They told him not to go anywhere near the Rosewood but he went anyway. And it turns out his name wasn't Brian. It was Euan.'

'*Euan?* I don't understand. Why would he lie to me?'

'He wasn't lying to *you*, Walter. He had his reasons, good reasons. But it wasn't about lying to you.'

'Do you know what happened to the laddie?'

'Not yet. But I've got some other things I want to ask you that might help. I don't want you to grass on anyone and I don't want you to get into any bother with the others in the Rosewood. If you don't want to then it's fine.'

He considered it for a moment then breathed hard. 'If it's not grassing, we'll call it helping and I'm fine with that. What's the worst that can happen to me anyway? I'm well past halfway to dying, so they can bugger off. Pardon my French, lass. What do you need to know?'

'Do you know a man called David McGlashan?'

'*Davie* McGlashan? Aye, I know him. Used to stay in the Rosewood till some bam beat him up for the sake of a packet of fags. He left the next morning and never came back. That'd be about ... hell, I don't know, all the days run into one after a while.'

'It would be about two months ago.'

Walter scratched at his head. 'Aye, I reckon that would be about right. What about him?'

'He died, Walter. Was he a friend of yours?'

Tears came to the old man's eyes. 'Jeez, hen. You're kidding. Him as well? Me and big Davie got on just fine. I liked the guy. What the hell happened to him?'

'We're not certain yet. It looks like it might have been a heart attack. I'm sorry, Walter.'

The man aged in front of her eyes. Another friend lost and not many left. His pain hurt her too and she couldn't help but think of her dad.

'What can you tell me about Davie? Anything might help.'

He looked confused. 'You said it was a heart attack. So what do you need to know?'

'It's probably nothing but I'm just checking everything out. It might help me find out what happened to Euan. To Brian.'

Walter shrugged and looked lost. 'Davie was all right. A daft boy with a drink in him but they're all the same. He wasn't a fighter or a thief. Just a poor soul. Never much to bother anybody.'

'So no one would have had reason to do him any harm?'

'You think somebody did?'

'I'm just making sure, Walter.'

'Nobody that I know of, hen.'

'Davie had been sleeping in an abandoned building, an old saw works in Anderston. Why'd you think he'd be in there?'

'Was it warm and watertight? Nobody to bother him? As good a place as any then and better than most.

231

Better than the one he left, that's for sure. It's no rocket science, Miss Narey. If Davie had found somewhere free, safe and dry then he'd be as happy as a pig in shit. Pardon my French.'

She took it in and nodded. It did make sense.

'There was something else I wanted to talk to you about, Walter. I hope you don't mind but I did some digging after I spoke to you last time.'

'Oh?' He didn't look best pleased.

'You said you'd had to leave the place you lived in. I got the impression you were forced to leave. Is that right?'

All she got was a non-committal shrug of the shoulders.

'Well I made a call to social security and your last address was in Charleston Street in the East End. Except it isn't there any more. There's new housing in its place, mostly rentals. Rent probably about four times what you were paying.'

'And the rest. Why are you interested though? It's nothing to do with the laddie dying and what's done is done. I'm in the Rosewood now and I'm no blaming anybody but masel'.'

'No, it's nothing to do with the case I'm working but I get angry when people are treated badly. What happened? Did they make you move out?'

Walter squirmed uncomfortably and lifted his shoulders. 'What could I have done, hen? No one was going to listen to me. I took some money to give up my lease and I left the place.'

232

'Were you threatened, Walter?'

He looked away, not keen on letting her catch his eye.

'Were you?' she repeated.

'Ach, listen, it's not as simple as that. It's not like I could prove anything. Not like they came straight out and said it. It was more how they said it.'

'What did they say?'

'Without putting it in so many words, if I stayed I might have found myself pretty unlucky. Like having my house burn down while I was still inside it. I didn't fancy that much. Get paid off or get burned alive? It was a no-brainer.'

She could feel the anger rising in her.

'Did you report it to the police?' She knew it was stupid even as she said it.

He laughed. 'Aye, right. No offence, hen, but just how was that going to work? Do you think your lot were going to listen to me? Even before I got put out on the street, I was a drinker. That housing mob just put enough money in my pocket to make me float in it. No, that's no right, it was enough for me to drown in.'

'Who were they, Walter? The ones that talked to you?'

'No, lass. Forget it. Even if I remembered names, I wouldn't want to tell you them. The ones that talked to me weren't the ones that ran the show. They were just the thugs that did the dirty work. The kind that make the real money, they keep their hands clean.'

233

'Okay, Walter. I understand. But I'm looking into this company anyway. I've got a friend in the insurance game. He'll want to know what they're up to. I'll not drag you in though.'

He shrugged. 'Up to you, hen. I can't stop you. And if you can pin something on them then good luck to you. Why are you trying to help an old soak like me, anyway?'

She smiled and, as she did so, she knew how sad it looked. 'Let's just say you remind me of someone.'

They'd walked round in a circle and were back almost at the Rosewood. She tried to palm another twenty-pound note into the old man's hand but he wasn't having it.

'No thanks, love. I'll feel a lot less like a grass if I don't take your money. Anyway, the way my head's feeling you wouldn't be doing me any favours.'

'You could buy aspirin.'

He laughed loudly. 'Aye, I could, hen. And I could be the next winner of *The X Factor*. It's just as likely.'

As they approached the steps of the Rosewood, Narey saw a tall, broad man standing at the entrance. It was one of the dosshouse's two owners, Thomas Kilgannon.

'This is harassment. My lawyer will be making a complaint to your superiors.'

'Be my guest, Mr Kilgannon. There's plenty of them to choose from but I doubt you'll find one that will agree with you.'

The man glared at her and did the same to Walter.

The old man tipped his head towards Narey then slipped past Kilgannon and into the building. The owner watched him every step of the way.

'A friend of yours, is he? He'd do well to remember who owns this place and puts a roof over his head.'

Narey walked right up to him and put her head close enough to his to smell the cheap aftershave that clung to his pores.

'Listen carefully to me, Mr Kilgannon. You'd better take special care of that man. Because if he so much as cuts himself shaving then I'll be coming after you. Do you understand? And I'll be coming with everything I've got.'

Chapter 31

Thursday evening

Remy was nervous. Seven of them, assuming everyone turned up, were going to walk the length of the old line to the abandoned railway station at the Botanic Gardens in the West End. The afternoon had been dry but a wind had picked up now and there were brooding dark clouds threatening overhead. It suddenly didn't seem a very good idea. Maybe it never had.

He couldn't even swear that he knew what his idea was. He needed to know what had happened in the Molendinar and the Odeon. He needed some way of ridding himself of the sights and smells and fears that were constantly replaying in his head. And maybe in some deluded moments, he thought he might just be able to uncover a killer.

His message to them had been clear enough but there was a message to one of them in particular.

Nothing too difficult, not the Molendinar or anything stellar like that, he'd written. It was bait and Remy's biggest hope and fear was that someone would take it.

The plan was to meet at the site of the former Kirklee station which was the next stop on the line to the Botanics before both were closed just before the start of the Second World War. There were blocks of apartments over the site now but the platforms were still there, even though they were completely overgrown. If you didn't know any better, you'd miss them but anyone who'd done any exploring in Glasgow could tell you where they were. If marijuana was a gateway drug then so was the Kirklee to Botanics line.

Gabby said she'd meet him there and sure enough there she was, standing on the old platform next to a tall, slim, younger guy with shoulder-length dark hair. He was wearing a blue-collared fleece zipped up to his neck and looking down at Gabby with more interest than Remy liked and she seemed to be laughing at his jokes.

They were on the part of the platform where the old bridge used to be. It was now bricked up and covered in vivid graffiti. Weeds sprouted by their feet and trees grew where the tracks once lay. Nature had reclaimed this for herself.

Gabby and the guy both looked up at his arrival and their chat stopped. She seemed pleased to see him though. 'You found the front door then?'

'You guys know each other?' asked Mr Tall and Athletic before Remy could answer.

237

'A bit, yeah. This is Remy. He organized this.'

'You're Magellan? Oh right. I'm Finlay Miller. My forum name's Astronut. How you doing, man?' He walked over to offer a handshake that Remy returned.

'Fine. Thanks.'

'Good, good. I was just saying to Gabby that this should be a nice wee stroll. I haven't done any tourist venues for a while.'

Tourist venues. Remy disliked the guy already. Gabby saw it – he could tell by the smirk that was spreading across her face as she stood behind Miller. She was teasing him, daring him to respond.

'Finlay works in an art gallery,' she told him, obviously trying to annoy him more. 'And he helps support emerging talent through a foundation. Isn't that great?'

'Really? That's interesting.' He'd done his best to make his voice suggest it was anything but interesting.

They were joined by three more people before anyone could reply. Voices back on the path made them look up to see a stocky, shaven-headed man in his thirties alongside a pencil-slim, younger woman with curly fair hair, both in denims and trainers. They turned out to be Ally Aitchison and Lorna Jessop, a.k.a. PencilPusher and NightLight. A few yards behind them was another man, a six-footer wearing a black beanie hat and crew-neck jumper. He was David Haddow, forum name Spook.

While they were all still introducing themselves, a young ginger-haired guy came running into the clearing, a checked shirt open over a white T-shirt. The latecomer was Gopher and preferred to be known as that rather than Donald, a name he admitted he wasn't very fond of.

'A couple?' NightLight was laughing. 'Me and Ally? No. We just met on the walk here and got chatting. Do you guys all know each other?'

'Gabby and Magellan know each other,' Miller jumped in, smiling at her. 'They're not a couple either though. Seems we're all young, free and single. Right, should we get going?'

'No!' Remy was louder than he'd meant to be. 'Not yet. We're still waiting on a couple of people. I think we should give them a few minutes yet.'

Miller shrugged amiably. 'No problem, man. It was just a suggestion. Let's wait, guys.'

They stood, mostly in silence, for five long minutes. Miller looked round at the group every now and again, shrugging his shoulders. Remy stared back at the path, willing the others to appear. He'd just about had enough when a guy in his mid-thirties appeared on the path.

He was about six foot tall with dark brown hair and had a backpack slung over one shoulder. He was looking round the group as he approached, as if he wasn't sure he'd come to the right place.

'You guys walking the line to the Botanics station? I'm Tony.'

Ally Aitchison stepped forward, smiling, his hand out. 'Hey, mate. Metinides, right? Good to finally meet you. I'm Ally. PencilPusher. Glad you could make it.'

'Hey, Ally, how you doing? Hi, everyone. Sorry I'm late. I hope I didn't hold you up too long.'

'No problem. Tony, this is Remy, he organized it all. Remy, this is the guy I invited along. He's been off the scene for a while.'

Remy waved hello.

'Metinides? Where does that come from?' David Haddow seemed confused.

'He's a Mexican photographer,' the newcomer replied, fishing a nice bit of Nikon kit out of his back-pack as if to explain. 'I like his work and it seemed as good a name as any.'

'I think we should get going,' Remy announced. 'If anyone else appears then they can catch us up in the tunnel or the pub.'

They all seemed happy with that and the group made their way to the tall metal fence topped with barbed wire that would have barred the way into the mouth of the Botanics tunnel but for the fact that it wasn't padlocked. They passed through the gate, leaving it ajar behind them, and strode into the brick mouth of the tunnel.

It was pitch black inside but they walked for a while without using torches, the way backlit by the last shards of daylight filtering through from the entrance. Remy looked back over his shoulder and saw the curve of the walls seemingly tinged with green, the reflection from the foliage outside. They had to pick their way carefully as the remains of the line were strewn with bricks and wood and various

240

bits of junk. There were hollows too and the odd puddle of water.

Remy got himself next to Ally Aitchison and drew him into conversation. 'So if you're PencilPusher, that mean you work in an office?'

The man nodded. 'Wouldn't be my choice really but yes. Don't judge me but I'm an accountant.'

'Not judging. I work in Tesco. I can see why you'd need to get out for a bit of fun though. You done this before then? The Botanics, I mean.'

'Maybe six years ago. It was probably the first explore I did. Me and a couple of mates did it on a Sunday afternoon after talking about it in the pub the night before. We nearly did it on the Saturday night but had the sense not to.'

'And you got the bug?'

'Yeah. My mates enjoyed it as well but that once was enough for them. I got the bug and have been doing it ever since. I go out maybe a couple of times a month. What about you?'

This wasn't about him. 'Much the same. Few times a month. So do you just go on your own then if your mates aren't into it? Or do you know other people in the city that go?'

'No. Don't know anyone else really. That's why I was keen to come along today. Meet some other nutters that did the same thing. Swap some war stories.'

Remy drifted away from Ally not long after that. Not much point in talking to him if he didn't know anyone else. That meant he didn't know Tunnel Man from the Molendinar. Instead, he sidled over towards the young guy, Gopher.

'You just made it today then. Saw you running in.'

'I'm always late for stuff,' he grinned. 'I couldn't get away from work in Dennistoun till five. I didn't want to miss this though so caught the bus over then jogged the rest of the way.'

'You been doing this for long?'

'Since I was sixteen. I'm nineteen now, so three years. I love going into these old places. It's a sin when they demolish them or let them rot. At least we get to go in and see them though.'

'You know any of the others?' He nodded at the rest of the group.

'Not really. I've seen the big guy before. Finlay. Seen him around. And I've swapped messages with a few of them on the forum. I only really know them from on there.'

'Anyone else you've chatted to on OtherWorld who isn't here today?'

Gopher shrugged in thought. 'One or two. There's CardboardCowboy. He's never off the forum. He's posted quite a few explores and takes good photies.'

'Do you know him?'

'Nope. Never met him.'

'There's also someone called Ectoplasm. You know him?'

The boy laughed. 'He's a she. I've never met her, like. But I remember commenting on one of her photographs and she told me. I think I said "Great picture, man" or something like that. Said thanks but she wasn't a man.'

'What about JohnDivney?'

A shrug. 'Don't know that name at all.'

They were getting towards the other end of the tunnel now, another green semicircle of quickly fading light just a hundred yards or so away. He could see Gabby ahead chatting to Finlay Miller but couldn't make out what they were saying. Their voices just mixed with everyone else's, a hum that reverberated round the tunnel walls.

By the far wall, two of the others were talking. Tony whatever his name was and Ally Aitchison. Remy wanted to split them up and interrogate each in turn. Interrogate. Listen to him. Really, what the hell did he think he was doing?

Winter caught the young guy Feeks looking over again and couldn't help but notice how nervous he seemed. He was jumpy, chatting to everyone in turn and moving around the group. Maybe it was just his nature, maybe it was something else.

They were an odd mix but that was the nature of it, he guessed. He'd never explored with anyone other than Euan Hepburn but knew enough about the type of person likely to do it. Youngish, mostly single, adventurous, fit, loners sometimes, sociable others.

David Haddow had told him he was in sales. Kitchens and bathrooms. He was maybe mid-thirties with something slightly flash about him that probably came with his job. He seemed friendly enough though and happy to chat.

'So what do you do? That camera for work or just a hobby?'

'Bit of both. This one's just for play but yes, I'm a photographer for my day job.'

'Yeah? What sort of stuff?'

Winter paused just long enough to sound casual. 'Weddings mainly. Some portrait stuff.'

'Don't think I'd have the patience for that. Arranging whole families into position, getting them all to smile, trying to make the bride look good. Must be a load of kids to deal with too. Doesn't sound like fun.'

'It's not that bad. And it pays well.'

'You never think of doing press photography, newspapers and stuff?'

'Not my kind of thing. I don't need the hassle. Weddings, people are usually in a good mood. How's the sales business?'

Haddow shrugged. 'People always want new kitchens but they can't always afford them. My job is to persuade the wife to persuade the husband that they can afford it. I always go after the woman.'

'Bit sexist, no?'

'It's the way of the world. I don't sell, I don't earn. You do what you have to do.'

'I guess so.'

The group emerged together onto the underground platform at the Botanics, the gardens themselves above their heads. For all that this was kid's stuff compared to most of the explores in Glasgow, Remy couldn't deny that it was still an eerie sight.

Sure, the place was defaced, overgrown, decrepit and a bit dangerous but it also took you back a hundred and twenty years to when this place bustled with people making their way from the West End to the city centre.

Now it was a ghost station. Bare and windswept, century-old brick covered in graffiti and a rustic lane where the track used to be. The lightwell above them ran almost the length of the platforms, letting moonlight slip through the gaps left by the great girders.

A lot of the scrawling on the walls was just mindless stuff but there was some pretty good art as well. One section of brown brick was daubed with the white-painted inscription *Meat For The Beast* and beside it was a drawing of some poor screaming soul being devoured by a ghoul. The dripping maw of another fearsome creature was further along, only the feet of a victim sticking out of the mouth. On another dark section was written *When The Wolves Come Out Of The Walls*. Simple but effective if you want to scare the shit out of people.

Of course it made him think of the Molendinar and the man left in there. How could it not? It also made him think of the beast that cut the man's throat. Demons and victims.

They milled around both platforms and the line in ones and twos. Gopher, Ally and Lorna were taking photographs, lining up arty shots using the lights by the look of it. Metinides was working his camera too, taking shots of graffiti and down the platforms into the tunnel but also photographing the group. No one else seemed to notice and it looked like that was the way that Metinides wanted it.

The longer Remy watched, the more he was sure of it. The guy was snapping a piece of graffiti or the line but he was always doing it as one or more of the group crossed his path. What the hell was he up to?

Chapter 32

Narey's incident room had changed out of all recognition. Three new faces on the wall and a host of new faces, not all exactly friendly, in front of her. In not much more than twenty-four hours, she had gone from having one murder case and the probability of losing another to holding the hottest ticket in town. The danger of that was getting her fingers burned.

She turned her back for a moment on the assorted detectives of MIT, and looked at the five faces on the wall. Euan Hepburn, looking straight at the camera in a press accreditation shot. Jennifer Cairns, smiling in a publicity picture taken for her website. Derek Wharton, young and stern in his driver's licence photo. Then two police mug shots. Christopher Hart with a scar on his cheek and a smirk on his face. Davie McGlashan appearing soft and bashful with a thick grey beard.

As she looked at all five of them together, she began to lose the courage of her convictions. Could they really all be linked and was the connection really urbexing? Some of the bastards sitting and waiting behind her would doubtless be ready to laugh it out of court. Shit, part of her was wishing she'd never made this happen. Too late now though.

Addison was going to kick it off. It was officially under his command but they knew she was running the investigation. It was her half-baked theory and it would certainly all be hers if it went wrong.

'Okay, listen up. DI Narey is going to bring everyone up to speed on where we are with Euan Hepburn and Jennifer Cairns. The enquiry has widened and we are looking at three other possible, I stress *possible*, deaths in connection with this investigation. You'll all be going away from here with leads to follow so pay attention.'

She rose, feeling unusually nervous, and began going through the five victims one by one. Some of it was old ground for a few of them but that didn't matter. It would be much more of a mistake to leave something out than to repeat it. She began with Hepburn and worked her way through them.

She saw a few faces wrinkle in scepticism and made a mental note not to forget who they were. DS Aaron Petrie, sore at her getting promoted rather than him. DI Bill Storey who probably thought the case should have been given over to him. DS Lewis McTeer who had just never liked her and had probably never liked any woman. Fuck them.

Not everyone had been so antagonistic though.

She'd already made phone calls on the other three deaths and the lead officers had been keen to help. Actually doing so proved more difficult though.

DS Dugald Lindsay had talked to her about the body found on the ruined floor of the seminary but couldn't provide much in the way of answers.

'I just don't know. I always felt there could be more to it but I couldn't find anything to prove it one way or the other. Maybe I was always bugged by the fact that if someone did want to stage an accident then a place like the seminary, which was remote even before it fell into ruin, would be perfect. It just seemed too neat, you know? No chance of witnesses or CCTV.

'Wharton did have gambling debts and I looked into it but didn't get anywhere. It wasn't a lot of money, just a few grand. And plenty of people owe that without getting killed for it.

'His family said he did visit abandoned places as a hobby but they didn't really understand it. I wish I could tell you more but I can't.'

DI Martin Telfer at Organized Crime had filled her in on what they had on Christopher Hart's death but had to confess it was nothing concrete.

'Crispy Hart worked for the Mullen brothers, did a bit of everything, basically whatever they told him to do. Thief, bagman, hard man, dealer. Whatever. It's possible he stepped out of line and Mullen punished him but we don't think so.'

She thought it best not to mention that she'd just heard the same thing from the horse's mouth.

'Mullen was having troubles with Jack Hulston around that time. The usual territory crap, turf wars. Maybe Hart was done as part of that but we've no intel to back it up. A guy like that would have had a hundred enemies and a handful of mourners. Often with these gangland killings, we know who did it and we just can't stick it on them. Usually someone's shooting his mouth off and that gets back to us but there was none of that this time. Not a word. I can't see how it fits with these other cases of yours though.'

Maybe it doesn't. Maybe it does.

The death of Davie McGlashan hadn't even merited a detective on the case. She spoke to Constable Elaine Paton, one of the two who'd been called when the man's body had been found. She was surprised to get the call from MIT, thinking the matter was closed.

'We did a sweep of the saw works, ma'am. There were bundles of clothing and little things like a tooth-brush and empty food tins that certainly made it look like he'd been there for some time. Certainly more than one night. No sign there had been more than one person there though. Just Mr McGlashan as far as we could see. Forensics came in, took photographs, did their stuff then moved the body out. It was all pretty routine.'

'Nothing strange about it at all that you can remember?'

'No, ma'am. Like I say, it was . . . Well maybe there was one thing. Maybe nothing.'

'What was it?'

'Well it seemed likely that the man had died in his sleep. The way he was positioned, still under his blanket. But there were two bottles of Buckfast near the body. Neither of them had been opened and that struck me as a bit odd. I don't know many drinkers that wouldn't have had at least some before they'd gone to sleep. Most would have had at least one of the bottles.'

'Were there empties? Maybe he'd drunk something else.'

'No, ma'am. None. He hadn't had a drink.'

That little nugget didn't seem to impress many of the detectives in the incident room. One or two took notes but most seemed to shrug it off. Seeing it, she gave them the lecture about every little thing being important even though she knew it would just turn a few further against her.

As she spoke, she saw Detective Chief Superintendent Tom Crosby, the lead on Major Crime, slip into the back of the room. Great. Just what she needed. Crosby, known obviously enough as Bing, stood with his arms folded across his chest and listened intently. A couple of heads turned to see him standing there but she pulled them back.

'There is a community out there in Glasgow, right now, continuing to explore old buildings, enter abandoned premises and disused tunnels. They are doing this out of sight and by the nature of it, out of our protection. We have no reason to think that whoever is responsible for these deaths will kill again but equally, we have no reason to think they have stopped.

251

'We're on the clock here. We need to work all sides of this and get a result as quickly as possible. Becca Maxwell has information sheets for everyone on urbexing, who does what and where. Read them.'

She saw a couple of them, Petrie and McTeer, whispering to each other and both had grins on their faces. Arseholes, the pair of them. She'd sort them but doing it in front of Bing Crosby wasn't the way.

Minutes later, the briefing was over and the detectives were dispersing with varying degrees of enthusiasm. She allowed herself to catch McTeer's eye, just enough to let him know she was on to him.

She turned back to see Crosby deep in conversation with Addison. He was shaking his head a lot and occasionally gesticulating with his right arm. For his part, Addison was bending his head forward and speaking quietly so no one else could hear. It looked for all the world like a pissed-off Detective Chief Superintendent and a defensive DCI. She didn't like it.

Crosby left with a final shake of his head and, once he was out of the room, Addison approached her.

'Let me guess, he wants to offer me a promotion.'

'Not quite. It was all I could do to stop him reprimanding you. He's gone to cool off and you'd better hope he does.'

She wasn't sure she wanted to know but had to ask. 'What's he so mad about?'

Addison loomed over her. 'Not just him. I *told you* not to go near Bobby Mullen. What the hell did you think you were doing, Rachel?'

252

'Ah. That.'

'Yes, *that*. He got a call from Ken Bryson to say you'd been seen going into Mullen's pub. It's a toss-up whether Bryson or Crosby will have you sacked first. You were talking about a ticking clock on this case, Rachel. Well it's ticking for you too. You'd *better* get a result.'

Chapter 33

They'd gone straight to Oran Mor for a drink after the walk to the Botanics. It had been Remy's idea. The place used to be a church before it was turned into a pub so what better for them than an old building that had survived more or less intact after it hadn't been wanted any more. Okay, so it had been tarted up inside but it wasn't quite gentrified. They'd also be able to get in a corner and talk without too much chance of being overheard.

It was all dark wood and panelling inside, pillars and pews and low ceilings. It was shadowy, intimate even. Like another tunnel but this time with alcohol. Remy would be going easy though; no boozing for him but he'd make sure everyone else had plenty. He got the first round in, encouraged a 'proper' drink for those that said no and got himself a lager shandy that looked like a real pint.

When he came back with the tray of drinks, he saw

Gabby and Miller were sitting next to each other, heads tight together in conversation. He didn't like that much but maybe later he could get something out of her of what the arse was saying. He needed to get whatever he could from all these people because he wasn't sure he'd be seeing them again.

He handed out the glasses and parked himself next to Lorna the NightLight who had ordered a glass of white wine. She'd actually asked for a small glass but he'd got her a large. She was so skinny that he couldn't imagine she'd be able to hold much alcohol at all. That made him feel bad, but he needed people to talk.

'That was fun,' she said. 'Thanks for organizing it. I'd only ever been there with an ex-boyfriend before. It was good to do it as a group. It felt like we were occupying the place.'

'You usually go on your own then?'

'Oh no. I go with a couple of friends. My pal Lizzie and her boyfriend Gus. They don't post on OtherWorld though. We all do the urbexing but I do the photographs and stick them online. Probably why you wouldn't know to invite them along.'

'Yes, probably.' He sighed inside, wondering how many other part-time explorers were out there who didn't use the forum. Clearly neither of Lorna's friends could be Tunnel Man though.

'So you only know the two of them?'

'Just those two. People have posted after seeing my photos but I don't know them. Still, now I know five other people that do it.'

255

'Six.' The voice came from above them, someone standing. They all glanced up.

'I take it you're the muppets that walked the Botanics line this evening?'

They were looking at a lean, flint-cheeked guy in his early thirties with sleek black hair. He tried to switch to a smile when he saw everyone staring but didn't quite pull it off.

'Only joking. I'm Crow. Or Murray Bradley if you like. I thought I'd give the tourist route a miss and come straight here. Can I get anyone a drink?'

Bradley wore a black-leather jacket, T-shirt and jeans to match his hair. If he *had* walked the tunnel from Kirklee with them then he'd have disappeared in the darkness. Everyone said they were sorted for drinks and the guy headed off to get one for himself.

He came back with a pint of lager in his hand and squeezed himself into a space between Ally Aitchison and Gopher. 'Cheers.' They all raised their glasses without much enthusiasm. The newcomer had managed to piss them all off with just a couple of sentences.

'Walking the line too safe for you then?' Aitchison seemed happy to take him on aggressively.

Bradley shrugged, clearly not fazed. 'Been there, done that. Happy to come for a beer though and see what you guys are all about. So where else have you done?'

It sounded like a challenge and Gabby, not surprisingly, took it that way. 'Anywhere that's worth doing in Glasgow. What about you, big man? Surprise us.'

256

The man sneered and Remy wanted to slap him. There was more chance of Gabby doing that though. 'Finnieston Crane, the old Transport Museum, the black building at Gartnavel, the Hydro when it was being built. Like you say, hen, anything that's worth doing.'

The next question was out of Remy's mouth before he could stop it.

'Have you ever done the Molendinar Burn?'

Bradley paused then pushed his lower lip over his top one and shrugged. 'No. Not yet anyway.'

'What's that?' Lorna looked confused.

'There's a tunnel where the Molendinar Burn runs under Duke Street,' Miller answered. 'It gets really tight and you wouldn't want to do it if you were claustrophobic. Only one person's supposed to have done it.'

More than one, Remy thought. Definitely more than one.

He knew there was a risk he was about to overplay his hand but they were the only cards he had.

'Did you read about the body found in the tunnel last week?'

They all looked at him and he tried to take in the expression on their faces. Confusion mostly although a couple of them, Aitchison and Miller, obviously knew. Haddow too. Not Gopher, that was for sure. His eyes widened and his mouth bobbed open. 'Body? As in, dead body?'

*   *   *

257

Winter struggled to keep conflicting emotions under control. This guy Feeks was asking all the questions for him. They were all staring at Remy so that left Winter free to look at them. Trying to read them. And what about Feeks? Nervily chatty and obviously interested in the Molendinar. But then they all were now.

But the kid's words, *body, dead body*, made him picture Hepburn in a way that he didn't want to. It messed with his thinking. He sat and watched, trying to take it all in. Underneath he was in knots.

'Yep. Some guy was found under Duke Street,' Miller told Gopher. 'I saw it on the news and read about it. The newspaper said it was suspicious circumstances.'

'Seriously?'

'Was he urbexing?'

Shit. Was he?

'No one knows.' Miller stated it as if it was a fact even though Remy knew it wasn't. 'He could have been in there for any reason. Might have been living rough. Might have been hiding from the cops. If he *was* urbexing, he probably just slipped and banged his head.'

'Probably that,' Haddow agreed.

'So who was he, if he was urbexing?' Remy knew he was pushing his luck. 'Anyone know who he might be?'

'What did he look like?'

'Newspaper said he was about five foot eleven, medium build, reddish-fair hair.' Miller seemed to know everything or think he did. The rest mulled this over or just shrugged. Remy wanted to shake them upside down till their memories popped.

258

'But if the newspaper said it was suspicious . . .' Lorna sounded scared.

'Maybe someone just took the guy down there to sort him out. Nice and out of the way. In space no one can hear you scream and all that.' Bradley made it sound as if he knew what he was talking about. 'Was he just inside the entrance to the tunnel?'

'Paper didn't say.' Finlay Miller knew it all. 'Probably. Wouldn't want to go further into there than you had to.'

'Anyone remember the guy that broke his neck at the seminary?' Aitchison asked them. 'It was about a year ago.'

They all either nodded or said yes. In a community as small as urbexing, something like that didn't go unnoticed for long.

'Poor guy.' Lorna shivered. 'Gus, my friend's boyfriend, he knew him. Said he was a really nice guy. They think he just slipped.'

Bradley chipped in. 'And there was that guy who supposedly fell from the Finnieston Crane. Except I'd heard that wasn't an accident.'

'Yeah?' Aitchison sounded sceptical. 'Who did you hear that from?'

'Can't say. Someone who knows someone. But they reckon the guy wasn't an urbexer.'

There was a lot of silent nodding and quiet supping. Remy saw they were happy to believe it was nothing to do with urbexing. All sitting there with that thought on their faces. All except Gabby. She was looking straight at him.

Chapter 34

Winter waited in the doorway and watched the two of them speaking, the girl Gabby and Feeks, the guy who'd organized it and was asking so many questions. He held back until he saw the girl walk off then stepped out of the pub, catching Feeks before he too could leave. He didn't know what he was going to say to the guy but he knew he had to talk to him.

'Remy?'

Feeks nearly jumped out of his skin. He turned, alarm in his eyes. 'What?'

'I just wanted a chat. That stuff you were saying about the body in the Molendinar. It's interesting. You fancy another drink?'

'Well, I should really—'

'It's just that I've been down there. The tunnel, I mean.'

Feeks blinked. 'Really?'

'Yes. It gets weird in parts. At one point there's this

tunnel of spiral steel piping. Then it opens up into this beautiful redbrick section before it all gets really low. Like I said, it's interesting.'

The younger guy just looked at him. Long enough for Winter to know he'd been right.

'Um, sure. Maybe one more.'

'Great.'

They went back inside and Feeks found a quiet corner while Winter ordered a couple of pints. He looked back from the bar and saw his new friend fidgeting nervously, his eyes flitting left and right.

He placed two drinks on the table, as happy as Feeks seemed to be that there was no one else in earshot.

'Cheers.'

'Oh yeah. Cheers.'

Winter raised his glass and took a better look at the guy over the top of it. He was in his mid to late twenties, with a mess of fair hair and a light sprinkling of freckles. He had bony shoulders and skinny arms, barely a pound of fat on him anywhere. Seen more meat on a butcher's pencil, as his Uncle Danny would say. He seemed an unlikely candidate to slit another man's throat.

'So where you from, Remy?'

The guy hesitated. 'East End. You?'

'Charing Cross. Like I said, I'm a photographer. What about yourself?'

Remy looked wary. 'I work in a supermarket. You really been down the Molendinar Tunnel?'

'Aye. Till it got so low that there didn't seem a way

through without getting on my belly and crawling. Was it in the papers that you read about the guy they found down there?'

'Uh huh. I saw it on the TV news too. There's not been much about it since though.'

'You been keeping an eye on it?'

'What? Yes, I suppose so. Just interested.'

'Yeah, me too.'

'When did you go down there, Tony? I mean you didn't say when the others were talking about it.'

'Quite recently. I didn't want to mention it when we were talking about the poor guy being killed. Didn't seem right. Would have made me sound like a suspect. You know?'

Feeks laughed uncomfortably. 'I guess it would have. Did you take photographs when you were down there?'

'Yeah, I did. Quite a few.'

'Right. Cool.'

'You ever explored the Molendinar yourself, Remy?'

'Me? No.'

His reply was just too quick and just too hollow. Winter let it simmer for a bit, sipping his pint and noticing that Remy had barely touched his.

'So what do you think happened to the guy they found?

Feeks shrugged, his pointed shoulders rising and falling like a kid who'd been asked how his school day had been.

Winter tried again. 'Suspicious circumstances according to the cops. You think that's right?'

He reddened ever so slightly and the hand that went to his pint glass had a tremble in it. 'I don't know. I guess the police should know so it must have been.'

'Yeah. That makes sense.'

Feeks didn't say anything more for a bit. He looked around the room and Winter could see his mind was in overdrive.

'Do you know a lot of people who urbex?' he asked at last.

'Not many,' Winter told him. 'Most of them I met this evening.'

'Do you know anyone that might fit the description of the guy in the tunnel? I mean, he might not have been exploring but he might have been. You know?'

Winter nodded. 'Yeah, he might. There was one guy I knew years ago I did some explores with. He was about the same height, same hair colour.'

'Really?'

'Yes.' Winter watched Feeks intently. 'His name was Euan Hepburn. Probably a different guy though. The one I knew moved to England.'

The name meant nothing to him. That was obvious.

'Maybe you should tell the police, Tony.'

'Yeah. Maybe I should.'

Another awkward silence fell on them. It was like they were in a competition daring the other not to speak. If they were, Feeks lost. He quickly downed some more of the pint and all but jumped to his feet.

'I've got to go. Do you want me to buy you a drink before I go?'

'No, no need. Listen, are you okay, Remy? You seem upset about all this.'

'Eh? No. I'm . . . I'm fine. I'd better go. Sorry.' Feeks looked like he wanted to say something else but couldn't find the words.

'No worries. I'll get you out. Time for me to go anyway.'

Chapter 35

It was raining by the time the two of them left Oran Mor together, the ones named Winter and Feeks, but it wasn't difficult to see them. From the shadows of a doorway across Byres Road, they were lit up like Christmas trees under the orange glow of the street light.

They stood on the steps, speaking and shaking hands like old friends before going their separate ways. Had they known each other all along? It hadn't seemed like that in the pub but maybe they'd been hiding it.

Feeks and the blonde girl, Gabby, had hung back at first after everyone else had left. She went off and then the older guy had appeared. He and Feeks had gone back inside. That had been a worry.

The temptation had been to follow them inside again. Try to hear what they were saying. But the risk was too great. Too hard to explain if noticed.

So there had been no choice but to wait. It was an

uneasy, enraging wait. Not seeing, not hearing, not knowing. It just made for a headache, a brain-pounding pain that throbbed black and dull.

They were in there for a long time. Twice, the urge to check on them nearly became too much. Twice, feet started to follow heart before head said no. Wait, just wait. Try to stay calm and wait.

It was impossible not to wonder though. What were they talking about? What information were they sharing? What did they know?

The stone steps outside Oran Mor were dappled with the first spots of rain and still there was no sign of them. Willing Winter and Feeks to appear through the arch of the door did no good either. It worked as well as trying to wish things away.

The pain had grown thicker and darker, feeding on frustration and anger, becoming blacker and bigger with every pulse. Then, finally, they showed. Smug and conspiratorial on the steps. Sly handshakes, a wave goodbye and slipping off into the night thinking themselves out of sight. Thinking themselves clever. They weren't, not clever at all.

Only one of them could be followed though. Which? Eenie meenie miney mo. It was Winter.

The man turned and headed down Byres Road towards Hillhead underground. It meant a quick dash out of the shadows and across the road, trying to stay close but not too close. A late hop onto a different carriage of the same train. Winter went only two stops, getting off at St George's Cross. Over the interchange and along the length of St George's Road, hugging shop fronts and darkness. Finally, along North Street past the Koh-i-Noor and to the corner where the dome of the Mitchell Library shone like a lighthouse in a rough sea. But when the corner was turned, Winter was nowhere to be seen.

Had he gone inside the library? The building was still open so it was possible but the entrance was far enough away to make it unlikely. Across Berkeley Street in a weird panic, standing in the shade of the sandstone and looking around. There. Back across the street. Just in time to see a light go on and a figure closing blinds at the window.

It was him.

It was where he lived.

Chapter 36

Narey had parked up outside a house in Rowallan Gardens in Broomhill and had just stepped out of the car when her phone began ringing. She cursed the timing of it but pulled the mobile from her pocket and looked at the screen. The call was from her dad's care home. At nearly eight in the evening? It was unlikely to be good news.

She nibbled at her upper lip, debating whether she really wanted to hear whatever it was they had to tell her. There was no argument to be had. She opened the car door and fell back into the driver's seat.

'Yes?'

'Miss Narey? I mean, Inspector Narey? '

'Yes. Who's speaking?' The voice was familiar but it wasn't Mrs McBriar, the home owner. It was someone younger. It was . . .

'Jess. Jess Docherty. From Clober Nursing Home. I look after your dad.'

She breathed deeply. 'Hi, Jess. What's wrong? Is he okay?'

'Yes. Well, no. I mean he's *okay* but he's a bit stressed. He's been asking for you and I can't calm him down. I usually can but he's agitated and worried. He keeps going on about Huntly Avenue. You used to live there, didn't you?'

'Huntly Avenue? When I was about thirteen! What is he agitated about?'

'He keeps asking when you'll get here. Or there. He thinks he's in Huntly Avenue. He's worried about buses being off and you not being able to get home. It's really upsetting him. I've told him you'll be fine but he's not having it. He wants to pick you up in his car and I'm having to say no. Could you maybe come over and see him?'

Narey looked through the car's window at the house she was about to visit, the home of Jennifer Cairns' best friend. This wasn't a choice she wanted to make.

'There was a bus strike when I was in second year at high school. I had to walk nearly three miles to get home and he was out of his mind with worry. I'll get there as soon as I can, Jess. What time do you finish your shift?'

A pause. 'Forty-five minutes ago.'

'*What*? Why are you still there?'

'I told you. He's agitated. I couldn't go home and leave him like that. Wouldn't have felt right.'

Eileen McBriar had said that Jess wasn't the problem she seemed to be. She said that surly was just the way

269

her face was, just the way she spoke. She'd insisted to Narey that Jess was a good worker and that she genuinely cared. It looked like she might have been right.

'Jess, I need to do something before I can get over. But I'll be as quick as I can. Can you stay with him? I know it's asking a lot.'

'Course.'

'Thank you.'

Thank you, thank you, thank you.

Carrie Thomson was a good looking forty-something dressed as an early thirty-something but pulling the look off effortlessly and stylishly. Blonde and tanned, she was wearing money and it suited her. The only clue that anything was wrong was in her make-up, eyes smudged from running mascara and cheeks streaked with tears. Narey also had the distinct impression that she'd been drinking.

The strain in her voice was obvious and her slightly manic manner was testament to her insistence that she wasn't Jen Cairns' friend, she was her *best* friend.

'Of course I'll help you. Why the hell would I do anything else? I can't go five minutes without thinking about her and bursting into tears. What *happened* to her?'

Narey and Thomson were sitting in the front room of the woman's large and expensively furnished house in the West End, a couple of streets back from Clarence Drive. Becca Maxwell sat quietly to the side, letting Narey connect one to one with the woman.

'To be honest with you, Mrs Thomson, we don't know yet. That's why we need to talk to as many people as possible who can help us build a picture of Jennifer's life and movements. So you were close?'

'I think I was as close to her as anyone. We'd known each other for twenty years. Best friends isn't just a label, it's the way it was. She was godmother to my eldest. We didn't go a couple of days without speaking, rarely more than one. *Yes*, we were close. We knew each other better than anyone else did.'

'Better than her husband?'

Thomson laughed bitterly. 'Much better, I'd say. Douglas is a lovely man in many ways but he didn't always *get* her. There was ten years between them but it seemed that gap was growing. He was getting older quicker than she was. Jen could talk to me about stuff that he just wouldn't understand or be interested in.'

'Like what?'

The woman shrugged expansively as if there was so much she didn't know where to start. 'Fashion. Art. Music. Food. If we'd even mention a *celebrity* then Douglas would start muttering and leave the room. He has very fixed ideas on why people should be famous and they don't include much more than being a politician or a classical composer.'

'Did they get on?'

Thomson's eyebrows shot up and she moved back in her seat. 'What are you actually asking me?'

'Just what I said. Did Mr and Mrs Cairns get on well? Were they happy together?'

Carrie crossed her arms and locked them tight. 'Douglas was happy.'

'But not Jen?'

'I'm not saying that.'

'Then what *are* you saying?'

'He was happier than she was. Jen needed a bit more than Douglas seemed able to give her. That doesn't make her a bad person.'

Narey's voice softened. 'I'm not saying it does. Carrie, I'm not here to judge Jen in any way. I'm here to find who killed her.'

The woman stared for a bit then nodded, relaxing slightly. A thought occurred to her but she held on to it for a while, reluctant to set it free. Finally, she did.

'Do you think it was Douglas?'

'I'm sorry to answer a question with a question, Carrie, but do *you* think it could have been Mr Cairns?'

Thomson's eyebrows knotted in thought as her head made little sideway movements. 'I don't think he has it in him.'

'But you think he may have had reason to?'

'I didn't say that.' The answer was too quick.

Narey nodded, making it obvious she had read a lot into the woman's answer. 'Carrie, I know you're sitting here to defend your friend but I need to remind you that you are also here to help her. Was—'

'You *don't* need to remind me of that,' Thomson snapped.

'Was Jen having an affair?'

Carrie's mouth screwed shut involuntarily and

Narey knew she'd been right. She watched the woman's mind battle with itself, knowing it was just a matter of time.

'Yes.' The word came out laced with bitterness; she was angry at being forced to betray her friend. Narey felt sympathy for her but didn't have time for it.

'Thank you. I need to know this. I wouldn't ask otherwise.'

'I'm sure.'

'Was this the first time she had been involved with another man?' Narey knew she had lost any hope of the woman liking her enough to help her so there was little more to be lost on that score.

'No. She'd had an affair once before. Look, this wasn't her fault. She . . . Look, Douglas couldn't get it up any more. Okay? Too much stress and Shiraz. So I think she went for a younger, better-functioning model.'

'Carrie. I'll say it again. I'm not judging, I'm not blaming. I just need to know. If Jen had previous affairs then the man or men might be suspects.'

The nod of agreement was grudging. 'She saw a guy named Phil Traynor, a car salesman, for a few months but it ended maybe a year ago. He was married too and they both thought they'd pushed their luck far enough. There was no falling out. No recriminations.'

'Where can I find this Phil Traynor?'

A shrug. 'As I said, he's a car salesman. BMW dealership in the north of the city, I think. *He's married.*'

'I kind of think that's his problem, don't you? And we'll be discreet. We have done this kind of thing before. Anyone else other than the man she was seeing before she was killed?'

'No. And I'd have known. She wasn't some kind of slut. She was a good person.'

'Okay, what about the man she'd been seeing lately? What can you tell me about him?'

Thomson stood up, her hands going back through her straight blonde hair. 'I think I need a drink. Can I get you something?'

'No, thank you.'

Narey heard glasses clinking from the next room and a fridge door opening and closing. She could also hear nerves fraying. Thomson returned a couple of minutes later with a glass of white wine held shakily in her right hand. Narey gave her time to drink some courage from it before asking her to continue.

'I don't know his name. I'm sorry.'

Narey's heart sank. 'How long had she been seeing him?'

'A few months. Four months, I'd say.'

'From now or from when she was killed?' As soon as the words were out she regretted how harsh they sounded but it was too late.

'She had seen him for four months.'

'And yet she never mentioned his name?'

'No. She just called him The Man. I think she found it exciting that way. An extra edge of whatever. It was always just "I saw The Man last night" or "I'm going to sneak off tonight for a few hours with The Man". Never a name.'

'You must know something about him though. Any little thing might help.'

'Well he had quite a big thing apparently but I don't see how that's going to help. He had some kind of job where he could get away at any time. His own boss was how I'd taken it. He was younger than her. The sex was good, adventurous. She said he was a bit of a bad boy and she liked that.'

'How do you mean, adventurous?'

Thomson frowned. 'She didn't go into the juicy details, Inspector. I got the feeling it was ... thrill-seeking? Definitely out of the norm that she is used to with Douglas. *Was* used to.'

'Okay, I'm sorry I had to ask. What else can you tell me? Was he married?'

'I don't think so but he was definitely in some kind of relationship. He was sneaking away as much as she was. When I think about it, it was odd how little she told me about him. As if it was some big secret that was even more exciting because she didn't tell me more.'

'Okay, any clues in how she met him?'

She took a long sip of wine as she thought about it, a realization dawning. 'Well ... yes, it was work-related. I remember her saying at the beginning how it had been a shitty work day but how it hadn't been all bad. She said it with a wicked grin on her face and I immediately called her on it being some guy. She just laughed and made this face as if he was really hot. Another time, she talked about how it couldn't be all

275

work and no play and she was definitely preferring the play side of it.'

'So it could have been a client?'

'Or a supplier or a designer or a delivery guy. It almost became a running joke that she wouldn't tell me. This man of mystery. I'd joke to her that he might be a spy or a ...' The woman's face dropped. 'Shit, I used to say he might be a spy or an international hit man. Christ. Do you think it *was* him?'

Narey wouldn't have answered that even if she'd known. 'We have to find him to find out. What other circles did Jen move in where she might have met someone? This man.'

Carrie's hands flew up in a despairing gesture. 'God, it could have been anywhere. She was really ... sociable. She got out whenever she could. And her work took her all over. Lots of houses, contracts for developers, magazine work. Her business was going really well. People liked her and her work.'

'Okay. On the night that Jen disappeared, she was supposed to be seeing a client in the West End, at Kensington Gate. Was she?'

Carrie looked distinctly uncomfortable. She stared at her feet. 'I don't know. But I don't think so.'

'You think she was seeing this man? Did you not think to tell the police that?'

'I didn't know for sure. Of course I suspected that she was going to see *The Man* rather than some unknown customer but I didn't know. And I didn't want to ... I couldn't go tell the police or Douglas in case she turned up. It occurred to me that maybe she'd lost her mind and actually run off with this guy. *I didn't know.*'

Narey's stare left her in no doubt that she wasn't impressed. She didn't push it though as she needed a bit more from the woman.

'Okay, I'm going to leave you my card and if you can think of anything else about him then please call me. Anything at all that might lead us to him.'

'Yes, of course. I'm sorry I was . . . I just didn't want to . . .'

'It's okay. I understand, Carrie. Really. Okay, there's just a couple more things I need to ask.'

Thomson sank some wine back, draining the glass. 'Okay, hit me.'

'This might seem strange but did she ever mention urbexing?'

'*What*? I don't know what that means.'

'Did she ever mention exploring abandoned buildings or places like that?'

She looked aghast. 'No. Never! Why would Jen want to do something like that?'

'Okay. Then finally, do you think Douglas Cairns knew his wife was having an affair?'

Carrie Thomson blew out her cheeks and pushed her hair back on her head, holding it there, her knuckles glowing white through her tan.

'I obviously don't know the answer to this . . .'

'But?'

'But yes. My guess is that he did.'

*   *   *

Narey drove to the nursing home with the woman's words echoing through her head. Betrayal was a powerful motivation. People would do a lot for those they loved but they'd do a lot *to* those who threw that love back in their face.

The door to the home was opened by a tired-looking woman in her fifties. She looked how Narey felt. Her name was Avril or April, something like that. She nodded a greeting and held the door wide.

Narey walked the corridor to her dad's room, blinking at the awful yellow walls. Were they meant to be cheery? If so, it wasn't working.

She was just about to push open the door to his room when she stopped, hearing voices inside. His familiar tones, older and weaker now but still the same comforting, loving voice, and he was using her name. God, it always felt so good when he did that. But something wasn't quite right. He was talking *to* her. And she was seemingly answering.

'I'm so glad you made it, Rachel. I was so worried about you. I don't like you having to come home on your own like that.'

'I'm fine. Don't worry. I'm here now. We're both fine.'

'Yes, both fine. All's fine now you're home.'

Narey pushed the door ajar quietly and saw her dad sitting on the edge of his bed with his arm round Jess. She looked up at the door opening and smiled sheepishly. Narey wasn't sure if what she was feeling was gratitude, anger or jealousy. She gestured outside with her head and waited for the girl to follow. When they were both in the corridor, she closed the door again.

'You're pretending you're me?'

A flush came to Jess's cheeks. 'I'm not *pretending*. Sometimes he thinks I'm you. Maybe because we've got the same hair colour, I don't know. But he does. It's not good to keep correcting him on things. He only gets worked up. So I let him think it. You're not always here and it comforts him. I'll stop if you want.'

'No. Don't. It's . . . it's okay. If it makes him happy. I can't be here as much as I want to and—'

'I wasn't having a go at you for not being here. Honest. I know you have more important things . . . I mean, like an important job. I—'

'I get here as often as I can!' She was angrier with herself than the girl but that probably wasn't the way it sounded. 'Look, Jess, thanks for staying to look after him. I really appreciate it. But I'll take it from here. You should head off home.'

'Fine.' The girl shrugged sulkily and turned to leave.

Narey didn't know what to do but knew she shouldn't leave it like that. 'Hang on.' As Jess spun back towards her, she took her purse from her pocket and took out a twenty-pound note. The girl's eyes widened with surprise and her mouth fell open.

'What? I don't want your money! That's not why . . . No, just . . . just go see your dad. He might like it if you sing to him. *Money*?'

Shit. If there was a way of making things worse then trust her to find it. Some days she just shouldn't bother getting out of bed.

Chapter 37

Unable to sleep for thinking about her dad and the way she'd messed it up with Jess, Narey was sitting up in bed with her laptop in front of her. She was deep in OtherWorld, a notepad at her side.

She considered joining the forum under some dumb user name and fishing for the information she wanted. If she dropped the right bait then maybe she'd pull up the person that found Hepburn and called the cops or find out that Hepburn himself had used the site. And maybe she'd catch a killer.

It was a long shot but she was sure she was fishing in the right pool. She signed up, called herself WeegieGirl and posted.

Have any of you ever walked the Molendinar Burn? I've been thinking of exploring it but not sure how doable it is.

It probably wouldn't get any points for subtlety but she was in a hurry and it just might flush someone out.

She looked at it, not at all convinced it was a good idea, but closed her eyes and pressed enter.

Well there it was. Up for everyone to see. No going back from that and she just hoped someone would tell her something useful.

She flipped from section to section through the forum, bringing up all the Glasgow posts again. She'd read through most of them the previous time but knew it had to be done again. There was so much of it. Asgarten Youth Hostel, the cathedral, the subway, the West End tunnels, Gartnavel Royal Hospital, Gartloch Asylum, Holmlea Primary School. So much to get lost in.

She jotted down all the names, counted up how many posts they'd made and where they'd been. It was a slog but she didn't know any other way. *Astronut. LilythePink. CardboardCowboy. Digger9. Magellan93. Hermit. Spook. JohnDivney.* Bloody *Metinides* again. *PencilPusher. NightLight. BigTomDog. Ectoplasm. Crow.*

The forum had a search function and she put in the names in turn and brought up every post they'd made. It varied hugely. With Divney, it wasn't much at all. He'd made only three posts and those were all just remarks on other people's photographs.

However she immediately saw that CardboardCowboy was a different story altogether. Fifty-two hits in a little under a year. Eleven of those were posts that he'd started, each of them a report of an explore he'd done along with photographs. The guy was prolific.

He was a regular commenter too, enthusiastic about explores that others had done. He'd talk up people's photographs, remarking on their reports. She jotted down dates and ticked off posts. The Cowboy had been active online every day or two.

Until it suddenly stopped.

Just over six weeks ago, he'd posted a compliment about a photograph from inside an office block that was to be flattened. And then nothing. His posts just dried up completely without explanation. As if he'd disappeared. As if he was dead.

It was him. It had to be.

Something bothered her though and she went back and re-checked the posts by the user who called himself JohnDivney. Sure enough, he'd only ever commented on three posts. All three were about six weeks earlier. And all three had been originally posted by CardboardCowboy.

She was simmering with that thought when the buzzer went at the front door and it made her jump. She stepped naked from bed and pressed the intercom.

'It's me.'

'Hey, me. Come on up.'

Walking to the front door, she took it off the latch and left it slightly ajar. She padded back through to the bedroom, closed the laptop and slid it under the bed.

The computer and everything on it was business and she didn't want to mix it with pleasure.

Winter was up the stairs in a minute and she heard him close the front door behind him. By the time he had walked through the living room and the hall, he was as naked as she was. He slid in beside her and she flinched at the cold chill he'd brought in with him.

'Sorry.'

'That's okay. I can warm you up pretty quickly. How was your night with these mysterious old friends?'

He slipped his arms round her and kissed her. 'It was fine. I went home first and picked up a change of clothes for the morning and then headed over.'

'Beer,' she told him as her lips slid from his.

'I *did* brush my teeth.'

'I can still taste it. It's okay though, you know I like it. Kiss me again. In fact, don't stop.'

'Bad day? I know I still owe you that hug.'

'Bad day, shitty night. I'm afraid a hug isn't going to cut it now.'

'More?'

'More. Much more, please.'

He pulled her closer and ran his hands down her body. 'How much more?'

'As much as you've got.'

He released her from his arms, letting her go enough for him to catch her by the shoulder and arse and flip her over onto her front. She lay beneath him, her body pushed into the bed as he began to kiss her neck then work his way down.

He squeezed and licked, teased and probed, making her move to his touch and forget the day she'd endured. This would last as long as they wanted but he had a feeling it was going to be urgent and swift, needs fulfilled and bodies sated. Her hips were writhing below him and he pressed against her, matching her movements. She arched her back, pushing up at him, inflaming him, welcoming him, encouraging him.

He slipped a hand between her legs, found her more than ready and knew neither of them wanted to wait any longer. A moment later, he was inside her and they were moving together. He had one hand on the small of her back and one entwined through her hair. Hers were pressed against the bed, bracing back against him.

She urged him on and he did as he was asked, losing himself in the moment and the act, letting everything go. When the end came it was together and breathless.

He lay on top of her, bearing what weight he could on his elbows and kissing her neck. She managed to twist a hand back and stroke where she could.

'I needed that.'

She'd said it but it could have been either of them.

'Want to talk about it?'

A long pause for thought then a heavy sigh. 'No. Just hold me and kiss me. Tell me about your night if you want though.'

'No. I'd rather kiss you.'

'Suits me fine.'

Chapter 38

Friday morning

The incident room was buzzing in a way it only could when everyone was under pressure yet secretly enjoying it. You couldn't go around admitting that you got a high when there was a murder, better still more than one. But it was why they did what they did. No one signed on to find lost cats or give road-safety talks to schoolkids.

The phones were ringing off the wall, detectives were running in and out, keyboards were being hammered, the humour was black and rife and there wasn't a single moment of silence. Narey loved it. Even under all the pressure she'd managed to create for herself, she revelled in it.

She'd spoken to Hepburn's sister who told her that a DNA test was being done that afternoon. No one doubted that it was him but everyone needed the final confirmation. Rico Giannandrea had been in and out like a fiddler's elbow, working with Johnny Jackson and turning over every stone to see if Saturn Property might be hiding underneath it. They were also forensically examining other companies to see if Saturn had morphed again.

They were looking again at Davie McGlashan's post-mortem results and maybe, just maybe, there would be something they'd missed. Maxwell had drawn up a list of Jennifer Cairns' charity commitments, including a breast cancer support group, a homeless charity and an arts foundation. Narey had lined up a phone call with someone who was supposedly the UK's leading urbexer. Others were trying, so far in vain, to find a link between Hepburn and Cairns. It was buzzing.

She was looking at her computer screen when she became aware of Fraser Toshney standing up and waving at her, his hand clutching a pen. He had a phone in his other hand, clamped firmly to his ear. Toshney was manning one of the hotlines and had been fending off well-meaning nutters all morning. This time, he seemed to have something more interesting.

She pushed out of her chair and walked over, just catching the tail end of the conversation.

'Are you sure you don't want to give your name, sir? You might be eligible for a Crimestoppers reward and . . .'

He stopped to listen. 'It would really help us if . . .'

He looked at her and shrugged. 'He's gone and

wouldn't leave a name. Said he wasn't interested in a reward and didn't want to get involved.'

She just looked at him. 'Well? I'm assuming this is something worth me getting out of my chair for.'

'Yes, boss. Definitely. Well, if this guy's telling the truth. He says he's got a name for the person that found Euan Hepburn in the Molendinar.

'This guy says he was in Oran Mor last night and overheard some people talking. One of them was a guy named Remy Feeks. He spelled the name out for me. He says this guy was talking a lot about the body in the tunnel, knew a lot about it. He said, and get this, that this Remy Feeks said he went urbexing. We haven't said anything public at all about urbexing, boss.'

'I know that, Fraser. Go on.'

'The guy that phoned said Feeks seemed really interested in the Molendinar and said he'd been in there. He was asking lots of questions about it.'

'Did he give an address or a description?'

'No address but said, from what he heard, he lives in the East End and works in a Tesco. He said this Feeks sounded scared. He specifically said' – Toshney checked his notes – 'that he didn't sound scared of getting caught. More like scared that he'd be next. He said the guy was maybe twenty-six or so with fair hair and freckles. Skinny guy about five feet ten.'

Narey glanced down at the scribbled note. 'Good work, Fraser. Go and get that typed up into something legible then get your coat. We're going to the East End.'

Chapter 39

They were driving out to the East End to see the only Feeks listed in the Glasgow phone book. The phone call might have been genuine or it might have been another crazy or just an attempt to get someone into trouble. There was only one way to find out.

Adelaide Street was like an oasis in reverse. Its short row of grey sandstone buildings was isolated among green swathes of wasteland where other tenements used to stand. Now the remaining homes, weathered and shabby, stood like the last couple of teeth in an old man's mouth.

This part of the Calton used to be home to hundreds of families but they and their houses were all long since gone. The buildings, the single-ends and rows of closes, had been demolished and the infertile scrubland was the only reminder of where they had stood. Many of the buildings had become unfit for habitation by twentieth-century standards, lacking the little luxuries like inside toilets and heating. All that hung on were the better-class and later-built tenements that had sprung up in a 1920s overhaul. They were better then but they weren't all that now.

According to both the phone book and the electoral register, Archibald Feeks was the only person in the city with that surname and seemed to be an obvious enough place to start. If he wasn't the right Feeks then he was likely to know who the other one was. Narey and Maxwell parked up in front of the downbeat row and stood for a moment to take it in.

There was only a handful of flats in the block whose windows weren't either boarded up or smashed in. Most were shattered, open to the wind and rain and to anything or anyone else who fancied crawling in. Take away the lack of curtains in a couple of those whose glass had thus far escaped the sticks and stones that broke their bones, and that left just three that might still be lived in.

They pushed open the scruffy door to Number 2 and walked inside, finding the air thick with the smell of neglect and the stairs as steep as the climb out of poverty. The landing outside 2f was different though. It was swept clean and a neat little green mat sat outside a door that, unlike the others, had been painted while the present Queen was on the throne.

Narey knocked and they waited. Finally, a shadow appeared and they watched a head duck to the spy hole. The person on the other side of the door must have been wondering whether they liked what they saw as the door catch still didn't budge. Finally, the door swung open about six inches.

'Can I help you?'

The man was probably in his mid-sixties but his skin was about ten years older, with the dull mustard glow of a lifelong smoker's. His brown eyes were bright but tired and his hair curled back grey on his forehead. He was looking at them as if he feared they were there bearing bad tidings by the stretcherload. This was a man used to hearing bad news.

'Mr Feeks?'

He huffed and the door moved an inch or two nearer to them and the lock. 'I said I wasn't going to talk to you people any more. I told them you'd be wasting your time coming to my door.'

Narey held up her warrant card. 'I don't think it was our people that you talked to, Mr Feeks. Police. I'm Detective Inspector Narey and this is DC Toshney. May we come in?'

His face turned to confusion and then the habitual worry turned even deeper. The door edged back towards him. 'What's wrong? Is it Remy? Has something happened?'

Well, that answered one question: they'd come to the right place.

'It would be easier if we could speak inside, Mr Feeks.'

That didn't do much for his optimism but it did get them in. The man pulled the door back and grimly waved them inside. Once he'd shut the door behind them, he led them to a busy but well-ordered sitting room where he turned off the television and showed them both into a chair.

'So *has* something happened?'

'Not as far as we know, Mr Feeks. I take it Remy is your son? We'd like to speak to him. Do you know where he is?'

'Is he in some kind of trouble? Sorry, but I think there's been a mistake. Remy's never been in trouble in his puff. What's this all about?'

'We just need to speak to him, Mr Feeks. There's nothing to worry about but we think there's something he may be able to help us with. Do you know where he is?'

The man leaned forward, eyes narrowed. 'He doesn't live here. *Something he may be able to help you with? What does that mean exactly?* If that's like helping the police with their inquiries then I don't much like the sound of it. I'm sorry but I'm not saying anything until I know what's going on.'

Feeks was getting louder as he got more worried by the situation and he finished his statement by exploding into a coughing fit that didn't sound like it was being fuelled by much in the way of breath. He was reaching deep into his lungs and only producing a rasp.

'Are you okay, Mr Feeks? Can I get you something?'

The man shook his head and barely managed to say, 'What's this about?'

'We think Remy might be a witness, Mr Feeks. That's all it is. He isn't in any trouble but we'd like to

291

speak to him. He isn't in the phone book or on the electoral register. You are so that's why we came to you.'

The man started to speak but she could see he hadn't the strength for it. 'I think Remy might be worried about talking to us. He doesn't have to be. It might help if you can tell him that. I'll leave you my number but I'd like his address too if that's okay. Has Remy been okay recently? Maybe worried or acting differently?'

He shook his head, the cough continuing.

'I'm also interested in what Remy does at night.' She saw the man's eyes widen in surprise. 'Do you know if he has hobbies that take him out late?' She could hear how bizarre it sounded but she couldn't take it back. 'Mr Feeks, do you know if Remy ever goes exploring?'

'*Exploring*?' He barely squeezed the word out. 'Who the fuck do you think he is? David Livingstone? Remy works in a supermarket, for God's sake. *Exploring*?'

'Calm down, Mr Feeks. Please. There's nothing to get upset about.'

'What are you talking about, hen?'

'We think Remy may have seen something and might be able to help us. He's not involved. And if he's interested in visiting old buildings, that would fit with what we're looking for.'

Feeks looked old and confused. 'He's into history. Of old Glasgow and stuff like that. The boy's proud of his heritage but I don't understand what else you're talking about. You'll need to speak to him. He's got his own place. 619 London Road. He doesn't have a phone. Not a proper one anyway. He just uses his mobile. Listen, I don't know what he does at night but I know it won't be anything crooked or anything weird. He's not like that.'

Narey nodded at Toshney, their cue to leave. Both stood and Feeks also got to his feet.

'That's it? You scare me half to death and now you're going?'

'I'm sorry, Mr Feeks, but that's all I can tell you for now. As you say, I'll need to speak to your son. But you don't have to worry.'

He stood frowning but finally gave in with a shrug. 'Okay, but whatever it is, go easy on the boy, will you? He's a good lad.'

'We'll take it very easy. Mr Feeks, when we arrived, you said you'd told our people we'd be wasting our time coming to your door. Who did you think we were? Are you getting hassled?'

'Ach. It's nothing. Nothing I can't handle anyway.'

Narey heard more behind the dismissive words. 'It doesn't quite sound like nothing. You looked worried when you saw us. Who did you think we were?'

'Och it's just some crowd who want to move me out. But I'm going nowhere and I've told them that. Told them there was no point coming round trying to change my mind. I'm a stubborn old sod.'

'Who are they?'

'Developers, I suppose you'd call them. Got all these big plans. Going to make the East End the new

West End or some bollocks like that. It's a lot of nonsense.'

Narey asked the question just in case. 'They're not called Saturn Property, are they?'

'Eh? No. Never heard of them. This lot are called Orient Development. Bunch of chancers, if you ask me.'

'How many of you are left here, Mr Feeks?'

'Two houses. The McCanns left last week so that leaves the Meiklejohns at 4c and me. Tam Meiklejohn says he's chucking it and taking the family away. So it will just be me.'

'It's not going to be much fun for you if that happens.'

'I'll not be the first. A pal of mine knew a guy called Jamal. He was the last resident of the Red Road flats. He was an asylum seeker, poor bugger. They were knocking the flats down but he was going to get deported if he left his house so he refused to go. For four months. He was the only person in his entire block and they were demolishing the other towers round about him. The guy was terrified. Living alone on the fourteenth floor all that time. Well if he could do it then so can I. I'm only on the second floor. Should be a doddle.'

'But they knocked the Red Road flats down.'

'Eventually. I'm going nowhere though. This was the first house my wife and I had together, bless her soul. My laddie was brought up here. I still think it's his home even if he doesn't. There's too many memories for me to leave it. I'm staying.'

'Stick to your guns, Mr Feeks. But watch yourself, okay? And if the hassling goes over the top then you call us.'

He gave a throaty laugh. 'Hen, I used to be a welder. Made cups of tea with a blowtorch and worked with guys who knocked rivets in with their foreheads. I'm not going to get bothered by some guys in pinstripe suits. You just do me a favour and look after that boy of mine. Okay?'

'I will, Mr Feeks. Promise.'

Giannandrea answered immediately.

'Rico, I've got something I want you to look into. A company called Orient Development. They're working on a project in the East End around Adelaide Street. Jacko might know about them.'

'Sure. What am I looking for?'

'Find out if they're full of Eastern promise.'

Chapter 40

Her phone rang when she and Toshney were driving back to the station. It was Winter.

'Hi. Listen, I know you're busy but could you find some time this afternoon?'

She glanced at Toshney but he had his eyes dutifully glued to the road. He'd been warned more than once for listening to her conversations and maybe he'd finally learned a lesson.

'Busy's an understatement. Some time for what?'

'Well not the same thing as last night, if that's what you were thinking. Although if you can find time for that too then I'm more than willing.'

She kept her voice level and didn't indulge in the flirting by her tone. 'Well that would be good and we should schedule that as soon as possible but it won't be this afternoon. What was it you wanted time for though?'

'Your dad. Could you get over to the care home for about three o'clock?'

'*My dad?*' She forgot Toshney instantly. 'What's wrong?'

'Nothing. Sorry, didn't mean to alarm you. Nothing's wrong, honestly, but it's still important. Can you make it?'

'Why can't you tell me what it is? I'm not in the mood for guessing.'

'I'm not asking you to guess. There's nothing wrong and I think you'll want to see this. Please.'

'Okay, okay. I'll be there.'

When she pulled into the car park of the nursing home, having deposited Toshney at the station, she saw that Winter's car was already there. She looked to the front door and instead of the usual depressing sight of it staring back at her, he was standing there waving and with a smile on his face.

She had no idea what was going on and that wasn't the way she liked it. Surprises didn't impress her as a rule and even less so when it involved her dad. She preferred to know what was coming despite or perhaps because of his condition meaning that wasn't often possible.

'Right, what's going on? You know what I'm in the middle of. This better be good.'

He slid an arm round her waist, kissed her and pulled her close.

'I think it will be. Just come and see. But be quiet, okay? It will be better if your dad doesn't know you're here just yet.'

297

They walked down the corridor together, his arm round her and easing some of her misgivings. As they neared the door to her dad's room, he slowed and made her do the same. The door was open and she could hear voices coming from inside, one of them unmistakably her dad's.

Winter put a finger to his lips and an arm round her shoulder to guide her into the open doorway. Her eyes widened to see her dad sitting upright in the chair by his bed, quite animated and deep in conversation with a man in his sixties she didn't recognize. Behind the stranger sat Tony's uncle Danny.

'I was *there*,' her dad was saying as if proving a point. 'Me and my brother and our pal Bill. You scored and you would have had another couple but that big goalkeeper of theirs made some cracking saves. Big baldy fella.'

'Gordy Gillespie. He was a good goalie. Nice bloke as well. We played together at Morton for a season.'

'Did you? I don't remember that.'

The stranger laughed. 'Typical supporter. You only remember us when we played for your team.'

'Aye, right enough,' her dad laughed. 'I always had those blue-tinted glasses on. Always the Rangers for me.'

'Who *is* that?' Narey whispered to Winter. She had a smile spread across her face though. 'What's going on?'

He nudged her back from the doorway and whispered a reply. 'The guy is Bobby McDonald. He used to play centre-forward for Rangers and your dad and your uncle Brian used to watch him from the terraces at Ibrox. He was your dad's favourite player.'

'Right . . . So what the hell is he . . . what is he *doing* here?'

Winter grinned. 'He's been to see your dad a couple of times now. There's a scheme called Football Memories run by Alzheimer's Scotland. The idea is to stimulate memories by talking about football. I read about it online and thought it might work for your dad. I didn't want to say anything and get your hopes up but it seems to be helping.'

'He's like a different person. But how did you get the player to come in? Wait, don't tell me, Uncle Danny knows him.'

'Of course. Come on, let's go in.'

They walked into the room and her dad looked up at the sound of their footsteps.

'Rachel! Come in, come in. I need to introduce you. This . . . is Bobby McDonald. The prince of poachers. He played for the Rangers. Bobby, this is my wee girl Rachel.'

They all sat, Narey with one hand holding her dad's and the other squeezing tight on Winter's, chatting like it was yesterday – which it was.

She leaned in on her dad while he was in full foot-balling flow and kissed him on the cheek then turned her head to do the same to Winter.

'This is amazing. Thank you for doing this.'

'Shush. You don't have to thank me. Seeing that silly smile on your face is thanks enough.'

She kissed him again and turned back to listen to talk of a Cup Final when her dad had managed to get the afternoon off work and got home drunk as a lord. For an hour, it was the late 1970s and she was a girl and her dad was her hero and all was well. Murders and bogeymen were kept at bay and the real world could wait till tomorrow.

Chapter 41

Remy had sat with the laptop in front of him for a full hour without hitting a single key other than to wake the computer when it began to snooze. He'd thought a lot in that time but hadn't actually done anything. It struck him that the same could be said of his entire life.

The home page of the OtherWorld forum sat waiting patiently for him to say hello but he'd shied away from reintroducing himself. Instead he just sat and stared like the awkward, gawky teenager he'd been since he was eight. So much he wanted to say but didn't dare.

He'd read that you don't regret the things you have done but the things you haven't done. There was some truth in that, right enough. If he made a list then top would be failing to ask Gabby out. Properly, that is. Second would be not going to university but that was different. He had to make a choice and he did what he had to do. After that? He wished he'd gone to Machu

Picchu, the ancient Incan site in Peru. Or the great Pyramid of Giza, the only one of the seven wonders of the ancient world still standing. There was smaller stuff too. Bigger in some senses. He'd never told his dad that he loved him. Because you just don't, right? Not if you come from Glasgow you don't. He'd never flown in a helicopter, given blood, owned a dog or drunk real champagne. Regrets, he had a few.

But to say you don't regret the things you *have* done ... well, that just wasn't true. He still mourned the day he wet himself in Miss Johnson's class aged six. He bitterly regretted the day he ever thought it was a good idea to try to grow a moustache aged twenty-one. He hated himself for being in the library the night his mother died from cancer. And he wished he'd never walked down the Molendinar Burn.

Maybe it wasn't about regrets at all. There was nothing you could do about those other than choose to live with them or not. You could, maybe, possibly, avoid future regrets though. By not *not* doing the thing. By doing it and to hell with the consequences.

After that hour of thinking and no typing, he had finally worked out what he was going to write. It wasn't much, just a few lines, but he'd convinced himself they were what they had to be. What he hadn't decided, not quite, was whether he had the guts to send them.

He was nearly there though. One last push. He forced himself to think about why he had to do it, not why he shouldn't. His fingers fretted over the keyboard and got as far as creating a blank message ready to be filled then hopefully dispatched to the two recipients he had in mind.

He knew it was about his dad, about his mother, about Gabby, about himself. It was about the feel of the dead guy's body against his. About being a loser his entire life and wanting, aching, to change that. It was about doing the right thing. About doing something. He could stay in the same crappy job, live in the same crappy flat, live the same crappy life and wait till it was time to die or he could do something. It was about him.

He typed. He pressed enter.

Fuck. He'd done it now.

Chapter 42

Saturday morning

Narey had made up her mind to have another chat with Douglas Cairns. The suggestion from his wife's friend that not only was Jennifer having an affair but that Cairns knew about it made him interesting again. An angry husband and an unfaithful wife made for motivation. He was certainly worth another visit and she wasn't in the mood to care whether he minded or not.

She made her way to his firm's offices, and again unannounced pushed through the double doors. The assistant, Chloe, rose to meet her and clearly remembered who she was.

'Are you here to see Mr Cairns? He's in.' Talk of what happened to his wife was clearly the only story in town for the staff.

Narey told her she was and the girl led her to Cairns' inner office.

Douglas Cairns didn't seem exactly overjoyed to see her but was polite nevertheless. Dressed in a black suit with a black T-shirt underneath, he rose from his black-leather sofa like a man escaping from a tunnel and asked if he could have anything brought for her.

'A glass of water, please.'

'Still or sparkling?'

'Still.'

Cairns nodded and Chloe left to return just moments later with a decanter of water and two crystal tumblers. Cairns nodded again and the girl left. Narey waited until she had closed the door behind her before she spoke.

'Thanks for seeing me, Mr Cairns. I realize this is a difficult time for you.'

'That's an understatement. Do you have any news on the investigation?'

'We're making progress. There's a couple of definite leads we're looking at.'

Cairns wasn't giving much away, no matter how closely she studied him. There was a nervous air about him but that was hardly surprising given the circumstances.

'What are they?'

'Well we've spoken to some of your wife's friends to establish a picture of her movements. That's opened some avenues we're exploring now.'

She was being deliberately vague, teasing a reaction out of him. His mouth twitched: he was suitably exasperated.

'*And?*'

'Mr Cairns, one of the people we've spoken to has suggested that your wife may have been having an affair. Do you know if that is correct?'

He reacted this time okay. His eyes widened, either in shock at what she'd said or that she'd said it. His face darkened and his lip curled in anger.

'How dare you come here and ask me that at a time like this?'

'I know this must be upsetting, sir, and I'm sorry for that. But it is something I have to ask. Was Jennifer having an affair?'

Suddenly, Cairns was on his feet and shouting. 'Who told you that?'

Narey remained calm. 'Who told me isn't what's important. I'd like to establish if it was the case and if you were aware of it.'

'Don't fucking tell me what isn't important.' Cairns plucked the glass of water from the table and hurled it across the room where it smashed against the Perspex wall. An ugly crack appeared in the black frosted screen and, beyond it, Narey could see shadow figures standing up to see what had happened.

Cairns' mouth was hanging open, as if he didn't believe that he'd actually done it. He was shaking with anger or nerves. 'Get out of my office!'

'Sit down, please, Mr Cairns.' She kept her voice as low and as composed as possible.

'Get out!'

The door opened and Cairns' partner David

McCormack hurried inside looking suitably anxious. He stared at the hairline in the frosting and the shattered glass on the carpeted floor.

'Douglas? What the hell's going on? Are you okay?'

Cairns shot him a furious glance, ready to take his anger out on anyone. 'Yes, I'm okay! I'm just . . . just—'

'What is all this?' McCormack waved a hand at the broken glass.

'I'm asking Mr Cairns some questions relating to his wife's death.'

He stared at her, as if not making sense of it. 'Does this really have to be done now? I'd think Douglas has been through enough.'

'I sympathize with that, Mr McCormack, but I have a job to do. And sometimes, like now, that means asking difficult questions. I'm sure we all want to find out what happened to Mrs Cairns. If you could leave us, please, then I can get on with trying to do that.'

The man looked between Narey and Cairns, clearly unhappy at the situation and unwilling to leave.

'If you could close the door behind you, please, sir. I won't keep Mr Cairns any longer than necessary.'

There was a brief stand-off while the two men considered their positions but finally some of the air and defiance went out of Cairns. He nodded at his colleague that it was all right and he should go.

'Okay.' McCormack didn't seem happy at all. 'But I'll be outside. Call me if you need me, Douglas. And Detective Inspector, I'd appreciate it if you remembered that Douglas has just lost his wife.'

'It's why I'm here, Mr McCormack. You can leave us now.'

The man glared but said nothing. He closed the door and left them alone.

Cairns was dragging his hand through his long, greying hair and looking decidedly agitated. 'Okay, ask me your question.'

'Please sit down, Mr Cairns.'

He resisted like a sulky teenager but then parked himself angrily back on the leather sofa.

Narey nodded, satisfied. 'Was your wife having an affair, Mr Cairns?'

His jaw clenched and he took in a lungful of air. 'I think so, yes.'

'How sure are you of that?'

The question made him scowl. 'I'm not *sure*. I just . . . I had my suspicions. I want to know who told you that she was. Was it that bitch Carrie Thomson?'

'I can only repeat what I asked you. It isn't important who told me. I'm more interested in whether it was true and what you knew of it.'

'Why don't you tell me what you've been told?'

'Okay, I will. I am told that your wife had an affair once before. And that she was having an affair at the time she was killed. Does that fit with what you know?'

Cairns gripped the side of the sofa, clawing at the leather with his fingers, and she thought he was going to push to his feet again. He was clearly furious.

'I told you. I didn't *know*. I suspected.'

'Okay, what made you suspect?'

He huffed irritably. 'She was out a lot, vague about where she was, dressed up to the nines. She'd be putting her mobile away when I came into the room. There was something *different* about the way she was acting.'

Narey nodded, making a show of taking it in. 'The person who told me that Jennifer was having an affair also said that you were aware of it. That you *knew*.'

'I already told you—'

'Okay, if you suspected, was there anyone in particular you suspected your wife was seeing?'

This time he did stand up. 'This interview is over. You can leave now.'

'I'd like to ask you a few more questions, Mr Cairns. I'm not—'

'*Get out!*'

His shout brought McCormack back into the room at the double. 'What's going on? Douglas, are you okay?'

'No I'm not. This . . . this woman—'

'Right, I think you should leave. This is harassment. Unless you've got some kind of warrant, you need to go now. The man's wife has just died.'

'Murdered.'

'What?'

'Mr Cairns' wife has been murdered. I think it's important that we remember the difference.'

'Get out! Get out before I throw you out.'

'I seriously suggest you do not attempt to do that, Mr Cairns. But there's little to be gained from taking this any further today so I will go. We can take this up another time.'

'Chloe!' It was McCormack's turn to shout. Moments later, the young, black-clad woman reappeared looking quite startled. 'Chloe, show this lady out, please.'

'Thank you, Mr McCormack, but I'm no lady. And I can find my own way out. Mr Cairns, I apologize for any distress this has caused you but murder investigations work that way sometimes. And this one isn't over.'

Chapter 43

Saturday evening

Winter had spent a long, frustrating day chasing sirens but with his mind most definitely elsewhere. None of it had been the sort of thing to get his pulse racing. A break-in at an off-licence, the bruised remains of a mugging and the burned-out shell of a stolen Ford Focus. If the day had had a flavour it would have been vanilla.

The job was beginning to feel like work and he didn't like it that way. He'd never wanted routine, never been interested in any job that was done by the numbers or meant drowning in bureaucracy. Whether he'd changed or the job had, that's how it seemed now. Frame a shot, push a button, fill in a form, go home, start again. It wasn't enough.

He'd just completed the going-home part of his day, albeit that he was still on call, and was ready for something more. The something that had never been more than a thought away the whole time he'd been on the clock. Euan Hepburn. Jennifer Cairns. The Molendinar and the Odeon. Remy Feeks. Rachel.

He was worried, perhaps even scared. He'd been taking a risk from the moment he'd got involved in this but the stakes were getting higher. It wasn't a game, wasn't a step into a building where he could back out if he felt unsafe. He was in deep and the door behind him had been locked.

There had been a couple of times he'd felt someone was following him: Friday as he went home after work, and the night before as he'd left Oran Mor. Nothing he could be certain about, just shadows that were there and then weren't. Footsteps that stopped with his, a feeling that he couldn't shift. He'd have put it down to paranoia but that was defined as irrational and there was good reason to think he really had put himself in danger.

Not just him, Remy too. Winter worried for the kid even more than himself. He'd take his own chances if he had to but Feeks didn't seem to be able to look after himself. That was why he'd made the anonymous call to the station, knowing that Rachel would know what to do, knowing she was much more capable of looking after Remy than he was.

Rachel. The biggest risk of all. His greatest fear.

When your mind was as messed up as his was then even doing something good could leave you confused as to why you did it. Like the day before when he'd taken her to the nursing home to see her dad with the old Rangers player. Had he done that because it was the right thing to do, because he loved her, or because he was guilty of betraying her by interfering with the case?

He fired up his laptop and went straight to OtherWorld. There really was no going back so there was nowhere else to go. He had to sort this. Warn the kid to stay out of it, maybe tackle the others he was suspicious of. Something, anything, risky or not.

The moment he'd logged in and the home page had built, he saw that he had a message in his inbox. He went straight there, opening it up as quickly as his fingers could fly.

The subject field contained just one word. *URGENT.*

He took it all in at once. The sender was *Magellan93.* It was Remy's user name. The message was opened in an instant.

He read it twice, blood pumping. Then read it again.

I know more about what happened in the Molendinar than I said. I know why you're asking and if I'm right then it's about the Odeon too. Can't say more on here, too risky.

Meet me at the Gray Dunn building in Kinning Park. The old biscuit factory. Saturday night at seven. I'll tell you all you need to know.

The message had been sent the night before and it was already nearly six. This meeting, this whatever the hell it was, was a little over an hour away.

What the hell was Remy up to? Why the cloak and dagger routine? The Gray Dunn factory was right up the boy's street though. Winter had never been there but knew of it – an urbexer's paradise, all maze and mystery, secluded and vulnerable. It was the last place either he or Remy should be going. The one thing it wasn't was safe.

Why couldn't he just have told him in the message? Why was it too risky to tell him? Did Remy think OtherWorld private messages were being hacked? Winter had to wonder who'd be capable of doing that. And he really had to wonder how it could be more risky than pitching up in an isolated ruin like the factory.

No matter, his choice was simple. Go now and meet him or don't. And that was no choice at all. He had to go.

Chapter 44

Carrie Thomson didn't look entirely pleased to see Narey standing on her doorstep for the second time. She looked hard at her for a while before nodding silently, mouth tight, and standing back to let her inside.

The woman closed the door behind her then stood with her back to it, her arms folded across her chest and an expression made of ice on her face.

'I've had two phone calls from Douglas Cairns, bawling and shouting and accusing me of spreading rumours about his wife. I assume I have you to thank for that.'

'I didn't mention any names to him. So if he thought it was you then he guessed. It didn't come from me.'

Thomson turned her head and smiled sarcastically. 'Well he seemed pretty fucking sure when he rang and called me an absolute bitch.'

'I think it might be better if we sit down and talk about this calmly.'

'Well I don't. I'm happy talking about it right here. Why did he think I'd told you?'

Narey wasn't for giving the woman much room or sympathy. 'Perhaps because you *did* tell me. I refused to tell him where my information had come from. I didn't tell him if it was a man or a woman. He leaped to that conclusion all by himself.'

Thomson simmered, trying to decide whether to believe her. 'Well he called me a few choice names, including a whore. Said that I'd encouraged Jen to sleep around because that's what I was doing myself. He demanded to know who it was that she was fucking. His words, not mine.'

'And what did you tell him?'

'Well I told him that it wasn't me who gave you the information. Although I'd have been as well saving my breath. I told him I didn't know who she was seeing. Which of course he jumped on as confirmation that I knew she was seeing *someone*. I hung up on him but he called back about five minutes later.'

'What did he say that time?'

'He was shouting. I think he'd been drinking. He said something along the lines of how he'd known all along. He called Jen some vile names too. I told him to shut up and get off the phone. He went on and on, asking me who it was. He started asking if it was the car salesman. He kept saying, "Was it the fucking car salesman again? I'll kill him if it was." So he must have known about Phil Traynor.'

'He said he'd *kill* him?'

She shrugged. 'Figure of speech, I guess, but yes, he did.'

'Did you tell him anything?'

'No. Nothing. I told him to sober up and that I was hanging up and taking the phone off the hook. Which I did.'

'Okay. Well I'm going to ask you some of the same questions. We've spoken to Phil Traynor and we're satisfied that he hadn't seen Jen in over a year. Do you have *any* idea of who it was she was seeing?'

Thomson looked somewhere between fury and tears. 'We've been through this! I've told you all that I know. She only ever called him The Man. It was this big secret. She shut me out of it for whatever reason. Believe me, I've wracked my brains and there's nothing I can tell you or Douglas.'

Narey nodded, believing her. 'Okay, but if you *do* think of something, please tell me before you tell Mr Cairns. Okay?'

'*Okay*. I'll be happy if I never have to speak to Douglas again.'

She then threw Narey a look which left no doubt that the same thing applied to her too.

Chapter 45

Even from the other side of Stanley Street, in the industrial warren of Kinning Park, Winter could hear traffic roaring by on the M8. Only the ruins of the biscuit factory stood between him and fifteen lanes of motorway. It felt strange, the silence of redundancy all around him in complete contrast to what was beyond the building.

He knew a bit about the place even though he'd never been inside. There had been a biscuit factory on this site since the mid-1800s. It was eventually taken over by Rowntree's and they churned out millions of Blue Ribands, caramel wafers and custard creams until the company went bust in 2001. The place had been shut since then and he'd heard it was in a sorry state. He'd soon find out.

He'd taken the subway to Kinning Park and made his way through the industrial estate on foot. There were one or two people about but he kept his head down and avoided eye contact with anyone. Ten minutes later, he could see the motorway elevated on the horizon and a big building on his left. A succession of arched windows on the ground floor were boarded up and the frontage was fenced off. *Danger Keep Out*, read the sign on the fencing. Sure thing. He lifted, moved, breathed in and squeezed through.

He was inside and half an hour early. He wanted to scout the building out, maybe find a good place to stand where he could watch Remy come in. See before he was seen.

Immediately, he saw that was going to be easier said than done. The factory was enormous, six storeys high, a desolate labyrinth of a place that would have made a good set for a post-apocalyptic movie. It was graffiti central too. Every wall seemed to have been scrawled over with names or drawings. It was a huge, tangled mess.

He found himself standing in a central courtyard area with the building rising high above and around him on three sides; a one-storey building behind him let the rush-hour sounds of the motorway flood in. It was like standing in the worst council housing estate imaginable; somewhere no cop would be crazy enough to come no matter how much trouble was reported. Rubbish and rubble were strewn everywhere, so much so that he could hardly find a spot to stand. There was brick and concrete, broken chairs, twisted metal frames and discarded trolleys. Above him in the darkness, the building glowered down like it was ready to eat him.

Daylight had slipped away but he could still see that almost all the windows on the floors above had been smashed. An army of people could have been standing behind the broken panes and he'd have been none the wiser. He felt small and vulnerable standing down there. He needed to get up higher and out of sight.

The concrete stairs corkscrewed up, past flaking walls painted in battleship grey. He got off on the first level and wandered into a vast, cavernous room with bare concrete floors, a forest of support pillars as far as the eye could see. The floor was damp and cracked in places and nothing seemed particularly safe.

The ceiling felt low even though it wasn't, dirty white-painted girders over his head squeezing down on him and reducing the feeling of space. He followed the beam of his torch as the room stretched on forever, dotted with empty aerosol cans, broken glass and pieces of wood. He came across an old wooden writing desk and he counted three large Avery weighing machines, two of them tipped onto their sides.

Finally, the level came to an end and he climbed once more, skipping the second floor and making for the top. On the way up, he passed a couple of open lift shafts and couldn't help but stare down into the gloom. The brick walls dropped straight down away from him, rusting metal rungs descending to the bottom.

The top floor was the same dark concrete that had presumably once been covered in linoleum or carpet. Now cabling snaked across it and loose stones made an untidy line down the middle. Girders ran above his head here too but there was no ceiling and the room rose up past them to the underside of the roof. Further on, a white computer workstation and chair sat isolated in the middle of the room, a monitor perched precariously on the top shelf.

He turned a corner and picked his way through a minefield of half-bricks, his way barely lit by his torch. Stepping in water, he stopped and strobed the area in front of him and saw it was flooded, dotted with discarded metal and planks of wood. He shone the beam on the wall ahead and stepped back. What the hell?

Inching warily forward into the puddle, he cast his torch across the wall and a vicious alien face with sharp teeth appeared out of the gloom. It had large green eyes, pointed ears, dark green scaly skin and drooling jaws. As graffiti went, it was pretty scary in the dark. Scarier than he needed right now.

He moved away from it, eager to get onto the roof and find himself a viewing spot. He breathed what he realized was a sigh of relief when he got into the open air again and stood facing out with his back flat to the wall, the brick shrouding him in darkness and the M8 in front of him. It was stirring to see so many cars rush past, so near and yet no one aware that he was there.

A long-forgotten feeling came back to him. The notion that if he was still enough for long enough then he could become part of the structure. Building and bones and bricks and blood. The factory was part of the city and so was he. It wasn't easy to separate the people from the place.

It was like the thundering motorway before him. It ran through the city like an artery, pulsing night and day, cutting east to west on the northern fringes then plunging south like a dagger into its heart. The motorway was a stranger to the old factory, a stranger it saw every day. That's the way it was when a city constantly reinvented itself without moral planning permission.

He shook himself out of it and stepped away from the wall, walking round until he could look down from the roof into the central courtyard. It was pitch black and he couldn't see the ground below, reluctant to use his torch for fear of giving himself away just yet.

Was that something or someone moving down there? A darker shadow from the left corner. It was under the eaves now and he couldn't be sure what he'd seen. There was a crash of metal and the noise made him jump. He stood still and listened but could hear nothing.

Another crash. Like metal being thrown onto the concrete. Or the other way round. It was harsh and reverberated through the darkness, even cutting through the noise from the M8. This noise was further to the right, near the stairs. And closer. Then another noise, quieter but way to the left. Two people? Or one moving very quickly?

Suddenly, it all seemed like a bad idea. He didn't even know where exactly in the vast building he was going to meet Remy, even if he was really sure that's who the message had come from. Shit, this was stupid. The building seemed even more claustrophobic than it was just a few moments before. He had to make a decision, to stay or go.

There were more noises below, more movement. Maybe the decision was being taken out of his hands. He just had to calm the fuck down. This was what he was here for, to meet the guy and get the information he needed.

Someone screamed. A floor or two below. It stopped almost as soon as it had started. He couldn't be sure but . . . there it was again. Longer this time. The sound cut through the night like a samurai sword.

Decision made. He was going back down there. He was shaking, balling his left hand into a fist as he walked, the torch in his right. Breathing fast, almost as fast as his heart was pumping. He began down the stairs warily, no idea what was round the next bend, his left leg leading the way but ready to brace and either fight or flee.

There was another noise. Something heavy crashing. It sounded like . . . his mind told him it was like a body hitting a concrete floor but then that wasn't a noise he'd ever heard before. He reached the second floor and passed one of the open lift shafts. He'd gone a full pace beyond the shaft when an inner voice told him to go back and look in it. Cursing himself, he turned.

He lowered the torch over the edge and sent a beam down the walls towards the bottom of the well. The circle of light began to lose its shape as it went but it still picked out the pale brick and then, finally, lit up the floor. There was a dark shape down there that was separate from the bits of rubbish he'd seen previously. Was it even the same shaft that he'd looked down before? He traced the outline of the object with the torchlight. It was square. Not body-shaped. He followed the outline again to be sure that it wasn't just wishful thinking but no, it was a table top or a suitcase or a box. It was something, anything, that wasn't a body. He breathed out hard and ran his free hand through his hair.

That's when he felt the pain in his lower back. Air rushed out of him and he buckled at the knees, the torch dropping from his hand. The realization that he had been struck hard with something extremely solid dawned on him only as he was falling. The pain became a fire that spread across his back and he had no breath with which to douse it. His legs had gone too, turned into useless rubbery things that couldn't hold him up.

He became aware, through the soup that clogged his brain, that someone was standing over him. Remy? Surely not. He saw the toe of a black boot just inches from his eyes and, beside it, something metallic scraped the ground. He'd got as far as working out that the metal object had been responsible for putting him on the ground when the thing disappeared from sight. Something inside told him to move and he curled and rolled, throwing an arm up for protection.

A split second later that arm caught a glancing blow that still managed to send pain shooting through him.

It had probably saved him though and he rolled again, away from the black boots and the metal pole. There was a clang against the concrete that rang in his ears, missing him by inches. He could hear heavy breathing above him and a muttered 'Fuck' as his assailant regretted his failure.

Winter rolled as fast as he could, desperately trying to save himself. It wasn't quite fast enough as another dull blow caught him on the side, pain flooding his bones and electrifying his senses. He rolled again and heard another miss. To his right he saw the top of the stairwell just a few feet away and made for it – no time to calculate whether it was a good idea or not. He spun across the floor until it fell away beneath him and the spiral of concrete steps took over. He dropped fast and awkwardly, painfully, every edge of step chastising him.

Footsteps sounded as the world tumbled, the noise coming at him as if filtered through a washing machine; it was impossible to tell if they were gaining on him or not. He worried more about tucking his head in and not bashing his brains out.

His initial spill had more or less run its own course but he forced it on, half falling, half jumping, further down the stairs until he hit the landing below. He immediately sprawled in the direction of some half-bricks that were strewn there and began hurling them one after the other at the foot of the stairwell. Not with any real hope of hitting anyone but more as a signal of intent, buying himself time to recover.

It seemed to have worked as no one appeared round the corner after him. Maybe the guy was less keen on a fight when Winter could see him coming. He stood there on shaking legs with an enormous pain in his lower back, his eyes at once on the stairs but also scouring the landing for a weapon. He saw a plank of wood and grabbed that in one hand and a fist of brick in the other.

He held firm, trying to shut out the pain, listening and waiting, ready to fight. Nothing came. No sound from above, none below. All he could hear was the background music of the motorway and the rush of blood in his ears. He waited and waited but his attacker, whoever he was, had either gone or was standing as still as Winter.

It was time to move. Down the stairs and out. The ache in his back was excruciating, dull and debilitating, but he had to get out of there.

He took the steps two at a time, reaching ground level to see the courtyard completely swallowed up by the dark. The walls loomed above and crowded in on him like prison guards. He stopped to listen, for screams, for movement, for sounds of metal. Still nothing.

He went to the middle of the courtyard, his feet stumbling on stone and wood. Then, abruptly, on something softer but still solid. He stopped immediately. Not daring to move. He cautiously put down the wood and the brick and wished that he still had the torch he'd dropped when he was hit. He reached into his back pocket, thankful to see that his mobile phone was still intact, and switched on the flashlight.

The beam of light was thin but strong and yet it trembled as he swung it round to his feet. At once he saw a hand, an arm, blood. He stepped back quickly, tripping over a brick and following it to the ground. The phone slipped from his grasp and he scrambled to pick it up.

On his knees, he could see the body stretched out unmoving. He shone the flashlight on it again and saw it was a man lying on his back, something long and thin driven through his chest. Winter's mouth was hanging open and he could only stare, hardly believing the horror of what he was seeing. He got to his feet and inched closer, seeing the iron spike spearing the man just below the ribcage, seeing his eyes wide open, his head slumped to the side. He was so pale and skinny. So young.

Remy. Remy Feeks.

Chapter 46

Something stirred in Winter's stomach and made a beeline for his throat and he had to cover his mouth and gag it down. He wanted to vomit, to cry, to scream, to run. He was the veteran of a couple of hundred dead bodies but this was different. Somehow, this was his fault.

He stared and saw the young guy, speared most probably with the same kind of railing that someone had used to strike Winter on the back. The aborted scream he'd heard earlier: *that* had been Remy. He'd been murdered and Winter was to have been next. All he could do was stare.

Stare and think. He saw Remy but thought of Euan Hepburn's decaying corpse in the Molendinar. It was his fault that Euan had been there on his own, his fault that Remy was lying dead. Winter was drowning in a pool of shock and guilt.

Maybe that's why he didn't hear the sirens at first.

By the time he was aware of them, he knew they'd been in earshot for longer. His head came up and he took it in slowly, his feet still glued to the spot he stood on. Police cars. Coming closer.

He ran to the lower back building. Lower but still maybe thirty feet high. The words *ACOS!* And *ALEK!* were sprayed in large white lettering near the top and he knew someone had managed to get up there to do it. Past the wall there was a pile of scrap and above it a second wall that might just let him scramble to the top of the first. He leaped onto a long piece of wood propped against the wall, falling back and trying again, driven on by the now deafening sirens. Succeeding this time, and from there onto a mess of loose metal that just about bore his weight. He stretched and jumped and clawed to the top of the wall, hauling himself up.

He picked his way over the flat roof, then a corrugated ridge behind. There was only a wide grass verge and a drop into the dark separating him from the motorway, cars still streaming along it. The only way out was straight down but in this light he had no idea how far it was. He'd no option. He turned briefly to face the biscuit factory before kneeling on top of the wall and slipping over the side where he held on with both hands. Do it. He let go and fell, the side of his face just avoiding the brick wall as he dropped. Falling until landing on soft grass and rolling head over heels towards the sounds of cars.

The sirens and the factory were on one side of him,

the M8 on the other. It made for an easy but crazy choice. He got to his feet, finding an ache in his right leg that almost matched the one in his back, and scanned the lanes in front of him. The traffic had thinned out a bit but was still scarily busy. He pulled up the hood on his fleece till it covered as much of his head and face as possible then waited, swallowed hard, and ran. He was halfway, still alive, still hurting, still scared. He halted then ran again. Into the middle and climbing over the barrier. Drivers were blasting their horns furiously but a gap came and he hurtled into the traffic once more, not daring to look until he made it across.

He was sweating hard, his back soaking, as he clambered over a wire-mesh fence to the other side. From there it was easy, down an embankment and onto a quiet tree-lined street on the farside of the industrial estate. He knew Shields Road subway was on that side, somewhere to his left, and he headed for it as quickly as his injuries would let him.

Chapter 47

The fleece was ditched in a bush just before the subway station and he managed to walk in as straight and unflustered as he could. On the outside at least. Inside, his guts were churning.

On the platform it was all he could do not to look at the cameras. He knew they were up there, following his every move. Instead, he stared at his feet or at the far wall, urging the train to arrive and get him out of there. When it did he got inside, found a corner seat and studied an advert above the window, avoiding all eye contact and trying not to picture Remy Feeks' broken body.

The kid had been caught in the middle of something he couldn't survive. Winter was sure that Remy had done nothing more than explore the Molendinar and find Euan Hepburn's body. He was the witness who became the victim.

Now Remy Feeks was lying in the rubble of the

factory with a railing stuck through his chest. His skinny frame was punctured and his freckled face was as grey as a gravestone. Winter was shaking with guilt and anger and fear, wanting to shout and punch and run.

He had to hide his hands so that people couldn't see them trembling. He wedged them under himself, trapping them there so they couldn't give him away. It must have been all over his face though. And if anyone could see the other side of his eyes then they'd see the face of the boy who had been in the wrong place at the wrong time.

Winter was on the inner circle, going anti-clockwise on the Clockwork Orange and turning back on himself to where he'd come from. If he could have turned back time as easily then he would have. He had five stops till Cowcaddens, five stops to pull himself together and make a plan. When he got out and within range of a phone signal then he was sure there would be a missed call waiting for him. Telling him what he already knew. Dead body at the old biscuit factory. Get there now.

Except he couldn't go like this. He had to sort himself. Get a change of clothes and a new head. He had to be able to go in there and do a professional job without stinking of sweat and fear. Without giving himself away in two minutes flat.

Of course, it might not even be as simple as that. He had no idea what they'd seen or what they knew. Someone had obviously called them, most probably the someone who had killed Remy and had tried to do the same to him. Had the bastard passed his name on to the cops? Had the cameras seen him arrive or leave? He knew nothing and didn't like it being that way.

Shit, where was the subway train now? Stops had passed and he hadn't noticed. He looked up and saw the carriage was pretty busy, late-evening shoppers or people heading home. Maybe the police were already checking the stations, looking for a man in a hooded fleece. He caught his reflection in the window opposite and saw himself staring back, wide-eyed and dishevelled.

Someone had killed Remy Feeks and tried to frame *him* for it. Kill him or frame him.

This was crazy. He couldn't get his head round it and was sick to his stomach. He felt hot and cold at the same time and was sure his breathing was in overdrive. He needed to slow down his thoughts, get them into some sort of order.

Then the train lurched to a stop, catching him by surprise and causing him to topple forward. His nerves were shot. The sign on the wall outside the carriage read *St Enoch's*. They were in the city centre, just two stops from Cowcaddens where he'd get off for Stewart Street cop shop and his car.

A woman got on and sat down directly opposite and he knew she was looking at him. He glanced up despite himself and saw a large, older lady wrapped up in a warm coat with a scarf round her neck. He was in just a T-shirt and in a state. No wonder she was staring.

He studied the floor and decided that, whatever else, he wasn't going to look up to see if she was still watching. Then he felt someone sit down beside him, the cushioned seat sinking.

'Are you okay, son?'

He didn't look up. Pretended he thought she was talking to someone else. Maybe she would go away. Please, go away. Give me peace and go away.

A hand rested on his arm and squeezed it gently. 'I hope you don't mind me sitting here, son. I'm not being nosy but you look like you need help. *Are* you okay?'

No, he wasn't. He wasn't okay at all. Despite himself, he looked up and saw that the woman's face was a picture of maternal concern. He must have seemed even worse than he thought. He had to pull himself together quickly.

He wondered how old she was. Early sixties maybe. Hair greying at the fringes and probably dyed elsewhere. Lines around her eyes and her mouth. His mother would be about the same age if she'd lived. His mother. He realized how long it had been since he'd thought about her. Probably three months, that long since her birthday.

'Have you got somewhere to go?'

Shit, did she think he was homeless?

'Yes. Look, thanks but I'm fine. Just been a long day.'

She nodded but didn't believe a word. The train lumbered into Buchanan Street station but she didn't budge. She sat there with her warm hand on his arm. It felt good. Wrong and utterly fucked up but good.

The train moved off again and he edged more upright in his seat. 'My stop next. I'm fine, honestly.'

'You take care of yourself. Do you need anything? Money?'

'What? No. I mean . . . no thanks. I don't. Look, I need to . . .'

He got to his feet, the movement making her hand slide off his arm. Looking down at her, he felt the need to say something but words didn't come out. His mouth started a conversation that his brain couldn't finish. The poor woman looked so worried for him. And maybe she was right.

He went to the doors and stared through the glass at the walls flashing by until they changed into the platform at Cowcaddens. He got off without looking back.

He had gone no more than a couple of paces from the subway entrance when his phone flashed at him. Two missed calls. He stood still for a few moments, gathering himself together then called one of them back, desperately keeping his voice as steady as he could.

'Hi. It's Tony Winter. Is that Siobhan? I missed a call.'

'Hi, Tony. Yes, I was trying to get hold of you. You've got a job in Kinning Park. A murder. They'll be waiting for you. Can you get there sharpish or should I tell the SOCOs to handle it?'

Maybe that would be the easiest thing. Leave it to them. But it would look odd. He'd never turn down a job like that. Never. He had to go.

'Siobhan, I'm only two minutes from my car. Tell them I'll be there in under ten minutes. And don't let them start without me.'

'Okay, Tony. Will do.'

'Thanks, Siobhan.'

'Um, Tony? Don't you want to know *where* in Kinning Park?'

Shit.

The good news was that there wasn't much traffic on the Kingston Bridge and he was able to hammer it from the station car park to the factory in just seven minutes. His camera gear was in the boot and so was a jacket that would cover his sweaty, dirt-streaked T-shirt.

He was no more than halfway along the adjoining street when he could see that the place wasn't as it had been on his first visit. The low whitewashed walls of the building on the corner were flashing blue. When he turned into the street itself, he was greeted by a small army of emergency vehicles and the hurried to and fro of organized chaos.

The car sealed off most of the noise and it was like gliding into a silent movie that was just waiting for him to star in it. He pulled up and parked, breathed deeply and opened the door to let the sound of the scene burst in. No going back now.

He hustled to the boot quickly, pulled the dark green waterproof over his T-shirt and grabbed his gear. The cop at the tape gave his ID the once-over and nodded him inside. There were footsteps clattering everywhere and urgent voices calling through the darkness. Beyond those were the edges of lights that would have led him to the actual scene if he hadn't already known just where to go.

The inner courtyard was less than a minute away. He had no idea who'd taken the call but hoped to hell it wasn't Rachel. That would mean more questions than he had answers to. Anyone, anyone but her.

He pushed his way into the light, dazzled by it and having to shield his eyes until they adjusted. At first all he could see were the lights themselves and the white suits that flitted through the glare. Shapes began to form but not before a voice called to him through the shimmer.

'Winter. Get your arse over here pronto. Come on, we've waited long enough.'

It was almost as bad as it being Rachel. It was DCI Denny Kelbie, one of the most carnaptious little shits ever to join the police force. Five foot five inches of perpetual malice and grudge. At his side was his regular DS, Jim Ferry, a lazy sod who had adopted his boss's antipathy to the world.

One thing though. Kelbie had called him by name and acted just the arsey way he normally would. If the call to the cops had mentioned Winter then Kelbie would have had him by the throat.

'Hurry up. Get this done and get out of my way.' Kelbie was always itching for a fight but this night, more than any other, Winter couldn't give him the satisfaction of one. He needed to protect himself.

'Yes, sir. Just let the dog see the rabbit.' He had to control himself, not let any of it show. Kelbie would be all over it if he even suspected Winter had something to hide. He didn't look the DCI in the eye, didn't dare, just brushed past him and took up position over the body. Kelbie was snapping away at him like a Jack Russell but Winter shut the words out, tried his best to shut *everything* out, and do what he always did.

Remy Feeks was colder now, paler too. The last traces of life had drained away in the time it had taken Winter to flee and return. He was *more* dead. The kid hadn't stood a chance. He'd been caught up in something that he wasn't equipped to deal with and it had killed him.

Winter managed to get his camera to his eye and forced his finger through the shutter release. He photographed Remy laid out in full, the iron railing through his chest, his head resting on a broken brick in an ugly concrete graveyard. The building had died years ago and now it had another ghost to walk with its own.

He looked so young, even younger than he had done in the Botanics or Oran Mor. His freckles stood out against the alabaster of his bloodless skin, making him look like a teenager. He had no right to be lying there dead. None whatsoever.

Winter focused on the cold edge of the railing where it entered the kid, seeing it pierce his shirt and rip his skin. Remy had been dead before the spike was hammered into him: that much was obvious from the lack of blood on his chest. The railing had been an afterthought, a statement.

The death blow had been to the head: a fierce wound on the right temple was testament to that. It had rattled his brains, a fatal blunt-force trauma. Most probably using the same railing that was stuck through him. There was another wound that had smashed his left cheek, leaving the bone shattered like eggshell. A swing to the killer's right then the same to the left. One stunning, one killing.

The boy's mouth hung open, mid-shout, mid-scream, mid-plea. Maybe he was just asking why. Why him. Why this. He was so skinny, all angles and ridges. It couldn't have been any sort of fair fight. Someone bigger and stronger, armed with the iron railing and a hunger to kill. Winter knew he should have done something to stop it before it got to this.

A pair of black shoes with thick heels stepped into the shot beside Remy's head. They tapped impatiently and there was no doubt who they belonged to. Winter let the camera drift up with his eyes, the shutter hammering as he went, photographing Kelbie until he caught the twisted impatience on the DCI's face. When he'd done so, he switched his gaze and his lens back to Remy, saying nothing. He knew Kelbie was mouthing off at him, spitting out words furiously, but he didn't hear and didn't care. He was doing his job the best he could. He owed that to Remy Feeks.

When he was done, he backed away from the body and stood to take the inevitable onslaught of bitterness from Kelbie. The little man was so angry with the world that it was probably a long time since he'd stopped to wonder why. For that minute it was Winter, for the next it would be the rain or the lack of it. It would always be something.

'You can't get to the job on time and then you arse around taking unnecessary photographs. Inappropriate photographs. Campbell Baxter is right about you. The sooner you get shifted out of here the better. You're a waste of fucking space.'

'Is that right?'

Kelbie bristled, his lips curling back into a snarl. 'Aye it is right, you cheeky shite. I'm going to see to it that your arse doesn't hit the door on the way out of Forensic Services.'

'Is that right?'

'Winter, you are asking to have your head kicked as well as your arse. Watch your step.'

'Is that right?'

He knew it wasn't wise but he could feel the anger rising in him and wasn't sure he could stop it. Euan Hepburn, Remy Feeks, it was all falling on top of him at once. And now this. Maybe he should just headbutt Kelbie and be done with all of it. He pulled his head back and waited for the DCI to say one more word.

Instead Kelbie beat him to the punch, stepping forward so close that Winter could feel Kelbie's breath on his face and he couldn't throw his head forward at him. The man's eyes were wild and Winter knew all he had to do was lean back and one of them would stick the nut on the other.

'Boss!' Jim Ferry's arm came between them and for a second Winter thought that Kelbie was going to take a bite at it. 'Back off, boss. There's a crime scene full of witnesses here. Think about it.'

Winter just stared at the DCI, daring him to make a decision. Kelbie snarled wide-eyed but didn't push forward, his DS's words percolating slowly through his fury. He raised a hand and pushed it flat against Winter's chest, shoving space between them and turning away with a final glare.

'This isn't finished,' he called over his shoulder.

'Is that right?' Winter knew it wasn't the time or place to be pushing his luck but he was beyond that. Reason had opened the window, jumped out and run for its life.

Kelbie paused but set off again just as quickly, Ferry's encouraging arm keeping him moving. Winter breathed hard and fast.

'What is it with you, Tony? You got a death wish? You know what a turd Kelbie is.'

Winter turned his head to see one of the scene examiners, Paul Burke, standing beside him. 'No death wish. There's enough of that without me wanting more. I just couldn't take any more of his crap.'

'Right. Well maybe you should remember that he's a DCI. And, if what I'm hearing is right, then your jacket is on a shoogly peg as it is.'

'What are you hearing?' As if he didn't know.

'That Baxter is gunning to get you made redundant and using the review to do it. Don't give him any more ammunition, mate.'

If only you knew, Winter thought. If only you knew. 'Yeah. I'll try not to. Have you guys got anything else inside this place that needs photographed?'

Burke lifted his shoulders. 'We're running the rule over the whole building but it's massive. They might have something on the upper levels but they'll likely have photographed it themselves. We *can* point the camera in the right direction, you know.'

'I know. I'll go check it out anyway though. See if I can lend a hand.'

The truth was he couldn't care less about helping out. The only job he cared about was lying amid the rubble. He had to get upstairs though and retrace his steps as best he could, at least enough to be able to say he'd been there if he was ever asked. If his DNA ever turned up somewhere it shouldn't.

He made his way back up the concrete spiral and over the same floors as he had before, working his way between the white suits that were doing fine thanks without any help from him. This was a mess and he was in it right up to his neck and getting in even deeper.

Chapter 48

Narey didn't need to be told that Gray Dunn was an urbexing site. Of course it would be. From the moment the name of the place was put to her, she knew. It was Rico Giannandrea who had picked up on the possibility of the connection and called her to flag it up.

'. . . body found at Gray Dunn in Kinning Park. The old biscuit factory. It's been abandoned for . . .'

It was all she heard and all she needed to know. Her mind was lost in a turmoil of possibilities, Rico's words going unheard until a name jumped out from the shadows.

'Remy Feeks.'

'*What?* What did you say, Rico?'

'There was ID on the body. A photo driver's licence. The victim's name is Remy Feeks.'

'Shit.'

'You know him?'

She slammed her hand against the desk and Rico must have heard it on the other side of the line.

'Rachel? Ma'am?'

'I don't know him as such. I think he was the person who found Hepburn's body in the Molendinar and phoned it in.'

'Christ . . .'

'I'm going to the factory. Phone them and let them know I'm on my way and I'm taking over. Phone DCI Addison for me as well, Rico. Thanks.'

She saw the cars and ambulances massed outside the building as soon as she turned into Stanley Street. The sight of the lights made her stomach turn over and the reality of it kicked in.

Her warrant card was in her hand the moment she'd locked the car door and she hurried to the tape and was glad to see uniforms on it that she recognized. They waved her through and she climbed into protective clothing as quickly as she could, scrambling to put on gloves, hat and overshoes.

Spotlights had already been rigged up and she stepped into their harsh glare, instantly taking in the stark desolation of the place. The lights threw macabre graffiti shadows onto the walls and made giants from broken stonework and twisted metal. It was like the factory was lying in wait for her.

Or maybe it had been waiting for Remy Feeks.

She saw a small army of forensics slipping by, upstairs and down, flitting across boulders and picking their way through debris. They were moving quickly

344

but without a moment of rush. It was a measured haste that she'd seen a thousand times.

There were still two of them hunched, all but motionless, in the clearing left by the parting of the swarm of bodies in the central courtyard. She was suddenly struck by the bizarre thought of them all standing there like Wise Men and shepherds, the spotlight above the body leading her to it like a guiding star.

One of the shepherds looked over his shoulder, saw her approaching and spun on his heels towards her. Denny Kelbie looked like a man whose numbers had come up on the lottery when he'd forgotten to buy the ticket. He was furious as he stepped up into her face.

'This is a piece of shit. It's no way to run an investigation and you're way out of your depth.'

'Anything else, sir?'

The DCI clearly had plenty more he wanted to say but she was sure that the phone call he'd have received from Addison or perhaps even from higher up had left him in no doubt that he had no say in this any more. He spat on the ground at her feet and stormed off without another word. That suited her perfectly.

She walked over to stand above the two forensics working on the body and saw the kid stretched out beneath them. Fair hair and freckles, his face young and bloodless, and a railing puncturing his chest. It was as if someone had murdered the Milky Bar Kid.

The SOCOs became aware of her presence and looked up as one. She knew them both by sight, Keiran Hardie and Matt McGowan.

'Give me a minute, guys, please.'

They both got to their feet without dissent and stepped back.

'I take it photographs have been done?'

'Yes, ma'am,' McGowan confirmed. 'Tony Winter has been and gone. Probably left about twenty minutes ago. We told him you were on your way but he didn't want to hang around. Said he was done.'

Something about that made her uneasy but she didn't have the time or space in her head to debate it. The main thing was the job had been done. Now she had to do hers.

She could see something of the boy's dad in his damaged features. This was Archie Feeks' son, no doubt about it. A face without a lifetime of smoking or working in a shipyard, a face that wouldn't grow any older.

Words came back to her. A promise. She'd been trained not to make promises she couldn't keep but she'd still made this one. She'd told Archie that she'd look after his boy. Fine job she'd made of it.

Any doubts she might have had that it was Remy who'd found the body in the Molendinar had vanished. Just where it fitted into the whole mess wasn't so clear though.

She glanced around and saw that Jim Ferry, Kelbie's DS, hadn't scarpered with his boss. She outranked him and she'd make use of the fact.

'DS Ferry. What do we have?'

Ferry huffed theatrically but didn't have much

choice. He grudgingly filled her in. 'Someone phoned 999 and said there was a body in here. That was all they gave. No name, no explanation as to how they knew. Uniforms were here in minutes and we followed on. We've searched the place, best we could in a maze like this, and there's no one else here.'

'The person that phoned, male or female?'

'Male.'

She turned to McGowan and Hardie. 'How long's he been dead?'

'We can't . . .'

'Best guess.'

'Not much more than an hour.'

'And how does that compare to the time of the 999 call?'

Ferry shrugged but looked at his watch. 'The call was made fifty minutes ago. So maybe ten, fifteen minutes between death and the guy calling it in.'

Whoever had killed Feeks had phoned the police. Why? *Why?*

She made up her mind to look round the rest of the factory, not expecting to see anything that had been missed but just because she had to do *something*. Also, it gave her time to think and a little more time before she had to make a visit that she was dreading.

Narey breathed deeply as she stood in front of the door of the flat in Adelaide Street. It really *didn't* get any easier but this was going to be more difficult than most. She became aware that she was feeling the same depths of anxiety she did before she stepped into her dad's care home. Not knowing what reception she was going to get but doubting it would be good. She paused again, made a silent prayer then knocked.

After a few moments, the door swung back but, rather than Archie Feeks, she was greeted by a rounded, middle-aged woman wearing a raincoat over a black turtleneck jumper. Narey held her warrant card up.

The woman responded by lifting the card on a lanyard round her neck. She kept her voice low. 'Jill Henderson. Family Liaison. I only got here five minutes ago. As requested I haven't said anything but he's very worried. He's asked me three times if anything has happened to his son.'

She cursed herself for getting there after the FLO. It wasn't going to have helped the old man's state of mind to have been kept waiting and worrying.

'What have you told him?'

'Only that you were on your way and you were in a better position to talk to him. That you had all the relevant information.'

'Okay, thanks. But I wish that were true.'

'Sorry?'

'*All the relevant information.* There's far too much that I don't know. He's in the living room?'

Henderson gave the briefest of nods.

Narey went through the door and saw the man sitting in his armchair, his body small and tight with the fear of anticipation. He looked up to see her standing there and she saw him shrink even further.

'Mr Feeks, I'm really sorry to—'

'No!' He was on his feet, his eyes wide. 'No, no, no. *Don't*. Not in my house. No. You *can't*.'

'Mr Feeks, your son . . .'

His hands flew to his ears, his eyes screwed shut and his mouth twisted in pain. He must have been sitting imagining the worst since the liaison officer turned up and now it was ticking in front of him, ready to explode. She recognized the signs of denial: he was like her dad when he was corrected on things he didn't want to believe.

Archie spun on his heels, unable to look at them. Henderson moved warily across the room towards him, her arms seemingly changing their minds as to whether to reach out to him. She stood close but let him breathe.

Narey had no choice but to finish what she'd started.

'Mr Feeks, I know this is not what you want to hear but I need to tell you it. A body was found tonight in the former Gray Dunn building in Kinning Park.'

'No!'

His yelps were painful and she wanted to soothe them but, for the moment at least, could only make them worse.

'We believe that the body is your son, Remy.'

The man doubled at the waist, his arms hugged round himself. His breathing was convulsive, drinking from a well that was suddenly empty. All colour drained from him and Narey feared a heart attack as well as the loss of breath.

He was as pale as the horse that death rode, ageing before their eyes. His hands trembled and silent tears streamed down his cheeks as he coughed. He sucked in air hard, expelling it again just as quickly as his body went into overdrive. Narey was well used to holding her emotions in check but this was hard. She just wanted to hug him.

It was a couple of minutes, every second of it an age of agony for all of them, before Archie had settled enough to speak. He looked at the liaison officer beside him.

'Is it definitely him?'

Narey answered. 'Yes, Mr Feeks. It is.'

He got shakily to his feet, his face contorted in anger.

'I didn't ask you.' He jabbed a finger towards Narey.'You said you'd look out for my son. *You* said you'd look after him. *You* told me not to worry. Well how's that worked out for me, eh? Not so fucking good, I'd say. So don't mind me if I don't want to listen to what you've got to say.'

'Mr Feeks—'

'I don't want to hear it, hen. I don't want to hear anything from you. Not a word.'

Jill Henderson stepped between them, the FLO taking the man gently by the arm. He shrugged her hand off but still let her guide him back into the chair. Henderson kneeled to talk to him but the man's eyes were beyond her, glaring at Narey.

'Is there anyone you'd like me to call, Mr Feeks?' Henderson was asking. 'Someone who can come and sit with you. A relative or a friend, maybe?'

'No. I just want to see my son.'

'I understand that and DI Narey will make sure that—'

'No! I don't want *her* to do anything. I don't want her near me or my laddie. Do you understand that? I just want to see my son and I want *her* the fuck away from me. Get her out of my house. Now.'

She was helpless and scorned, knowing she'd let him down and could do nothing to put it right. All she could do was have someone else care for him. Someone to do what she couldn't.

The FLO turned and looked at Narey, both of them knowing Henderson didn't have the authority to tell her to leave as the man wanted. There was a higher authority though and Narey knew it. She wouldn't stay.

She wanted to tell the man that she was sorry for his loss, that she'd do everything in her power to bring him some justice and that she burned with guilt for letting it happen. She couldn't do any of that though, not to any good purpose.

She nodded at them both and let herself out, a little piece of her dying inside as she crossed the threshold.

Chapter 49

Sunday morning

She managed four hours in bed and slept for maybe three of those. She couldn't shake the tortured image of Archie Feeks any more than she could rid her thoughts of his son lying murdered amid the rubble.

Half-awake or half-asleep, she hadn't been able to tell the difference. Her mind worked it over and over in both states and when she was finally sure that she was awake and getting up, she was exhausted before the day had begun.

It was still dark when she rolled into the station, flipping the lights on in the incident room and watching them flicker slowly into life. The place would be buzzing before long, full of bodies and shouts, people demanding to know what had happened and where the hell it left them. She didn't know what she was going to tell them.

She had to be in first, to get her thoughts into some sort of proper order. If she didn't know the answers then at least she had to be aware of the questions. And she'd ask more of the team, get them to ask more of themselves. Some of them would be on board more than others and some of them would wallow in it, relishing seeing her fail. Fuck them. This all had to stop and she'd be the one to do it.

She fixed a poster-sized portrait of Remy Feeks to the wall, standing back to see him alongside Euan Hepburn, Jennifer Cairns, David McGlashan, Christopher Hart and Derek Wharton. Below each was a photograph of the site where they were found, urbexing sites all. She stared at them for an age, weighing up what she knew and what she didn't. The latter was way too much for her liking.

Her guts told her to change the set-up. She rearranged the displays, pushing Hepburn, Cairns and Feeks to one side, and the remainder to the other. It wasn't what she knew, it was what she *felt*. She'd just finished and was looking at the faces afresh when she heard footsteps behind her.

A constable had walked in, mug of tea in hand, and was waiting to speak to her.

'DI Narey? You'd asked for CCTV footage to be pulled overnight. We've got some images for you.'

She felt a rush that she knew was the first sign of good news in a long time. 'Great. Let's go see them.'

The constable, Tom Brightman, stood beside her as another, Lyndsay McEwan, operated the video. The image that came up was typically grainy and not helped by the falling light at the time it was filmed.

'We have shots of three people, we think all men, all going separately towards the Gray Dunn building on Stanley Street,' Brightman explained. 'None of the images are particularly good and I'd say at least two of them were making an effort to keep their heads down and faces out of sight.'

'Show me.'

One by one, the operator showed the stop-start images. The digital time display in the top corner stated that there were eighteen and then twelve minutes between the men appearing on the corner of Stanley Street. The first was about six foot tall and wore a light blue fleece with his head kept low. After him came Remy Feeks, his fair hair obvious and the only one of the three not shy of being seen. Maybe he ought to have been. Finally, came a taller man wearing a hoodie and what might have been a dark balaclava.

The camera had picked each of them up a couple of times and had done the same for two of them, Feeks and the hoodie-wearer, on Milnpark Street.

'I can hopefully pick them up elsewhere and trace them back a bit but it's a real needle in a haystack job,' McEwan told her. 'There's not a lot of cameras down there so it will be a case of guessing where they'd come from. I'll do my best but it will take time.'

Narey said nothing. Her mind was working overtime, joining dots and hoping against hope.

'This is what we've got of them on the way out,' McEwan continued. 'Just man number three. He's in a hurry and goes onto Admiral Street and that's where we lose him. He's probably headed for Paisley Road West but as yet we haven't picked him up again. If he changed his jacket or ditched the balaclava—'

'What about man number one?' She hardly dared to ask.

Brightman shrugged. 'If he came back out onto Stanley then we haven't been able to see him.'

'Show me him again.'

It was the way he walked, hunched and hurried. It was the fleece he was wearing. It was the height and the build.

More than that. It was Euan Hepburn. It was the forum user with the login name of Metinides. It was curtailed conversations and a feeling of distance. It was a lack of questions about a case that would normally have produced far too many. It was the feeling in her guts that had been niggling away at her for over a week.

She excused herself and hurried back to the incident room, to the phones where the anonymous call had been received about the witness in the Molendinar. The tip-off about Remy Feeks. She checked the log then called up the recording.

The voice was slightly muffled and deliberately low. The man was putting it on, trying to disguise himself. It might have fooled most people but not her. Not for a moment. She felt her stomach sink and lurch. The

355

room had shifted on its axis and her throwing up was a distinct possibility.

'DI Narey?'

She put the phone down and stepped away from it before she turned. Constable Brightman was by the door.

'Sorry, DI Narey, but do you want me to get these images on Stanley Street enlarged and sharpened up so they can be made available for posters or media use?'

She looked back at him. The question should have been expected but it managed to take her by surprise.

'Yes. Please.'

'All three men?'

She paused just for a heartbeat. 'Yes. All three.'

Chapter 50

Winter woke on Sunday morning with the biggest hangover he'd ever had without touching a drop of alcohol. Sleep had come late if it had come at all and he'd tossed and turned the whole night, plagued by memory and guilt as much as by the pain in his leg and his back.

He'd dragged himself into the shower and suffered the sting of the jets of water against his bruised and broken skin. However painful it was, he deserved it.

Somehow, when the buzzer went at the front door, he knew instantly who it would be. It didn't occur to him that it could be anyone other than Rachel.

A couple of minutes later, he stood at his open door and watched her come up the stairs with the wind at her back. Her speed didn't mean that much in itself; for her that kind of urgency could mean many things. He sought clues in her eyes but couldn't quite read her. She wasn't happy but he could have told that without looking. The question was whether she was unhappy with *him*. And how much.

She paused briefly as she got to the door, a hand rising unexpectedly and caressing the side of his face as she looked into his eyes. Her touch electrified him as if she'd plugged his veins into a power socket. He was still trying to work out just what it signified when she walked past him into the flat. He trailed in her wake, trying to ignore the throbbing pain in his leg and doing his best not to limp. She slipped off her coat and dropped it onto a chair before dropping herself onto the sofa.

She let her eyes slide shut and air escape wearily from her lips like someone who'd been told they'd only have to run one more marathon that day. When she opened them again, her eyes were full of questions. She kept them to herself for a bit, weighing him up as if deciding whether to kiss him or kill him.

When she finally spoke, she sounded tired but there was also a low flame under her voice that scared him. 'What the hell are we in the middle of here, Tony?'

Truth or lies? Maybe it was too late for either. 'Nothing good.'

She laughed softly and with no humour. 'Oh I'd figured that much out. I've had a lovely night and a fun morning. Do you want to hear about it?'

He was a mouse and she was the cat, flicking him from one clawed paw to the other.

'Sure.'

'*Sure?* Okay. Well last night I got called to the Gray Dunn biscuit factory. Maybe half an hour after you'd taken your photographs and left. Someone had the sense to realize that the location fitted with my investigation. I had the pleasure of dealing with that little shit Denny Kelbie but he was the least of my worries. I had another urbexing death. At least number three, possibly number six. The pressure I've been under ratcheted up another notch. But even *that* wasn't my biggest problem.'

His stomach fell a couple of feet and he wasn't sure he could swallow.

'I managed to get a couple of hours' sleep and got back in this morning to find the nightshift had called in all the CCTV we could get our hands on. The interesting images were of three men walking, separately and at different times, towards the factory in the hour or so before the services were called. The images weren't great quality but one of them was recognizable. If you knew them very well.'

He said nothing. He couldn't speak.

'I think it was the fleece that gave it away. I bought that for you last Christmas.'

He found a small voice. 'Rachel . . .'

'Still, lots of those fleeces, I'm sure. And probably lots of people on urbexing websites that might call themselves Metinides. You know how it is though. I'm a stubborn cow. So I listened to the tape of the call that Toshney took, the man who phoned in to say that Remy Feeks was the Molendinar witness. The caller had tried to disguise his voice a bit. Couldn't hide it from me though. *Could you?*'

'No.'

She took in a lungful of air and he recognized the sign. She was composing herself, or trying to, doing her best to keep her temper in check. It was barely working.

'So you'll understand then why I'd quite like to know just what exactly is going on. I'd like to know what the fuck you've done. And why. And I'd like to hear it right now or I'll have to walk out of here for good and drive to the station to tell what I know.'

His skin was tingling as if someone had set it on fire and he wasn't sure his throat was connected to his lungs any longer. He said a prayer to a God he didn't believe in and began.

'I'll tell you but I need to work out how to do it. I need to tell you this properly.'

'Damn right you do. But first I'm going to ask you a question that you won't need time to think how to answer. Did you kill Remy Feeks?'

She saw his reaction. It was as if she'd slapped him or punched him in the stomach. His mouth bobbed open in shock and his eyes widened. He couldn't believe she'd asked. It was written all over his face.

'No. No, Rach. I didn't.'

She stared hard at him, looking deep into his eyes and searching for signs of a lie. She didn't want to see any but nor would she be fooled into just seeing what she wanted. She needed the truth from him, whatever it was.

How long had she known him? Six years. You had to know someone by that length of time. Know their nature and their mannerisms. He was holding her gaze, not trying to look away or dodge her.

'I didn't kill Remy Feeks, Rachel. I didn't – *couldn't* – kill anyone. You should know that.'

She did. She was sure she did. Yet she needed more from him than that. Much more.

'Tell me where you were last night.'

He hesitated and she didn't like that. She didn't want him to think, she wanted him to talk. He didn't get to decide how much of anything he told her. She had to make sure he really knew that.

'Okay, wait. I'm not sure you're getting this, Tony, and that's where we're going to have a problem. Because you only telling me half a story or some edited version is not going to work for me. And if it doesn't work for me then you'd better start understanding that it's not going to work for you either. Do you get what I'm saying, Tony?'

'You want to know everything. I get that.'

'No! I *need* to know everything. And if you and I are going to have any chance of getting through this then that's what's going to have to happen. You lie to me here or hold back on me then we are in big trouble. The kind of trouble that means I can't do my job. The kind of trouble that means I could lose it. The kind of trouble that means we're done or you go to jail. Do you get *that*?'

He did. Suddenly and forcefully, she saw that he did. There was a flash of fear in his eyes and that scared her too. He nodded.

361

'Okay, where were you last night?'

'I was in the Gray Dunn factory. I had gone there to meet Remy Feeks. He'd messaged me to be there and I turned up. Someone else was there too though. I don't know who he was but he murdered Remy. He also called the police and I ran.'

She had done this for a long time and knew truth and lies when she heard them. Sometimes though, the truth was still bad news.

'*Why?* Why were you there? What the hell did you think you were doing?'

'What I had to!'

He knew he probably had no right to shout back at her but he couldn't help it. Her being right just made him more annoyed for being wrong. More than that, it was all falling on top of him. Euan, Remy, the guy that had attacked him in the factory. All of it.

'What the hell is that supposed to mean? Don't give me any cryptic shit. Tell me. Now!'

'I wanted to find out what happened to Euan Hepburn. I owed it to him. Yes, I shouldn't have stuck my nose in but I did. I'll deal with the fall-out from that. I don't want any of that fall-out to be me and you.'

He paused, waiting for a response to that, but she didn't indulge him beyond a hard stare.

'I knew Euan better than I let you think. He was my friend. For a while, he was my best friend.'

He saw the disappointment in her face and it hurt him. She wasn't impressed and he knew it was about to get worse.

362

'So you lied to me.'

'It wasn't so much a lie as not telling you everything.'

'Sounds like a lie to me. How did you know him?'

'I didn't mean not to tell you. When you told me the dead guy was Euan . . . I panicked. And I was shocked. It brought lots of old memories back and I didn't know what to tell you.'

'But you knew you should have.'

'Yes.'

'Tell me now.'

So he did. And she didn't like it.

Knowing someone so well that you are on the point of committing to spending the rest of your life with them. Then finding out something. She wasn't sure she could take many more surprises for one day and it wasn't yet noon.

'Why did you never tell me that you went urbexing?'

'Because I'd stopped. There didn't seem much point in telling you, seeing I didn't do it any more. And it didn't finish well. Euan and I fell out badly and I hated the idea of urbexing. Hated to think about it, far less talk about it. The longer we were together, the harder it was to mention it. It was much easier not to.'

'And that's it?'

'That and guilt. It was my fault that Euan and I stopped talking but I put it all on him. I hate myself for that. If we hadn't stopped then he might still be alive.'

She was mad at him but loved him. She was mad at him but felt his pain.

'You can't know that.'

'No. Not for sure. But it doesn't stop me feeling it, thinking it. *That's* why I had to do it. For him. To make up for what I'd done in letting him down.'

He wasn't getting away with this. Guilt and self-pity couldn't be an excuse for fucking everything up.

'You did it for *you*. You got right in the middle of a police investigation, *my* investigation, for yourself. Your guilty conscience isn't a passport to playing at being a policeman. Or to screwing up everything between us.'

'What if I did? What if I fucking did do it for me? Am I not allowed to do something for myself?'

'Not if it messes with us. It can't just be about you. Can't you see that?'

'I had to do it, Rachel. And *you* need to see that. If you can't understand that I had to help my friend, that I had to get this out of my system before it fucked me up completely, then we are in trouble. Of course it's not just about me but it *is* about me too.'

They were nose to nose now, both shouting. They were standing on the same tightrope and if one fell then they both would.

'I did this for us as much as for me. Look, I couldn't live with knowing that he'd died and I could have been in a place to have stopped it if I hadn't been such a prick to him. I had to put that right so that I could be right for us. And because it was the right thing to do.'

'Right thing? You think you did the right thing? Christ, Tony, that's crazy talk. I need to know you're with me. That you understand what can and can't happen. I need to be able to trust you.'

'And you need to *know* me. Euan was murdered. From the minute the body was found in the Odeon, I knew both were connected and both were connected to urbexing. I know that world and I could use that. I could do something about it. What kind of friend, what kind of man would I be if I didn't want to help make it right for him?'

She wanted to slap him, shake him, grab him and send them both falling off the rope without a safety net.

'You'd be *my* man if you just told me what you knew rather than buggering about on your own. You'd be on my side.'

'Of course I'm on your side. Always am, always will be.'

'Christ, Tony, you don't know what you're doing or what you're talking about. You say Hepburn and Cairns are connected but we *don't* know they're related to each other. All I know is that they're connected to urbexing.'

'Yes we do. I do.'

She stopped breathing for a second. It wasn't just what he said, it was how he said it. Certainty.

'*What?* How can you know that?'

'I went into his flat.'

'Hepburn's flat? You *broke in*?'

'Yes. Like I said, I had to.'

'We searched the place. There was nothing to see.'

365

'You didn't look hard enough or in the right places. I knew what I was looking for.'

She didn't like the sound of that on any grounds. 'Which was what?'

'Euan's second camera. He used two. I figured whoever killed him had one of them. I wanted to see the other and I found it. It had photographs taken at the old Odeon.'

She held her breath again and said nothing. She thought he could hear both their hearts beating over the silence in the room.

'The Odeon? Photographs that *he* took at the Odeon?'

'Yes.'

'You think Euan Hepburn . . .' She was trying to take it all in. 'Are you telling me he killed Jennifer Cairns?'

'Well . . .' He paused, not quite sure where to go next. 'Maybe you should take a look at the photographs.'

Chapter 51

Winter opened his laptop and brought up a file of images that he'd copied from the memory card on Hepburn's camera. He set the laptop on the table in front of them and began to slowly scroll through what was there. Her eyes were wide.

He could see why the building had drawn Euan: a part of Glasgow history that was about to be demolished and a small window of time in which to do it. It was a perfect urbexing location, intriguing and forbidden and right in the heart of the city centre. The kind of site that would have had him itching to explore back in the day and the sort that Euan would have found irresistible.

Winter worked his way through a series of images showing the inside of the cinema, nothing particularly exciting but enough to let her see that that was indeed where it was. The call to the discovery of Jennifer Cairns' body was all too fresh and left no doubt that the narrow corridors, steeply banked rooms and wide staircases in front of them were the Renfield Street site.

He moved on to what looked like an entry shot, a window that didn't seem to have any merit but showed how Euan had got in.

Then back further through the timeline. A couple of exterior shots. One highlighting what might have been the other side of the same window, a few feet above a red-metal exterior door that itself sat at the top of a fire escape, perhaps round the rear of the building. Winter himself would have looked at that as a likely entrance. Places with nothing in them weren't as secure as they might otherwise have been.

Back another frame. The same fire escape, the same door and unguarded window. But this time there was someone making their way down the stairs. Winter had checked the digital time stamp and knew this was just a few minutes *before* Euan had gone inside. He'd taken two photographs of this other person, one at the top of the stairs then another halfway down, then had entered the building once the mystery figure had left. The person walking down the stairs was wearing a dark hooded sweatshirt and jeans. The hood was up, covering their face.

His face. It was a man. A second look had made him sure of it and Rachel no doubt thought the same now. The width of the shoulders, the size. Euan had photographed this man leaving via the fire escape then had gone inside by the same route.

The photographs were all dated 10 September. Right on the money for the time they thought Jennifer Cairns was murdered.

He watched her rub at her cheekbone as she processed what she was seeing. Her eyebrows were knotted in concentration and he wondered if she was debating the same things he had.

'Okay,' she said at last. 'I'll repeat my question while I try to make sense of this. Do you think Euan Hepburn killed Jennifer Cairns? And who is that in the hoodie?'

'Well . . . first of all you'll have noticed the date on these.'

'Of course I have! It could be coincidental but let's assume that it's not. It's when Jen Cairns was murdered.'

'Yes. So there's two potential scenarios here. Basically either that Euan was with this guy or he wasn't. It could be that the other man was checking out a possible entry and then gave the thumbs-up and Euan went in too. If that's what happened then yes, maybe he killed her or helped kill her.'

'Or?'

'Or Euan photographs him, just out of curiosity or his sense of mischief. Thinks, this guy's been in there and I'll be doing the same. Probably thinks nothing more of it. But maybe the other guy turned for one last look before he left and saw Euan go in, camera in hand?'

She was nodding. 'If he saw Euan go in then maybe he'd be worried about what he might find in there.

And he'd be scared that Euan had almost certainly seen him.'

'And then it would have been easy enough to track Euan down. Wait for him to come out maybe. Or place a message on the forum asking about the Odeon, drawing out anyone with even the slightest temptation to brag about being inside. Euan would have come running. He wouldn't have been able to help himself.'

'This mystery man befriends him, goes urbexing with him. Persuades him to explore the Molendinar Burn. Then cuts his throat.'

'Yes.'

She stared at the screen for a while longer. 'Who's the man in the hoodie?'

Winter didn't reply but brought up an image from the black building at Gartnavel, the photograph showing the pale blue room and the wooden-panelled walls. The one showing the photographer and his companion reflected on the glass doors. The other person wore a dark hooded sweatshirt and jeans.

'That's all you have?'

'It's all there was. One, probably accidental, photograph. Dated ten days after the ones taken at the Odeon. And a few days before Euan was killed.'

'So why do you think Hepburn wasn't involved in killing Cairns? Seeing as he seemed to be there.'

'A few things. First, I just don't think Euan was capable of something like that, murdering a woman. Second, it doesn't add up that he'd hide and photograph while his pal checked out the entry. That's not what he would do. Third, there is no sign of him knowing this other guy until after the Odeon. But also, most of all—'

'The killing hasn't stopped.'

'Yes. I'm sure this guy' – he jabbed a finger at the laptop screen – 'killed Jennifer Cairns then killed Euan to cover it up.'

She didn't take her eyes off the screen, seeing the similarity between the hooded figure and the third man heading for the factory the night before. She finished off the picture. 'And Remy Feeks stumbled across the body that hoodie guy thought would never be found. Then he – and you – went sticking his nose in. And Feeks got himself killed.'

There was recrimination in her voice. Anger and fear too. It could as easily have been him. She just looked at him for an age. He curled up inside under her gaze and felt her unpicking him at the seams.

'How long have you had these photographs?'

'Just a few days.'

'A few minutes was long enough. You should have given them to me.'

'I couldn't have told you how I got them. It would have put you in a bad position.'

She couldn't help but laugh. 'And I'm not now? Have you any idea how much pressure I'm under and how many people are just dying for me to fall flat on my face? Forget that though, forget that I could lose my job and the case. Think about what this could do to you and me. Have you stopped to think about that at all?'

'Yes! Of course I have.'

'Good, because, God help me, I love you. If I had to choose between you and keeping my job, then, even though it probably makes me crazy, I'd choose you. But I'd really rather not have to choose. You understand that, right?'

He was stunned. He honestly didn't think she would choose anyone or anything over her job with the possible exception of her dad and his health. He nodded without being sure he really did understand.

She put her hand against his injured side and pushed, hard enough for it to hurt. It showed on his face and she nodded in satisfaction.

'Remember how much it hurts. People are getting killed, Tony. You can't put yourself in the way of that.'

'It's *because* they've been killed that I've *got* to do this.'

'No, no way. You're not going all John Wayne on me. I've no time for a dead hero right now. I need you alive and well and I need you to remember what I've said. This is about *us*. Do not mess it up. Do not do something so stupid that we can't get back from it.'

'I won't.'

'Don't keep trying to get involved in this. Do *not* lie to me. Do *not* go behind my back. Do *not* break the law. If you do, we're done.'

'I won't.'

The words sounded hollow in his own head so he could only guess how they sounded to her.

* * *

She didn't believe him. She was sure he wanted to mean it but it didn't sound like he could keep that promise, to her or himself. *Got to do this*: that's what he'd said. Promises were easy after that but they didn't come with the same feeling. She felt sick. Deep in her stomach it felt like something had ended.

Chapter 52

Narey dragged herself back into the station where the team had gathered to be brought up to speed with the events of the night before. Exhausted and nursing emotional bruises, she ached for the comfort of a hot bath or her bed but she had time for neither. Everything was on the line.

Addison was waiting for her outside the door to the incident room and took her by the arm into a corner.

'Okay, what the fuck is happening?'

'That's what I'm about to tell everyone.'

'You can tell them what you like but tell me what *is* going on. What are we looking at here? I don't want questions from Crosby I don't know the answers to. Are we looking at *six* murders? Because if we are then you're taking a back seat, whether you like it or not.'

She really didn't need this. 'I don't think so. I think it's three and I'm getting a lot closer to getting a handle on it.'

'You sure about that? Because all I see are bodies piling up. Give me what you have. I'm on your side, remember.'

'It kicked off with the murder of Jennifer Cairns in the Odeon and the other two, Hepburn and Feeks, were done to cover it up. The killer is running scared and was worried they were a threat to him.'

Addison digested the information. 'And the other three that you brought to me? Wharton, McGlashan and Hart?'

'I don't think they're connected. Certainly not Wharton and Hart. Whatever it's about, it's happening *now*. Hepburn had been at the Odeon and photographed Cairns' killer. Feeks found the body in the Molendinar.'

Addison's eyes narrowed. 'How do you know Hepburn was there?'

'I've got his photographs.'

'*What?* How? Where the hell did you get them?'

She hesitated. 'An informant. Someone who can be trusted. The photos are genuine.'

He wasn't happy with that. It was nowhere near enough and they both knew it. He was trying to work out what she wasn't saying and whether he dared let her run with it. She hoped he couldn't read her mind but feared how well he knew her.

'You're taking chances, Rachel, and it's not like you. Are you sure about what you're doing? Don't leave yourself somewhere I can't help you.'

'I need to clear this case.'

His voice hardened into a fierce whisper. 'If you're gambling your career on this because the pressure's got to you then you're not the person I think you are. You're better than that, Rachel, so act like it. Use your head and do the right thing. What do I need to know?'

He was right, about all of it. In the instant of realizing that, she felt a relief she hadn't known all morning.

'The photographs came from Tony.'

Addison said nothing but just looked at her, waiting for the rest.

'He had been best friends with Hepburn years ago and he . . .' She paused. 'He felt the need to find out what happened. He found Hepburn's camera. He also went out with a group of urbexers to the old railway line at the Botanics and got photographs of them.'

Addison rubbed at his eyes and swore quietly under his breath. 'Remind me to kill him if you haven't already done it. Where is the camera now?'

'Back where he found it in Hepburn's flat. He just took copies from the memory card.'

'Did he wear gloves?'

She nodded.

'Okay, so your informant told you where the camera might be. Go get it and find the photographs for yourself. Anything Tony took at the Botanics is fine – he did it as a member of the public. And as a twat.'

'What about the briefing?'

He looked at his watch. 'Get back here in an hour

and I'll postpone it till then. They can moan all they want. Just make sure you get this right.'

She was back in forty-five minutes, the camera found and bagged, the relevant photographs made ready to show to the troops on the PowerPoint. The break, and Addison's words, had given her back some control. The pressure was still there but she was in slightly better shape to handle it. She had to do her job.

DCS Crosby was there, standing at the back of the room with his arms crossed and a sombre expression. She avoided his gaze and tried to forget he was there at all.

She took the squad through everything they had on Remy Feeks and where she thought he fitted into the timeline. She laid out her theory and watched them take it in. One murder, two more as cover-up. It was her best guess, her gut feeling and the logical conclusion.

Not everyone was impressed and she saw the same sceptical faces wrinkle in doubt: Petrie, Storey and McTeer chief among them. There was chatter and shoulders being shrugged, whispers and shared looks.

It was Storey, not surprisingly, who stood and challenged her. He made a point of looking troubled but she could see he was loving it.

'What about these other deaths?' He pointed over to the three faces to the right. 'Last time we were all in here you were telling us how they were all part of this and now we've to forget about them. I'm a bit confused. How much are you just guessing here?'

'*DI Storey!*' Heads turned to see it was Crosby who was shouting at him. 'If you were listening you'd know the answer to your question. DI Narey is giving you the best analysis she can of a changing situation. If you're taking advantage of that to score some points then maybe this team isn't the place for you. Is that what you're doing?'

Storey shrank. 'No, sir. Understood, sir.'

'Good. I trust the rest of you are in the same position. Eyes front, shut up and listen.'

She looked at Crosby and gave him a small, grateful nod of the head and carried on. Even as she did so, she knew his intervention was a mixed blessing. All well and good as long as she was right and some more rope to hang by if she wasn't.

She took them through Cairns, Hepburn and Feeks, point by point. She went through everything they knew about the locations, the motives and the photographs. Almost everything.

Since the meeting had broken up, she'd gone back to basics herself. She went over it all in her head, brainstorming and questioning every decision she'd made, making a list of names and scribbling notes against each.

She had already been through Winter's muddled set of notes twice. She'd read each name and nickname from the Botanics and the forum, looked at the photographs and checked out the website again. She'd made a new list, scoring names out, adding them back in again. She'd searched everything available to try to ascertain just who these people were.

There was too much she didn't know. Did they have one account on this bloody website or two? How could she be sure of their movements at any given time when they could say they were crawling around in some old school or exploring a tunnel somewhere under the city?

She was sure she had a handle on many of the forum user names. Euan Hepburn was CardboardCowboy, Remy Feeks had been Magellan93 and Tony – bloody Tony – was Metinides. Others – PencilPusher, NightLight, Gopher, Spook, Astronut, Vixxxen and Crow – she was able to tick off thanks to the Botanics trip, assuming anyone was telling the truth about who they were. She didn't know who JohnDivney was but desperately wanted to. He, or possibly she, had interacted with Hepburn just before he was murdered. Narey's nose was bothered each time she looked at the name.

There was also a strong possibility that the person she was looking for wasn't among those names at all. She knew why Hepburn and Feeks had been in a recognized urbexing site when they were killed but Narey just couldn't picture Jennifer Cairns making a habit of breaking nails or getting covered in cobwebs. Much more likely that someone had taken her there. What about her husband? Could Douglas Cairns have been one of these people? There were far too many questions and not enough answers.

She'd secreted herself away in a small, underused office in the depths of the station seeking some peace in which to think. She had only one small lamp switched on over the desk in the hope that no one would realize she was there.

She'd uploaded the photographs from the Botanics to her iPad and sighed at the prospect of going over them a third time. If there had been some magic button, some glamorous short cut, then she'd have pressed it or taken it long before then.

Tony had taken a bunch of scene-setting photos, graffiti on walls, rubbish and foliage where the old track had been, huge girders overhead, moonlight and the odd spot of rain making their way through the ventilation shafts from the park above. Then, increasingly, people appeared in the shots. They were there in ones and twos, occasionally in larger numbers, but always seemingly unaware that they were being photographed.

There weren't many of these, which was frustrating but understandable. Too much of it and Tony would have become obvious. They would have had to wonder about this guy in their midst who was intent on recording them all.

Remy Feeks was seen staring at the group, his eyes keen but his body language tight and nervy. His friend Gabby was there, a little blonde bundle of energy, flitting from one person to another. The tall, athletic-looking guy who Tony had said was Finlay Miller, Astronut, was frequently by Gabby's side. Some of them were photographed while they were using their own cameras. He watching them watching him.

He hadn't managed to get all the group into clear shots but there was something of each of them even if they were partially obscured by the others or seen from behind. She worked her way through them, ticking them off, mentally trying to stitch together the various angles and half-images that there were.

Wait.

She had to look again. There. Half-hidden behind one of the others. And there. Just turning away from the camera. And there. Just half a face but enough. Was it? If it was, then a few things would make sense, pieces of the puzzle would slot into place. Don't do wishful thinking, she told herself, wait and see.

She enlarged the photographs as much as she could but lost the focus and had to step away from them again. There, that was the best she was going to get. And it was good enough.

Without taking her eyes off the screen, she picked up the phone.

Chapter 53

Sunday evening

Winter sat staring at his laptop for an age, his fingers almost arthritic, tight with anger. The last time he'd sat looking at this screen, this very site, it had ended with Remy Feeks dying – no, not dying, being murdered – while he was just yards away. He knew he was boiling up a seething, simmering rage but he couldn't put a stop to it even if he'd wanted to.

There was a thing called survivor guilt. He'd once lived next door to a guy named Colin Hurst who was a passenger in a car crash. Colin and a colleague car-shared to get to work and this day it was the other man's turn. The guy's Mazda was mown down by a lorry that had lost control. Colin suffered broken ribs and whiplash. The driver was crushed to death by his side. Inches more and Colin would have joined him. Not in any way his fault but he didn't drive for over

382

two years, which was probably just as well as he hit the bottle hard. He became anxious, depressed and guilty. He didn't like himself much and seemingly set out to make sure other people didn't like him either. It was no way to live your life.

The driver hadn't deserved what happened to him but neither had Colin Hurst. Neither had Remy Feeks nor Euan Hepburn. It wasn't about whether you deserved it. It was about how you dealt with it.

The home page of OtherWorld stared back, daring him, telling him to just do it, to go for it.

There was a series of photographs at the top of the page which switched every thirty seconds or so, each one calling out to him, challenging him. They reached into that central core that made all explores irresistible to those with the bug. Each one screamed climb me, enter me, photograph me, save me for posterity.

The longer he looked at the page, the more common sense crumbled. He knew what he was proposing to do was a very bad idea but he also knew that he was going to give in to it. The voice of reason, the conscience sitting on his shoulder, was there on the orders of Rachel. It chirped away at him, telling him to keep safe, to leave it to the cops, to hide nothing from her, to do nothing that would threaten what they had together. However, the other voice came from deep inside him. It told him to remember Euan and Remy.

There was no contest. Bad idea it definitely was but he was going to do it anyway.

* * *

He played with the wording, changing it and deleting it, making sure he got it just right. He had to get the response he wanted. The message had to spook him, challenge him, flush him out once and for all.

I have Hepburn's photographs. They show you and your friend going into the Odeon on the day she died. I think the police would be interested in those. Don't you?

It wasn't quite right though. It sounded too obviously like blackmail and not enough like he actually knew what he was talking about. Try again.

I know who you are. I know what you did.

Too vague. Too much I know what you did last summer. The guy had to know that he was serious. Maybe the photograph would be worth a thousand words.

He attached it. The shot of the man clambering down from the Odeon. Euan's snapshot that cost him his life. Winter couldn't know if the man was aware that Euan had photographed him at the site but he must have feared that it was a possibility. Winter needed to tap into that fear.

I have this. And I have more. Much more.

That should get his attention but he also needed to make the arrangements. That, as much as anything, was what was scaring him.

Meet me at the Glasgow Tower. Not at the bottom.
At the observation deck. Tomorrow at midnight.

He gave it one last look-over and shook his head at the craziness of it. Before he could change his mind, he clicked post and it was done.

Chapter 54

Monday evening

The next day seemed to have lasted for ever. Twenty-four little hours, the song said. It had seemed so much longer than that.

Winter had watched the weather turn, seeing clouds roll in and gather over the city as if they were lying in wait. Big and dark, full of rain above the grey, just killing time until it was the right moment to unleash everything they had.

He'd seen the light come and go, seen day turn to night and night to something even darker. The moon was hidden by a wall of cloud and the sky over the Clyde was a murky, murderous black, like a raven's wing or a killer's soul.

No matter how much quicker he'd wanted the clock to tick, the hours had dragged as if weighed down by everything that had happened and everything still to come. At last, at long and weary last, it was time for him to be there.

It was an hour earlier than he'd said in his message. He had said midnight but wanted to be there by eleven, content to wait and desperate to get there first. He stood in the shadow of the tower, hidden in a city full of shadow, and wondered just what the hell he was doing.

It had come to this though and there was no going back. Maybe it had always been leading to this from the day he and Euan Hepburn had climbed this bloody tower and he'd nearly killed himself in the process. Maybe it had been inevitable from the moment Euan had been found in the Molendinar. Whatever, it was finishing tonight. That much he was sure of.

His heart was beating fast and he could feel the nerves bubbling, coming slowly to the boil. He'd done some stupid things in his time but this was right up there with the best of them. Right up there with the last time he climbed this.

As if on cue, the rain started. He looked up and saw it falling in big, heavy drops from the black. It came thick and fast, like the clouds had been unzipped and the whole lot couldn't get to ground quick enough.

He pulled a black woollen balaclava from his pocket and dragged it over his head and face, put on gloves and finally zipped his waterproof jacket to the neck. There was nothing to be gained from waiting as it wasn't going to stop raining any time soon. He began to climb.

He moved slowly and deliberately, feeling the pain in his leg from the injury he'd acquired fleeing the factory, and trying to ignore the hammering in his chest and the memories that were pulling at his mind. He made sure every hand on every rung was secure before he moved a foot from the rung below. At this rate, it was going to take most of the hour that he'd given himself just to get up there but the alternative was a quick and bumpy return to earth.

The rain was constant, lashing down as if defending the tower. In no time, his clothes were heavy and sodden, his jacket slick and soaked through. Juicy raindrops sat on each rung, waiting to be squashed by his hands or sent slipping and spiralling. He clung on, skin through wool to water to metal.

There was no sound of other feet on the metal rungs and he couldn't hear another person's laboured breath from the exertion of the climb, but he felt the presence. Someone else was climbing as he climbed, matching him step for step and hiding it by keeping in time with him. He slowed and stopped, tried to fox them, but all he could hear were his own feet and the howl of the wind. He knew though the other man was there. He shut the thought out and climbed.

With every step up, his head got heavier and lighter. More memories and less sense. He tried to look straight ahead, see only the rungs, focus only on the rungs. Don't look down, don't think about anything else. Don't think about falling. Don't think about the last time. Don't think about when you fell.

388

His pulse was a drum roll. The more he tried to shut it out, the louder it got. He squeezed his eyes shut hard and it was a mistake. A flare of phosphene danced behind his eyelids. Bursts of yellow and white made him dizzy as the pressure worked on the cells of his retinae and created a light show that he really didn't need. He gripped tighter on the rungs and hugged his face against the ladder, the metal cold and wet against his skin.

He knew the world was spinning around him: he didn't need to open his eyes to see that. He tried to stay as still as he could and let it settle back into place. Blowing out a long, steady stream of breath seemed to help. Taking in a big lungful to replace it definitely did.

When his eyes did open, Glasgow shimmied before him. A million lights waved hello through the rain and not one of them seemed capable of staying in the same place even for a second. He took his right hand away from the ladder briefly and waved back – drowning not waving – then clung on once more.

His right leg was the first to find the courage to move again. It climbed to the rung above and shoved the rest of him into action. He had to get up there. There was no other way.

He pulled with his arms and pushed with his feet, onwards and upwards. He could still feel the other climber although he couldn't tell if he was above him or below. He tried to look both up and down but, between the rain and his own fear, he could make out only shapes and blurs. Was that the sound of someone laughing? Or coughing maybe? He was there, no doubt about that, just far enough out of sight and hearing to taunt him, to watch him.

The rain was getting heavier and the city was almost impossible to see through the veil. He could just make out the nearby neon-lit outlines of the BBC studios, the Armadillo and the Hydro, the big beasts of the new Clydeside. The rest was a flickering blur of yellows and reds without much shape or sense. He climbed higher.

The observation deck had only been a shadow in the rain but now it began to loom real and reachable, though looking up caused his head to spin again. The deck was there in the clouds, waiting to be boarded like a ghost pirate ship sailing in a sea of dirges.

What had made him think this could possibly have been a good idea? His head was full of Euan Hepburn. Full of guilt and fear, of falling and consequences. His head was full of Remy Feeks and Rachel. Rachel. His promise to her echoed between his ears. Don't lie. Don't mess it up. Don't keep it from her. Don't do your own thing.

Of course he shouldn't have looked down again but he couldn't help himself. He strained to see through the murk but there was no sign of anyone else, just the vertical drop he'd once taken without the aid of parachute or safety net. It spiralled through the night and the rain to the small, firm circle of grey concrete that he'd started from. His hands were strangling the rung of the ladder somewhere just under his chin, clinging on in case it slipped through his fingers and disappeared.

There really was no one else on the climb up the tower. Not in the sense that he'd thought. No living, breathing being. He realized that now. He was still there though, watching, maybe waiting to catch him if he fell. If you believed in that kind of thing. Euan Hepburn made an unlikely guardian angel but Winter felt him there nevertheless.

Higher and higher. The underside of the observation deck was clearly in sight, a giant metallic eye looking out over the city. He pushed on, bolder now, sure he was going to get there.

The deck itself was fully enclosed, a space for the public reached by the internal elevator, assuming it was working. From there they could look out over the city in comfort and safety. Winter's destination was immediately below it, the maintenance platform that shared the same view as the deck above but was accessible, with some effort, from the ladder. He hauled himself up, over and in, collapsing onto the metal floor, enjoying the shock of the cold against the sweat on his back. He was tired and soaked through. His hands were numb with cold and the stress of holding on for his life. His head was a mess of worry and wonder. But he'd made it. He'd actually made it.

Now all he had to do was wait.

Chapter 55

Narey was sitting with the lights off, waiting for something to happen. Not just anything but a very particular something that was as much hope as expectation. She knew the place well but everything changed in the dark. Furniture seemed bigger, closer. The room itself seemed smaller but without end.

The lights outside the window were sneaking their way in, casting shadows and playing with her mind, making things stretch and twist. It gave her time to think but it was an elastic and unhelpful form of time. Thinking in the dark wasn't generally to be recommended. Your mind went places it shouldn't, running through doors that you knew were shut for a reason.

There were doors marked *Dad, Tony, Work, Future*. She was crashing through them all, even the ones that shouldn't be linked but were. It wasn't exactly helpful given the circumstances but she couldn't help herself.

The more you thought about why you shouldn't go there, the more you were thinking about it.

She'd given Tony an ultimatum but had basically left him to choose whether to go along with it or not. It meant she'd given him the option of completely destroying what they had. It was like giving a chimpanzee the keys to a Ferrari. Men weren't good with decisions, she knew that. They'd rather not make them and they certainly didn't like being made to make them. What other choice did she have though? She had to trust he had the sense to see what was important. If he didn't then they were wasting their time.

It didn't come too naturally to her to sit still for any length of time. It never had. As a kid she would devour books but always on the move in one way or another. She'd sometimes walk and read, through the park or down by the river. Even if she read in one spot, on her bed or in the living room, then she'd roll and wriggle, move from one place to another, never giving the world the chance to take root beneath her. Ants in her pants, according to her mum and dad.

She had to try to stay still now though. Still and quiet and unseen and patient. The only things allowed to move were the doors that opened and shut in her head. There was no guarantee that this still-waiting would have the outcome she was hoping for, but there was no other way to find out. She'd sit and she'd wait. And she'd think.

In the end, it took a bit less time than they'd thought. She'd sat in that familiar chair in the dark for less than forty-five minutes when she heard three little words whispered in her ear. 'Here we go.'

Her pulse quickened and her hands gripped the sides of the chair. She'd been ready from the moment she sat down but now she felt the need to reinforce that. Feet flat to the floor, ready to brace against it even though she probably wouldn't have to.

She mentally crossed her fingers and hoped their man wouldn't change his mind or chicken out. The words in her ear meant he was on site and ready to move in. It didn't mean that he'd definitely be coming through the . . .

The creak of weight outside the door filtered through the apartment just a moment before the sound of something jangling at the lock. Surely he didn't, couldn't, have a key. Although in his line of work maybe it wouldn't be too difficult for him to get his hands on some kind of skeleton key. Whatever he was using, a key or a jemmy, it had worked. The door edged open and the person on the other side stood quietly, testing the temperature.

She held her breath, sitting tight. A potent cocktail of anticipation, adrenalin and apprehension coursed through her veins. Don't switch on the light, she silently urged him. Not just yet. Let's both savour this.

Footsteps padded through the hallway, and the door to the living room, which she'd left ajar, was slowly eased wider still. A tall shadow appeared in the doorway, its outline framed by the street lights shining through the window. It was him. Surely it was him.

The shadow's owner carried a torch and in seconds a slim beam of light arced across the room, settling first on the desk against the far wall where Tony's laptop sat along with the external hard drive which held many of his photographs. She'd let him go a little further, until he was within touching distance of what he'd come hoping to find.

Pausing for a moment to sweep the torchlight over the desk, he reached out to flip open the laptop's lid. Thinking better of it, he closed it again, picking the laptop up and stretching to do the same with the hard drive.

'That's a better idea,' she called from the gloom. 'Don't waste time trying to get into them here. Safer just to take them with you.'

He jumped at her voice and threw the laptop across the room at her. She dodged it easily but suddenly regretted the theatrics and knew Tony would be furious if the laptop was damaged.

'Who's there? Who the fuck is there?'

He sounded scared. Desperate.

'We've met before. Don't you remember?' She was enjoying the moment but she also wanted to push his buttons as much as possible. Anything that made him lose his cool would be a good thing. 'I told you then that I wasn't a lady. You've got to believe me now.'

The torch wavered in her direction and she raised a hand to shield her eyes. He gasped when he saw her.

'You fucking bitch. I'm going to kill you.'

Those were the magic words. Giannandrea and

Toshney emerged from the shadows and crossed in front of him and two uniformed cops piled through the door to take him down from behind. He struggled against them but could do nothing against the superior numbers. He writhed in frustration, his face contorted, spitting in fury.

'I'll fucking kill you,' he raged. 'I mean it. I'll fucking kill you.'

'Like you killed Jennifer Cairns?'

'Fuck you! Fuck you!' He'd lost it completely. 'Get off me!'

She stood over him as he looked up, screaming obscenities.

'David McCormack, I am Detective Inspector Rachel Narey of Police Scotland and I'm arresting you for the murders of Jennifer Cairns, Euan Hepburn and Remy Feeks. You do not have to say anything but anything you do say may be noted in evidence. Do you wish to say anything, Mr McCormack? Or do you prefer David Haddow?'

His head shot up and he stared hatred at her, his face turning a blood-boiling shade of anger.

'I'm saying nothing. Get my lawyer. I'm demanding my lawyer.'

'You did kill her though, didn't you? Your partner's wife. How long had you been having an affair with her? How long?'

There was no reply.

'You broke in here looking for the photographs that prove you were at the Odeon. Didn't you?'

McCormack glared but still said nothing.

'Take him away. And get his lawyer. He's going to need one.'

The ring of his mobile phone made Winter jump, the noise rattling round the high night air and cutting through the whistle of the wind. He sat bolt upright and stared at the screen, the lights of the city below and beyond him.

Rachel. His finger scrambled for the screen and hit receive.

'We've got McCormack. He came looking for the photographs as you thought he would, once he saw you were up there out of the way.'

'Well, I didn't know it would be him. That was down to you. And I couldn't be sure I'd been followed that night from Oran Mor and another night. It was just a feeling. Has he confessed?'

'He hasn't admitted or denied anything. But he will. Now, can you get yourself down from there safely without breaking your neck or do I need to send a helicopter?'

He laughed. 'A helicopter would be nice, but no thanks. This is something I need to do.'

'Exorcize some ghosts?'

'Yes. Exactly that.'

'Okay, we'll pick you up at the bottom. And please, be bloody careful.'

'Didn't I promise I would?'

Chapter 56

Tuesday afternoon

David McCormack sat in interview room 2 in Stewart Street, his back firmly to the chair, trying and failing to give an impression of calm. By his side was his solicitor, Patrick Doull, and opposite were Narey and Addison.

Doull came with a reputation as hard-nosed and aggressive. He looked like a middleweight boxer in an expensive suit, well-schooled in confrontation and doing whatever it took to keep his clients out of jail. The word was that you couldn't mark his neck with a blowtorch. They both knew he'd be hard work.

The room was deliberately small and claustrophobic. Anyone with a sense of smell could still make out the countless cigarettes that had been smoked in there. No amount of bleach or fresh paint could remove that any more than it could get rid of the twin spectres of sweat and fear.

The interview had already lasted ten minutes. Doull had made his mark early, stressing his client's clean record and professional standing, questioning the legality of the process that led his client to the flat in Berkeley Street and making loud noises about entrapment being illegal in Scotland since the incorporation of the European Convention on Human Rights into Scots law. In terms of the interview, it was bluster. Narey led the attack.

'Mr McCormack, officers carried out a search of your home earlier today. They found a number of items of interest. Do you know what they might be?'

Doull answered as she'd expected. 'My client isn't a mind reader, Detective Inspector. Why don't you just tell us what you found?'

'Okay. In a small rucksack in a cupboard, we found three torches, spare batteries, a Swiss Army knife and a street map of Glasgow. In the same cupboard, there was a pair of waders. Can you explain why you have those, Mr McCormack?'

The man didn't look worried or surprised. 'There's nothing unusual about any of those things.'

'Okay. We also found this camera. Is it yours?'

She placed a Nikon SLR on the desk between them.

McCormack was wary, as if fearing a trap. 'It looks like mine. I can't be sure.'

'We've already dusted it for fingerprints.'

Doull nodded at his client, who answered, 'Yes, it's mine.'

'Good. There were a considerable number of images

399

of empty buildings on the memory card. Can you tell us about them?'

McCormack looked troubled but gathered himself. 'I like to explore abandoned places. It's legal.'

Narey smiled at him. 'Not entirely. Anyway, let's leave that for now. We also found these.'

She placed a clear evidence bag on the table. Inside were a pair of black-silk panties.

'Do you recognize them?'

'No. I . . . They belong to an ex-girlfriend.'

'What's her name? We can check with her.'

'I don't remember.'

Narey looked across at Addison who duly laughed.

'You don't remember. Must be plenty of exes then. Mr McCormack, were you having an affair with Jennifer Cairns?'

Colour drained from his face at the mention of the name.

'No. I wasn't. They're not Jen's. You can't prove that they're hers.'

'Which is it, Mr McCormack? That they're not or that we can't prove it?'

'Either.'

'But we *can* prove it. DNA tests might take a couple of days, no longer. I'm confident that they will match to Mrs Cairns. Aren't you?'

McCormack's eyes flitted to his lawyer, looking for help. Doull recognized the gesture for what it was. 'I'd like a moment alone with my client.'

Narey and Addison nodded to each other in

agreement. 'Interview suspended at 14.42,' she told the tape. 'DCI Addison and DI Narey leaving the room.'

'Two minutes,' Addison informed Doull. 'That should be long enough to tell him what he needs to do.'

The solicitor ignored Addison's remark and the door was closed on Doull and McCormack as the officers left. When the door reopened, less than ten minutes later, it was clear that the atmosphere inside the interview room had changed.

'Are you ready to continue, Mr McCormack?'

'Yes. And I wish to make a statement.'

'Good. Then let's get going again. Interview resumed at 14.51. Those present as before. David McCormack has intimated his wish to make a statement. He will now do so.'

The man drew a deep breath and let it back out slowly. With a final look to his lawyer, he began. 'I wish to confirm that I was involved in a sexual relationship with Jennifer Cairns. This began three months ago. It was mutually initiated and consensual at all times. I did not kill her and I was in no way involved in her death.'

Narey nodded slowly at him as if grateful for the information. The man's lawyer had obviously told him not to deny something if it could be easily proven. Deny everything else. That was going to be their strategy.

'How often did you and Mrs Cairns see each other?'

McCormack looked uncomfortable. 'When we could. Maybe two or three times a week.'

'And was Douglas Cairns aware of your relationship?'

'No. Of course not. It would have destroyed him. Jen said that he could never find out.'

'So Mrs Cairns said your affair would *always* be a secret. *Always* just be an affair. Were you happy with that or did you want more from your relationship?'

He flushed slightly. Just a hint, a little poker tell. Then he shrugged.

'I don't know what you mean.'

'Yes you do. Did you want to take it further, be a couple, have her split from her husband, be with you full-time?'

'No.'

'You sure?'

'My client has already answered—'

She ignored him. 'She'd have been better off with you, wouldn't she? Younger, better-looking, more what she needed. Give her what her husband couldn't.'

'Maybe but I . . .'

'Is that what you argued about in the Odeon?'

'No.'

'But you were in the Odeon with her?'

'Yes. No, I . . .'

'You were in the Odeon with her, you argued and you killed her.'

'*DI Narey*, I must speak to my client alone.'

'You argued, you lost it and you killed her. Maybe you didn't mean it. Was it an accident?'

'Yes! It was an accident. I swear.'

Doull was red-faced with frustration. 'Don't say another word! This interview is suspended until I speak to my client. I insist.'

Narey looked to Addison who stood up, smiling, and spoke to the tape. 'Interview suspended . . . again . . . at 14.56. Doull, maybe you can find out what else he hasn't told you and then we might not have to stop every five minutes. I'm going to the pub at six.'

The lawyer scowled but said nothing.

On their return, McCormack was sitting pale and clearly rattled. When the tape was restarted, they found he'd changed his tune again.

'I went to the Odeon with Jennifer Cairns on the night she died.'

'Why were you there?' Narey gave him no time to relax.

McCormack glanced at Doull who nodded. 'We went there to explore the building.'

'You're an urbexer. An urban explorer.'

'Yes.'

'And why did you take Mrs Cairns along?'

'I . . . she wanted to know what it was like. I'd told her what I did.'

'Showing off? Playing the big man?'

'*DI Narey*—'

'It's okay. Yes, maybe that. But she was interested. Excited. She wanted to try it. So I took her to the Odeon. She enjoyed it. She liked the fact we were in there all alone. No one could know we were in there.

Especially her husband. His ... *our* offices were just a few hundred yards away and yet—'

'Did you have sex in there?'

He hesitated before nodding.

'Out loud, please, Mr McCormack.'

'Yes. Yes, we had sex. Being in there ... it turned us on. We had sex. It was natural.'

'That's so lovely. It didn't stay very lovely though, did it? You began arguing, is that right?'

More hesitation. Tears began rolling down the man's face.

'We argued. We had a fight. About telling Douglas. I didn't want ... it wasn't that I wanted her to leave him there and then but maybe one day. That was all. She lost it. Began shouting and screaming. Completely irrational. She started to run and slipped on the stairs. She hit her head. Twice. From one step to the next.'

No one else in the room said a word. They all just looked at McCormack.

'That's what happened. I didn't do it. She fell.'

'She hit two steps?' Narey asked. 'Are you sure it was two?'

'Yes I ...' McCormack froze mid-sentence. 'Maybe not. I'm not sure. It all happened very quickly.'

'So maybe more? Or maybe fewer?'

'Don't answer, David.' Doull put an arm out in front of his client, part protection, part speech barrier.

'I'm not sure,' McCormack repeated. 'I was in shock.'

'Right. Of course you were. Let's leave that for now. But we *will* come back to it. Maybe once you've had a chance to think of a number. What did you do next? You didn't phone for an ambulance and the police. Why not?'

'I panicked. I was scared. I covered her up and I got out of there. I know it was wrong but I didn't know what to do. After I'd left it was too late. Anyway, it wasn't going to bring Jen back. It wouldn't have helped anyone.'

'It might have helped your partner. He was left with no idea of what had happened to his wife. He was left not knowing her body was rotting away just that few hundred yards from his office.'

McCormack's head fell to his chest, as if he was unable to face it or her.

'Look at me, Mr McCormack. Please.' He did so. 'Did anyone see you leaving the building? Did you then or later discover that anyone knew you'd been there?'

He looked her straight in the eye the way people do when they are lying and trying to convince you otherwise. 'No. At least if anyone did then I never knew about it.'

'Okay. Do you or did you know a man named Euan Hepburn? Don't bother looking at your lawyer, Mr McCormack. He doesn't know whether you knew Euan Hepburn or not. Only you know that. So, did you?'

'I don't think so. I may have met him through urbexing but we don't always know someone else's real name so I can't be sure.'

Deniability. She knew that was the game he was playing. And he'd play it again.

'What about Remy Feeks? Did you know him?'

'I don't know.'

'You really don't seem to know very much, Mr McCormack.'

'*DI Narey*—'

'Do you think you ever met Remy Feeks?'

'I might have done, yes.'

'And where do you think you might have met him?'

'I'm not sure.'

Narey nodded and nibbled at her lip. She made a show of looking down and checking her notes. 'Were you in Oran Mor last week, Mr McCormack?'

She saw the reaction in his eyes. Surprise. He began to turn towards his lawyer but he stopped himself and took a breath instead.

'Yes I was.'

Now it was Doull's turn to react. He again didn't know where the questioning was going and he didn't like it. Narey saw him on edge and ready to dive in. She'd make sure she beat him to it.

'Why were you there, Mr McCormack?'

'I was having a drink with some friends.'

'Friends?'

'Acquaintances. I didn't know all of them.'

'Was Remy Feeks among them?'

He tugged at his collar, his hands betraying him. 'I can't be sure.'

'Was there a man among your group of acquaintances who identified himself as Remy Feeks?'

The question seemed to prove difficult. McCormack

deliberated, weighing up his options and finding that he had none.

'Yes. I think there was. I barely spoke to him though.'

'Mr Feeks was murdered in the grounds of the former Gray Dunn biscuit factory. Are you familiar with that site? Have you heard of it?'

'I think so, yes. I'm an architect. I know buildings.'

'Uh huh. You know buildings. Do you also know the Molendinar Burn?

'Of course.'

'So you know of the Gray Dunn building, you know of the Molendinar, you admit you were in the Odeon. These are all known urbexing sites, are they not, Mr McCormack?'

He shrugged. 'Yes, I suppose they are.'

'You suppose. You *know* they are. Here's what I think happened. You left Mrs Cairns' body in the Odeon and on the way out you were seen by Mr Hepburn who was also there to explore the building before it was demolished. You either saw him and knew he'd seen you or you later found out he'd been there at the same time.'

'No.'

'You knew he could put you at the scene of the death and you were scared.'

'No!'

'You befriended Mr Hepburn through the OtherWorld site. We know you had two aliases on the site, Spook, which you'd used before, and JohnDivney, which you created exclusively to talk to Hepburn. You went urbexing with him then either you or he suggested exploring the Molendinar, probably you. You both went down there and you murdered him, leaving him there because you thought he'd never be found.'

'No.'

'Say nothing, Mr McCormack.' Doull looked fit to burst.

'You thought that might be the end of it but then Hepburn's body was found and suddenly people were asking questions, other urbexers sticking their noses in. You knew Remy Feeks found the body, you wondered what else he knew. You were terrified now. Two bodies on your hands. You couldn't take the risk and you killed Feeks as well. Am I right?'

McCormack looked to Doull and then turned back, his mouth stuck firmly shut and his eyes wide. The lawyer looked like he'd taken a few punches along with his client and he'd had enough.

'My client is exercising his right to silence and will continue to do so. This interview is over.'

Chapter 57

Wednesday morning

The buzz had gone from the incident room. The buzz had gone from the whole team.

McCormack had been given bail.

Addison had taken the call from the Procurator Fiscal's office and relayed the bad news first to Narey then the rest of the team. The Fiscal wasn't convinced they had the physical evidence to justify holding McCormack in custody. He was pleading guilty to leaving the scene of a crime but not the three murder charges they'd stuck on him. His passport had been taken from him and he was not considered a flight risk. He would face trial but wasn't being held on remand.

It was a body blow to every one of them. The adrenalin-induced elation of getting their man was gone, replaced by disgust at him being allowed home and having perhaps months before a trial. Worse, there was a gnawing fear that he might never be convicted for the murders of Hepburn and Feeks.

Everyone was in a bad mood, not least Narey. She knew she was grouching at people when it wasn't their fault but it didn't stop her from doing it. She snapped at Maxell and shouted at Toshney. She later did both with Addison as if to prove she wasn't just taking it out on the ranks.

Doors were being slammed everywhere; a despondency spread through the building and threatened arguments wherever it went. They'd already started anew on making sure they could find sufficient evidence to guarantee a conviction in court but it couldn't take away the frustration in the meantime. They *knew* he'd killed all three and it stuck in everyone's throats.

Which is partly why Rico Giannandrea found himself in danger of being lynched when he came into the incident room with a smile on his face and a whistled tune on his breath. The DS was a naturally buoyant character, laid-back and taking the world as it came, but this time it wasn't appreciated. Misery loves company, not a cheer.

'What the hell are you so happy about?' DS Lewis McTeer was still hanging around like a bad smell. Given that everyone else was pissed off, it was inevitable that miserable sod would be even more unhappy than the rest. Rico wouldn't be dissuaded by a prat like McTeer though.

'Happiness that lasts too long spoils the heart, eh, McTeer? No danger of that happening to you.'

'*What?* You taking the piss?' McTeer was itching for a fight.

Rico just smiled and spread his arms wide. 'Old Italian proverb that my granny used to say. Don't worry, be happy.'

Narey wasn't going to side with McTeer but neither was she up for light-hearted banter. 'Leave him, Rico. No one's in the mood.'

'Well I am,' Giannandrea countered. 'And while it's not going to make up for McCormack walking, it might just put a smile on a couple of miserable faces.'

If he meant hers, then Narey wasn't going to take it well. But she was listening. 'What have you got?'

'You asked me to look into a company called Orient Development. Told me to see if they were full of Eastern promise.'

She'd almost forgotten amidst everything else that had been going on.

'Well, as you probably suspected I would, I found connections to Saturn Property. Johnny Jackson and I did some digging and found links between Orient and both Valhalla Homes and Hastings Developments. Directors of Orient include Barbara, wife of Dominic Hastings, and June, wife of Valhalla's Jason Grieve. The husbands being barred from taking directorships. The day to day running of Orient is done by one Mark Singleton. They and Saturn are basically the same company.'

Now she was interested.

'We went to Saturn's office in Skypark and there on the wall was a framed artist's impression of Orient's planned development in the East End. Full of Eastern promise.'

'So two companies are owned by the same people,' McTeer sneered. 'So what?'

Narey thought she had already figured it out, or at least what she'd do from there, but it was Rico's show and she was content to leave the stage to him.

'Well, Lewis, my happy little friend, *so what* is that it gave us two seemingly different companies that had put the frighteners on at least two tenants to leave their properties so they could be demolished. Archie Feeks and Walter McMeekin. Neither wanted to stand up on their own. Thought no one would listen to them. But together?'

'Walter's going to do it?' Narey was smiling but could barely believe it.

'He's already done it, boss. He and Archie Feeks both gave statements and descriptions of the man who intimidated them. In both cases the threat to burn them out of their homes was implicit but unlikely to stand up in court. Together, it's much stronger. And we got photofits done from both of them and the two images could be twins.'

'Anyone we know?'

'Yep. A fire-starter by the name of Martin Tully. Jacko says this guy is reckoned to be the best in the business. The insurance companies and our guys have been after him for a few years and never been able to lay a finger on him. Now we have something. We're going to haul him in and squeeze his nuts till he decides whether he goes down or Singleton does. I'm looking forward to it.'

'Walter isn't going to make the most reliable witness. Saturn's lawyers will go gunning for him.'

'I know. Which is why I was hoping we could get him out of the Rosewood and into somewhere better. Let's face it, anywhere would be better. And maybe encourage him to lay off the drink or at least cut it back.'

Narey ran her hand through her hair as she thought about it

'That might be easier said than done. Let me go speak to him. And I'll try Malcolm Colvin at the City Mission. He knows Walter and should be able to help. That's great work, Rico. Terrific. You hear that, McTeer? A reason for even you to smile.'

'Yeah. Great.' McTeer's face called his words a liar.

'Well if you can't smile then beat it. Go on, find some work to do somewhere else.'

'If you say it's important, hen, then I'll do it. If I can. I'm no promising anything though. I've been drinking for a long time. I've got too good at it.'

'I'm not looking for miracles, Walter. I know it's a big ask. But if you try, that's good enough for me. I figured that if we get you into a better place then you'll just maybe have one reason for staying sober a bit longer.'

The old man smiled at her, his eyes crinkling round the edges. 'I'll not be sad to leave the Rosewood though. I've been in there near enough a year. That might be a new record to be there that long and still be breathing.'

She laughed, seeing something of her dad in him, probably not for the first time. A thought occurred to her.

'Do you follow football, Walter?'

He shrugged. 'Not so much these days. The game's all about money. Average players earning millions, it's ridiculous. But aye, I like the football. Why?'

She hesitated. 'It depends. Who do you support?'

He narrowed his eyes as he tried to work out what she was after. 'I'm thinking I should say Partick Thistle so as no to ruin something.'

'Ha. No, tell me who you support.'

'I'm a Celtic man. Always have been.'

'Ah that might be a problem. But then again it might just be perfect. My dad's a Rangers fan, you see.'

'Och I'm no a bigot, hen. I'd argue with anybody.'

'Well, good. How would you fancy spending some time with my dad? Say once a week, to see how it goes. Just a cup of tea and a chat about football. I think it would help him.'

Walter shrugged again, easy with the world. 'Sure, why no? Is he no keeping too well?'

'Alzheimer's.'

'Och that's a sin. Count me in, hen. If you think it will help then I'll tell him all about how his team's been cheating mine for years.'

She had a tear in her eye as she bent over and kissed him on the cheek.

Chapter 58

Wednesday evening

Narey and Winter were in the back room of the Station Bar on Port Dundas Road, a Guinness and a vodka and tonic in front of them. The bar was quiet and they had the raised rear area to themselves. It was a mixed blessing because although they didn't want to be over-heard, they were having this discussion in the pub rather than at home as it would reduce the chance of them shouting at each other.

It was the first opportunity they'd had to sit down and talk about it. About them.

Just less than forty-eight hours since Winter had scaled the tower and McCormack had walked into the trap they'd set for him. Two days of interviews and legal argument, elation and frustration. Two days in which they'd been able to do nothing more than hug each other. He was drained and she was working furiously. Catching her man was one thing, keeping him was another.

Rico's work with Orient and Saturn had managed to take the edge off her exasperation at McCormack's bail and her talk with Walter had put a smile on her face. She was ready for this conversation, even if Tony wasn't.

'Look, it's worked out fine. We got him and you'll put him away in court. Can't we just leave it at that?'

'*No*. We need to talk about it.'

'I'd rather not.'

'Of course you'd rather not. It means talking about emotion and feelings. And you'd rather run a mile than do that. But sometimes you have to. Like now.'

He drew deep on his Guinness and nodded glumly. 'Okay. Go.'

She shook her head, knowing she was probably going to have to do all the work, but fine, it was better than it not being done. 'Okay. Do you understand why I was so angry with you when I found out what you'd been doing?'

He sighed. 'Yes I do. But do you realize it was a two-way thing? I was angry too.'

She let out an incredulous gasp. 'The difference is that I had a *reason* to be angry. You'd gone behind my back, broken the law, risked your life, endangered my investigation and risked everything we had together. And you *knew* you were doing all that.'

He tilted his head to one side and blew out air. 'But apart from that, what have the Romans ever done for

416

us, right? *Okay* . . . I get it. I really do. And I didn't
want to do any of those things. I wasn't thinking about
the consequences, only what I felt I had to do.'

'But—'

'And I'm not saying that's right. I don't want to do
anything behind your back. And I definitely don't
want to do anything to harm us. It's too important to
me.'

'So why do it? It's easy to say but I can only go on
what you actually did.'

'Because Euan was my friend and I let him down. I
treated him badly and I wasn't there when he needed
me. I had to put that right. I owed him. Look, I don't
want to drag your dad into this but you know what
it's like when it's too late to help someone you care for
but you still feel you have to do something for them.'

She narrowed her eyes at him but conceded the
point. 'That's a bit of a cheap shot but yes, I get that. I
do. But—'

'But nothing. You're asking me to change my nature
and I can't do that.'

'What? How did this turn round so that it's my
fault? I'm asking you to change your behaviour, not
your nature. I'm asking you not to be such a dick.
Above all, I'm asking you to be honest with me.'

'Honest I can do. But it might mean telling you
something honestly that you won't like.'

'Fine. I'd rather it was that way. If you're going to
kill yourself or get arrested then at least I'll know
about it.'

'Fine. So we're sorted.'

She laughed. 'No we're *not*. Look, you're who you are and I love you. So fine, I accept there's times you will need to *be you* and do what you need to do, however crazy and risky it is. I can live with that but what I still can't live with is it crossing into my professional life. I've got a career and you can't mess with that. Take your own risks, not mine.'

He pulled a hand through his hair and exhaled hard. 'Okay, so it's the problem it's always been from the start. I work with the police, you *are* the police. That line that's always been there *will* always be there.'

'Yes. And I don't think I can change that.'

'Maybe I can.'

'*What?*'

'If that can be sorted then we can be sorted. If whatever I'm doing doesn't cross that line, doesn't interfere, doesn't compromise your job then we can make it work. Right?'

'Yes but I don't see—'

'I don't want to explain right now but if I can . . .'

They were so in the middle of it that they didn't hear Addison approach until he'd placed two pints of Guinness, a vodka and tonic and a newspaper in front of them.

'Evening, campers. That bastard McCormack may be at home with his feet up but here's a reason to celebrate and the drinks to do it with. Don't say I'm not good to you.'

The newspaper was the *Scottish Standard*. Plastered

across its front page and two inside were a report and photographs of the Rosewood Hotel. The words were Winter's, the photos were Euan Hepburn's and the headline, *Hellhole*, was the newspaper's.

'Nice work,' Addison admitted grudgingly. 'I didn't even know you could write sentences.'

Winter shrugged it off. 'The work was all Euan's. I just wrote it up from his notes and from what I saw in the photographs. And from what Rachel told me about what it was like in there. It was easy enough.'

Hellhole. The shame of the Rosewood Hotel. Exclusive investigation by Euan Hepburn.

'Were they okay with putting a dead man's byline on the piece?'

'They didn't have any choice. I told them it was the only way they were getting the story.'

Addison nodded. 'How much did they pay?'

'A thousand for the front page and the two-page spread inside. I gave the money to the City Mission. Seemed the right thing to do.'

'Very generous,' Addison raised his glass in salute. 'I'm sure that guy Colvin at the Mission will be pleased. He might even take Rachel out to show how grateful he is.'

Narey sighed theatrically. 'Very funny. You did do the right thing, Tony. I'm sure Euan would have been happy with the Mission getting the money. And he'd have been even happier knowing the place is going to be closed down.'

'It is?'

'Yes.' Addison confirmed it. 'Your story, Hepburn's story, kicked it all off this morning. Local MSPs and a couple of MPs have jumped on the bandwagon and they've forced the council to act at last. They've said they'll review the Rosewood's licence and privately they've let it be known they'll withdraw it. The Department for Work and Pensions is feeling the heat too so basically the shit has hit the fan as far as the owners are concerned. Kilgannon and Wells are going to pull the plug and close the place down before they're told to.'

'Great but . . .' Winter's glass was still half-empty. 'Kilgannon and Wells still get away with having run that place the way they did.'

'No. They won't. Thanks to Rachel, they'll still pay a price.'

Winter looked at her questioningly. Wondering not only what Addison meant but why she hadn't told him.

'I only got the word this afternoon,' she stressed it as if anticipating his complaint. 'David McGlashan, the homeless guy whose body was found at the old saw works in Houldsworth Street. He did die of natural causes but we've been able to put a time of death on it plus check when he last stayed at the Rosewood. Those bastards had been claiming his housing benefit for eight weeks after he died. They'll be charged and there's no way they'll be opening up anything similar. We might even manage a bit of jail time for them both.'

'Nice. So why was he sleeping in the saw works? No urbexing thing, I take it?'

'No. We can't be sure but it seems he just wanted somewhere dry and warm, a roof over his head that wasn't the Rosewood. The poor sods that are there just now will be looking for the same once it's closed down. We don't know who's going to look after them.'

Addison shrugged. 'The City Mission will be glad of Tony's donation. And council services will have to take up some of the slack.'

'And that's *it*?'

'What do you want me to do? Arrest them? Look, the Rosewood is being shut down, Rico and Johnny Jackson are on Saturn Property's case and we'll be asking Bobby Mullen some very difficult questions about torched buildings. Let's just be happy about that for now. And we'll make sure McCormack's put away for life. I'll drink to that.'

'There might be a complication with McCormack,' Winter began slowly. 'He and Remy Feeks weren't the only people in the Gray Dunn factory that night.'

They both looked at him. Until that point it had gone unsaid in Addison's company but he didn't seem surprised by Winter's statement.

'I saw the CCTV images,' Addison told them flatly. 'The third man looked familiar but I couldn't make any definitive identification. Too blurry. If McCormack has something to say in court then we'll contend with it then. For the moment, he's saying nothing so let's leave it like that.'

'If I could give evidence —'

'Just shut up, Tony,' Addison told him firmly. 'Don't say another word. We'll have to deal with your photographs from the Botanics as it is. That's enough to be getting on with.'

Winter shrugged. 'So be it. I'll take whatever's coming my way.'

Anger flashed in Narey's eyes and it could be heard in her voice. 'You made a mistake. Playing at being a detective and nearly getting yourself killed. Lucky for you that you didn't make that mistake twice.'

'No, I got good advice and I paid attention to it.'

'I'm glad you did.'

Addison laughed. 'Do you two think I'm daft? You think I can't hear the private messages in amongst what you're saying to each other? Or that maybe I'm blind?'

'No idea what you're talking about, Addy.'

'No, of course not. Anyway, you've got bigger problems than what I know about your relationship. The Chief Constable knows about you taking those photographs and your relationship with Hepburn. He's put two and two together and it's fair to say he isn't impressed.'

'Great. Where does that leave me?'

Addison and Narey looked at each other again, not a smile or flicker of hope between them. He'd feared as much. Campbell Baxter had been building a funeral pyre for him for some time and now Winter had given him all the fuel he needed to set it alight.

Narey was about to speak when her phone began ringing in her pocket. She pulled it out and her face wrinkled in surprise when she looked at the screen.

'Hello?'

'Detective Inspector Narey.' The voice was instantly familiar. 'I think you'll want to speak to me. I suggest you come right away.'

Chapter 59

David McCormack lived in the West End in half a million pounds' worth of blond sandstone on Lancaster Crescent. The first patrol car had beaten them there and two uniformed officers were standing guard outside the open front door.

They'd called for a car of their own, none of them being able to risk driving. Narey sat up front with the constable while Addison and Winter sat in the back, the latter with his camera bag on his lap. They said little in the few minutes it took them to get there, preferring to let the sound of the siren drown out their thoughts and words.

Narey was first out and up the short flight of steps to the glossy black front door before the others had got out of the car. She talked to the cops on the door and waited impatiently for Addison and Winter to catch up.

'He's inside. They've kept an eye on him through the

window but haven't been in. They've left him to us, as instructed.'

'Okay, let's do it. Let me go first.' Addison was the senior officer and the responsibility was his. He pushed at the door and it swung back to let him stride into the hallway. Narey and Winter followed in silence and single file. The two constables went in behind them.

The hall was dark and minimalist, McCormack clearly taking his work home with him. Dark blue walls and black flashes but no clutter whatsoever. It looked unlived in. Maybe it was.

Addison held his right hand out to the side as he neared the first door, slowing them down. They eased to a halt behind him and let him work his way round so that he was face on to the door, so he could see as much as he could of what he was walking into. He stepped inside and although he pulled up quickly at the scene in front of him, they followed hard on his heels.

David McCormack. In a room of virgin white, an interior designer's orgasmic fantasy. White walls, white carpet, white furniture. A snowstorm of statement. Spoiled only by the violent splashes of red.

McCormack lay on his back on the white shagpile carpet, his arms and legs wide as if he was making a snow angel. You might have thought it was exactly that but for the blood spatter that formed a sickly halo round his neck and head and beyond. The sticky red clung to the thick white pile of the carpet like an invasion from another world.

Winter eased past Addison and Narey as they stood looking at McCormack, slipping between them and taking his first shot. The contrast between the room and the blood was a photographic gift. The man was sprawled helplessly, his life seeping into his living room, his skin draining of colour till it was beginning to fade into the surroundings.

The man's throat though . . .

It was a riot of red. Winter's internal shade chart put it at crimson, meaning it was as fresh as it was warm, no more than twenty minutes since it was spilled. It had soaked into McCormack's shirt and through it to his skin.

Winter zoomed in, seeing the throat ripped, stabbed, cut, destroyed. This wasn't one slice of a knife, it was a succession of frenzied assaults. The knife had been wielded savagely long after life had gone.

A tilt of his camera brought it all into focus. On the white-leather sofa above McCormack's body sat Douglas Cairns. A large knife, its blade still dripping blood onto the once pristine carpet, was clutched in his hands. Winter fired off a succession of shots, catching the open-mouthed, distracted wonder on the man's face. He'd done this yet he seemed barely capable of believing it. He might have worn the same expression to gaze at a goldfish bowl.

'Mr Cairns? Douglas?'

The man lifted his head lazily, roused from his deliberations. 'Detective Inspector Narey. And you've brought friends. That's nice.'

She spoke calmly. 'Douglas, I need you to put the knife down. Slowly, please.'

'What?' He looked down at the kitchen knife in his hands as if surprised to see it there, so easily forgotten amidst everything else. 'Of course. Sorry.'

He bent forward and placed the blade on the carpet by his feet. Winter couldn't help himself and caught a close-up of the black-handled knife as it settled into the white carpet, the remainder of the blood drenching the fibres.

Cairns sat back and they could all see that his shirt was as soaked as McCormack's. The other man's blood was all over him, drenching his hands and splattering his face and streaking his beard. He leaned against the white leather behind him, breathing hard as if relieved. His work was done.

'Tell us what happened, Douglas.'

His face screwed up in bemusement as if she'd asked why the sky was blue or why five followed six.

'I know what you're thinking,' he replied at last. 'Have I killed him because he fucked my wife or because he killed her? Or because you let him go free and I was scared he'd get off in court? I'm right, aren't I?'

She answered for all of them. 'You're right, Mr Cairns. I was wondering that and I do want to know why you killed him. But first I need to read you your rights. Douglas Cairns, I am arresting you for the murder of David McCormack. You do not have to say anything but anything you do say may be noted in evidence. Do you understand?'

427

'I do.'

'So what's the answer?'

He laughed. A high-pitched, highly stressed laugh that didn't suit him. 'I don't know. I really don't know. *All of it?* Because he fucked her, because he betrayed me, humiliated me. Because as angry at her as I have been since I found out, I loved her and he killed her. He admitted it was no accident. He admitted all of it.'

Narey and Addison looked at each other, hoping and fearing in equal measure. She had Cairns' attention though and she spoke for both.

'We only have your word for that, Mr Cairns.'

The man smiled weakly and picked up the mobile phone by his side and held it in front of him. 'I recorded it all on this. I made him confess.'

'With a knife to his throat?'

'Yes. But it's the truth. He was too scared to lie. He killed my wife then he killed two men to cover it up. I didn't know anything about them but he told me anyway. It spilled out of him like . . .'

Cairns faltered, staring at his business partner's body, seeing the blood that was everywhere but where it should have been. His mouth jammed, lips trembling. The reality of it had suddenly bitten him hard. Unable to work words that would make any sense, he pushed one button on his phone, waited a few moments, then pushed another. McCormack's voice filled the room.

'. . . I didn't want to do it. I didn't *mean* to do it! I was terrified, Douglas. Terrified. The boy was asking

428

too many questions and I didn't know what he knew. Didn't know what he could tell the police. I arranged to meet him and . . . It just happened. I couldn't have it all come out. Jesus Christ, Douglas, I didn't want any of this! You have to understand!'

Cairns pressed the button again and McCormack stopped talking as surely as if his throat had been cut.

'He thought I might let him live if he told me it all. I couldn't do that though. I couldn't. He disgusted me. He . . . he betrayed me.'

'You did this? You killed him? I need you to confirm that, Mr Cairns.'

'Yes. I killed him. I meant to kill him. I'm glad I killed him. I did it alone. I came here intending to kill him. Is that enough? I won't deny any of this if that's what you're worried about. *I killed him.*'

Narey nodded, rarely unhappier at getting confirmation of what she needed to know.

'You need to come with us now, Mr Cairns. You know that, don't you?'

He smiled at her and let his head bob in agreement. He made as if to push himself up from the sofa but let his hands slide off the leather and made a grab at the floor where the bloodied knife still lay. He managed to grasp the handle and turned it towards himself. He got as far as lining it up with his heart when Addison swung a boot viciously into his ribs and caused his arms to drop. The two constables were on him in a second and his wrists were twisted until the knife fell from his grasp.

429

'Don't touch the handle!' Narey shouted. 'Just get him away from it.'

She stood above Cairns, seeing the fight drain from him. He had no interest in hurting any of them, just himself. With that chance gone, he'd collapsed.

Addison stood by her side, shaking his head at the stupidity of it all. He turned to Winter who was standing a few feet away with his camera in his hands. 'Did you get that?'

'Every frame.'

Chapter 60

Monday morning

Winter was on one side of the table; on the other sat
Two Soups Baxter and a blonde-haired woman in her
early thirties who said she was from Human Resources.
There didn't seem to be a whole lot human about her
though. Winter wasn't convinced that she wasn't some
form of advanced robot with fake tan, peroxide hair
and a designer business suit. He dismissed the idea on
the basis that a robot would exhibit more intelligence
and certainly more emotion than the HR woman.

She was doing most of the talking; Baxter just sat
smirking behind his whiskers. The fat bastard was
clearly loving every moment of it. He was getting what
he'd wanted since the day Winter started on the job.

The woman was using words like *expediency* and
streamlining, *efficiency* and *lean*, *needs* and *excess*.
Winter wasn't really listening: he already knew what

the bottom line was and just wanted her to get there. He was out. It was cost-cutting but it was also just that his face didn't fit any more. Perhaps it never had. Specialty was always going to take a distant second place to multi-tasking when accountants ran the world. Why pay two people to do two jobs when you can pay one person to do both?

Now she was thanking him, actually thanking him, for his service. He wondered if she was allowed to deviate from her script at all, if she even knew what she was saying. Gratitude and regret were thrown into the same sentence as if they were compatible when it seemed to him that they weren't. If they were so grateful for what he'd done and so sorry to let him go then don't do it.

He had to sign a compromise agreement as part of the settlement, basically saying that he wouldn't tell anyone where the bodies were buried. Neither the literal ones nor the metaphorical. In return he got a year's salary and a pat on the head before they slammed the door in his face.

'I imagine you will want time to consider and have this agreement seen by a solicitor but I must tell you that you have four days to decide whether to accept this offer or else it will be withdrawn and replaced by another, likely lower, offer of redundancy.'

Winter laughed, his eyes on Baxter rather than the woman from Inhuman Resources. 'Four days? I don't think I'll need that long. Have you got a pen?'

Baxter's jowl wobbled as he seemed to struggle in

choosing between delight and surprise. The HR woman's eyes widened and her mouth bobbed open but she composed herself enough to push a silver pen across the desk. Winter picked it up, gave a cursory glance at the page in front of him and signed his name at the bottom. He shoved the paper back across the table and lobbed the pen towards Baxter who fumbled but caught it at the second attempt.

Winter smiled at Baxter for long enough to make him uncomfortable, nodded at both of them and turned on his heels and walked out of Forensic Services for the last time.

Chapter 61

'Baxter is a self-righteous prick. A pompous, arrogant—'

Narey was stalking around her flat, propelled by the anger of hearing his news from a few hours earlier. Winter caught her right wrist as she passed and pulled her back down onto the sofa beside him.

'He's all those things, Rachel. No doubt about it. But this wasn't down to him. I dug my own grave. The most he could have done was give me a nudge in the direction of it. Baxter probably thinks he engineered this but he didn't. I did. I knew my job was hanging by a thread but I still went in search of a pair of scissors. In the end I did them a favour by saving them from making the redundancy compulsory.'

'I still want to slap that smug bearded face of his.'

'There's a queue of people waiting to do that but thinking like that is how sad tossers like Baxter win. He is never happy unless someone else is as miserable

434

as he is. This is a positive, Rachel. If we want to make it one.'

She looked at him, bemused. 'When did you become the glass half-full guy?'

He smiled sheepishly. 'When I realized how destructive it is to dwell on the things you can't change. How guilt and resentment just eat you up from the inside. Stuff like that.'

'Am I getting a new man? I was just getting used to liking the old one. Anyway, how do you plan on making this a positive? It doesn't look all that sunny from where I'm standing.'

'Well . . .' He took a deep breath and she could see that he was suddenly nervous. It scared her a bit. 'It struck me that seeing as how I don't work for or with the police any more, then the line's gone. The one that stood between us and caused us problems. There's no reason I can see that we can't become a couple. A proper couple. No secrets from the world. You and me together and everyone knowing about it. What do you say?'

It felt good to be asked. She smiled widely.

'Yes. I say yes. Now that you're—'

'I haven't finished.'

'What?'

'I haven't finished explaining how we can make this a positive. Do me a favour and don't stop me in case I lose my nerve. I want us to take my pay-off from the job and put a down payment on a house with it. I've . . . shush . . . I've been looking and there's a conversion in Bellhaven Terrace, back of Great Western Road. I think we should buy it.'

'Seriously?'

'Seriously. It's a ground-floor and garden apartment. Built around 1870 in solid brick. Private rear garden. Four bedrooms.'

Her mouth opened wide. 'What do we need with four bedrooms?'

'Well I thought your dad could come to us a couple of days a week. It's big enough to hold all of us and we can—'

She moved forward and her mouth was on his before he could say another word. It was a while before she let him go. When she did it was to tell him to stop talking.

'It's been a perfect pitch. Don't ruin it by saying anything else.'

'That's a yes then?'

'It's a yes. You do know it's not going to be easy having my dad live with us even for a couple of days and that it will only get more difficult?'

'I know. But we'll manage.'

'We'd need some help but there's a carer at the home. Jess. We could maybe ask her to come out part-time. Tony, I love you. But, hang on a second, how can we afford a four-bedroom in Bellhaven Terrace when only one of us is working?'

He smiled. 'Ah. That's my other bit of news. I've got a job.'

'You've got a *what*?'

'Photo journalist with the *Scottish Standard*. I start in two weeks.'

'But that's fantastic. I mean, how? What do you know about journalism? And how long have you known about this?'

'Which question do you want me to answer first? I knew about it two days ago. Just in time to take the redundancy package. The timing couldn't have been better. The *Standard* liked what I did with Euan's piece on the Rosewood and they know I can take photographs. I'm a money-saver and seeing as newspapers are run by accountants just like everything else these days, then it's a no-brainer for them. It's just a six-month contract but it's down to me to make a go of it. They also like the fact that I've got police contacts . . .'

Her eyes widened. '*What?* You mean *me?* No chance. Have you not got us into enough trouble? Have we not been through this? You can take your new notebook and pen and shove it.'

He grabbed her by the waist and pulled her close. 'Can I quote you on that?'

She smiled. 'No comment.'

THE END

Acknowledgments

The nature of exploring abandoned buildings often means doing so in a limited window of opportunity before they are either demolished or refurbished. The same complication applies to writing about them. For that reason, and for my own convenience, I have changed the dates that some of the buildings written about lay empty. For example, the Odeon Cinema was demolished in 2013 rather than 2015 and the Central Hotel was temporarily closed in 2006 rather than 2009.

Given that I was writing about exploration, it is perhaps appropriate that I managed to get hopelessly lost halfway through the creation of this book. I owe a huge vote of thanks to those that rescued me, most notably my agent Mark 'Stan' Stanton, my editor at Simon & Schuster, Jo Dickinson, and my patient and brilliant partner Alexandra Sokoloff.

My greatest thanks go to those that went before: the urban explorers whose reports and photographs opened up a hidden world that cried out to be written about. In particular, I'd like to express my gratitude for the time and knowledge of the only urbexer known to have walked the Molendinar Tunnel, Ben Cooper.